IMPACT

JACK LIVELY

Marie, she comes to me in the twilight
When the wind blows down 'cross the river, so cold the fishermen cry

-Bruce Springsteen

CHAPTER ONE

The Lincoln handled like a boat, loose and easy and relaxed. The road was wide and I could have floated endlessly among the green lawns and houses, but I'd reached my destination and the long drive up from Alabama was over.

I turned the wheel with two fingers and guided the car to a stop beside a clean curb. The automatic shifter nudged into the park position. I twisted the key back in the ignition and the engine hum fell off. The windows were down and the smell of fresh-cut grass and the faint odor of a two-stroke engine passed pleasantly into the car. Given the quantity of grass in view, I figured the mowing of lawns was a common occurrence in the town of Promise, Indiana.

I leaned forward in the driver's seat and pulled my shirt away from the leather. My lower back had gotten a little hot and sweaty. I stretched. The street was empty. Both sides of it had medium-size houses separated by generous lawns. There was nothing going on that I could see. Nobody walking around either purposefully or aimlessly. Nobody visible at all. It was late afternoon and hot for early summer, maybe eighty degrees in the shade. Humidity was high and the air was close.

I ducked my head and looked to my right through the passenger window at 1250 Springhurst, my destination. Its only distinguishing feature was a sprinkler in the middle of the lawn, doing its rotation. The water hissed and the mechanism ticked as it cycled and spun back to start all over again.

I stepped out of the car and opened the rear door. The guitar case was in the back seat. I reached in and pulled it out by the handle. The sprinkler at 1250 was spitting water in my direction, so I waited for it to finish another circuit before starting up the lawn. White lace curtains were drawn across the two windows, one on either side of the front door. I didn't know who was going to be receiving the instrument, but my job was almost done.

The sprinkler finished its turn and wound back with a rapid clicking sequence. I was about to step off when I heard two gunshots fired in quick succession. After a slight pause, the shooter squeezed a third shot.

The shots were small arms fire, probably a pistol. The triple booms bounced off the facades of the houses facing me, which didn't mean that the weapon had been fired from that direction. Across the street was a good-size yard with bed linens hanging on lines. The white sheets caught whatever meager air currents they could hold, billowing ever so slightly to reveal a woman standing still, looking at something in front of her that I couldn't see. She did not appear to be holding a weapon. There were no other sounds. Nobody was reacting to the shots, and not even an airplane was in the sky.

I opened the Lincoln's rear door and returned the guitar to the back seat. The door clicked quietly shut. I glanced at 1250 again. Whoever this instrument belonged to could wait a couple of minutes, since apparently they'd been waiting for decades.

I turned away and crossed the street to the yard with hanging laundry. A jogger appeared, pounding pavement on the opposite sidewalk, oblivious and sweaty with a bare torso. When he came by, I could see his ears plugged with electronics. I waited for the jogger to pass. The heat was keeping everyone else inside, either in front of a fan or in a sealed, air-conditioned room within easy reach of cool beverages.

I came through the first line of drying sheets and got a good look at the woman before she noticed me. She was in her late forties and wearing a loose summer dress. Her glossy black hair was pulled back into a ponytail. She was slim and tall with dark-brown skin. Her hands hung empty at her sides. Her eyes were fixed on a point on the ground maybe fifteen feet in front of her. I moved forward and saw what she was looking at.

A second woman was face down, her body splayed in an awkward position.

I ignored the standing woman and moved to the casualty on the ground. She had a small pistol loosely held in her right hand, muzzle in the grass. Her fingers moved across the grip, which meant that she was alive. I had a moment's hesitation before I touched the weapon. The police wouldn't like that, but the police weren't there.

I removed the gun from her hand and dropped the magazine. I cleared the chamber and put all the pieces down. Beneath the woman's head, blood pooled among the rich green stalks and seeped into the black soil. Insects had already gotten involved, interested, hungry, insistent. She was breathing raggedly. Her body was moving in a repetitive way, slowly twitching, fingers grasping at nothing.

I turned to the one standing.

"What happened, ma'am?"

Her eyes shifted to me. "She tried to shoot me, then she shot herself."

"Call 9-1-1." The standing woman ignored me. I said it again, "Ma'am, please go inside and call 9-1-1."

The woman on the ground made a sound, something between a moan and a howl, but with meaning and syllables. Two words. "No police."

I examined her dispassionately. Definitely wounded, but conscious and able to express herself. I turned her carefully into the recovery position and took a better look. She'd blown a hole in the left side of her face from the inside out. The wound was engorged with blood, the exposed tissue scorched and inflamed. It probably looked worse than it was, but she might have internal bleeding or hemorrhaging inside her skull from the explosion.

She needed medical attention. I turned to the one standing, tried to figure out if she was in shock. The standing woman gazed into my eyes like she was looking for something.

She said, "Who the hell are you?"

"I was across the street and heard the gunshots."

"That right? Normally people move away from gunshots, not closer to them." She stepped toward the wounded woman. "And don't call me ma'am. Makes me feel like a grandmother and I'm nobody's grandmother."

The wounded woman's eyes were open, staring straight ahead, which for her was into the grass. Her breathing was shallow. She looked to be in her late thirties. Blond hair cut in a bob.

The tall woman knelt down to look. "She doesn't want us to call 9-1-1. Maybe she's got a reason." She motioned to the ground. "She's got a purse." The wounded woman moaned again. This time not as loud. But her words were clear and there was no confusion. "No police. Please."

Which made no sense. If you don't want to attract police, why go out in public firing a weapon at another person, then yourself? But that's exactly what she had done, which meant that her making sense wasn't a reasonable expectation. As a veteran combat medic, I knew that I could provide some form of care right there and then. None of it would be enough if she had brain trauma.

I looked around at the scene, getting my bearings and visualizing what had happened. The younger woman had come up from the street. Maybe first to the front door, then over to the yard when she noticed the tall one hanging laundry. She'd pulled the pistol from her purse, fired twice and missed both times. After that she had inserted the barrel into her mouth and blown her face out.

I was operating under the assumption that the woman had hoped to put a bullet through her brain, not her cheek. It looked like a couple of teeth had been caught up in the blast, which made a tough day even worse.

The wounded woman coughed loudly and rolled into a seated position. She looked ghastly with half of her face shot off. She put out a hand to steady herself and moaned again. I could barely understand the words. "Help me."

The tall woman said, "We can bring her into my house through the side."

I said, "Okay."

She looked surprised that I had agreed.

She said, "But then what?"

"Then you'll see."

CHAPTER TWO

THE GUN WAS A SMITH & Wesson subcompact. I put it together and slid it into the waistband at my back and pulled the t-shirt over it. The tall woman took the purse, and I helped the wounded one to the house, my arm firmly around her waist. She was walking unsteadily, one arm slung over my shoulder. Her eyes were bulging and gray below finely trimmed fair brows. Her cheek was flayed and puffed, giving her a distorted profile. She wore hanging gold pendulum earrings shaped like tear drops.

I knew what was going on with her, chemically speaking. The adrenaline hit must have been intense, and she wasn't trained for it. I figured the only reason she was able to walk and talk was that the chemicals hadn't dumped yet. That would happen soon, then we'd see.

The tall woman walked in front of us and climbed a short set of steps to open a screen side door. She held it as I brought the other one through. It was cooler inside by a couple of degrees. A standing fan was going full speed on rotation. The homeowner threw a spare blanket on the sofa and nodded at it. I laid the wounded woman down and propped her head carefully.

I looked at the tall one. "You have a first aid kit?"

By the time she'd come back the woman on the sofa was out. The adrenaline was gone, and her body was depleted of oxygen and energy. It was a contact wound, which made it easier to treat. The burning gasses had cauterized exposed flesh.

I set the woman's gun on the dining table between the living room and kitchen. Dressed her wounded face with a large square of gauze and tape. The wound would heal and leave a bad scar, but there wasn't much else to do about it and the bleeding was minimal. I'd seen several people with holes in their faces, mostly involuntarily. But once I had known a guy with a hole in his face he'd put there on purpose, for fashion. I'd seen him enjoy smoking through it.

The unconscious woman didn't look good. If it's possible to look confused and asleep at the same time, she was doing it. It wasn't a fashionable look. The tall woman was standing looking at me, like she was still expecting something.

She said, "You were across the street when you heard the shots?"

Which reminded me of something. I held up a finger. "I'll be right back."

I walked out the side door, through the hanging sheets, over the lawn, and across the street.

I hadn't locked the car and the windows were open. I had a sinking feeling that only became worse as I got closer. The guitar was gone.

In the scheme of things, compared to a human life, a musical instrument is unimportant. I had been careless leaving it in an unlocked car. Modern cars lock all by themselves, like jealous guardians or paranoid property owners. This car wasn't modern enough for that; it was a Lincoln Town Car that had missed the era of automatic locks by a couple of years. It was the kind of car you had to lock on purpose, like you meant it. I rolled the windows up manually, locked the car, and turned back across the street.

There might be people watching from the windows and not showing themselves, hiding back behind the curtains observing me.

Maybe they'd seen someone take the guitar, maybe not. Perhaps it was the kind of neighborhood where people are suspicious of strangers. That was all fine and understandable, nobody wants to stick their neck out. But I was going to get that guitar back and make the delivery. That was for damned sure.

Promise, Indiana, had gotten a little more complicated.

I LOPED BACK across the street and studied the green yard for a while. The sheets swayed in the breeze. It was still weirdly quiet out. Near the side door was a rectangle of aged cement about fifteen by ten feet. Two ventilation pipes stuck out of it, one of them had a rotating turbine, the other was straight.

The tall woman was seated at a kitchen table when I walked inside. The contents of her attacker's purse were spread out in front of her. A red leather wallet was open and she was staring at something in her hand. The woman held it out to me. "Look."

It was a photograph of the tall woman with an address written across the bottom: *1247 N. Springhurst Road.*

I said, "She had that in her purse?"

"Yes."

"So you know her."

She shook her head. "I've never seen her before."

"But she knows you."

"I guess."

Among the contents on the table was a large mobile phone in a pink case studded with fake crystals. The black screen lit up and a tropical rhythm kicked off. We both watched the phone ringing. The screen showed a number. No name, no picture, which meant a number that wasn't in the contact list. The woman reached for the device and snapped a switch with her long fingernail, which was painted in a complicated pattern of red and black. The ringing stopped.

She scooped the wallet toward her and popped it open. The left side had rows of credit card slots. She pulled a card out and held it so that I could see.

The credit card belonged to Donna Williams.

From the front of the house came the sound of knuckles rapping on wood. The tall woman looked at me, her eyes wide. I looked back at her. She made a gesture, between a shrug and a negative, like she wasn't expecting anyone. Another couple of knocks came from the front. The person was insistent.

The woman said, "Can you get that, please? Tell them I'm not home."

"Who is it I should say isn't home."

She gave me a dead-eyed look. "Linda Cartwright."

I left the living room and entered a long hallway. The look Linda Cartwright had given me was one practiced by law enforcement officers, seriously organized criminals, and certain military types. I didn't ruminate on that reflection.

Whoever was at the door knocked a third time. Insistent and impatient, not my favorite combination. I reached the front door and opened it.

Two men stood on the doorstep, one in front of the other. They were both small but sturdy, with the high cheekbones of Mestizo Hispanics. They looked like they had exposed their faces to the sun and the wind for a sizable proportion of their lived years, which I estimated at sixty or less, combined between the two of them.

The guy in front had been knocking. "Donna Williams here?"

"No. Nobody with that name lives here."

"I know she doesn't live here. But she's here. We need to get her."

Which pissed me off. As if the woman lying unconscious on the couch with half her face shredded was some kind of property that he was going to fetch.

I said, "There's no Donna Williams here."

The guy made a move to get past me, aggressive and dismissive. He ducked like he was just going to pass between me and the door. I stepped into his path, which made him come real close to touching me. That would have been an error, but he managed to stop midstride and fell back on his heels. I took advantage of that moment of imbalance. Just a single step toward him and the guy had to scamper down the stoop. His eyes were leveled at my chest, like he'd been planning to look through me. Then he turned the eyes to meet mine and I saw in them a dull indifference.

He said, "That's how you want to play it?"

I had already evaluated the man. He wasn't going to be a problem in close combat. I couldn't help thinking that way; it came involuntarily, a quick judgement. I came down the steps and crossed my arms over my chest. "That's how it is."

He looked at me hard and said something in Spanish to his friend and they turned and walked away. Both of them wore jeans over dusty boots and button-down shirts tucked loosely into leather belted waistbands, as if they employed the same stylist, maybe taking advantage of two-for-one specials when possible. Each of them had large sweat spots pooled at the small of their backs, which made their shirts translucent. When they got to the sidewalk they turned to look at me in unison before crossing the street. I watched them climb into a silver van with paneled sides.

Guys like that wouldn't go for unarmed combat. If they came back they'd come heavy.

I waited until they were down the block.

Linda Cartwright came up behind me. "What did they want?"

I jerked a thumb inside. "They wanted to take her."

"You didn't give her up."

"No."

She pointed at the Lincoln. "That your car?"

"Yes."

"Well now would be the right time to get back into it and drive away."

I turned to look at her. "I can't do that."

CHAPTER THREE

I LOOKED at the open door next to me. The number plaque was set diagonal and read 1247. Linda Cartwright was gazing across the road at my car, squinting from the glare.

"Those aren't Indiana plates. You from out of state?"

"Car's from Alabama. I'm here to make a delivery to your neighbor." She didn't say anything. I was looking at 1250, the house with the lawn sprinkler. "Do you know those people across the street?"

She shook her head. "There's a lady who lives there. I don't think I've seen her for a couple of years. A younger woman takes care of her sometimes. Is that who you're making the delivery to? Far as I can see the old lady doesn't leave the house so you can deliver that package and get on your way, mister."

I looked at her. "That's the issue. While I was busy in here, it looks like the package was stolen out of my car."

Linda Cartwright looked at me. "Oh. I'm sorry to hear that."

"Which is why I won't be leaving just yet."

She was looking at me with a flat but sympathetic expression, like my stolen package was more of a concern than the bleeding woman on her couch who had attempted to kill her just a little while before.

Cartwright lowered herself into a chair set on the stone patio out front of the house. I let the screen door close.

I said, "You don't seem to be too affected."

She said, "What's your name?"

"I'm Tom Keeler."

"Okay, Keeler. Sometimes, there isn't anything to act on at a certain moment in time. You've done what you can, and anything extra would be unwise."

"You do know her, then."

"Like I told you, I have never seen her before."

"But you know something about her, or you suspect it."

Cartwright kicked her feet out in front of her. They were brown with hardened skin on the soles. She licked her lips before speaking. "I recognized the photograph of me she had in her purse. I know that only one person had that photograph, my husband. And I know that the handwriting on it was not his."

"Which tells you what, exactly?"

She laughed sharply. "Well, for one thing, that woman in there doesn't seem to be a very proficient assassin, which leaves the option of her being involved with my husband."

Pretty much what I'd been thinking. "That doesn't seem to disturb you much."

Cartwright's face immediately blushed and became shiny. "First of all Mr. Keeler you don't know me, so you are in no position to judge my mental state. Secondly, you don't know my husband."

I said nothing.

She said, "So, thank you. I appreciate the help. I'll take it from here and good luck with finding your package. I mean that. If I were you, I'd start with the kids."

"Which kids?"

She pointed her chin across the street. "Kids from back there. No doubt they've got it. You'd be best off getting it back quick, before they move it someplace else. Is it something valuable they'd want to sell?"

"Presumably it's valuable to someone, subjectively speaking." I was looking out at the street, empty and hot.

Cartwright said, "Packages get stolen all the time these days." She shook her head. "I kid you not. Folks are just driving around looking for packages left by impatient delivery people on doorsteps."

I turned to Cartwright and gestured into her house. "What are you planning to do with Miss Williams?"

She scraped her heels on the paving stones.

"I don't know. I'll have to think about that. Maybe wait to see what my husband's got to say for himself. If that isn't satisfying, I might just call the police. We'll see what happens when that woman wakes up."

I said, "There's something else you need to think about, in my opinion."

"What's that?"

"The two guys who were just here. You have to wonder how they knew she was in the house."

"She might have told them she was coming."

"I don't think so. They'll be back."

"So what do you think I should do?"

"Call 9-1-1."

Cartwright bit her lip and looked down at her hands. She was twisting and knotting her fingers together. "Now with the photograph and everything, I don't know what that would lead to. I'm afraid it could get complicated. And you heard that woman, she definitely didn't want us to call 9-1-1."

I said nothing and watched Cartwright's face. She was torn. There was something about her husband that made her reticent to go to the cops. It wasn't any of my business what happened between Cartwright and her husband, but the woman on the sofa needed looking after.

I walked back inside and Cartwright got up from the chair to follow me. I knelt down to look at Donna Williams. She was out cold, half her face covered by the medical dressing. The uncovered part was engorged and distorted, objectively bigger than before. The pain would hit as soon as she regained consciousness. But the adrenaline dump was going to keep her out for a while, possibly hours. She'd be unconscious until her body had managed to recover from the initial shock. Cartwright was standing over me.

I said, "Tell me about the kids."

She sighed. I imagined patience being summoned behind those intense eyes. Cartwright said, "If I were you, I would sit in my front window and watch the street for a while. They'll come out when they need to, when they think nobody's watching."

"Aren't kids supposed to be in school at this time?"

"These kids don't go to school."

SHE PUT me in the front room, on an easy chair set up at the window. Over on the sofa, Donna Williams snored gently.

A couple of hours later I hadn't seen any kids. I'd seen several cars and one old guy on a bicycle. A compact red Honda had pulled into the driveway of 1250, and a young woman had come out of the car. I supposed it was the woman Cartwright had mentioned, the caretaker. I was too far away to see her clearly. She was carrying flowers and had her own key to the house.

During the hours of watching and waiting, I'd consumed two cups of coffee and twelve cookies. The cookies were chocolate chip, and homemade, but not by Linda Cartwright, who told me that she didn't bake. She'd received the cookies at work, leftovers from a birthday celebration in the staff room. She was a substitute teacher for several local schools. She'd spent the time moving between her bedroom upstairs for a nap, and the kitchen table, where she was deeply absorbed by a thick paperback novel.

Like me, Cartwright took her coffee black and strong. I was beginning to like her. From what I could see so far, she was an intelligent woman with a strong sense of independence. Three hours is a long time to look out a window at nothing much. But I'm a patient watcher.

Two teenage boys emerged from a gap between houses across the road. The kids.

They'd come out of the wooded space between 1248 and 1246. I watched the kids saunter along the sidewalk, inspecting the cars parked on the street. Even from that distance I could see that they were experienced thieves, eyes scanning the important elements, door locks and windows. Other eyes scanning the surroundings. No obvious targets presented themselves and the kids walked on. When they came past my car they didn't so much as look at it. I stayed put and waited. Ten minutes later they came back, each clutching a plastic shopping bag. I could see the outline of a large soda bottle in one of them. No doubt they had secured the required sustenance and were returning to base.

I watched the kids go back through the wooded alley between the two houses. When I stood, I saw that Cartwright was watching me from the kitchen doorway.

She said, "You know anything about teenagers?"

"Nothing."

She nodded. "You go indirect. Oblique, like you're looking for anything except what you're actually looking for."

I stood there for a second, letting that piece of advice seep in. Then I went after the kids.

CHAPTER FOUR

I WALKED up the driveway of 1248, where they'd come through, and pushed through the bushes into the backyard. I trudged over grass to the rear and came to a wire fence. On the other side was a line of trees through which I could see a narrow road, then more trees beyond that. I found where the fence had been cut vertically along a post and carefully squeezed through so I wouldn't rip my shirt.

I was out on the narrow road five seconds later. It wasn't a regular road for traffic, more like an access road of some kind.

I paused to look left, then right, then straight ahead. The woods were dense, which made it easy to spot where the kids had trampled the bushes. I followed their path for a minute and came to a set of railroad tracks. Across the tracks was another wooded area. I crossed over the rails and the gravel bedding. The woods weren't any kind of a picnic spot for families. More like a forgotten zone between the train tracks and the garbage dump, dirty with discarded junk and debris.

Behind me, a train came around the bend. There was no wall of pressurized air hitting the trees in advance of the locomotive, like with a Japanese bullet train, or something modern in Europe or

China. This was a rusty American freight train composed of linked box cars inching slowly down the track. It made only a slight creaking sound from the shifting of weight along the carriages.

Maybe the train was bringing commodities south, out of Chicago, bound for the southern states and the port cities on the Gulf of Mexico. Or foreign freight west, out of New Jersey, goods unloaded from container ships and distributed across the United States by rail. Whatever freight was on board, there was a lot of it.

There was no way back just yet, so I persevered into the junk-filled woods.

The narrow path had been beaten down to hard dirt, which signaled that the trail was an important one. The path branched around an oak trunk and I took the fork on the left.

After about twenty feet I spotted a clearing.

When I entered it, I saw three kids: the two from before and a girl, who was dressed in a black jogging suit with gold trim, black sneakers, and a black baseball hat. All three were seated on tree stumps and were digging into the pile of junk food laid out before them. There was no guitar case to be seen.

I remembered what Cartwright had said about talking to teenagers. I figured nutrition might be a good subject to begin with. Then I could move into music and get to the stolen guitar that way. The kids looked up in unison when I entered the clearing. I examined the alimentary choices: potato chips, chocolate chip cookies from a box, and a large bottle of coke.

I said, "Potato chips are good. I like plain. What do you have there?"

They said nothing, looking at me like I was an idiot uncle. There were two open bags.

I persisted. "Sour cream and onion." I peered at the second bag. "Barbecue. Problem here is you'll have to deal with the residue. You either have to lick it off your fingers or wipe it on something. You'd need napkins, or you'd have to be satisfied with wiping your fingers on your pants, just one more thing to have to think about."

I got no response, nothing in return from the kids. They held me in their collective gaze for a couple seconds, then dropped back down to the important matter at hand, salt, fat, sugar, carbs. I figured they still had some growing to do. Maybe walking had been strenuous. The trip to the store alone was probably enough of a justification for eating, if justification was required.

The girl wiped her fingers carefully on her black jogging pants. She finished chewing, and swallowed. "What're you waffling about?" She glanced back at her friends. They were looking at her with blank faces, chewing with their mouths open, like holes in a donut. She returned her gaze to me. "Huh? Why do old people bullshit so much?" She was smiling, but her eyes were sharp and merciless. She stood up and spoke aggressively. "Speak up, man. What'd you have to say?"

"Am I old?"

"You are to me. What are you, fifty?"

"Between thirty and forty."

"Yeah, old."

"Well it's all relative, I guess. I've got a problem."

"What a coincidence, so do I. My problems don't mean much, but that don't make them go away."

"Mine is a musical kind of a problem."

She kicked dirt.

I continued. "Musical as in a musical instrument. Problem as in a missing musical instrument."

She shrugged. "That doesn't mean anything to me."

"Also relative. Actually the object itself wouldn't mean much to me either, if I wasn't its moral guardian."

The girl laughed harshly, amused despite herself. She flashed her eyes at me. "So what, you lost it, mister moral guardian?"

I had to admit to myself that she spoke the simple truth. I had allowed the instrument to slip away from me, distracted by the situation across the street.

I said, "I wasn't going to put it into those words, but, yes, something like that."

She kicked more dirt, like a little dance. "You failed in your primary mission to take care of property. You were supposed to be a guardian, and now it's gone. Too bad for you. Now you want to take that personal failure and blame it on someone else. Maybe you should go see a therapist."

"This isn't any old musical instrument," I said. "It's an important one, not to me, but to somebody else. I made a promise that I'd safely deliver it. I've come far to do that. I'm not a professional courier, just a guy doing a favor to someone in a bad spot. You see the issue now? If a third party were to try and make a financial gain from this predicament, I would consider it a serious breach of my basic code of ethics."

The girl stopped kicking dirt. "Which you define how?"

"The code isn't complicated; it has simple but practical manifestations."

She said, "I don't think I've ever seen anybody sustain an ethical code. Maybe on TV, but not in real life."

"You're young. Don't lose hope."

The girl nodded. She was maybe seventeen years old and looking me up and down. "I can hear that."

"Okay, then."

"But here's the problem," she said. "Say somebody did take possession of this valuable musical instrument while you were being neglectful. Say they wanted to return it on ethical grounds. You have to be open to the possibility that the item in question might have moved on by then, or at least become temporarily unavailable."

I nodded. "I can be patient. What kind of a time scale do you think we're looking at?"

She looked at the sky. The sun was just over the treetops on the southwest side. "To be safe, let's meet again when the sun is almost at its highest point tomorrow. Between now and then I'll ask around, see what I can find for you, as a courtesy."

I thought about that for a second and a half. The sun's highest point would be high noon; it would be below the highest point twice during the day, once before, once after.

"Roger that. I'll be here when the sun is just below its highest point for the first time."

She said, "Good."

I looked past the girl. The woods continued for a while, merging into an industrial area. There were at least two ways out of the place, the way I'd come in, and out the other side. I heard the tail end of the train finally pass. The rails squeaked badly and the sound receded.

"I'm Keeler. What's your name?"

"Sherisse."

"I'll be back, Sherisse, and I'll have expectations."

"Yeah. I bet you will."

"I hope that won't be a problem."

She shook her head. "I prefer people with expectations."

CHAPTER FIVE

I CAME BACK to Springhurst Road through the yard of 1248. I could see Linda Cartwright's house across the street. The door was slightly ajar, like she'd been out on the patio sitting and had gone back inside for a glass of lemonade. I thought about the woman on the sofa, Donna Williams, a strange and tragic story. Williams being the presumed mistress of Cartwright's husband. That guy was going to have a lot of explaining to do. In the best case scenario Donna Williams would heal her face and all three of them could move on with their lives.

I didn't know if Sherisse would come up with my stolen guitar. I'd find out soon enough. Until then, I would need to find a place to sleep. I could hope for a motel with a pool, or perhaps a B&B with homemade breakfast included.

When I hit the sidewalk I took a right to my car. 1250 Springhurst was separated from its neighbor by a line of bushes. When I got clear of them I saw someone crouched at the lawn sprinkler, struggling with it. It was the woman who'd come in the red Honda. The one Cartwright had said was a caretaker for the old lady. I saw her in profile, on my way to the Lincoln. She was hunched over trying to get something loose. Maybe the hose was screwed on at an odd angle.

The caretaker shrieked and jerked her hand away from the sprinkler, as if she'd been hurt by something inside the mechanism. Her cry stopped me in my tracks. I had the car keys out of my pocket and they made a clinking sound. She turned and we locked eyes. She was good-looking, in every possible way. I felt like I'd been captured in some kind of magnetic force field. She smiled. "Sorry for yelling, that thing pinched me."

It took a while before I absorbed what she had said, that she was sorry for making a noise. By that time she was back at work pulling on whatever was giving her problems. I considered offering a hand, but then she made a satisfied grunt, like she'd achieved her goal. She stood up and looked back at me standing in front of the Lincoln. I saw her eyes flick down to the keys in my hand, then back to my face. A look of concern cast itself over her symmetrical features. She had dark hair with green eyes a couple shades lighter than her skin, which was like polished bronze from the heat and effort.

She pulled her hair back from her face. "That your car?"

"Yeah."

"You should be careful with it, nice vintage car like that. I saw two guys checking it out."

"Which two guys?"

She wore a flannel shirt with sky blue and white squares and pale blue jeans. The light blue clothing contrasted with her skin and did aesthetically pleasing things for the parts of her not covered, like her wrists and forearms below the folded sleeves, and the hollow of her neck. She came to the edge of the lawn and took one step out to the sidewalk. She had a powerful presence and seemed completely oblivious to its effect. I tried my best to remain cool and leaned back against the Lincoln.

She put her hands on her hips. "Well I don't know them, but they came over to the car and looked at it. You know, checking it out. I saw them from the window and I stopped watching them when they walked back across the street. I would have called the police if they'd broken in or anything."

I said, "They come in a silver van?"

"Yeah, maybe there was a big silver van." She considered. "But it's not here anymore." She had slowed down her speech and was examining me. "Do you live around here?"

I shook my head. "No."

"Oh."

We were entering some kind of psychic tunnel together, but given what she'd just said, it wasn't the time or the place. I let the keys jangle in my hand again. She stepped back on the damp grass. I got one last engagement with her cool green eyes, and then she waved at me and walked backwards two steps before turning to 1250. I took a deep breath and watched her enter the front door and close it behind her.

I crossed the street to Linda Cartwright's house. The door was open, the interior visible as a wedge of darkness. I was putting the pieces together in my mind and they didn't join up in a pleasant way. The caretaker had described two men, who I assumed were the guys from earlier. Now, Cartwright's front door was open.

Cause and effect?

WHEN I GOT to the house I could see that there were issues. The bandage that I'd carefully taped over Donna Williams's wound was lying on the doorstep, blood stained on the inside. I toed open the door and called in. "Hello. Anyone home?"

No answer.

I moved into the house. "Miss Cartwright? Tom Keeler. I'm coming inside." I had a good memory of that small Smith & Wesson 9mm. I didn't want to be accidentally on purpose shot with it.

Again, there was no answer, just my own voice echoing off the walls. There was nobody on the sofa, only a dull impression in the blanket where Donna Williams's weight had been. I stepped back to the kitchen. A cup of coffee sat on the counter. I heard a sound and turned. Linda Cartwright stood in an open doorway. Past her were stairs down to a basement. She was pointing the Smith & Wesson at me.

"What happened?" I asked.

Cartwright lowered the gun and her shoulders shuddered in relief. She had changed clothes since I'd been gone. She now wore a pair of long shorts and a polo shirt. "I was here in the kitchen. They came through the front door. Didn't even knock. I heard them speaking before they got to the door, so I had a few seconds to act before they came in. I got down to the basement."

Her eyes were wide and she was visibly shaken by the experience.

I said, "You did well." She said nothing, her teeth bared, mouth open in a rictus. I put a hand on her shoulder. "Breathing is good, try it."

She exhaled and then inhaled deeply. I looked down at the pistol in her hand. Her finger was not threaded through the trigger guard. She looked at the kitchen table, where I had seen her examining the contents of Donna Williams's purse. There was nothing on the table now.

"I guess they took her phone too." Cartwright pulled the red leather wallet from her back pocket. "I grabbed this when I went down into the basement. Do you think they can track it?"

"Probably not."

She put the pistol and the wallet on the kitchen table and lowered herself into a chair. "I heard them from down there in the basement, speaking in Spanish. I don't speak Spanish. I don't think the woman was awake. I guess they just took her out, you know, unconscious." She glanced up at me. "Do you think they'll take her to a hospital?"

"I don't know. They didn't seem very charitable, at least that's not the impression I had." I examined Cartwright, weighing the situation.

She was clearly involved in something dangerous, yet she didn't seem to want assistance. I said, "Now would be the time to call the police."

She stood up and moved to the sink, keeping her back to me. She loosened the faucet and splashed water over her face. I used the opportunity to pick up the Smith & Wesson and slide it open. She had put a round in the chamber, which meant at least that she knew how to operate a gun. I put it down before she noticed. She finished drying herself off. She regarded me through a fold in the kitchen towel.

"I already told you. I'm not calling the police."

"When does your husband get home?"

Her eyes slid to the left for an instant. "He's working." She turned her head to me and then glanced into the other room. "He sells insurance to the hospitality industry. Restaurants and stuff. Usually he isn't away more than a week at a time. You think I need a babysitter?"

The thought had crossed my mind, but that's not what she wanted to hear. A couple of things were crossing my mind and tangling. For one, Linda Cartwright was lying about her husband. Out working. More likely that she didn't know where he was. The other thing was she seemed pretty self-sufficient, a resilient woman who didn't want to take advice from anyone. If she didn't want advice, perhaps she could give it.

"Listen, I need a place to stay for the night; a motel would be fine. A room with a bed and a bathroom, air-conditioning, breakfast."

"Yeah, well, you'll have to go over to the south side. There's nothing decent north of Main. Two choices on the south side. Do you want decent or tolerable?"

"What does the tolerable option look like?"

"Like the decent option without the breakfast or the coffee. They have instant coffee and a kettle in the room. You'd tolerate it if you had to, but you'd need to travel for nutrition and real coffee."

"That's a tough sell."

She blinked at me, no smile, no humor, nothing ironic about the conversation in her opinion. She pointed south. "Drive through town, it becomes one way at the municipal building. Go around the circle and follow the road straight down. You'll get to the Silver Inn, that's where I'd go. There's a third option, a fancier hotel in town on Main, but I wouldn't stay there."

"What's wrong with fancy?"

"The coffee comes complicated. They use some kind of an expensive machine that spits it out cold and weird. Plus the Silver Inn has the better restaurant."

"Complicated coffee won't do."

"Ask for Nancy at the Silver Inn and tell her Linda Cartwright sent you."

"I'll do that. I know you're not interested in advice, but personally, I wouldn't feel comfortable staying here. Certainly not at night. You might want to consider making another arrangement until you've figured out the situation."

She looked down at the table. "Yeah, maybe." Then up at me. "I'll stay with my sister for a couple of nights."

Which was my signal to leave. I took another glance at her sitting at the table looking worried. I left her there and went out to the car.

CHAPTER SIX

THE DRIVE TOOK ten minutes and change.

I'd originally come in from the west. The city center was due south from Cartwright's house. *City* was a glamorous word for the place. The four blocks surrounding the municipal building hosted restaurants, bars, and businesses, but you could miss all of that if you blinked slowly. Like Cartwright had said, the way in forked to a one-way street, which sent me on a tour of downtown Promise before spitting me out onto another long and straight suburban road going even farther south.

A couple minutes later I saw a tall sign on my left with *Silver Inn* on top and *Grill and Banquet* below. The motel was a brick two story building set back from the road by a parking lot accessed from a side street. I hung the left and pulled the Lincoln into the motel lot. The Silver Inn had nine rooms on the ground floor, and nine above. Both sides of the building had recessed stairwells to access the rooms up top. I got out of the car, locked it, and retrieved my backpack from the trunk.

The office was reached by going back around the motel and turning the corner past the Grill and Banquet, to a separate building.

I passed the street-front windows of the restaurant and looked in. I could see a generous counter with grill and griddle. The rest of it was booths and two family-size tables. The window side hosted a couple of two-tops. Each table was furnished with a cylindrical sugar dispenser, a salt shaker, ketchup bottle, and paper place mats covered in printed advertisements for local businesses.

In other words, I was looking at some real potential in that window.

A door in a wall of aluminum siding led to the office. I was expecting Nancy, but I got a pale adolescent boy of around sixteen. He was courteous and efficient, no showboating, no delay. I asked for a second-floor room for the night, preferably a corner unit so if there was noise I'd only get it from one side. The guy said I could have a room without any neighbors to start with and he'd keep it that way as long as possible.

He slid me a check-in form. By force of habit I invented a name to put on it. I quickly scanned my brain for possible combinations and came up with Robert E. Lincoln. The guy at the counter wanted a credit card and I said I'd come back down with it later. I pulled three twenties from my wallet and slid them over to him. I suggested the cash could handle any contingencies and smiled like a trustworthy person.

Five minutes later I was lying on the floral bedspread of a queen-size mattress in room number ten, first door in from the stairs. The sun was low and coming in through a crack in the orange curtain. The ceiling was painted sky blue. The room smelled clean and fresh and the sheets felt crisp.

It had been a long day and I was happy to lie immobilized on the bed. The blue ceiling made me think of weather and the guitar, and the sequence of events that had led me to Promise, Indiana.

~

FLORIDA HAD BEEN ABOUT AS close to perfect as seemed possible. There was more than enough beach, plus fresh seafood, boats, suntans, and tropical sunsets. And when it got too hot, there was always the water. Clear and turquoise like something out of a travel brochure. In the evening there was good company, if I wanted it. When I didn't want company, I had my own rented bungalow. I was working hard at perfecting the art of doing nothing much at all and was getting pretty good at it.

There's a whole lot of Florida in the Air Force Pararescue pipeline. Combat diving in Panama City, and then a long stint at Air Force Special Operations Command at Elgin AFB. All that exposure to the Florida climate makes guys want to come back—not to base, but preferably to somewhere more given to a recreational mode of existence. Down on the Keys, it wasn't just the retired guys from the units, it was them and their wives and girlfriends and their girlfriends. Like a happy daisy chain of connections that I was able to move in and out of according to my mood.

As usual I was up at five. Not like some kind of an ambitious person who gets up to work out, or to get their laboring in before the heat of the day. I was up early because I like to get a good start on leisure; you never know when you're going to run out of it.

My plan wasn't complicated. I walked along the beach for about a mile, then cut over to a twenty-four hour diner one block in from the water. I took a stool at the counter and ordered two eggs over easy with well-done hash browns, bacon, and rye toast. There was no need to ask for coffee. A mug slid into position before I'd settled onto the stool. It was a good mug, thick and capable of capturing heat and holding it.

I was watching the griddle man flip my eggs when a guy stepped up to the counter next to me. I recognized him. We'd met a couple of times socially. His name was Terence Kilroy, but people called him Drain. Some military nicknames are kind, some aren't. I remember not liking the one he'd been stuck with and deciding not to use it. Maybe that's why I remembered his real name.

Kilroy dropped a heavy backpack onto the platform next to the stool and took a seat. A mug of coffee appeared in front of him. When he'd gotten comfortable, he turned to acknowledge me with a thick hand. "Keeler."

We shook and I gave him a nod. The griddle man wanted Kilroy's order, so he turned away and gave it. Same as mine, except he got sausage and wheat toast. He also put milk in his coffee, which I didn't judge. Kilroy looked tired. Like he'd been up half the night. He had a very tightly trimmed afro so the hair wasn't the problem, it was the eyes and the lines of his mouth that showed strain. I looked down at his backpack and noticed that he was wearing hiking boots. Looked like he was going somewhere.

"Had enough of the sunshine, Kilroy?"

He sighed. "Short answer is no. You heard about the tornado up in Alabama, right?"

I shook my head. "Negative. I don't watch the news."

Kilroy accepted that. "Big storm up there. I'm going up to help my folks. We live in part of the country where you get bad tornados. The storm hit last night, and I haven't heard from them since, so I'm assuming that when the update does come, it'll be bad. I'd rather be there when I get the details, so I can be of use to them."

"No cell phone signal?"

"Nope. Cut off about oh three hundred hours."

I said, "Hope for the best, plan for the worst."

"You got it."

I turned my head to look out the window. Nothing but blue sky. A clean and crisp horizon line with only a touch of humidity coming off the placid ocean. Alabama was almost a thousand miles north from my current position, give or take a couple hundred. Clearly that was a distance that made a difference.

"What's the worst look like, Kilroy?"

Kilroy sipped at his coffee. I couldn't help calculating that the milk meant the coffee was no longer hot, just tepid. To each their own.

"Worst is bad. Last outbreak, a force-five twister came down and tore through Shottsville like a buzz saw. When it was gone there was nothing left standing. Just splintered wood and people's torn-up junk."

"You were there?"

He shook his head slowly. "I was on deployment. My folks rode it out in the shelter. Eventually they got FEMA money. I was deployed for a *while*—you know how it was—so I couldn't help out with the reconstruction. I'm no longer deployed."

"You tell the other guys that you're going?"

Kilroy shook his head. "Negative. Didn't want to disturb anyone's vacation." He bit into a triangle of toast dipped into egg yolk.

"What're you going to do, take the bus?"

"Yup."

"When's it leaving?"

"Forty minutes." Kilroy looked at me over the brim of a raised coffee mug. His eyes were clear and brown. He was alert and oriented. I could see that his mind was sharp as a barracuda's smile. There wasn't much more to say, and no questions needed asking. He just said, "All right."

Forty minutes later we were on the bus. I'd paid the rent on the bungalow in advance. They could keep my toothbrush and clothes, maybe they could auction them online. The bus took about twenty hours, give or take a couple. We got off in a city and tried to take another bus, but the line wasn't running. The woman at the ticket counter said that all travel in that direction was disrupted because the governor had declared the area a disaster zone. The highways were closed to all civilian vehicles north of the county line.

So we walked.

Twelve hours later we were trudging across a highway overpass, a couple of hours' hike from our destination. The overpass looked down on a giant shopping complex. One of the stores was a big-name pharmacy chain. I nudged Kilroy to look in that direction. He grunted, affirmative. We came down off the road to get supplies.

It took us only about twenty minutes to build up two decent emergency medic kits in the pharmacy. We were walking away across the parking lot when a pickup truck pulled alongside us. It had a fire department badge on the door. An old guy was in the cab next to a woman his age. They looked at us with glowing eyes, sharp and concerned, pumped up with motivation to help.

"You boys heading out to Marion County?"

Kilroy stepped up. "Yes, sir."

"Well jump in back."

We climbed into the back of the truck and the guy took off. He looped the vehicle up onto the overpass and joined the freeway going north. The sky was lead and rumbled. The dark green leaves on the trees had turned inside out. There were no cars or trucks coming south and only emergency vehicles headed north.

Twenty minutes later we hit the zone.

CHAPTER SEVEN

THE OLD GUY slowed the truck when we crossed the county line. The world had gone upside down, and we became slack-jawed spectators in a weird and compelling movie.

Trees had been ripped out and flung around like a game of pickup sticks. Some of them had landed upside down, others had impaled houses. Surviving trees in touch with their roots had still been affected. I saw a huge oak with a woman's underwear collection spread up in its branches, the carcass of a deer and a car bumper on top. Cars were propped atop collapsed roofs. Surviving horses wandered around, seriously deranged.

It hadn't been just a single tornado. Six of them had touched down across the tristate area.

The old guy dropped us off in what used to be Kilroy's hometown near Shottsville, Alabama. He didn't wave goodbye, we were all too busy trying to make sense of what we were seeing. Both myself and Kilroy had deployed in some bad places. But the destruction had been over there. Now it was over here.

The first thing we did was hike to where Kilroy's house had been. The roads hadn't been cleared. The neighborhood was a pile of splinters. But the Kilroy residence didn't even have the splinters. It was like a giant vacuum hose had come in and sucked it all off. The only thing left of Kilroy's house was a bare concrete foundation, slick and clean. Not a single belonging remained, not even a piece of wood framing or an electrical wire, not even plumbing lines. Everything had been ripped out and taken up into the tornado, a direct hit at the peak of its ferocity. The concrete foundation itself had been sucked three feet out of the ground, and sat at an oblique angle.

I stood there shoulder to shoulder with Kilroy looking at the spot where he had grown up. The faint footprint of family life with all its complexities had been reduced to a two-dimensional plane that couldn't even be the foundation for a new build anymore. The dream was over.

The house had been a modest three bedroom, which would indicate a sibling. I looked at Kilroy; he looked at me. Neither of us said it, but both of us thought it. Shit happens, and then you die. We swiveled our heads over the street to the neighbor's house. There was a true pile of wreckage, like some kind of careless giant had pushed it hard with a thumb. The tornado had hit the Kilroy place dead center, and the edges of it had wrecked the surrounding buildings.

We got to work helping the neighbors. For three days we pulled belongings from the wreckage of what had recently been secure domestic bubbles of comfort and shelter. The structure of their lives destroyed, folks were now trying to consolidate what they owned into little piles of order.

After three days, Kilroy went down to Birmingham to join his parents, where they'd been moved by FEMA. I stayed.

The Federal Emergency Management Agency had been busy. A little tent city was established in Shottsville with generators and satellite communication rigs. I had a cot to sleep on, food, and water. FEMA trucked in laborers to do the heavy lifting, so I figured my position on the team was like a running back. I stayed behind the lines with a clear view of the situation until I spotted an opportunity to help, then moved in and finished the job.

Which is how I came to be outside of a wrecked house on the county line looking at a weeping young woman clutching an old guitar case. It was raining and the woman's dress was soaked through. I took a knee and got into my backpack to retrieve one of the emergency rain ponchos I was carrying. She didn't hesitate to put it on, then she picked the guitar up off the ground and looked at me for the first time.

"Thank you."

"No problem, ma'am."

The woman stepped forward and thrust the guitar at me. I had no choice but to hold it.

"It's the only thing left from my grandparents. The only belonging that remains, and it isn't even ours."

I said nothing.

She gestured at the wreckage behind her. "I don't even know whose house that is. I've been searching for a week now and all I've found is the damned guitar, just now, under that carport. I have no idea how it ended up here."

I looked at where the driveway would have been. A carport had imploded onto a vehicle, now squashed by the collapsed roof and an entire tree.

"Where are your grandparents?"

"Refused to leave the house, so they got taken up with it."

Twelve people had died in the storm, which made this woman's grandparents members of the unlucky club. I had a brief image of their last moments, adrift in the vortex, sucked out of their living room and into the afterlife. They were on another journey now.

"Sorry to hear that."

She wiped her nose and looked at me. "They were in their late nineties. Born the same month a year apart. Wouldn't have been better any other way. My grandad fought in World War Two, faked his age to join up. He almost died three times in Italy. People always said he'd been born lucky."

Which made her grandfather a surviving member of the United States 5th Army, definitely a member of the lucky club.

The woman dropped into a crouch, like she was tired of standing. I matched her. She shook her head as if to clear it of grief and looked at me with blue eyes. "I've got to get back to California. I'm assistant manager at a burger place and they let me come out here no question, but my kids are with a neighbor." She looked at me. "You know what I mean." She touched the guitar case. "This needs to go to Indiana. Can you help me get it there?"

"What's in Indiana?"

"The rightful owner."

"Your grandparents were not the rightful owners?"

"No. Grandma won it off another woman in the eighties playing bingo. She always felt guilty about that and spoke about giving it back."

"I didn't know that bingo was a betting sport."

She rolled her eyes. "You'd be surprised what those bingo players get up to. It's a competitive sport, believe me. Grandma was a bingo hustler, man."

I said nothing as my mind sorted through other options. The United States Postal Service. It had come under some suspicion over the years, but I still considered it to be a reliable option for sending packages around the country. But would it be as reliable as me? Was the USPS completely immune to disruption and theft? To which I concluded, no it wasn't, never could be, and never had been. There were private courier companies that could guarantee delivery, but that would be expensive. This woman didn't seem to be a person who could afford luxury. Coming out here at the drop of a hat must have already stretched her finances.

I stood up. "Where's it going exactly, in Indiana?"

She pointed at the case. "Written right on there. Grandma had it ready to travel since the mid-nineties, just never got around to letting go of the thing."

I examined the case for the first time. It was constructed from leather that had been stretched and glued over a wooden shell. The leather was heavy duty and looked like it had been weatherproofed. The handle was stitched cowhide over wadding. The rivets were still good between the handle and the case. The edges were scuffed but intact. All of which was remarkable, considering the thing had been picked up by a tornado along with the other contents of the woman's grandparents' house, and then deposited miles away. The case was an object of solid workmanship, that was for damned sure.

"Strong case."

"Yes." She started to cry and then stifled the tears with her hands.

I thumbed the latch but it didn't give. Locked.

"No key." The woman was smiling through the tears and rain running down her face. "Grandma said they'd have the key in Indiana. Like that was some trick that the lady pulled when she lost her bet. The lady said there wasn't a key, but Grandma never believed her."

"So nobody's seen what's inside?"

"Nope. Look at that latch."

I looked. At first glance it was just a latch, but then I saw that it was more like a piece of sturdy jewelry, bronze and complicated. Not complicated like a Rubik's cube, but like something vintage and crafted by a practical genius.

She said, "You could rip out the latch, but you'd ruin that case. I don't know for sure, but the case could be more valuable than what's in it." The woman leaned over and kissed me on the cheek. "Thanks. I have to go now."

I watched her walking away in the rain. The poncho was fluorescent green. Her figure threaded through the wreckage like an emergency beacon disappearing at sea. There was a tag attached to the handle of the guitar case, lettered in blue ink. The writing had blurred in places, but I could read the address.

1250 Springhurst Road, Promise, Indiana.

The S in Springhurst was smeared. Looking at it was like having double vision, like someone had let a single tear fall over the writing.

CHAPTER EIGHT

I opened my eyes.

The word *Indiana* entered my mind and then passed right back out again.

The sky-blue ceiling was now dark. Across from the bed, a vertical yellow line slashed the wall. I traced it to the harsh electric light from the Silver Inn's mezzanine, entering through a sliver of window left uncovered. It was quiet enough to hear the little things, like the humming vapor lights outside the room and the soft hiss of traffic on the main road out of Promise. I swung my legs off the bed and stretched. Joints cracked and ligaments worked out minor kinks, muscle tissue twisted and uncompressed.

I felt great and very hungry.

The Grill and Banquet wasn't busy. A guy sat at the far end of the counter, idly feeding soup into his mouth while looking at his phone. One of the booths along the wall was occupied by a couple of teenagers whispering in excitement over frothy flared glasses that looked ice-cream related. I took a stool, two in from the front door. A waitress was working the counter. She was a woman in her forties with smooth skin, trim and fit inside a pink uniform. When she came over I read the name tag, *Nancy*.

"Take your order?"

"Hamburger, cheese, pickle, hold the tomato, no lettuce."

"Onions?"

"Yes, ma'am."

"Grilled or fresh chopped?"

"Chopped."

"Okay, big guy." She flashed me the whites of her teeth, bright and fresh. "Anything else?"

"Coffee. Black, no sugar."

Nancy noted the order on her little pad. "Sure. I forgot to ask about the fries. We do gravy, cheese, waffle, regular, or everything."

"Regular."

Nancy walked back making marks in her order book. I watched her tear the page out and slot it into the order board by the grill. The operator flipped his spatula in the air, looping twice before he caught the handle. He spun away to the under-counter fridge. Nancy tore off the order duplicate and spiked it by the register. She turned one hundred and eighty degrees to the coffee section, both hands outstretched. A mug in the left hand, the pot in the right. They met in the middle and coffee was poured.

When she put the mug in front of me, I looked down into the steaming black liquid. Then I glanced up at her. Nancy was smiling, like something was going right in the world.

"Is that okay?"

"Yes, it is."

Her smile wavered when she saw me examining her. "What is it?"

"Just wondering if you're the same Nancy knows Linda Cartwright."

Nancy shifted her weight to the other leg and brought a finger to her lips. "Sure I know Linda. Are you a friend of hers?"

"I'm here on Linda's recommendation. She said to tell you she'd sent me."

Nancy's eyebrows went up about a half inch. "Well, Linda's right over there." She pointed to one of the booths tucked into the back. I couldn't see into it.

"In that booth there?"

She nodded. "Yup. Want me to bring your order over there?"

I stood up. "Thank you."

I didn't immediately recognize Cartwright. Gone was the glossy black hair. Now it was close cropped and natural. I realized that she'd been wearing a wig earlier. She was staring into a laptop computer. A mug of coffee was off to the side, halfway depleted. The red leather wallet that had been in Donna Williams's purse was on the table. I slid into the booth opposite. She looked up at me. "What're you doing here?"

"You're the one who sent me here."

"Yes, but what I meant is, it's late."

I yawned. "Is it?"

Cartwright tapped her teeth with a long fingernail. "It's two in the morning, Keeler."

I was mildly surprised. "I'm going to eat dinner and get back to sleeping."

She closed her laptop and proceeded to look at me while saying nothing. I looked back at her. Linda Cartwright was a hard lady to read, that was for sure.

"Am I disturbing you?" I asked.

"No, that's okay." She smiled briefly, showing teeth.

"I thought you said you'd be staying at your sister's place."

She shrugged. "Yes, but I should have remembered that my sister's a bitch."

I said nothing.

Cartwright looked me in the eye. Hers were brown and flecked with gold. I noticed that she'd plucked out her eyebrows and painted new ones on, which gave her a sculpted look. I supposed that was the point.

"She's older than me and we weren't close growing up. My only memories are of her messing with me. Now she pretends that we're close, but I know she doesn't mean it. She's that kind of a fake bitch. Do you have any siblings?"

"I've got a sister."

"And how do you get along with your sister?"

"I haven't seen her in a couple of years. But we get along just fine. I like her, and I think she likes me. We're both very independent people."

Cartwright looked at me for a moment before going back to her coffee. One sip and she put the mug down again and glared at me. "Yeah, well, lucky you."

Nancy came over with a plate and set it in front of me. She drew a cutlery set wrapped in a thick white napkin from her apron and placed it carefully on the right side of the plate. "Careful now, the plate is hot."

The burger looked good, substantial without being intimidating. I wouldn't need to use more than the single high-quality napkin provided. The French fries were looking equally good. Linda Cartwright wasn't interested. She was sliding the laptop into a woven bag. The red leather wallet went with it. Tough indeed, and definitely not looking like she was about to open up to me about whatever it was she had been getting into when I came in.

I said, "So what, you're staying here instead of your sister's?"

"Yes. I'll stay here, maybe until my husband comes back."

"You didn't speak to him about what happened?"

"No. Not yet." Cartwright stood up. "I'm tired. Good night. I probably won't be seeing you tomorrow, so good luck finding your missing package. I'm very sorry about that."

"Not your fault."

"Okay."

She reached her hand out for mine and we shook. Her hand was bony and tough, the skin dry and cracked. Cartwright went out into the night. I watched her make a left out the door and walk across the front of the Grill and Banquet, disappearing after four or five strides. She didn't look back. I took care of the burger slowly and with relish. When I was done I ran the napkin over my fingers and crumpled it onto the empty plate.

Nancy refilled the coffee. I sat for a while looking into it.

Over in the Middle East they make it differently. They don't use filters or fancy machines for their coffee. They grind it to a fine powder and boil it in water, leaving the grinds to sink to the bottom of the cup as sludge. Some people there have superstitions around coffee, in the way they prepare it and in the way it's consumed. Some folks read fortunes from the leftover grounds. When you're finished drinking you can turn over the empty cup and let the residue drip down along the inside of it. You let it sit for a while, then turn it back over and look at the pattern it left. You can see whatever you want to see, like one of those Rorschach tests the military shrinks use. Couldn't do that with a cup of Nancy's coffee; the filter had already caught the grounds with no consideration for their secondary uses. The dark liquid surface reflected back at me.

I thought back to Linda Cartwright.

A self-sufficient person, that was for sure. Maybe in over her head with problems that she didn't want to talk about, at least not with me. Which made sense, we didn't know each other. I thought of the missing husband. Cartwright had said she hadn't spoken to him yet. The question was, had she tried? And if she wasn't able to get in touch with her own husband after his maybe mistress tried to kill her, well that would speak volumes on its own.

I didn't know who Donna Williams was, but she wasn't a successful killer. She was clearly an aggrieved woman. Aggrieved, turned aggressive, then suicidal, which in other words meant desperate. And she didn't want the police involved.

Then I turned to the other part of the story, the two guys who had come for Donna Williams. First, they'd known that she was at Cartwright's house. Second, they had returned to get her after I'd sent them away. Those two men hadn't seemed like the type of guys to care about someone like Donna Williams, and if it wasn't about caring, the perseverance had to be rooted in something else, like money or loyalty.

Which made them paid agents of someone with more power than Williams or Cartwright. First person who came to my mind was the husband. He seemed to be in the middle of it, the way a hinge goes between the door and the doorway.

I paid the check, left a tip, and walked out of the Grill and Banquet. Linda Cartwright was here now. Question was, had trouble followed? I didn't go directly to the motel. The intuitive paranoid part of my brain was active.

I crossed the street and walked to a bus stop. The street was a major artery, a thick strip of asphalt all ready for two-lane traffic going both directions. But there wasn't any traffic now, at close to three in the morning. I sat down on the bench and looked over at the motel. I had a good view of the Silver Inn parking lot. There were four cars in it including the Lincoln I'd brought up from Alabama. I figured one of the others must belong to Cartwright. There hadn't been a car in the driveway earlier, so I supposed it had been in the garage or out on the street.

The motel and restaurant were located at the intersection of the main road I was on now and a side street. Across the side street from the motel, a line of cars were parked at the curb. I settled down to wait. For a long time nothing happened. Then a skunk scurried from between two of the parked cars, hustling across the street. A hand emerged from the darkened window of a silver sports car and formed into the shape of a gun. The guy inside fake shot the skunk and brought his hand back.

The silver sports car had been parked in that spot for as long as I'd been there and most likely longer. The guy inside was alert enough to notice the skunk crossing the road, which meant that he wasn't parked reading a book or listening to a podcast or having an argument with his boyfriend. He could be doing any number of things, or he could be watching the motel. I decided to operate on the assumption that Linda Cartwright was being surveilled. My second assumption was that she didn't know about it.

If I walked back to the motel now, they might take my picture simply as a matter of procedure, that's what I'd do if I were them. Then they'd have my photo and they could do whatever they wanted with it.

Therein lay the issue. It's a matter of principle in the end. You don't let a surveillance team get you on a list, regardless of the unknown unknowns of the situation. Worst-case scenario they run you through a facial recognition database. Best-case scenario they don't even take your picture.

I looked left, then right, then across the street at the motel office. There was a payphone outside the door. I jogged over the road again. The phone took quarters. I punched 9-1-1 into the keypad.

The operator answered. "9-1-1 what's your emergency?"

I spoke as clearly as I could. I wouldn't be repeating myself. "Silver sports car parked out front of the Silver Inn Motel. The driver just discharged his firearm into another vehicle. I think someone's been shot, so hurry please."

I wiped off the handset with my t-shirt and hung up the phone.

Three in the morning. Not much going on in Promise, Indiana. I waited five minutes, then walked past the Grill and Banquet. When I came around the corner to the motel parking lot, the first prowler was pulling in to block the silver sports car. The officer behind the wheel and her partner came out of the car in full tactical flow, operating in high gear, working it the way they'd been trained. There was abundant shouting, and the show from the police car's light bar was impressive. The last thing I saw before I entered my room was the driver waving his empty hands out the window of the silver sports car, desperate to show that he wasn't a threat.

Maybe he was, maybe he wasn't. At least he wouldn't be paying any attention to me.

Sleep came fast but didn't last long. Four hours later the screaming started.

CHAPTER NINE

A FEMALE SCREAM, muffled by distance and intervening structures. It was coming from somewhere below the room, but not directly. I was out of bed before the first scream was finished and ripping the door open by the time the second one began.

The third scream was angry. By then my bare feet were pounding the concrete outside. The sun was low to the horizon, shining directly in my eyes as I leapt down the stairs four at a time and landed like a panther on the cool concrete below. I was focused and alert, looking down the row of rooms, numbered one to nine.

There was another outburst, but it was no longer a scream, more like an angry bestial howl. The sound came from down the row of rooms, which I figured made it room number nine. A hoarse yelp followed the angry howl, like a severely reprimanded dog.

A big man with long, thick red hair fell out of the room and stumbled across the walkway. He tripped on the curb and fell onto the ground of the parking lot, holding his head with both hands. Linda Cartwright came after him in her nightshirt, angry and disturbed. Her face was a harsh grimace, the mouth a thin line of intent. By then I had stopped moving so fast and started to admire her in action.

Cartwright moved well, balanced and low. Her legs were thin and muscled, her bare feet spread on the cold concrete. She looked stable, a credible menace. A hammer was held in her right hand, knuckles pale around the rubberized grip. Cartwright had it up above her shoulder, ready to go. I could see that she was calculating, looking for the best position, the most opportune angle to get a hit in. She pounced and brought the hammer down hard and fast, shoulders turned for maximum power. The guy was covering his head with his arms, but she wasn't going for the head. The hammer nailed him in the meaty part where neck meets shoulder. Steel drove into muscle and bone with a dull thwack.

Cartwright noticed me. She was breathing hard, nostrils flaring and eyes flashing. The weapon hand dropped to her side. Meanwhile, the big guy with long hair was digging something out from behind his back. Cartwright was no longer on the ball. I had distracted her. I took three steps to the guy and kicked his hand with my bare foot. A heavy pistol went sliding over the parking lot surface.

Cartwright muttered a curse and launched herself at him again. I stepped up and caught her, immobilizing the dangerous hammer arm. She struggled briefly and glared at me in anger and frustration, like I'd become the problem and deserved the hammer. I tilted my chin back to her room.

A second man was framed in the doorway of room number nine. He was clutching his head with one hand. The other hand held a handgun. The new guy had blood running between his fingers and down his face before being absorbed by a gray t-shirt. Cartwright turned her head to see the man and stopped fighting me. The guy looked bad, like he was going to need a hospital bed once the shock wore off. His eyes were rolling back and forth, as if he was having a tough time focusing. It looked as if Cartwright had put in a good head shot with her hammer.

The man staggered to his friend and pulled the long-haired guy up by the collar of his black leather jacket. The gun wasn't steady, but it stayed more or less directed at us. I could see the man's finger already applying pressure. The chrome-plated revolver in his fist was ready to go. The red-haired guy retrieved his pistol, and the two men piled into a red Pontiac GTO, a throwback car that was a hell of a lot older than the Lincoln. The GTO roared and peeled out, bumping over the curb and swerving into the street with a loud tire squeal. In a couple of seconds they were gone in the early morning traffic.

When I turned back, Cartwright was slumped and breathing hard.

I looked around and checked out the overall situation. No onlookers that I could see, no open motel room doors, no witnesses. The only car in the parking lot was mine.

I said, "Go in and get dressed. I'll meet you at the restaurant."

She was staring at me like I was insane. "What?"

"They're not coming back, at least not immediately. And I'm hungry again." I turned back to my room.

Fifteen minutes later we were in the back booth. Cartwright's hands were shaking. I pretended not to notice. When the coffee arrived, she gripped the mug and inhaled the aromas. She took one good drag from the steaming cup and looked up at me.

"They tried to get me to go with them in their car. Plus they wanted to know where my husband was."

"And you just happened to have a hammer on you."

She looked me directly in the eyes. "Yes. Always within reach. Not a lot of bullshit a man can do to you if you've got a hammer ready."

"No doubt."

She held up her left hand, showing an angry welt on her wrist. "Guy who grabbed me was strong." Cartwright shook her head, like it was unbelievable what some people do.

"Any idea where they wanted to take you?"

"No."

"Could have gone bad but you turned it around. Nice work."

This elicited some movement around her mouth, the closest thing to a smile I'd seen on her face, subtle and hard to identify as pride, but real. "You think?"

"I do."

"You know, women like me have at least one advantage."

"What's that?"

"They underestimate us."

Nancy had been replaced by a short older Hispanic man. He brought much-needed sustenance in the form of eggs and hash browns, with bacon and sausage for me, not for Cartwright.

I said, "What now?"

She sighed. "I'm just really tired. I couldn't sleep in that motel room with so much stuff buzzing in my head. Probably lucky because I was half-awake when they came in."

"They came in with a key card?"

"I heard them scratching at the lock, so I was ready by the time they got through it." She shook her head.

"Did they say anything about the girl from yesterday, Donna Williams?"

"The one who tried to kill me? No." She looked up. "Think she'll be back?"

"I don't think so. But those guys you hammered will be."

She lowered her eyes to the coffee. Stubborn. "They're welcome to come back for more of the same."

Tough lady. But I couldn't help thinking that she was being overconfident.

"I'm not on top of the situation. I don't know the ins and outs of what's going on, but neither am I a complete stranger to problems. Far as I can see, this looks like the kind of problem that won't just go away by itself."

She laughed sharply. "My whole life has been a sequence of problems, and you are right, they don't go away."

"Ma'am, I can appreciate the abstract issue of problems in

general, but here you've got a more specific situation. Let me just bring your attention to the sequence of events as I've seen them unfold. This woman, Donna Williams, comes over to attempt your murder, ends up trying to take herself out of the game. Has a photograph of you that you say could have only come from your husband."

"Yeah, the little shit."

"But two men come to get her, and you're lucky they didn't come looking for you down in the basement, right?"

"I'm the lucky one?" She shook her head incredulously.

I looked at her for a moment and decided not to mention the silver sports car surveillance from last night.

I said, "Whatever. Next, here you are at the Silver Inn Motel and two new guys come for a conversation with a side of kidnapping. You got out of it once more, fine. And like I said, all credit to you. But this looks to me like a situation in which you're not the only one with a problem. Somebody else also has a problem, and they figure you have answers, which means they'll be back to ask again. In my experience, each time they come back, they'll come back harder." I took a swipe of egg yolk with an end of rye toast. "Many people would use their weapons if attacked with a hammer, but they didn't. So my question is, why not?" Cartwright was about to speak but I put out my hand to stop her. "And one more thing. Last night I was thinking that your husband was behind these events, but I don't think that anymore."

Which shut her up and stopped her from saying whatever it was she was about to tell me. Instead, she sipped at her coffee, took a bite of scrambled egg, and ruminated. "Yeah. That's true. They wanted to know where he is, which means the little rat's hiding out somewhere." She remembered something. "And don't call me ma'am. In the army they called me Cartwright, which should be good enough for you."

The word *army* got me thinking about the little Smith & Wesson that Cartwright had in her possession.

"What about Donna Williams's gun?"

"Left it at home."

I finished the last bite of eggs and looked up at Cartwright. She was looking right at me, waiting, knowing.

"You want to know what I did in the army, right?"

I said nothing.

Cartwright answered the question I hadn't asked. "I did nothing worth talking about."

CHAPTER TEN

Turned out that Linda Cartwright owned a car, but it was in the shop getting a new transmission. She insisted on going home, so I offered to give her a ride.

The tall, thin woman folded herself into the passenger seat and the belt tightened around her as she snapped it into the lock. During the drive through town she kept her eyes forward, lips pursed in a bitter scowl. The two-way road turned again into a one-way slingshot around the municipal building, this time going north.

I tried small talk. "You live here for long?"

"All my life. Long for me, short for other things, like asteroids and sea turtles."

I glanced over, she wasn't smiling. That hadn't been a joke. Cartwright clutched the woven bag in her lap, and I couldn't help wondering if she'd had time to clean the hammer she kept there. Or perhaps she preferred the steel well-seasoned for the next guy's head. The thought made me smile, which she noticed.

"Something funny?"

I kept my eyes straight ahead through the windshield. "Nothing at all."

We drove the rest of the way in silence, her looking blankly out the window while I concentrated on driving. I parked in front of 1250 Springhurst again. The sprinkler was gone, which made me think of the caretaker. No Honda in the driveway, curtains drawn. Cartwright unsnapped her seatbelt.

"Thanks for the ride, Keeler. What's going on with the kids and your package?"

"Found the kids. We came to an agreement, I think." I looked at the sky. The sun was slowly getting up there. The clock on the dashboard didn't work. I estimated nine a.m. I gestured behind the houses. "Going back there in a couple of hours."

"Oh, good." Cartwright climbed out of the car. She closed the passenger door and stepped onto the grass between the sidewalk and the curb. She stood beside the car for a moment before bending to look at me through the open window. She let out a sigh, like a taut balloon releasing air. "Thank you for helping me out. I know it doesn't seem like I'm grateful, but I am. I'm pretty stressed out, you know." Her forehead was creased with worry lines.

"I can understand that."

She rested her forearms on the car door. "If you need to stay another night to take care of your issue, I have a guest room. No reason to pay for the motel."

Cartwright looked at me, sincere. She was relaxed now. The invitation was thoughtful, but I was happy at the Silver Inn. I like motels, I can just pick up at any time without the burden of having to make a big deal about it. "I'll be okay. Thanks all the same."

She nodded and then laughed sharply. "I know you will. Tell you what, I half-trust you. Yesterday you helped me out in a bad situation, and then today same thing. I like to think I can take care of myself, but truth is I don't know what would have happened if you hadn't been there."

"You would have been all right." Which was maybe true, maybe not.

"I get hotheaded. Served me well today, maybe not tomorrow."

She pulled back out the window. "Listen, you change your mind, the key is under that flowerpot left side of the door. You don't need to notify me in advance, you can just let yourself in. I'd actually feel better if you stayed, but it's your call."

I locked eyes with her. "You could just tell me what's going on. I might be able to help."

She disengaged without comment. I watched her enter the house and close the door behind her. I looked to my right, through the passenger window, at the old lady's house. I turned again in the other direction toward Cartwright's house. I figured it was heads or tails she'd be all right. It all depended on what was at stake for whoever had ordered the creeps to invade her motel room.

I thought about that another couple of seconds. The two sets of aggressors who had been involved. One, the duo from the day before with the silver van, who had presumably taken the Williams woman. Two, the duo Cartwright had taken out with her hammer. Whoever was in charge had personnel at their disposal.

Then there was the surveillance team in the silver sports car. Number three. The explanation could be that they worked in shifts. Silver sports car on the night shift, Pontiac GTO guys on the day shift. Then there was the silver paneled van.

Organized.

None of which was my problem. She'd made that fact abundantly clear. I switched off the ignition and got out. It was a nice day, not quite as hot as the day before, which was a good thing. I had a meeting with young Sherisse at high noon, so I figured I'd go scout around a little before then. I like to be well-prepared when possible.

I WENT through the fence out behind number 1248 Springhurst, over the thin asphalt road and across the railroad tracks. I walked to where the footpath forked. The clearing was still there, but the kids weren't. I sat on a tree stump and looked around. Nothing really there to look at except for the discarded garbage that had been swept up by the wind to catch in the trees and brush. I decided to explore further. After walking for another minute I came to a high fence made of dented steel panels topped with a triple run of barbed wire.

It was an old barrier, with plenty of holes and cracks to look through. I put my eye to one particularly large hole and saw a junkyard with all kinds of refuse organized into piles. Looked like they had a mountain-sized pile of just about anything you could want a piece of. From that vantage point I could see distinct piles of washing machines, stoves, and rusted old bicycles.

I took a right turn and followed the perimeter. The junkyard was large and it took me a few more minutes to circle around to a road. I looked through another hole in the old fence.

Now the piles were rusted-out car bodies on one side, engine blocks on the other. A third pile had discarded tires. To my right I could just about see a building and two large dogs lying in the dust. No human beings in sight and no noise or activity. I couldn't tell if the dogs were chained or not. In any case, I wasn't going to be scaling the wall just yet.

A minute later I arrived at a gate. I was curious.

I considered the situation. There were dogs. But dogs aren't always mean, I reasoned, and a junkyard is a high-traffic area. Vehicles ingress with things to drop off, vehicles egress again with a lighter load. Some vehicles would be operated by the junkyard owner or employees, others would be strangers, which should mean that a junkyard dog had to be accustomed to strangers. If that was correct, then the corollary was that dogs ought to be friendly.

The gate was a panel of steel fencing on rollers. I pushed it in and walked through. My plan was to avoid returning the long way. I figured cutting over past the main building to the other side of the yard would be a shortcut.

About ten steps in, the two dogs I'd seen before were now looking at me, ears pricked up and alert. Five more steps, and they stood up from their lazy sprawl. Big dogs. The first one stretched and yawned.

The second one licked his balls. A third dog sauntered around the corner of the building. All three dogs were muscled and lean and looked hungry. Twenty steps in, I was surrounded by five of them, Rhodesian ridgebacks, tall and athletic dogs bred in Africa for keeping lions at bay.

I took my twenty-second step and the two dogs in front growled in unison. I stopped walking. The other three casually fanned out to surround me. Smart dogs with innate tactical sense and territorial instincts regarding that building. I made soothing sounds, but the dogs weren't impressed. The two on my flanks came in a couple of feet and growled low, with bared teeth. If they'd been cautious before, they were getting bolder.

I was thinking through the training. What to do if a dog-related situation turned rough. The answer was, try not to get bit in the thigh. If you're going to have to get bit, better on the forearm or shin, where you're less likely to bleed out. Also, keep the fingers safe inside fists. The other thing I remembered was, if you do have to get bit, you need to use that to your advantage and lift the dog up by its hind legs while it's latched on.

None of that seemed helpful, given that I was surrounded by five dogs.

I reversed gears and began to move back to the gate. Maybe the dogs wouldn't notice what was going on until I was out on the street again. I figured dogs would get bored of me once I was off the property, less interested when the territorial chemistry was diluted by distance.

A sharp whistle put a stop to that. All five dogs froze, ears perked up. The whistle turned melodic. Some kind of line with several notes in a row, like a theme song to a movie I'd never seen. The pack turned as one in the direction of the building. Sherisse was there, looking like a young widow in black. She was shaking her head, a slim smile on her face. She wasn't holding anything that resembled a guitar case. Her hands were empty.

But it wasn't high noon yet, so I still had hope.

CHAPTER ELEVEN

If dogs reflect their owner's feelings, then Sherisse was on the fence about me.

The pack stopped baring teeth and threatening to bite, but they didn't back down. I had to push through and take my chances. The fact that the dogs didn't bite must have meant that Sherisse wasn't feeling all that threatened by me. She raised her eyes to the sky. "Not exactly high noon."

"I was taking a walk. Didn't expect to find you here."

She shrugged and looked like she didn't know what to do or say. Her body language said enough.

I said, "You were going to blow me off."

Sherisse removed a splintered toothpick from her mouth. "Well you're here now. Truth is I might have been a little presumptuous yesterday."

I said nothing.

She put the toothpick back in and looked at me. I let the silence build.

Sherisse said, "I was over sympathetic. To be straight with you, I regret that."

"Or maybe something else happened, like you weren't able to get my guitar back."

"Well, it might be a combination of both."

"Where is it?"

She shook her head. "I was presumptuous in being so sure I could get it back for you. That's what I meant." Sherisse squinted at me. "What's your position on theft?"

"Biblical."

"What does that mean?"

"Means what it says, *Thou Shalt Not Steal.* One of the Ten Commandments, punishable by death."

"That's harsh."

"But the biblical origins of theft refers to the theft of persons, not guitars."

"Like kidnapping."

"Not exactly, but maybe close."

"Who would they steal?"

"Human property, women, children, and slaves. Castrated males were pretty valuable at a certain point."

Sherisse screwed up her face like the curves of a question mark. "The only people who know that kind of shit are ex-cons who've spent too long in the library. You an ex-con?"

"Ex-military, another disciplinary institution. I spent a long time in a hole with a very biblically minded guy."

"What kind of a hole?"

"The kind you dig."

Sherisse was looking at me like I was kidding. I wasn't. She knelt down and petted one of the dogs. "I don't know what to tell you, I can't get the guitar back."

"Not good enough, Sherisse. I promised that I'd deliver that instrument."

She spoke coldly, "Or what?"

I looked down at my shoes, a good pair of hiking boots, waterproof and breathable, the best of both worlds. The yard was pounded dirt, yellow and dusty. I looked up at the sky, not high noon yet, but blue. I figured it hadn't rained for a while. There were places where that mattered, like the place with the hole in the ground. Finally I brought my eyes back to Sherisse. I liked her; she was a tough kid. I didn't judge her for stealing the guitar, I just needed to get it back.

My silence must have made her nervous because she started to mouth off.

"Like, what're you going to do, torture me?"

"No. I won't torture you. I have no plans to harm you. But I won't go away either. I'm staying here until I get that guitar back and into the hands of its rightful owner. It's a matter of principle, Sherisse. It isn't a negotiable point. And since we'll be spending time together, there's something you need to know about me. I'm willing to go to any lengths to fulfill a pledge. I made that pledge quickly, but it wasn't an accident."

Sherisse kicked at a rock in the dust. She spat. "You know, you're kind of scary."

I said nothing.

She turned toward the building. "I'm thirsty. Come on inside and have a cola."

I followed Sherisse through to the building, which was more of an elaborate shack than any kind of permanent structure. There were walls and a floor, but the roof looked patchy and some of the windows were covered in plastic sheeting. The dogs settled back to lounge in the dirt. I came through the front door and into a dark room.

First thing I saw was a guy in a wheelchair, large torso with a gut, thick arms, no legs. He wore a baseball cap and sunglasses. If he had hair it was cropped tight to his skull. The wheelchair was backed against a wall facing the front door. I couldn't tell if the guy was conscious or not, but his bearing was upright.

"That's Uncle Dwight. He can't speak or do anything really, but he can hear what you say and understand most of it."

I nodded to the man in the wheelchair. "Nice to meet you." I got no response.

Sherisse was standing near a refrigerator, looking at me looking at her uncle. She said, "You want to see something cool?"

"Sure."

She picked up a baseball from a bowl on top of the fridge and threw it at her uncle. A good hard ball throw, like third base to the catcher when the other guy's trying to make home plate. Nothing changed in Uncle Dwight's demeanor, but his hand snatched the ball out of the air. The contact between hand and leather made a strong slap. The hand clutching the ball fell back to his lap and opened. The ball rolled off his thigh and onto the floor.

She said, "He can catch anything, but he can't throw anything, or hold on to what it is he's caught."

Her uncle didn't move. His mouth was a horizontal line below the sunglasses.

Sherisse opened a refrigerator door. The interior light gave her face a green cast. She came up with a couple of soda cans. Through another doorway was a room with couches around a coffee table. Sherisse put the Cokes on the coffee table and sunk into the sofa. I took a seat at the angle, dropped into the cushions, and went straight through to a hard board.

She pushed one of the cans at me. "Look, I'm not the problem, okay? I see your commitment and respect it. Maybe we can figure something out, although I'm not sure how."

I cracked the coke and took a sip. Crisp and chilled, just perfect. "That's the right attitude. Why don't you start by telling me who's got the guitar."

She said, "You're not from around here."

"No. If there's anything you need to tell me that relates to local issues, you're going to have to spell it out."

She took out the shredded toothpick and dropped it into an ashtray on the table. "Okay, Keeler, here's how it is. Remember the two kids I was with yesterday?"

I nodded.

"Yeah, well, they took your instrument and brought it back here.

They told me the car was wide open and it was like you'd invited them to help themselves. To be straight with you, I think you got lucky they didn't take the car itself. Those two are talented thieves. What'd they say it was, some kind of a Cadillac or something?"

"It's a Lincoln. There was a situation, I didn't lock the car. Who has the guitar, Sherisse?"

"I'm getting there." She lifted a chin to indicate our surroundings. "We get customers in here for all kinds of stuff. Sometimes buying, sometimes selling, sometimes they just need to get rid of something. Guy was here when they brought back the guitar. He was getting rid of an old Volvo. Like, his yuppie car from the nineties had finally died." She pointed out to the front of the building. "The guy sees the guitar and gets all excited. Wants to have a look. My friends were going to pop the latch but the guy freaked out and stopped them. He straight up gave them a hundred bucks for a guitar he didn't even look at."

I said, "I can pay him a hundred and fifty to get it back. No questions asked."

Sherisse shook her head. "No, you don't get it, Keeler. He's not going to give it back for a hundred-fifty, or even two hundred. I went over last night, but no dice. Wouldn't even let me in the gate, had to speak through the intercom."

"What did he say when you asked?"

"Never got past his wife or maid, I don't know which."

I shifted to the edge of the sofa. "As long as I know where it is and who's got it, there won't be any problem getting it back. Give me his address, and I'll be out of here."

Sherisse drained her Coke can, buying time. She put it down on the coffee table. "Believe me, the guy won't just hand it back. He thinks he got a lucky deal sight unseen, like he's hit the lottery."

"Sherisse, if you just give me the guy's address and whatever information you've got, we're square."

She sucked her teeth. "What're you going to do, steal it back?"

I said nothing.

Sherisse looked at me for a while. I looked at her, no expression. Neutral facial features, all muscles relaxed and feeling good and alert. Zero tension. She could see it. "It's against my policy, but I'll do it for you. And only because he's a south-side guy."

"South side?"

Sherisse looked at me with a faint smile. "You'll see what I mean when you get there."

I followed her to the other room. Uncle Dwight was holding position.

She said, "You know you got lucky. Guy brought his old car in, which is the only reason I was able to get his address. Had to switch the title from him to us, so there was paperwork."

She arrived at a desk, heavy with papers and grime and a calculator. Sherisse pulled a pink slip from under one of the stacks and set it before her. She peeled off a Post-it note and copied information onto two lines. She stuck the note to my chest.

I pulled it off and read out loud. "Gus Simmons, seven Sycamore Circle."

Sherisse nodded.

"How do I get there?"

"You go south through town, out the other side. Past the big church, keep going. Take a left at the second traffic light past the mall. Third right after that is Church Street. Sycamore Circle is off that."

"Okay."

Sherisse smiled. "I'm not kidding, that's how you get there. Want me to write it down?"

"No, I've got it. I first visualized it as a map, then put it away in a little place in my mind, back left, two compartments in from my tenth birthday party."

"Seriously?"

"No. Show me his old car."

We came out front. The dogs hadn't moved. She pointed at a faded Volvo.

"What's wrong with it?" I asked.

"Bleeding out. Got an oil leak from the engine block so it's all over."

I liked the way the Volvo looked, straight lines and nothing fancy. A utilitarian object for the purposes of transportation. Not as good-looking as the Lincoln, but good enough for a foreign car.

"He brought the car in, and what, took a cab home?"

"Came in with a new car and a woman driving the old one. Left with the woman in the passenger seat of the new car."

"What car is he driving now?"

Sherisse said, "Some kind of foreign car, like an Audi."

"Color?"

"Same as that one."

I looked at the Volvo. It had faded badly over the years. Right then it looked simply pale.

"What color is that?" I asked.

"Champagne."

CHAPTER TWELVE

I RETURNED to Springhurst Road through the backyard of number 1248. Cartwright was out front of her house on the patio chair, kicked back against the wall with her legs straight out looking very comfortable. In her hand was a tall glass of lemonade. She beckoned me over.

When I got up to the house, Cartwright curled her bare toes upwards. "So?"

"So what?"

"So what about the thing from your car?"

"Not yet. There are obstacles apparently."

"Oh." She sipped on her lemonade and looked up at me. "I found a clue, Keeler."

I said nothing.

"I told you I work as a substitute teacher. Well, turns out Donna Williams has a daughter in the ninth grade at Booker T. Washington."

"They let substitute teachers have access to student records?"

"No. But I have friends. They had her ID on file. I saw the picture, got a Xerox copy and everything."

"Okay. So what?"

"Well, there's an address attached to the student record. I guess my question is how much do I want to know? Do I want to go over there?"

I said, "That about sums it up. I hope you're not looking to me for answers. Any news from your husband?"

She shook her head. "No, and no again."

I examined her. She looked relaxed. You'd never be able to guess that she'd been attacked in her motel room that morning and fended off the armed goons with a hammer. I figured the army had missed their chance by keeping women out of combat roles back in the day, at least where Linda Cartwright was concerned.

I said, "Thanks for keeping me updated."

She looked at me for a while and finished her lemonade. "You know there's one thing that's true, like a lesson or something. Don't know if you want to learn it."

"What's that?"

"If you hadn't come over into my yard in the first place, you'd be gone by now. You'd be in another state or a city, or wherever it is you come from." Cartwright tipped her glass at me. "Put that one in your pipe and smoke it."

Which was true, but meaningless as a thought or a concept. I turned and walked back to my car.

She called after me. "I'll see you when I see you, Keeler."

I CROSSED the street to the Lincoln. The red Honda was now parked in the driveway of 1250, but there was no sign of life from the house itself. The curtains were still drawn. The initial stimulus of the red Honda was enough to begin forming an association with the good-looking caretaker, a cognitive process that quickly produced chemical secretions and combinations in my brain. Androgens like testosterone and androstenedione started firing off, alongside dopamine and norepinephrine.

I came to the driver's door with my keys out and saw her sitting right there in the grass. When she saw me, she made a little wave and pushed off with one hand to stand up. I came around the car to the passenger side and we met at the sidewalk.

She said, "I saw you across the street, so I came out."

I said nothing.

She smiled, confident and glowing. "Your name is Keeler? I heard the lady over there."

"Tom Keeler." For some inexplicable reason I stuck out my hand. She took it in hers, which only amplified the raging chemicals secreting out of hidden facilities in my body. Her hand was cool and a little damp from the grass.

"Keeler with a *K*?"

"Yes."

We were standing close.

She said, "That's a strong name. The keel of a boat is the most important part."

"I see."

She blushed. "Maybe you've got an ancestor whose job it was to build the keel, like in a shipyard. The original Keeler."

I was thinking of a comeback to that, but she saved me from it.

"I'm Tela Collins."

Collins was wearing a worn denim shirt and a pair of beige chinos. No jewelry, save for a bracelet that looked like a child had made it. She was even better looking than I remembered, if that was possible. There was a long moment of silence. She looked away from me, down and to the side, and bit her lip with perfect teeth. I could see that she was thinking, or more accurately, summoning a decision. I wasn't in a rush, just standing next to her was making my day. I felt relaxed and good. She glanced at me and saw it, the glow of happiness on my face. Her eyes were pale green.

She said, "You want to go out tonight?"

"Yes, definitely."

Her smile broadened. "You aren't from around here."

"No."

"Well then I'll take you to Le Petit Cafe. I hope you like French food."

"I like all kinds of food."

She brushed her hair back again. "Early okay?"

"Early is good."

"See you at six then. Le Petit Cafe." She tilted her head to the south. "In town. You'll find it."

"I'll be there."

She was still smiling when she turned away. I watched her go, this time she looked back at me before closing the front door and saw that I was watching. Her eyes flashed, then she was gone.

I climbed into the Lincoln. The sun was closer to high noon, give or take an hour. I stayed in the seat for about a minute to get my heart rate down. I thought of Tela Collins behind the curtains of the house, inhabiting her own beautiful body. Maybe cooling off in the air-conditioning, or in front of a fan.

I shook it off, got her out of the front of my mind and into the back. Still felt good back there, like a warm tingling sensation. A future promise to be fulfilled, I hoped. It was time to visit the south side, and Gus Simmons.

CHAPTER THIRTEEN

THE LINCOLN DROVE MELLOW, the suspension loose and easy. This was the full American experience, right there on a two-lane blacktop riding parallel to the longitudinal demarcation of a globe. Like strings along the neck of a guitar, which made me wonder what the old woman's might look like. I had never played a guitar before. I'd seen other people do that, and a few of them were competent. If the case was so special, I figured the guitar might be as well.

The two lanes split around the municipal building. The one-way loop swept out of town and south again. On the other side, the road widened just before I shot past the Grill and Banquet, catching a glimpse of the Silver Inn Motel at the corner. After that, the buildings thinned out until there were mostly trees and grass and a whole lot of flat Indiana land.

A couple miles later I passed the church, a mega structure on the other side of an artificial lake. I kept going until I got to a shopping center on my left. Like Sherisse had said, there were two traffic lights in short order after the mall. I took a left at the second, then the third right after that onto Church Street. Here, the houses were identical cookie-cutter copies of each other, the only differentiating factor being whether they had a flag outside the house or a basketball hoop. Some houses had both, very few had neither.

Sycamore Circle was different.

It was literally a single loop from Church Street out into the trees and then back again. I drove the loop slowly, looking for house number seven. It took a while because there weren't many houses. In fact, there wasn't a single house visible from the car, only high gates and fancy security cameras with intelligent entry technology and warning signs threatening anyone even thinking about breaking in.

The south side.

Number seven was about halfway around the circle. Getting there had taken almost five minutes' slow driving. I pulled the Lincoln to a stop on the opposite side of the road. The gate was a flat black steel barrier built into a stone wall. Both were high enough that you'd need a ladder to get over them. I got out of the car and walked to the intercom. There was no traffic on Sycamore Circle, just idle silence cut by the regular sounds of ambient life. I thumbed the button. The system returned a satisfying electronic ding to let me know that it was all working and my presence was being communicated to the house.

A half minute later I was addressed by a disembodied voice, possibly female with a possible accent. The sound was tinny and compressed. Whoever had designed the system had been cheap with the bandwidth. "Yes?"

I spoke into the intercom's grill. "Gus Simmons?"

"Mr. Simmons is not available. May I ask what this is regarding?"

"I'm here about a guitar."

There was a long wait with nothing going on except the sound of leaves in the wind and a couple of birds. Sherisse hadn't made it past the woman, so I didn't have high expectations. Neither was I surprised when, after a few minutes, a gruff voice came down the wire. "This is Simmons."

I decided to give Simmons the benefit of the doubt. I went slowly over the story, but left out the Alabama part of it. I told him how the guitar had been stolen from the back of my car, how it was destined for an elderly lady who would appreciate the instrument because of its history in her family. How it wasn't my guitar to give or to sell, and how if he wished to purchase the guitar, he'd have to do so from its owner, the elderly lady in question. I didn't embellish the story with any extraneous adjectives, just told it with the minimum relevant detail.

I offered him his money back plus extra.

Simmons didn't say anything for a while. There was another period of silence, shorter than the last one. The intercom blurted harshly before his voice came through with the brashness filtered out, a quieter and more subdued tenor. "I'm afraid I don't know the instrument you are referring to. If somebody has told you that I bought a stolen guitar, they're lying. I'm a collector, not a thief. Goodbye, sir."

And that was it.

I looked at the intercom, a vertical rectangular object with speaker grill, a small hole for a microphone, and a miniature camera eye. The guy had flat-out lied to me. Not a good turn of events. Things were going to be more difficult than I had hoped.

I thought, what else is new?

I tried with the intercom again, but it gave no joy, no more fake bell sound, only the dull physical sensation of pushing a button with none of the feedback. I pressed it twice, with the same result. On either side of the gate were security cameras mounted on stone walls. Both lenses were pointed at me. I noticed that the cameras were hard wired. No antennae sending out remote signals, just black wires looping up and then back down, presumably into cable conduits running vertically down the other side of the stone wall and into the ground.

Those reflections weren't voluntary, they were the habitual notes of a trained operator. If I had to return, there was one more thing I'd know about the place. I walked back to the Lincoln. It was quiet enough that my footsteps were loud alongside the bird song and the sound of leaves in the wind. Behind all of that was the gentle whirring of servo motors as the cameras panned and tilted to follow me.

That was a feeling I didn't like.

I continued driving around Sycamore Circle until I had completed the loop and come out on Church Street once again. Across the entrance to Sycamore was a section of brush. To the left of that was a long stretch of road bordering open pasture before the first cookie-cutter house. I took the left until I got to the first house and pulled a K-turn in the driveway. I came back toward Sycamore Circle and swung over the curb into the grass. I figured I'd wait and see if Simmons came out in his champagne-colored Audi.

I switched the engine off and racked back the seat. I was prepared for a long wait, even for nothing. Simmons would come out eventually, and I planned on being there.

CHAPTER FOURTEEN

I CAN BE EXTREMELY patient when necessary. I shut down the urge to do something and got in the zone. The zone is where you're alert and observant, with an active, critical mind. At the same time it's a mental space where you're calm and happy and satisfied. I'd seen someone meditate once. She had her eyes closed. In the zone you keep your eyes open.

There wasn't much to look at, but there was enough. The occasional car passing, the road, the trees and the grass.

Maybe Simmons was taking a nap, or maybe he was practicing the guitar or taking care of yard work or doing rich-guy stuff, like looking at his computer and making decisions about real estate investments or financial derivatives, or maybe planning an extended vacation in a place with fine sandy beaches. I don't know, but whatever he was doing, it took him three hours to do it.

An Audi station wagon vaguely the color of weak piss pulled out of Sycamore Circle and turned left. I figured that was what some people in Indiana thought champagne looked like.

I watched the car come by. I wasn't afraid of Simmons's seeing me. Most people aren't looking out for surveillance, certainly not a guy whose only issue seems to be collecting vintage guitars. The man driving the Audi was large, with a puff of gray hair and glasses. Besides that I didn't see much because of the reflection off the windshield.

I let Simmons drive on before starting up the Lincoln. I retraced the original journey up Sycamore Circle, back to number seven. This time, I stopped the vehicle farther down the road where there were no cameras. I got out of the car and stepped up onto the hood. One more step and I was on the roof. A languid leap got my fingers to the top of the wall, and I hauled myself over in a single move.

Boots landed in soft dirt. Knees bent to cushion joints and bones. Everything was working out as it should and it was a beautiful day. The stone wall at my back had been built on a rise. Below was young forest interspersed by several older oaks with impressive trunks. I looked around. No cameras on the inside of the wall, no obvious security measures.

I took a walk.

Gus Simmons's property was all that I had expected and more. The house was set into a glade in the forest. It was an incredible structure. The place looked light and floaty, constructed from long thin strips of wood and glass. There was zero structural material in sight, as if the wood and glass had been so perfectly combined that the whole thing was held together by the forces of physics alone.

The back end of it was literally floating, with no visible support. Underneath was a Japanese pebble garden. Beyond all of that was a big kidney-shaped pool. It wasn't turquoise blue like most of the pools I'd seen; it was dark blue and looked fancier for it.

I worked my way closer to the tree line until I was able to observe the interior. The floating thing was a gigantic open-plan living area with a kitchen at the other side of it. The living room was packed with guitars, maybe three rows of them. Each guitar was on its own stand. It all looked very expensive.

On the other side was a kitchen island with a counter and the stove in the center. Very fancy. There were high stools along the length of it, so guests could watch the cooking. The guitar case lay across three of the stools, unopened. I examined the corners, and the edges. Security cameras covered every angle. The big glass panes were cornered with contact sensors. This was a well-protected property, but nothing is impossible.

A woman walked out from the other side of the floating architecture. She was holding a double barrel shotgun and looking right at me. She walked confidently across the patio flagstones and hollered loud. "You've got thirty seconds to get your ass back over that stone wall, mister."

Her accent was indeterminate. I assumed it was the same person whom I'd spoken to over the intercom. There was no indication if she was wife or maid or sister or whatever. I opened my hands wide in surrender and shouted back. "Yes, ma'am. I was just admiring the architecture."

She smiled. "Well that's enough admiration. Next time you can call and make an appointment to take pictures, like everyone else."

She stopped walking, close to the tree line but sensibly keeping her distance.

I said, "How did you know I was here?"

The woman said, "Motion sensors. This place has the highest level of security available on the free market."

"Well," I said, "you have a great day."

She nodded, as if this was a regular occurrence. I shrugged internally. Nice try, but it hadn't worked out. I'd need to find another way, or the intervention of a higher power, like money, nature, or god. I came back over the stone wall with the help of a young sapling and dropped down beside the passenger door. I must have knocked the side mirror jumping off the roof, which had the effect of putting me into a confrontation with my own image.

I wasn't dressed very well. In fact, looking at myself made me realize that I hadn't changed clothes since I was in Alabama. The whole changing of clothes thing had slipped my mind. I was wearing the clothes I'd had on tearing up tornado-damaged houses. They were stained and torn in places, like items that had aged faster than they were supposed to.

What I needed was a clothing store. Because, I figured in Indiana it might be customary to wear relatively clean clothes on a first date.

CHAPTER FIFTEEN

By the time I was done shopping it was getting close to date time.

I'd gone to the mall. There I found what I needed, a clean button-down shirt with a collar and a couple of fresh sets of underwear. I threw in a three pack of t-shirts and a three pack of socks. The pants I was wearing would be fine, no use getting new ones when these were already broken in and comfortable.

I put my shopping bags into the trunk and got the Lincoln on the road back to the Silver Inn. The weather was perfect, no cloud in sight, warm breezes. I put a hand out the window and palm surfed the air currents. I found myself involuntarily humming a tune that I realized was the muzak they'd had on at the clothes store. Maybe it was an old standard, gussied up in a new way, perhaps by a robot living in a computer, spit out into the store because another computer had figured the tune would make people buy more and faster.

Looked like it had worked out as planned. It was the thought that it was so carefully engineered that made me stop humming.

Back at the Silver Inn I went to the office and paid in cash for another two nights. The guy was a new face and didn't bother me for a credit card. I brought my shopping up and stripped off the old clothing. A hot shower got me in a great mood. Cleanliness, combined with the fresh feel of a new shirt and the image of Tela Collins hanging there front and center like a flag of some kind, was as good a reason as any to get up and go. I wondered if Collins would also be wearing a new shirt.

I went down to the Grill and Banquet. Nancy was prepping for the dinner rush. She gave me directions to Le Petit Cafe. The guy behind the grill nodded to me. I figured it wouldn't be too hard becoming a regular around here. I was feeling good about Indiana.

Out in the parking lot the Lincoln waited, like my own private limo with me as my own driver. Good to go.

LE PETIT CAFE wasn't exactly downtown, as Collins had suggested. It was a couple of miles from the municipal building, down a winding road to the river. Not winding downhill, but west across the flat Indiana landscape. Sunset was hours away, but the light angled low on the water and made everything gleam and sparkle.

The restaurant was a converted house, painted green and white and tucked into a small track by the water. Tela Collins was leaning against her red Honda in the gravel lot out front. There were no other cars in the lot because the place was closed. I pulled the Lincoln in over the gravel. Collins waved. I looped around and stopped next to her.

"Not looking good, Keeler."

I stepped out of the car, careful with the new shirt. Collins was wearing a pair of faded jeans and a fresh red shirt with high-cut sleeves that showed off her arms. The same homemade-looking bracelet surrounded her wrist. Her hair was up and a little messy, which emphasized her neck in all the right ways. She wasn't wearing earrings.

I said, "Looking good to me."

She laughed and put a hand up to primp her hair. "Okay."

"More than okay."

I pointed to the bracelet. "You make that yourself?"

She blushed and held up the wrist. "My niece made it."

The bracelet was strung with four small ceramic blocks spelling out T-E-L-A. Collins put her head back and looked at me through a closed-lipped smile. "You know I only asked you out because of the car."

"This car?" I thumbed to the Lincoln.

"Yup. Pop the hood, I want to see the engine."

I reached in through the driver's side window and pulled the switch. She unlatched and raised the hood. I came around front and stood with her looking at the engine. To me it looked like a vaguely dirty bunch of parts which, when fed with gas, got me from point A to point B.

I said, "You see anything you like?"

"I like the fact that it's an unassuming but powerful and reliable machine. V8 engine with sixteen valves. Rear-wheel drive. Big damned fuel tank. What's it hold, sixty-eight liters?"

"No idea."

She glanced at me. "Am I boring you?"

I grinned. "Not even a little bit. I just don't know the answer to that question. I've put gas in the car, but I don't pay attention to how much."

She said, "You hungry?"

"Usually."

Collins laughed. "High-powered metabolic engine, that's what I expected looking at you, Keeler."

She was appraising me again, the way a farmer might examine livestock.

I said, "Your town. What's the plan?"

"Let's switch up to Mexican food. There's a place over on the north side. Can we go in the Lincoln? I'll leave my car here."

I twirled the keys and tossed them at her. "You drive."

She snatched the keys out of the air and we got back on the road.

She drove fast and happily. Not heavy on the pedal just calm and quick, anticipating the turns and the automatic gear changes. First thing she wanted was music. I hunted down a rock and roll station under her directions. An old Allman Brothers instrumental was playing. Collins cranked the volume and shrieked into a tight turn off the river road. I hooted out the window and we both laughed, already having a good time. On the highway back through Promise she accelerated in sync with Duane Allman's slide solo. I watched her driving and nodding her head to the beat. I liked what I was looking at. She glanced at me regularly, keeping track of me, always with a little half smile.

I thought that maybe we wouldn't even make it to the Mexican place. I had a hard time imagining sitting down soberly to a restaurant table and ordering burritos and nachos. But she took dinner very seriously. She guided the Lincoln into a slot at the Real Hacienda Three and led me inside. The place had candlelit booths in colorfully painted wood and black-and-white photographs on the walls.

A short woman seated us with two laminated menus. The ice water and tortilla chips came only ten seconds after we'd gotten settled, with hot sauce dipping bowls in three different colors.

Collins examined the menu, holding it between her hands and reading critically. I didn't touch mine, just watched her looking studious. She caught me watching her and blushed. She went back to the menu for a minute and put it down on the table between us. "I think we should order combination platter number six."

Which is what we did, along with two Pacifico beers.

I said, "I need to tell you something."

"Okay."

"You might think it's weird but bear with me."

Collins's happy smile reduced down to a hopeful question mark.

"Spit it out."

"The reason I'm here is to make a delivery to the lady you're taking care of."

"Only reason you're here, where?" She wasn't smiling anymore.

"Promise, Indiana." The question mark on Collins's face had turned to concern, which wasn't a good thing in the context. I held up my hand, a gesture meaning 'bear with me.' "I'm supposed to deliver a guitar to her address, 1250 Springhurst. Problem is it got stolen from my car. Now I'm trying to get it back." I spread my hands on the table and looked at them. "I was going to come over and tell her about it, but I figured it would be better just to get the instrument back and deliver it. Otherwise, there's a danger of making false promises."

I glanced up at her. She looked serious, like she was organizing her thoughts and feelings into boxes and compartments.

She spoke carefully. "Okay. Well, first of all she isn't any old lady I visit; she's my aunt. Technically she's my great-aunt and technically she is old, in relation to the average life expectancy of her gender and genetic disposition." She had moved her hands from the table to her lap. I pictured them twisting and torturing each other. She said, "Tell me how you came to have a delivery for my aunt. Ginny's about as far away from someone who would have a guitar as it's possible to imagine." She said the word *guitar* carefully, as if it were a strange object for her aunt to be involved with.

I told her the story of the Alabama tornado, and the woman who had asked me to make the delivery. I told her what I'd been told about the bingo game and the debt. When I was done she signaled to the waiter and ordered another round. I hadn't finished my first beer yet, but a second one slid into place anyway.

She drew from her bottle. "That's an interesting story, Keeler, and not only the part where you agree to deliver a guitar from one person you don't know, to another person you don't know."

I said nothing.

I saw by the way she looked at me that I hadn't screwed up completely. The story hadn't made her suddenly dislike me, which was a relief.

She was nodding to herself, as if she had decided to approve the way things had turned out. "I guess I'm a little surprised is all, about the guitar and my aunt." She looked up in the air and laughed sharply. Her eyes came back to mine. "Damn, Keeler. Maybe Aunt Ginny was some kind of a guitar player back in the day. I mean, I didn't know her at all growing up. She was always here in Indiana. Aunt Ginny from Indiana. I think I might have seen her a couple of times and that's it. I grew up out west in New Mexico with my dad. Mom died when I was young and Ginny's from Mom's side. So you see, I didn't know her really until a couple of years ago."

"Is that when you came out to Promise?"

"Yes."

"But you didn't come here for Aunt Ginny."

She squeezed lime into her bottle of Pacifico beer. "Came out here for a job. But, truth be told, I didn't really want the job."

"What kind of a job?"

"Swear you won't laugh?"

I put my hand over my heart. "Swear."

"I'm sort of a garden specialist."

I didn't laugh. "What's funny about that?"

"Just that it sounds mundane and boring."

"I worked as a landscaper for a while. I wasn't good at making things grow, only destroying them."

Collins laughed. "You were the hole digger."

I snapped my fingers. "You got it. Point me to the spot and I'll dig the hole. Not so good at planting the delicate flowers."

She nodded, like this was some kind of a philosophical point, but smiled as well, like all of that was ridiculous. "I work for the Indiana Department of Transportation, highways division. I run the teams that go out and do the landscaping. Most times I'm sitting in an office, with office clothes on. I use a computer more than a shovel, to be honest." She looked up at me. "I used to do fieldwork but then I got a master's in landscape architecture."

"That sounds like a good line of work to be in."

This made her smile again, a good thing. She looked relaxed and happy. I finished the first beer. Saw that the food was arriving. It looked and smelled good, steam rose from the hot tamales and enchiladas crowded into the dishes. I let Collins begin figuring out how to deal with the food.

We ate for a while in silence, out of respect for the aromas of spice and fresh ingredients. I figured I was far from suffering, that was for damn sure. When she was done, Collins wiped her hands carefully on a napkin and folded it next to her plate.

By the time we came out of Real Hacienda Three, it was getting dark. The night was fragrant and warm, and I felt exhilarated. Tela Collins was right there beside me, close, smiling and chatty. She was talking and laughing and bumping into me. Each slight physical contact was rich in promise. I avoided thinking about what might happen next. My plan was to leave that to her.

She was ruminating on her aunt. "Bingo, huh? I never even knew that Ginny played." Collins was going to say more, but shut her mouth and slowed down. I saw that she was looking at something ahead of us.

Two men were leaning against my car, one of them actually sitting on the hood. I didn't think I knew them, but I did recognize the car blocking the Lincoln into the spot. It was a silver sports car, same vehicle I'd seen surveilling the Silver Inn the night before. I looked more carefully at the faces of the two guys, leaning and sitting on my car and eyeballing us. I did recognize one of them. He was the guy I'd seen sticking his hands out of the car window when the police came the night before. The guy who'd fake shot the skunk.

I cracked my knuckles and Tela Collins drew in a breath.

I said, "What?"

She was watching me. "Nothing, it's just that you're smiling, Keeler, and your body language has shifted." She was examining me. "It's like you've made some kind of ultrafast animal shift from mating behavior to the posture of combat. Not only that, but you did it fast and it didn't put you in any kind of a bad mood."

I hadn't noticed any of that, but none of her observations were wrong.

CHAPTER SIXTEEN

"I'M BASICALLY A FRIENDLY GUY, until I'm not."

"Let's avoid unnecessary bullshit," Collins said. "I've got other plans for you this evening, Keeler."

Which was a significant upgrade to the night, at least in terms of its promise.

"Roger that, Miss Collins."

"Okay, so let me deal with them."

She nodded to herself, got her game face on and strode forward. I followed behind, wondering how she planned on handling the situation.

It looked like she was ready to kick some serious ass, and maybe the two guys on my car saw that and took notice. They slid down off the vehicle and separated themselves from it, like synchronized gymnasts. The guy I'd seen before put his hands up in a gesture of compliance. He was tall and muscular. The one behind him was the same size at the shoulders but a head shorter.

The tall one wore a light sweater and flipped up the hem to show a badge. He said, "Whoa there sister, we come in peace."

Tela Collins slowed down.

The guy looked past her and scowled at me. "You pulled a nice little stunt last night. Don't you know it's dangerous siccing the police on someone? I heard that getting stopped for a routine traffic violation gives you a higher chance of being killed than anything else in this fair country."

Collins turned to look at me with all kinds of questions written on her face. I glanced at her before speaking.

I said, "That's fake news, you left out suicide, cancer, heart attacks and drowning in the bathtub. I figure getting stopped by the police is just about one of the safest things that could happen to you. Up there with choking on a donut in terms of probable death."

He grinned. "Well, you may be right."

The shorter man coughed phlegm onto the asphalt. "Scumbag."

He pushed past his partner and got in my face. I didn't move. The shorter guy's breath smelled like green Tic Tacs. I turned away to avoid it. Which meant I was facing Collins again. I winked. She looked anxious and confused. I began to have doubts about the evening's romantic continuation. The body language was all wrong.

The tall guy put a hand on his partner's shoulder. "*Cálmate, amigo.*"

The shorter cop was more powerfully built than his partner, with a lower center of gravity and strong shoulders. I snuck a look at him, right there in front of me. He was gritting his teeth and clenching his jaw. The partner's gesture didn't seem to be having the desired effect. I decided to precipitate the level of tension and bring it all to a head.

I took a single step to the man and closed the distance. Now my chin was at the height of his nose.

I was alert to body language. The man's right bicep was engorged with blood, the fist and jaw clenched. The eyes had turned to pinpoints in a squint. I looked at his large, square head. The brain had already sent out signals to the rest of him. I had a hard time imagining them being retracted. I took a guess that he'd try an uppercut as his opening gambit. I figured he was hoping it would be a one-punch affair.

The man twitched into motion and it wasn't what I expected. Instead of going for an uppercut, he swung a forearm straight at my face. I saw it telegraphed like a slow-motion movie. His arm was big and heavy with solid muscle, lifting and floating at me. While it came, I switched focus behind the pointed elbow. The guy's face had turned crimson, the clenched jaw transformed into an open-mouthed grimace. He was holding his breath, instead of exhaling. That was going to effect the ability to project power. Worse, the attempted strike was also way too arm oriented. He hadn't put any waist into it, no power from the legs.

I shifted my shoulders about six inches to the left. The elbow whistled past my nose. In his attempt to get at my head, the guy had been forced onto his toes. I pushed the elbow along throwing him off balance. I wedged the steel toe of my boot under his foot and sent him tumbling into the Lincoln.

The short muscular guy staggered into my car, narrowly avoiding a face-plant. I addressed the taller guy. "That didn't look like a police badge. Mind showing it again?"

The man looked for a moment at his partner, who was grimacing after the impact of his palms on the Lincoln's chassis. The grin stayed on the tall man's face. "Did I say we were police?" He detached the badge and held it up for me to see. It was not a police badge, strictly speaking.

The man said, "Homeland Security Investigations."

Which was what the badge claimed. It was a shield capped with a screaming eagle, all in gold. The words *Special* and *Agent* floated on a banner at the bottom. In the middle was a more formal United States eagle logo with a *U* on the left and an S on the right.

I looked at him. "What can we do for you, special agent?"

"You can see that my partner is a little riled up. Apologies for his hotheaded behavior. I'm equally frustrated but choose to express that in a different way. Suffice it to say that we are in a small bind because of your actions last night."

The shorter partner squared up to us and glared at me. I kept the eye contact.

I said, "You can go ahead and apologize. I don't hold grudges."

The guy lowered his eyes for a moment and that was it.

Collins interrupted and spoke in my direction. "Mind telling me what's going on?"

The taller agent sucked in a breath.

"I'm staying at the Silver Inn Motel," I told Collins. "These two were outside last night, surveilling the place. I didn't want to become a photograph, so I got rid of them. I didn't know that they were *special.*" I pointed to the two agents. "Now they're upset."

Collins nodded once and turned to face the Homeland Security agents.

I said, "How was I supposed to know you were law enforcement, and how did you find out it was me who called?"

The tall one ignored the first question. He proudly answered the second. "Traced the call to the pay phone outside the Silver Inn. Got you on the traffic camera crossing the street from the bus stop and making the call." He looked back at the shorter man. "My partner here connected to the check-in desk at the motel." Both of them turned to me with hard eyes.

I said nothing.

The partner said, "But of course that wasn't going to be much help getting in touch with you, was it Mr. Robert E. Lincoln?"

I yawned. "My mother was on one side; my dad had other ideas. They compromised."

Collins was staring at me now, eyebrows raised. The tall agent patted the car.

I said, "So what, you got the plates from another camera?"

"Motel's got a camera on the lot." He looked at me curiously.

I knew what he was thinking. If he'd run the plates they would have come up with the old title and the fact that a transfer of ownership was underway. Car title transfers take around a month to process. They didn't have my real name.

I said, "That's truly special work. It marks you out as diligent special agents. Now if you don't mind, we're on our way out. It's a beautiful night." I gestured to Collins. "Let's go."

The stocky agent folded his arms across his chest. The tall one said, "Give me another chance here, bud."

I said nothing.

He opened his hands out at his sides, a gesture of peace. "Look, man, you are involved. You've got," he searched for the word, "operational inclinations and skills." He raised his eyebrows. "You can understand our position, given your actions. All the same, we've no reason to believe that you're on the dark side. Which is why we're here like this, all friendly." He glanced at his partner. "Mostly."

I was thinking about the incident at the motel that morning, with Cartwright's hammer. They must have gotten that on the parking lot camera too, or at least a piece of it.

The agent glanced at Collins. "We'd like to speak privately with Mr. Lincoln here."

Collins was looking at me with open curiosity. She said, "Do you want me to leave?"

That was the last thing I wanted.

I turned to the agent. "She stays, you can say whatever."

He shrugged. "Whatever. Last night, we were surveilling a person of interest in an ongoing Homeland Security investigation. Your actions impeded our surveillance and might have undermined the investigation."

"Which means what, exactly?"

The short agent looked at the tall agent, who looked back at him and shrugged. The short agent squinted, turned away, and spat into the dust. The tall agent took a deep breath.

"What is it they say about unusual circumstances?"

I said nothing.

He wetted his lips. "I need to see ID before we continue. Robert E. Lincoln isn't going to cut it. If you refuse to show ID, I'll have to get administrative on you."

I removed my driver's license from my wallet.

The agent's eyes dilated as he focused. He read out loud. "Tom Keeler, Hawaii driver's license." The tall agent shifted his eyes away from the license card and back to my face. "You're from Hawaii?"

"Negative. But the DMV there was less crowded than the one in New Hampshire."

He coughed with involuntary laughter. "And the surfing was a little better. Is that where you got those operational skills from, Keeler?"

"I was a PJ in the Air Force for a while."

The taller agent looked back at his partner and nodded at him, like they were confirming something they'd already discussed. "Special Tactics."

The shorter agent said, "My dad was in the Air Force. Served in Lebanon." They both looked for my reaction. I didn't react. He continued. "Dad worked doing mundane stuff on base."

"There's nothing mundane on base, particularly in Lebanon," I said. "Everything's important. You need to respect Dad."

He nodded. "I do."

I could see the tall guy making up his mind. He turned back to me. "Look, man. I'm going to speak to you in a way I'd never otherwise speak to a civilian. We're under pressure here trying to wrap this case. I'm going to treat you like, civilian plus. HSI are running a small op and we're out of time. If you served in a special tactics unit, you're cognizant of the manner in which branches of government operate. You will have experienced bullshit budget committees and the spreadsheet administration geeks, not to mention schedules and task priorities and other bureaucratic habits of the asshole desk jockeys who we answer to."

I nodded. "Roger that."

The guy had said a lot of words, like some kind of an orator. I guess he was done with the impressive speechifying because he sighed and started to speak plainly. "We need something better than we've got. I spent four hours last night dealing with the local police because of you. They crawled all over our shit. My boss is a prick and he wasn't happy. He's got beef from above him, so he gave me an ultimatum. Advance the investigation or they close up shop *tonight*." The man looked at his watch, as if we were actors in a movie scene where the clock is ticking on a hidden bomb. "Tomorrow morning the case gets sealed and filed away up in Virginia. Me and my partner here get yanked and spun into the next thing."

I said, "I don't understand what you think I can give you."

"Understand this: if you hadn't done your little dance last night, we'd have been there this morning when Linda Cartwright was attacked. Then, we might have the additional detail necessary to fill out the case file. Like we'd have the two attackers in separate rooms, with video and audio. As it stands we've only got security camera footage of you in your boxer shorts."

I said, "What's the deal with Cartwright?"

"That I cannot discuss."

Collins said, "So what are you asking him for?"

The guy pointed at me. "I need your friend to come into our operations room and talk about the Cartwrights on record. Linda and her husband. We also need a witness account of this morning's incident. Cartwright didn't file a police report, which means it didn't even happen. I need Mr. Keeler to describe the circumstances and the aggressors. We'll ask questions and you'll answer them."

"I can do that, but in return I want to know more about your case."

The tall agent said, "You come in, talk to us like regular people. I'll outline the case for you. I don't promise high levels of detail, but I'll give you an overall view of it."

I glanced at Collins. The timing was unfortunate, but that's life. I looked at the shorter guy. He was leaning against the Lincoln, examining his fingernails.

I spoke to the tall agent. "Homeland Security. What do you investigate, terrorism, illegal immigration, trafficking. Stuff like that?"

"All of the above."

Collins said, "Where's this operations room?"

The tall agent said, "We're at the Eight Ball Motel."

The shorter guy was shaking his head, as if the mere mention of that particular motel was getting him down. I recalled what Cartwright had said about the other motel in town. "Is that the place where they don't serve breakfast?"

The tall guy looked at me like I was clairvoyant. The short guy said, "Got to drive just to eat. Either that or you take your chances on foot. The place sucks."

I said, "I'll follow you over."

The tall agent saluted with his fingers. "Thank you, Mr. Keeler. If they were all like you, we'd be living in a better world, believe me."

The shorter one grunted to himself, as if something ridiculous had just happened. He rolled off the Lincoln and joined his partner. The two Homeland Security agents walked back to their unmarked car.

CHAPTER SEVENTEEN

I TURNED TO COLLINS. The night was still warm and heavy with possibility, fading out as the silver sports car's engine fired up.

I said, "You should get a cab back to your car. This might take a while, I don't know."

She shook her head. "No. You'll explain what's going on while we drive. Then I'll decide if I'm going to take a cab or not."

I walked to the Lincoln, opened the passenger door, and got in. I watched her through the windshield as she fixed the stray hairs that had come loose and walked over. I liked how she moved. We sat in the Lincoln for a minute, waiting for the Homeland Security men to move their vehicle out. She turned in her seat to look at me.

"Until now Promise, Indiana, was just a boring little, old town. Suddenly it isn't. Is that something that happens to you a lot, Keeler, do things just get interesting around you?"

I raised my eyebrows and shrugged, trying to look as innocent as I felt. I said, "I didn't actually do anything. Interesting things were already happening before I got here that have nothing to do with me."

She nodded to herself, a little personal secret. "Sure they were." She glanced at me once more before putting the car into gear and switching her concentration to driving. The little convoy got on the road. Silver sports car in front, Collins taking me after them.

Collins didn't know her aunt's neighbor, not even to look at. While she drove, I told her what I knew about Linda Cartwright and what had happened with Donna Williams. Then I told her about the motel and Linda Cartwright's hammer that morning. Collins listened to the story with a creased forehead and the occasional glance at me. She was focused on what I was saying and shook her head often, like it was an unbelievable story. When I was done speaking, her tongue flicked over her teeth and I knew she had questions.

Collins said, "Don't you find it weird that it's Homeland Security? They handle immigration and terrorism and stuff."

I had been thinking about that. "Linda Cartwright is a person of interest in their investigation."

Collins held up a finger. "They said both Cartwrights, not only Linda."

"Correct."

"You don't know who Cartwright's husband is? He might be the central figure here. The Homeland Security people could be after him."

"Cartwright told me he was an insurance salesman. She mentioned that he sells it to restaurants and that he travels for a week at a time. I don't think she wanted me involved."

The HSI agents had led us to a major artery with two lanes going each way. We arrived at a traffic light and pulled to a stop behind the silver sports car. I could see both silhouettes through the rear window. Looked like they were having a conversation. The shorter agent was driving. Collins looked over at me again and I met her gaze.

She said, "I'm curious why you didn't just call the police in the first place. You let both Donna Williams and Linda Cartwright make the wrong decision."

"Wasn't my place to decide that for them."

"Not even as a responsible member of the public?"

I said nothing.

She said, "I'm a close observer of behavior. I've got at least three indicators to peg you as a responsible citizen."

"Three is specific."

She tapped one finger on the steering wheel. "One, you agree to deliver the musical instrument. That's a tell right there. You've got a strong ethical core." She added a finger. "Two, you go across the street to the Cartwright house and get involved in something that isn't your responsibility, strictly speaking." She added the final finger. "And three, you agree to go speak on the record for these Homeland Security people, despite one of them attacking you. And that, Keeler, is the strongest tell of all."

"Oh, and why is that?"

Collins looked at me directly, no trace of a smile or even humor. It was the first purely intimate look between us. "Because by agreeing to go with them now, you're renouncing the opportunity to do the other thing. You're demonstrating a high degree of self-discipline and a transcendent sense of duty."

"What's the other thing?" I asked.

Collins was blushing and she didn't care. She was good-looking and confident. "You know what the other thing is, Keeler. The thing we were about to go do before this happened." She shifted in her seat and her look became even more direct. "Specifically, we were headed to my place. I don't do motels."

I said nothing, because there wasn't any funny or smart thing to say; there were only things to do.

The light turned green up ahead and the silver sports car's brake lights blinked off when the brakes were released. The car advanced into the intersection. I saw the wrong kind of movement coming from the left. It was only a fragment of a second, but in that small moment I recognized what was going to happen. The movement was a garbage truck coming through the intersection and running the red light. The truck was traveling maybe eighty miles per hour. It happened so fast that there wasn't time to say anything. I heard Collins inhale quickly. The silver sports car's brake lights flashed, and a moment later the truck slammed flush into the driver's side.

The impact made a flat sound, like a giant clap with no echo. There was a rushing noise after the first hit, as glass and plastics shattered and sprayed out onto the asphalt. The compounded force of impact propelled the small sports car through the intersection and out the other side for twenty yards. The wrecked car dragged with a terrible shriek. The garbage truck hadn't braked. The sports car's horn sounded and didn't stop. Collins kept the Lincoln motionless. We were both staring at the back of the garbage truck, there wasn't anything left to see of the sports car in front of it.

I came out of the daze quick.

Collins was unbuckling her seat belt, as if she was going to get out on foot and see what had happened. But in my estimation, there wasn't a question.

I put my hand on her arm. "Keep the seat belt on."

She gave me a quick look but complied. As her belt snapped back into place I inspected the surroundings. No traffic cameras that I could see. Not a major intersection and not in close proximity to any businesses. The garbage truck driver put it into reverse. The taillights lit up and the truck rapidly backed up fifteen yards. I knew what was going to happen next.

I said, "They're going to drive away. That was no accident. We need to follow them. You up for that?"

Collins nodded silently. A bar of light from the moving vehicle reflected off the rearview mirror, illuminating her green eyes for half a second. The truck accelerated and veered around the destroyed vehicle. Collins took her foot off the brake, hit the gas, and swung the Lincoln into pursuit. She was focused, her eyes fixed on the darkness ahead. Soon, the truck's receding taillights were drawn back within range.

She mumbled under her breath. "Scumbags."

The wrecked car had ceased being a vehicle and was now something else entirely. A warped and distorted perversion of metal and plastic and bone and flesh. Something that even the workers over at Sherisse's junkyard would have trouble taking apart. The Homeland Security agents were dead; there wasn't any way they could have survived that impact.

At the intersection, a couple of bystander vehicles were stopped in place, unmoving. I figured the civilians in their cars were stunned into paralysis. A man's voice came from the interior of a stationary car, muffled but excited, describing the location, probably to an emergency dispatcher on the line.

I considered the scene. For the garbage truck to have hit the sports car with that kind of speed and force, it was either an unlucky accident or a planned assassination. If it had been an accident, the truck would have stopped, which meant the hit was planned. And if it was planned, it meant the perpetrators knew where the agents were going to be, or where they were going.

The other thing was that the perpetrators seemed to be ignorant of me and Collins. Which made the situation interesting.

CHAPTER EIGHTEEN

The road was wide and dark and virtually empty. On either side, houses centered in wide lawns blurred past. The garbage truck accelerated and Collins touched the gas to keep up.

I said, "Stay back. We're not trying to catch up to them."

Collins said nothing for a couple of seconds, making up her own mind. She nodded once. "Right." She flashed her eyes at me quickly before turning back to the task at hand. "Were they dead, the agents?"

"One hundred percent."

Her hands gripped the wheel. "I can't believe they're dead. They were just there, talking and everything. Alive and doing their jobs." She looked at me again. "They weren't bad people, even the one who was angry with you."

I didn't respond. I hadn't formed any kind of opinion about the Homeland Security people either way. There were tears in Collins's eyes. She wiped them away with a sleeve pulled taut by gripped fingers. Up ahead was another set of traffic lights. As the truck came to it, the light went red. The driver plowed straight through the light without touching the brakes and swung left at high speed.

I said, "You need to run the light. Don't get us killed."

"Not planning on it." She made one last pass with her sleeve, wiping the tears from her eyes. Her expression cleared and her jaw clamped in determination.

The perpetrators in the garbage truck might be looking out for a tail. It's one of the things I would consider in their place. Run the light and see what follows. We didn't have a choice, either give up or do it. Collins blew through the intersection at around sixty miles per hour. She cut the wheel left and turned sharply. The Lincoln's tires squealed. A white SUV was coming through from the right and the driver panicked. The vehicle swung defensively onto the verge, mounted a front lawn, and flattened a mailbox. Someone else leaned on their horn.

That all faded into the background after a couple of seconds. Soon it was us and the speeding garbage truck and the surrounding night. The truck was far enough ahead that we could only make out taillights in the dark. The residential areas on either side broke into farm fields. A car whizzed by going the other way. A flash in the headlights revealed the strobed image of a guy with a beard and a woman looking down at her phone. I turned to watch our six and saw their taillights recede. After that it was a whole lot of dark empty road.

When I faced front again, the ambient light had changed. It took me a second until I saw that Collins had cut the headlights and was now running dark. Nice move. She'd allowed a good amount of distance to build up. The road was dead straight. I figured she was confident that whoever was driving the truck wouldn't be able to make us out. We'd be just a black shadow in the night, fading off into nothing in their mirrors. She drove like that for another two minutes, which felt like ten.

Straight road, two-lane blacktop heading east is what I figured.

I said, "You know where we are?"

"Southeast of town on Redding Road, heading straight east. Roads around here are like a grid. You want to call 9-1-1?"

I said nothing.

She said, "It continues like this for a while, then we get to East Travis and then a big intersection."

"What's there, another town?"

"No. Nothing's there. Same as this, forever."

"So what do you think, they're going to pull into a farm somewhere?"

She nodded once. "That's possible."

"In that case it's better if we just hang back and call in the coordinates. Let the police take it from there."

She looked at me briefly and in the darkness our eyes met. There was minimal dashboard glow since she'd flipped off the lights. The open fields rushed past like ghosts a shade paler than the trees. I listened to the sound of the engine and the tires, four points of contact on hard asphalt with gravel and sand spitting off into the edges. I smiled and so did she.

"You speak military talk, Keeler."

"Force of habit."

"My cousin was a marine."

"I'm sorry about that."

"He spoke like a military guy for a couple months after his discharge, then he became a veterinarian and started speaking differently."

"Started speaking dog?"

Collins laughed. Her eyes flicked up to the rearview and registered alarm. I turned around to check our six again.

Another vehicle had moved up on our tail. Just like us, it ran dark. But unlike the Lincoln, this was a large and powerful modern black SUV.

I said, "We've got un-friendlies."

She floored the accelerator and the Lincoln surged. The driver behind us kept pace easily. The big machine closed the distance and pushed into the back of the car, lightly bumping us. Not like a love touch, more like a cat playing with a mouse. I looked back again and could see nothing but a dark windshield above an imposing grill, which seemed to be level with my rear window.

She cursed. I knew what she meant, there was no way we could outrun them. The Lincoln had a good engine, big enough. Problem was that it would take a while to get fast, crucial seconds that we didn't have.

It was tough to see in the residual light, but I made out deep drainage ditches for the farm runoff on either side of the road. If we ended up dumping into that it wouldn't be pretty. I looked at Collins. Her eyes were darting back and forth between the side mirrors, the rearview, and the road in front of us. The truck's taillights were still visible far ahead.

"I don't know what I should do right now, Keeler."

"Don't look in the mirrors. Keep the car straight and focus on not dumping us in a ditch. Your job is to drive. I'll call out the moves."

"Okay."

Behind us, the SUV was coming up again.

I punched the rearview mirror away. "They're going to flash us."

Which they did about a second later. The high beams flicked on, along with a halogen light bar mounted on the roof. The combined luminance was harsh and powerful, strong enough to destroy a person's night vision for half a minute. I'd squeezed my eyes shut and still got the flash. But I understood what they wanted to do.

I called out to Collins. "Good?"

"Good."

"They're going to come alongside. Block the left on my call."

"Got it."

The SUV surged and swerved, trying to cut next to us. Their plan was to bump us off road into the ditch. Game over. I felt the timing, put myself in their position and anticipated.

I said, "Now."

Collins palmed the wheel left and the SUV fell back. Then she turned it to the right, anticipating a counter move. The vehicle behind us failed to anticipate the second block and bumped us again. Collins surged on the gas, which was impressive since it meant she had been reserving acceleration power. She was a good driver, balls out. That had been a risky and difficult move to make, even for a trained operator. I looked at her in the hard light from the SUV. A sheen had developed on her forehead and her green eyes were bright and glossy.

One option was to hit the brakes and force a collision. Then, I could egress and either counterattack immediately, or get us into cover. Either way we'd lose the garbage truck and be on the defensive pretty quick. I figured a combination of the two might work, but it was iffy, and I had Collins to consider. It wouldn't be appropriate to get her killed on a first date.

I was looking at the verge to see when the drainage ditch might end.

Collins said, "Shit."

I looked up.

The garbage truck was stopped a hundred yards away, blocking the road at a three-quarter angle. We were headed right for the wrong part of it. Impact in under two seconds followed by death or major injury. On the left I saw a cattle grid at the entrance to a farm road. I flicked my hand to move the steering wheel, but Collins was already there. She swerved the Lincoln off the road, skidding out, finding purchase, and jittering over the cattle grid. The rear door panel impacted an iron railing and screeched terribly. She managed to control the car and straighten it.

We powered up a dirt drive. Ahead of us were fields and darkness and the faint bulging outlines of a barn and other farm buildings. No lights, no cattle in sight. A shadowy line of trees behind the barn and, to the right, a fence and open fields. I glanced back. The Lincoln was bumping over the rough driveway, making it hard to see clearly. I could make out the garbage truck maneuvering but it was hard to say how. My situational awareness was muddled by the vibrating car.

The impact against the railing must have crushed the rear fender into the wheel, accounting for a harsh scraping sound and vibrations. Like teeth against an endless chalkboard. No more smooth ride.

I said, "Get behind the buildings."

I couldn't see if anything was following us, but I assumed they were. I was beginning to think that we'd entered a trap. Which made sense if you considered that the SUV people and the garbage truck people were communicating. They'd get us off-road first, then deal with us. Collins got the Lincoln around the other side of a barn and stopped. I reached over and pulled the ignition keys. "Get out, now."

The engine fan was ticking loudly. Otherwise there was no noise. I got situated. Barn to the right, looming over us. No moon in the sky yet. To the left I saw the shadows of smaller buildings, hay bales, and some large machinery.

I came around the car and moved to a big tractor. It had tires the size of the tallest person on earth and an insulated modern cab. I imagined it had all the refinements, like air-conditioning and satellite navigation. Next to that was another big object that I couldn't place, but the word *thresher* entered the front of my mind. None of which mattered because I pulled Collins into a sprint. My aim was one of the buildings about fifty yards away.

We slid across the external wall to an open door and got inside. Once into cover we kept still. Except for her short, hard breathing it was dead quiet. No vehicles following, no engines, no footsteps. There was wind from the trees and the smell of animal manure without the animals, as far as I could tell.

My mind drifted organically to all of the potentially interesting farm tools that I could repurpose. Some people say swords to plowshares; no good reason that couldn't work the other way. Collins was breathing hard, excited. It was very dark in there, but my senses were heightened. The predatory beast had been awakened. I wondered if it was the same for her.

For me it was an ecstatic moment, maybe the best day of the year so far.

I heard footsteps coming up the drive, fifty yards away on the other side of the barn. Collins stopped breathing. I put a hand on her shoulder and she started breathing again. I listened close. Four feet tracking across dirt and sand and stones. Two people were coming.

In other words, a whole lot of target opportunity.

CHAPTER NINETEEN

THE FOOTSTEPS COMING around the side of the barn stopped. I couldn't tell if they'd actually stopped walking, or if they were off the dirt and onto grass.

I was very close to Collins. We were just inside the door to the farm building, which wasn't a barn or a house, more like a glorified shed. The problem with that was I couldn't see much in there. The opening from the door let in only the faintest ambient light from outside. Enough that I could see Collins as a close shadow with body heat and scent and the sound of breathing, now calmer than before. I lowered myself so that our heads were the same level. I felt her loose hair, frizzy and tickling my face. Her hip was hard against me. I whispered very quietly behind her ear.

"I think I may have to do something about those people coming around the barn."

She backed even closer to me, intimate. Her head was touching my cheek. I felt her nodding. Her hand bunched my shirttails and she pulled me even closer. "What do you want me to do?"

"Stay here. Maybe deeper in. Find a spot and crawl into it until I come back."

I felt her nodding again. She pressed harder against me for a moment before detaching.

I felt around for something to use as a weapon. Searching within my operational reach. I didn't want anything to get dislodged and fall. I got my hands on a pile of bricks stacked against the wall. I used that as an anchor to creep around farther. Next to the bricks was a stack of sticks, which felt like bamboo. I was considering how they could be useful when my hand fell onto a wood handle. I lifted it and felt the weight of a heavy thing attached to the end of it. I hopefully visualized a shovel.

That could work. I pictured using the implement as a weapon. Steel blade, flat on one side, sharp on the edge. Oak shaft and sturdy handle.

I slid out of the building and into the cool night air, then went lateral across the external wall and crouched in the lee of a big machine with complicated parts like a metallic spider. I guessed it might be something that farmers dragged around a field behind the tractor, useful for tearing shit up. I looked at the shovel in my hand and saw that it wasn't a shovel but a pitchfork.

Interesting. Different concept, similar result but potentially messier. My new shirt might not make it through.

The exposed space between my hiding spot and the main barn was about twenty feet. I made a rough calculation, five strides and a couple of seconds. I was halfway across the yard when footsteps crunched again from the drive beyond the barn. I sprinted the last couple of yards and flattened against the exterior wall. There was no protection in that position, just me against a large external surface, like a fly against a sheet of paper. I moved. At the corner of the barn was a loose stack of wood siding, the planks leaned up against the wall. I got in amongst the planks and put my head around the corner.

Two silhouettes stood fifteen yards away. Big men in t-shirts with cropped haircuts and well-shaped beards. They were huddled in some kind of a whispered conversation. I saw three empty hands and one hand gripping an object, the shape suggested a phone. I saw no weapons but was going to assume they each had a firearm tucked away. I held the pitchfork shaft in my right hand.

Fifteen yards is a little far to go charging across open land and still expect to come out ahead. At the very least I'd meet some kind of lethal projectile coming my way, probably more than one. Chances were they'd miss, but the repercussions could be hard to justify in a cost benefit analysis.

What made it worse was Tela Collins tucked in the shed. I was trying to resist assigning her special treatment, but it wasn't easy. If I was taken out of the game it'd be that much harder for her to get to safety. I lowered to a crouch and felt around with my left hand. Dirt, grass, weeds, and a fist-sized rock. I brushed my fingers off that and unearthed a smaller stone. It wouldn't be good as a weapon, but that wasn't what I had in mind.

I looked around at the exposed area between the barn and the farm machinery. If I got those two men between me and the spider machine I estimated I could take them out and finish the job.

I played it through in my mind. Get them in there, looking at the spider. Between me and the machine the space was like a funnel, a choke point that I could use. I would creep up on them and use the pitchfork. The first steps would go unnoticed, then they would either get that special tingling of danger or hear me directly. Either way it would be too late.

Me with a pitchfork, in close against two men, was game over. I estimated that I'd have them neutralized within three seconds. Either that or I'd get shot.

There wasn't going to be screaming, talking, crying, or any other audible nonsense—just ultra-violence in velvet tones. For them it would be a brief moment of shock and awe before the vast nothingness. First up was the guy with no phone in his hand. Next would be the other one, reeling from what I'd done to his friend, conscious for another half second before it was his turn to be harvested.

But things didn't turn out that way.

The phone guy's device lit up in a garish blue glow that silhouetted his well-formed beard, jutting out from the chin. They both looked at the phone. The guy holding the device put it to his face and nodded once to his friend.

The two men turned and jogged down toward the gate.

A half minute later I heard engine noises and the screeching of tires on gravel, then the sound of vehicles moving away. After that there was only silence and the night. A minute later an owl hooted. I came around the barn. There was nobody there, nothing moving. It was like nothing had happened. The perpetrators had departed, and with them went all of the potential evidence and possible answers to my questions.

I heard footsteps behind me and turned to see Collins. Her face was pinched and anxious like she couldn't believe what had happened. "They're gone?"

I said nothing.

She exhaled and lowered her head to her chest. "That's a good thing."

I nodded. "I guess. I'm usually in favor of direct confrontation but in this case, you're probably right."

"So what do we do now?"

"We get out of here and get rid of my car, to start with."

She stood there, thoughtful, with burning questions of her own.

"You don't think we should call the police."

"No, I don't."

She looked at me with a serious expression on her face, forehead creased with concern. "Want to walk me through that for a second?"

"I've been thinking about that. Last night, I called the police to get the agents in the silver sports car distracted. I didn't know they were agents then."

Collins nodded. "And?"

"Two things. One, obviously the police got involved. You heard what the Homeland Security agents said. Local police kept them immobilized for four hours. That's a long time to hold back a federal agency's ongoing operation. I'd call that a hostile local response."

"Okay."

"Second, they got plowed by a garbage truck." I looked at Collins to see if she was with my train of thought. She looked back at me, her forehead still creased. "Cops get involved, agents die," I said. "Two moments in some kind of a bad composition."

She said, "Tangential logic."

"Correlation doesn't mean causation. I agree with you there. But in operational terms it's enough to get suspicious."

Her brow smoothed out. She was a decisive person. "I follow your thinking and I agree. We have to operate under the assumption that the police are an unknown variable."

"Correct."

"So we do what now?"

"We get rid of my car. Then we'll see."

Collins didn't make a fuss or ask any unnecessary questions. There would be time for that. To me it was an obvious set of variables, almost like a very simple math equation. These people had seen the Lincoln, most likely noted down the license plate number. I needed to get that car out of circulation. It wasn't only the killers I was concerned with; it was now the police as well.

I pulled out the crushed fender with my hands and got it away from the tire, then got behind the wheel. Collins sat in the passenger seat next to me. I kept the headlights off for the first couple of miles, then I flicked them on again. Nobody was following us. It was like nothing had happened, except it had.

After a while we were back in a place with streetlights and residential properties. There was late-night traffic and twenty-four-hour fast food restaurants with drive-through clientele. We pulled into an empty two-lane road and I saw the sign at an intersection, Church Street. We were on the south side.

The Lincoln blew past a familiar curve, and Sycamore Circle flashed by on the left. I recalled the floating architectural masterpiece and the woman with her shotgun. The image of Gus Simmons came into my mind's eye. That was something I'd be dealing with again,

Simmons and the guitar from Alabama, but that seemed far away at the moment.

Collins was leaned against the door gazing out the window. She pushed loose hair away from her face and glanced at me. "You know where you're going?"

"I think so."

She nodded and shifted in the corner of her seat. I looked over at her, beautiful in the yellow vapor lights. She felt me looking and smiled. I felt a renewed surge of energy and well-being. Despite all indications to the contrary, the world was improving all the time.

Some people call that progress.

CHAPTER TWENTY

The suburban landscape was dimly lit and uniform, differentiated in a slim way by fast food chains taking up prime real estate. Finally we bumped over railroad tracks and things got darker and less uniform. The houses there were scrappier, put together without the help of a cookie cutter.

The gates to Sherisse's family junkyard were closed. No sign, no name, only the anonymous steel-panel fence on rollers. Same as before except now the door was secured with a case-hardened chain. I nosed the Lincoln to the gate and leaned on the horn for a ten count. I got out and went to the slim opening where a door was hinged to the gate. At first there was nothing but shadow. Then the shadows moved and I saw the dogs.

All five ridgebacks were out, ears up and alert. They weren't barking in disarray, they were positioned in tactical formation. Two dogs prowled defensively, close in to the building, one was out in midfield being mobile, and the last two animals took an advanced reconnaissance position close to the gate, sniffing and listening. Weirdly, the two dogs out front were wagging their tails at me. The stiff appendages waved happily, like a third arm set back there for balance and communication. Looked like I was a much more popular guy now.

Not an obvious conclusion given how Sherisse looked and behaved when she finally dragged herself out of the house, still dressed in black, this time without a hat. Her hair was plaited into cornrows, coiled tight to her scalp like independent snakes, tails flicking out at the back.

Sherisse came to the gate and looked at me through the crack. "What happened, you got the guitar?"

I said, "Not yet. Different story. I need your help with this car."

She scratched herself and looked behind me at the Lincoln. "Who do you have in there?"

"I'm on a date."

She laughed quietly. "What do you need from me, big man?"

"I need the car to disappear. I figure you owe me a couple, so I'm not feeling too bad about getting you up out of bed."

Sherisse ignored most of that. "Disappear, as in how?"

"As in erased from the face of the planet."

The gate was unlocked and the two front dogs came running to scout the road. Collins climbed out of the car making happy noises at the dogs. No growling or other nonsense for her, the dogs were all wagging tails and licking tongues. I pulled the Lincoln into the lot. Collins and Sherisse introduced themselves and came inside with the dogs. Sherisse locked the gate and stood examining the Lincoln.

Sherisse said, "Got any practice in removing a gas tank, Keeler?"

I yawned and motioned to Collins. "She's the gearhead."

Collins shrugged. "You got an extra set of coveralls?"

Removing the fuel tank was a little more complicated than I'd have imagined. Sherisse directed me to pilot the Lincoln over to a pit. Collins got down under the vehicle with tools and a light. Sherisse sat on an old chair and smoked a mentholated cigarette. I handed tools to Collins as and when she demanded them.

Once she had drained the gas into a large container, Sherisse pointed over to something behind the building, which looked like a big iron dumpster painted in red. "Bring it over by the machine."

Collins got behind the wheel and steered while I pushed the Lincoln next to the dumpster. A set of elevated flood lights clicked and buzzed into service. Sherisse walked up.

I said, "I don't need it in a dumpster. I need it gone."

"Get over there and watch." She pointed to a steel catwalk platform surrounding the elevated cab of a mechanical grabber. Collins and I followed her up the steps and stood against the cab. I could already see that the dumpster wasn't a dumpster, it looked more like a box containing a barrel-shaped cheese grater.

Sherisse smiled when I glanced at her with questions. "Car shredder."

She pushed a button, and an engine fired up. Then a second engine. I figured one for the grabber, another for the cheese grater. Sherisse manipulated a joystick, and the grabber shuddered and growled. She sank its four iron teeth into the roof of my Lincoln, like an eagle's talons going into a rabbit. The car was lifted into the air and maneuvered above the machine.

Sherisse said, "Ready?"

Collins said, "Do it."

The cheese grating barrel began to move, undulating in weird ways as a multitude of teeth rotated and circled each other in complicated patterns. The grabber expanded and released. For a brief moment the Lincoln was in free fall. The car hit the shredder and it began to shudder and shake. Slowly, but inexorably, the vehicle was sucked into the machine and torn to pieces with mechanical violence.

The cacophony was intense, like a million pieces of metal being ripped against each other. The dogs began to howl. I wondered if Uncle Dwight was still seated in the same chair. Maybe Sherisse had put him to bed. Maybe Uncle Dwight liked the sound of metal thrashing. Five minutes later there was no more Lincoln. I wondered if it might be symbolic of something, like the end of an era. We walked over to the other side of the shredder to find a pile of fresh metal shards gleaming in the hard electric light.

Sherisse shut everything down and showed us the back way across the train tracks. She was tired and wanted to go back to bed. There was no incoming rail traffic and we crossed without incident. I turned to look and saw Sherisse watching me. She stepped back and melted into the enveloping darkness.

Collins and I walked in silence until we were past the tracks and into the woods on the other side. We came to the fence leading into the backyard of 1248 Springhurst. She stopped me in the darkness of the trees, put her hand out, and threaded a finger through the belt loop of my jeans, tugging gently.

"That was one hell of a first date, Keeler."

I allowed her to come close and brushed my fingers through the unruly hair at her neck, below the ear. I liked her smell. Her free hand came up flat against my chest, tracing the muscle and then around to my back. The nape of her neck was cool. She pulled me in and our lips touched. First it was delicate, brushing and testing. Her breath mixed with mine. It got more physical after that and we were lost in it for a while.

Eventually, she disengaged. "You busy tomorrow night?"

"No plans."

"Dinner at my place. No more distractions or excuses."

"Outstanding idea."

We went back in for another round of kissing, shorter this time. After that, she pulled me along the fence line and out behind her great aunt's house at 1250. We hopped the fence and came to the back door.

She whispered. "You got a phone number, Keeler?"

"Not a phone person. Give me yours and I'll call you."

Collins reeled off her number and I memorized it. She fished a key out of her purse and turned to open her great aunt's back door. She looked at me for a moment, framed in the doorway. "Call me tomorrow."

Then she was inside. I was left alone in the yard with the darkness, the insects, and her taste and smell lingering. There was a sound on the other side of the backyard fence. For a moment I held still and listened, alert to whatever might be out there. When nothing happened, I figured it was a skunk or some other nocturnal animal.

I came around the corner of the house and looked to the road. Across the street Cartwright's laundry still hung on lines like a yard full of ghosts. I figured she must have been too busy to remember to bring it in.

I used the key from under Cartwright's flowerpot and did my best to open and close the door quietly. I stood for a minute in the entry, listening to the regular sounds that the guest house made in the night, getting used to them. A minute after that I was stretched out on the sofa. Two minutes later I was asleep.

CHAPTER TWENTY-ONE

I WAS FALLING through the sky. It was a HAHO jump. High altitude, high opening. The parachute canopy was above me and everything was completely silent. The sun was just becoming visible at the horizon line, like a bright spark burning a hole in a featureless line. I knew where I was, because I'd been there before. Northwest Iraq above the Euphrates River; we were creeping down on a little town called Al-Obaidy. I could see the sun popping over the horizon because of my altitude, but down below it was still night. Even so, I recognized the dark outlines of the hospital complex that was our target.

But it wasn't real. There were no team members in formation with me, this time I was alone. I fell for much longer than seemed possible. It was peaceful, falling without falling. And then there was another jumper alongside me. Not one of my buddies with a beard and a smirk but my sister. I didn't get the chance to figure out what she was doing there because I woke up on Linda Cartwright's sofa.

Daylight was streaming in through the window. I was fully clothed except for the boots, which I'd removed before putting my feet up. There were no sounds of early morning plumbing or a homeowner shuffling around doing domestic chores like laundry and plant watering, sheet changing and breakfast making. No scent of toast and no sound of a percolator dripping coffee into a pot.

I swung my feet off the couch to the floor next to my boots. I looked up through the front window and saw two cars passing by in quick succession. Not too early for traffic. I'd slept late. A side table with a potted plant stood between the armchair and the window. I'd moved that armchair the day before. Now, the potted plant was on its side, the ceramic container cracked open and soil spilled out, dark and moist with little white specks.

My gaze drifted beneath the table and landed on a hammer which lay inert on the wooden floor.

It was Cartwright's hammer, with the rubberized grip, the same one she'd used on her aggressors in the motel room. The steel head caught the daylight with a dull gleam. The hammer alone was innocent enough, a tool used to convince stubborn objects to change their ways. The context changed all that.

I put on my boots and tied the laces. While doing so, I considered the recent journey of the tool.

Cartwright's hammer, projected across the room, hitting the pot and smashing it to pieces. She would have cleaned up the mess, given what I'd seen of her domestic habits. Which meant she was either unaware of the event, or incapable of cleaning it up. When I stood and started looking around, I quickly saw what had escaped me the night before in the dark: notably, dried blood stains on the floorboards at the front entrance.

Blood drops trailed back to the bottom of the stairs.

I went up the steps two at a time. At the first landing was an open door into a bedroom. Linda Cartwright was not present. I continued to the top floor. From there I conducted a basic search of the house, top to bottom. I was only looking for people, living, dead, or in between. A methodical effort would wait for later. I didn't find anyone home, dead or alive. What I did find was a dented bannister column a couple of steps below the master bedroom. It wasn't visible going up the stairs, only coming down. The surface had been chipped off. I looked closely and found fragments of varnished wood on the stair carpet.

In the master bedroom I found damage on the inside edge of the door, six inches below the top hinge. The bed linens were disordered, as if someone had flung off the sheets in a hurry. Cartwright had an army background, which pretty much guaranteed that she'd be fastidiously making her bed every day for the rest of her life.

I replayed the events in my mind.

Cartwright had told me she was a light sleeper. I figured some kind of sound disturbs her, she flings the sheets off, and gets her hand around the rubberized hammer handle positioned next to her bed, or under her pillow. When an intruder enters the bedroom door. Cartwright's ready and waiting and attacks. I had already witnessed her in a violent rage the morning before, and I could imagine its playing out again. But, this time it's dark. She swings and misses her target. The hammer slaps into the door and chips off paint and wood. Undeterred, she follows up. The intruder backs out of the door, she lunges between the door and the stairwell. Cartwright lands a shot on the surprised guy, sends him tumbling down the stairs. On the way down, the intruder hits something on the bannister.

I moved down the stairs to the entrance. I tracked the narrative.

Cartwright pursues the guy downstairs. She's relentless. Another tussle in the entrance. The guy isn't underestimating her anymore and this time she's overcome. In the struggle, the hammer is sent flying across the room. It was probable that a second intruder had been downstairs and helped to get her under control. Once they have her subdued, they bundle her out of the house and into a vehicle.

There had been blood. I thought of them taking her out and the silver van came to mind. That would be the obvious choice as a snatch vehicle. The Pontiac GTO had other purposes. Silver van meant the two guys who had come earlier for Donna Williams.

After doing a first pass searching the house, I made coffee in the kitchen. Cartwright had a French press system. I leaned back against the kitchen counter to let my thoughts percolate while the coffee settled. The basement door was right there facing me. I hadn't been down there yet.

The door opened onto a set of wood stairs and a bannister. I found the light switch behind a mess of raincoats hung on the wall. I thumbed the switch and a couple of bare bulbs flicked on. The stairs went down in the direction of the front of the house and ended approximately at the middle of the foundation footprint. The basement was a large space with cement flooring and shelving units. At the bottom of the stairs was another door. I opened it to see an empty garage with a closed garage door, which I assumed led out to the driveway.

I came upstairs again and sat at the kitchen table, sipping the hot coffee and ruminating. Cartwright missing. The hammer and the broken plant pot. The bloodstains. None of it was looking good for her. All of it put her and Donna Williams into the same boat. When I'd finished the first cup of coffee, I poured a second and took it upstairs. Time to do another search, this time for nonliving things.

CHAPTER TWENTY-TWO

On a dresser in the master bedroom was a photograph of Cartwright and a man. They were smiling and standing close together. The man, presumably her husband, was handsome and rakish with a thin mustache. He had vaguely Mediterranean features. I estimated him to be about ten years older than his wife.

I pulled the photo out of the frame and slid it into my pocket.

The husband had his own closet in the bedroom. I'm no fashion expert and I've worn a suit only on rare occasions, but this guy's suits didn't look cheap or formal. They looked like expensive casual wear bordering on flamboyant. In the bathroom there were two sinks, each with a mirror cabinet. The one on the left was his, with shaving items and male-specific grooming products.

I ruminated for a couple of seconds.

The guy lived in the house, but didn't dominate the domestic space with conventional masculine traces like sports memorabilia, guns, a well-stocked liquor cabinet, or plaid house slippers waiting in the entrance. In the basement it had been the same thing, no obvious traces of a conventional masculine presence besides a well-organized toolbox with all of the necessary items, including another hammer.

Maybe they had a his and hers agreement regarding the hammer, but I doubted it. I figured Linda Cartwright was the one who'd organized the toolbox, not her husband. Maybe he was simply incompetent. I wouldn't be surprised. She seemed competent enough for two.

The guest room was decorated in neutral tones, a simple room with a bed, a window, and a dresser. The window looked out to a rectangle of grass. I pulled open the dresser drawers: empty. There was nothing in there indicating recent human habitation.

The Cartwrights were middle-aged. There was no sign that they had produced any children.

Opposite was a small office with a white desk set in front of a window with a view to the street. The office was minimal in every sense. Minimal surface space, minimal contents. The desk surface hosted a computer, keyboard, and mouse. Nothing else. The desk cavity for legs and feet was bordered by rows of drawers either side. Three on the right side, and one triple-sized drawer on the left.

The top right side was dedicated to the utility bills, all in the name of William F. Cartwright. Looked like somebody was keeping clean records. The drawer contained six months of bills. The middle drawer was all about paper management. Clips and staplers of all kinds, along with a ruler and two pencils side by side with a steel sharpener. Bottom right hand drawer was shallower than its upstairs siblings. I found an extra mouse pad and a couple of cables.

I pulled open the triple-sized drawer on the left to reveal a hanging file rail with a bunch of neatly organized folders. The first folder was filled with a relentless series of property tax documents. After that were two thick sheaves of documentation related to a home improvement project that must have taken up the Cartwrights' attention for at least half a year. I skipped quickly through schematic drawings and construction permit applications.

Next in line were a bunch of folders relating to vehicle ownership and a couple different kinds of insurance. After those I pulled another thick folder. The contents turned out to be Cartwright's military documents, a whole bunch of bureaucratic nonsense and a couple of important papers related to her veteran status. I thumbed through the files until I found the separation form. DD Form 214 is what you get when you're done with an active duty contract. I was familiar with the jargon. Linda Cartwright had been honorably discharged from the United States Army in 2004. Her last job was listed as unit supply specialist with the 10th Mountain Division.

I sat back and allowed my mind to do a little mental time travel.

The army's 10th Mountain Division had been the first troops into Afghanistan, around 2001. Cartwright had separated in 2004, which put her smack into the initial deployments. Unit supply specialist is an important job dealing with inventory and logistics issues. Essentially, Cartwright had been in charge of making sure the important stuff arrived and got dispatched to the guys in her unit who needed it. There was a high probability that she'd been stationed at the division headquarters with the Combined Forces Land Component Command in Karshi-Khanabad, what they'd called K2.

I slotted away the military files and crawled my fingers over the remaining hanging folders. These contained documents related to the ownership of the house. The deed for the home on Springhurst road was in both William's and Linda's names. Date of purchase was 2006. I closed the drawer. The office had a narrow closet. Two shelves packed with boxes and empty space. The boxes contained more old computer hardware and cables and things of that nature, discarded office stuff.

Back in the living room I looked through the front window again.

There was no sign of life in the house across the street. I wondered if Collins had already left and gone to work. I figured she'd have taken a cab to get her car. There was no more Lincoln Town Car parked out there either, which meant I would have to find another means of transportation.

I contemplated the view for a minute.

Cartwright had discovered that Donna Williams's daughter attended one of the local schools. The name surfaced in my mind, Booker T. Washington High School. The kid was in the ninth grade.

She had told me there was an address attached to the student records, along with a photo ID scan. Cartwright had said it had been printed out for her, but I hadn't found any printout. I assumed it had been taken, along with Cartwright herself.

That was potentially interesting information.

I went upstairs and fired up the desktop computer in the office. The machine whirred and buzzed and clicked. Once I was looking at the internet, I typed questions into boxes and eventually found a white pages website where I searched for Donna Williams in Promise, Indiana. I got three versions of Donna Williams. Each version had an age attached, and none were younger than sixty. Either she wanted her information unlisted, or her domicile was in somebody else's name.

A car door slammed outside. I looked past the computer screen and saw nothing but sky. The sound of female voices traveled up from the street. I got out of the chair and leaned forward, looking down through the window.

A small white van was stopped in front of the house. The van had a custom logo decal on the side, *Lopez Cleaning Service.* There were soap bubbles behind the words. Four women with matching blue t-shirts were emerging from the vehicle. The cleaners got the back of the van open. Two of them extracted boxes filled with spray bottles and cleaning rags. The other two each had a vacuum cleaner in hand. I pictured the four of them policing the dust mites and stray cookie crumbs. This was looking like one hell of an efficient cleaning operation.

The team started up the walk to the house. They looked happy. I could hear them chattering in Spanish. I turned off the computer.

CHAPTER TWENTY-THREE

THE DOORBELL RANG while I was coming down the stairs.

I made it to the entrance area just after the second ring. I was about to open the door when one of the cleaning women did it herself, with a key. When the door opened, she was a little surprised to see me standing right there looking at her.

The cleaner recovered fast and turned to say something to a colleague behind her. I have enough of a Spanish vocabulary to get me through a restaurant menu, and even a little further. I recognized the word *marido*, which means husband. The woman in front stepped aside for a more important colleague. She came through and faced me. She was one of the two with a vacuum cleaner, held in one hand. The other hand was gripped securely around a large screen internet device with a rubberized case.

The boss woman set down the vacuum cleaner just inside the door. I watched her hands fret over the screen.

She spoke without looking at me directly. "You the husband?"

"No. They didn't tell me the cleaners were coming."

She looked up. "No, as in you're not the husband?"

"Right. I'm not a *marido*."

She smiled, blinding me with white teeth set in a perfect double row. "That's okay."

"What were you supposed to do, if I was the husband?"

"They just said to let them know if the husband was home. I guess so that he wouldn't be disturbed. I don't know."

"Who said?"

She said, "My client."

A confusing answer. I looked at the lit screen of the phone she was holding. "Show me."

People with expensive phones don't like other people looking at their screens, as if their interior secret life was in danger of being put out there for everyone to see. That was at least half true. Seemed to me like people with fancy phones had somehow agreed to take important parts of their brains out of their skull and put them into the phone to be leeched into someone else's computer. Doing so meant that it wasn't going to be secret or private anymore.

"It's our app." The cleaner showed me her phone and I looked into the screen.

The rectangle was filled with a series of smaller boxes. The client name was listed on top. I read out loud, "J&S Services." There was an address below the company name, 2174A N. 3rd Street. Interesting information.

I said, "Regular client?"

"Yes."

"And they gave you the keys to my friend's house."

She smiled at me, like she was eager to be transparent and above board. "That's right."

"What is that, some kind of a property management company?"

"I guess so. They have several properties. Is that all right, sir?"

The cleaner was trying to get rid of me. I said, "This is your first time cleaning here?"

"Yes, it is."

I nodded. "How did you get the keys?"

The woman wasn't happy anymore. Nobody likes to be interrogated. I could see the thought process playing itself out in her mind. Like a game of computer pong. She was wondering to what extent she needed to answer my questions. I helped her out by not smiling or moving. After a couple of moments she realized it was going to be better if she played it straight. The woman held up the phone as if it had all the answers.

"They book it on the app." She looked at me to see if I understood this advanced and important terminology. I didn't do anything. She continued patiently. "With these guys, I swing by the office and pick up keys to the property on the day."

"All your clients give you keys?"

"Regular clients sometimes give me the keys, sometimes they don't. J&S manage multiple properties, a good client." She grinned, showing me perfect white teeth, like money. "I make an exception and go by their office. I guess your friend didn't tell you to expect the cleaners. If you like we can come back later."

"There's a person there at J&S Services who hands out the keys to you?"

She nodded and looked into her phone vacantly.

The other three cleaners were waiting for the conversation to be over. What was interesting was the fact that Linda Cartwright's house was being cleaned at the behest of a property management company. I'd just seen the deed for the house in her name. I'm not a homeowner myself, but I did know that people usually hire cleaners on their own.

I said, "Thank you. Have a nice day."

I stepped aside and let the cleaners enter the house. They passed me with lowered eyes, latent banter ready to bubble from their lips. It didn't take long before they were doing their work. I went out and shut the door behind me. I crouched to put the key back under the flowerpot where I'd found it.

I turned and walked away

I thought about the situation, making a little checklist of events in my head. It soon turned into a checklist of disappearances. Donna

Williams, gone. Linda Cartwright, gone. Add William F. Cartwright to that list, check. The ghosts were adding up. Now the cleaners, tidying up. Making everything smooth and quiet. Somebody was running a slick operation, like they had it all figured out. Do the dirty work, send in the cleaners. Even the cleaners looked wholesome, like they didn't know. The more I thought about it, the less I liked it.

I didn't know what was going on, not entirely, not yet. But I did know that when I had it figured out, I wasn't going to be finding some kind of a morally confusing situation. When the truth came, it was going to be clear as the blue water on that Florida key. The bad people were throwing trouble around and getting away with it so far. It was about time trouble came their way. We'd see how they liked it.

There were two places to start with. Donna Williams's daughter's school and now, J&S Services.

THE BUS STOP on the corner wasn't exactly heaving with passengers fighting for first place, but there were three older men seated together. I addressed them as a unit, asked how to get to Booker T. Washington High School, thinking there was a thirty percent chance that even one of them would know. I was wrong, it was one hundred percent on all three. Turned out the high school was on the same bus route, just going the other direction. So they pointed me across the road to the other stop.

Which made it the route south to downtown Promise.

I asked about the other address fresh in my mind, J&S Services at 2174A North 3rd Street. Two of the men spoke together, same words at the same time. "Same direction, different bus."

The third man said, "It's out east. If you're going to do both you should go to the school first, then get back on to the same bus and keep going. Get off at the municipal building. North 3rd is a couple blocks away. Find that and take the bus out of town a mile or so, the bus driver should set you straight."

"A mile?" I asked.

They shrugged. "Yes, at least a mile."

On the bus I decided to do it the other way, go to J&S Services first, then think about the school.

I got off the bus at the municipal building and walked five blocks to North 3rd where I caught another bus out of town. Initially I was able to keep track of the numbers moving out of town. The buildings were spaced out comfortably, and each of them displayed its number like a well behaved product in a catalog. I sat back looking out the window, lulled by the ride and tracking the numbers in a regular rhythm.

That all changed as we got out of town. The last number I saw was 799, right before the bus carved a turn, slunk down under a railroad bridge, and came out in the countryside. A mile out I was looking at corn fields. Thinly distributed among the fields were buildings set back from the road. None of them had their street number prominently displayed.

Two miles out of town we came around a turn and there was a whitewashed brick building with J&S Services painted front and center in blue, just above the closed double-wide doors of an auto-service garage. I pushed the button to get off. The stop was about three hundred yards past J&S. I walked back along the grassy verge. The corn grew on my right. On my left were trees. The sun was high, I reckoned past high noon at that point. Lunchtime.

I assumed that was the reason J&S Services was all closed up, staff were eating lunch somewhere. I pictured a restaurant at the side of the road, maybe at an intersection a few miles away.

Thoughts of lunch made me remember that I hadn't eaten breakfast.

J&S Services was a two-story affair with windows above the garage. There was a commercial office on the ground floor accessed by a glass door. The sign was turned around to read *Closed*. The parking lot out by the side of the building had five cars positioned diagonally facing the road. The used cars had prices scribbled in white on their windshields. It was an optimistic scene, rooted in a hope that someone passing by would find the offer attractive, maybe someone tired of taking the bus.

Closer in to the brick structure, a clutch of cars were packed tightly together. These would be waiting for their turn in the shop. Other cars would be out to lunch with their owners. Nobody was walking around, except for me.

I circled around the side of the building. The asphalt parking lot broke up and merged into the edges of a neighboring corn field. A couple of large oaks marked out the border with grass growing between them. The oaks looked like they'd been there forever, even before the building and the corn. The rear was a solid brick wall, whitewashed like the rest. On the far side was a window into the garage. No doubt it had been left open to ventilate exhaust fumes and auto mechanic chemicals.

I pulled the window open all the way and vaulted through to the garage.

CHAPTER TWENTY-FOUR

I LANDED SOFT AND SILENT, knees folding to a lithe crouch. I was feeling dangerous, like a leopard with nothing to kill, yet.

There wasn't anything happening in the garage. Nothing moving and no objects of interest at present. Two cars waited for lunch to end, open hoods and distended parts spread on grease-stained work rags. Tools were organized on peg boards and inside the open drawers of shop tool stations. The place smelled of grease and lubricant.

I moved into the small office next door. At the far end was a spiral staircase going up to the second floor. The office consisted of an old steel desk in front of an equally ancient chair with foam stuffing duct-taped in. The desk hosted a modern cash register and the kind of electronic gizmo they use to suck down financial information from cards and phones without anything having to actually touch anything else.

Contactless, like a new way of living.

Behind the desk were shelves of things like spark plugs, replacement batteries, lubricants, cables, and aerosols, all jockeying for real estate with air fresheners and accessories for plugging devices into cigarette lighter sockets. The desk surface hosted a stack of invoice slips and a blank order book. There was a calendar pad front and center. The top sheet had the current month and bookings penciled in.

Behind the desk was a key cabinet in dirty gray steel, the cover swung open. Car keys hung on hooks, each key had an associated tag attached. Each tag had a license plate number written in ballpoint pen on a paper slip tucked into a plastic sleeve. Approximately a dozen car keys, no house keys. Facing the desk was a wall of industrial shelving stacked around the front door. The shelves held more car-related items in boxes.

At the foot of the spiral staircase hung a chain with a red sign in the center. It read *Private* in bold white lettering. I stepped over the chain and made my way up the stairs, spiraling in a full circle before I arrived at the second floor. Upstairs I was facing out to a big loft space above the garage. To my left was another desk. To my immediate right was another key cabinet, installed shoulder height one step away. It was the same box as downstairs, only cleaner.

I flipped open the cover and looked inside. Same color, same material, same brand, same hooks. All the same, except this one had seven sets of house keys and a tiny camera bubble glinting at me from the back. I looked into the bubble and saw a wide angle reflection of myself. I wondered if there was anyone on the other side watching, or if my face was just being filed away into a computer system somewhere.

It made me think of the camera doorbell at the Cartwright house and the security cameras following me around at Gus Simmons's gate. I looked back at the little bubble in the key box. My experience with closed-circuit camera systems was that the footage just went into storage before anyone could actually look at it. But then there were new developments to account for, like automated motion detection and recognition systems.

I closed the cabinet door. The loft space stretched the width of the building, light streamed in through four south-facing windows. First up was an area with a coffee table and two black leather sofas angled around it. A waiting room where visitors were sent to cool their heels. Facing that was a desk with a luxury leather chair, also in black. Farther in was a recreational area with a lot of space around the pool table. A refrigerator and a large antique cabinet were pushed back against the wall.

The green felt on the pool table had been worn in the right places. The coin drop for quarters told me that once upon a time the table had belonged to a bar, but then someone had tricked out the mechanism so that the quarters fell into an open box, available to be used again.

I walked back to the desk up front, a glossy surface in black wood, completely clear and spotless. Being so clean, it showed a layer of settled dust.

I sat in the chair and swiveled around. There were drawers either side. I pulled them open, one by one. The top left drawer featured a half-depleted pack of chewing gum and three screws. The drawer below it contained a flat box in glossy cherry wood. I pulled the drawer out all the way and thumbed open the box. A breech loading pistol from the eighteenth century was nestled into the velvet-lined interior. The pistol looked nice, but the box didn't contain any of the required accessories, like paper wadding, gunpowder, or a lead ball.

I went through the other drawers. Nothing of further interest. Just as the last drawer was closing on silent rollers, I heard the jangle of keys out front, followed by the front door opening. I stayed quiet in the leather chair. Downstairs, someone walked in and let the door swing back on its hinges. Ten seconds later music filled the space. A bouncy tune that came out of the speakers mid-song. I assumed the person below had just hit the switch on a radio.

I glanced around the office. There was nothing there to keep me. I only had one real question, and now I had someone who might be able to answer it. I opened the top drawer and removed the old pistol. Lifting the gun revealed a small slip of white paper pressed into the velvet. I turned it over. On the other side were three numbers printed in black ink. 30-43-92. I glanced around the room once more.

Nothing there spoke to me. No painting hung up to hide a wall safe. No closet that I hadn't looked into. I got out of the chair and onto my hands and knees. Under the desk was a small hotel-style safe built into the wall. A dial sat right in the middle of it. I had some experience with safes. They were different, but not all that different. I spun the dial left a bunch of times to clear it. Then landed on the first number, 30. Right turn past 43 until I landed on it the second time. I made a left turn to land directly on 92.

The door flipped open. A single pile of cash rested quietly inside. No little sachet filled with diamonds, no handgun, nothing but extra space.

I removed the cash and flipped through it. The wad contained fifty hundred-dollar bills held together by a rubber band. Five thousand dollars. I shoved the money into my front pocket alongside the photograph of Linda Cartwright's husband. I closed the safe and locked it.

The pistol felt nice in my hand, heavy and authentic, all wood and steel. The butt was capped with a solid metal knob, engraved with an angry face. Someone had kept the antique weapon in good condition. It was oiled and clean, at least on the outside. The barrel was substantial, the bore smooth and round, the exterior an elongated octagon of steel.

None of which would make any difference because there was nothing to shoot out of it. The radio was playing something modern and jazzy, good music. I heard the guy down there humming the tune. I returned to the key cabinet near the stairs and removed the seven house keys. Those went in my other pocket.

I winked at the small camera and closed the cover.

Downstairs, I walked through the little office to the car repair bays. A man was facing away from the entrance, putting on mechanic's overalls. He was still humming along to the music when I came through the doorway. I coughed and he froze. The guy was big, with exaggerated musculature, no stranger to the gym. He'd managed to feed his legs into the overalls, but the arms hadn't made it yet. They were defined and taut, tapering out to shoulders bulging with muscle. A clean white tank top contrasted to the guy's skin, ebony and gleaming blue with the fluorescent light.

I figured he'd flicked the switch and the lights had come on, along with the music. Even as he turned to look at me, he didn't stop humming. Cool, calm, and collected. The man let his eyes take a tour of me while he tied off the jumpsuit arms around his waist. He flicked a look to the ancient gun in my hand, then to the window I'd vaulted through, nodded gently to himself. "Thought I saw that window just a little more open than I'd left it."

I said, "You the owner?"

The guy said nothing until his boots were tied. When they were, he stood up and advanced toward me, flexing his shoulders. He gave his head a shake, neck joints crackled and popped. "I don't own anything except my car and my tools. I'm just a guy who works here and you are a man who doesn't."

I nodded. "That's good. You have no skin in the game if you're not an owner. Did you have a nice big lunch?"

He shook his head. "Not big, but nice. Thank you for asking."

"You don't like to eat with the others."

"They eat different food than me."

I grinned. "You're vegan?"

He did the opposite of grin, which was to square his jaw and frown. "What do you want?"

"I've got a question."

"Only one?"

"To start."

He shook his head. "Not going to be answering any questions from you, mister. You might as well get on out of here, before I'm obliged to help you do that."

I shook my head. "Not going to happen."

His eyes got harder still. "Like I just said, no answers, no cooperation." The guy pointed at the breech-loading pistol. "You know that's not going to be doing much for you, at least not today."

I said, "I wasn't planning on firing bullets with it. Mostly these things don't work anymore. Firing it could be dangerous to the person doing the shooting."

I laid the gun in my hand, like I was examining it for an auction. I picked it up by the octagonal barrel. Felt the weight of it, the butt engraved with that unhappy expression. I showed him the angry face.

"You know why they put these angry faces on the butt like that back in the old days?"

The man was close to me now, looking at the gleaming metallic scowl. "Can't say that I do."

I moved very fast, something between a flinch and a twitch. I swung the handle and gave the guy's head a light rap with the angry faced steel knob. The impact with the guy's head made a hollow sound, like a percussion instrument.

He jumped back and put his hand to his head. "What did you do that for?"

I said, "Always wanted to try that. Back in the day you'd take your one shot with a gun like this, then you'd need to spend two minutes loading it again. Obviously that isn't going to be sufficient in a combat situation, which is what the handle was made for."

"For what, to hit the other guy with?"

I said, "To beat him to death with."

"Thanks for the history lesson."

"I didn't hurt you did I?"

"Not the point. That wasn't a sporting thing to do." He picked up a heavy ratchet extender from the tool station. "You want to go like this, or you want to do it clean? I'll go either way."

I said, "I'd rather just ask you the question and then go away, buddy."

He shook his head. "Can't do that. *Buddy*."

I put the antique pistol on a work surface to my left. "Whatever."

The guy flung the ratchet extender at the tool station. It was heavy, clanging against the steel cabinet. He put his hands up like a boxer. "Let's go. Haven't had a bare knuckles experience in a couple of years. I'm damned excited."

I appraised him. Amateur boxer, very fit, strong positive mental attitude. About six feet four and change. The size and height made him confident. The guy was moving his feet, lightly dancing them in place. He'd fight orthodox, which was a disadvantage in my opinion.

CHAPTER TWENTY-FIVE

I WATCHED the guy doing his boxing routine for a moment. He looked light on his feet, which only meant I'd have to knock him off them. The problem was that I was liking the guy. He had a good spirit. I didn't figure him for someone who needed to learn about retribution.

I said, "You sure? It doesn't have to be like this."

"I'm a hundred percent sure."

"Not exactly a fair deal."

He said, "How so?"

"I have questions, you don't want to answer. If I break your face and you can't speak, I won't get my answers."

He grinned. "True. Tough shit."

The guy shuffled his feet in a flurry of deceptive movement. One foot in, another out, two up, two back, a split step popping in then out. He jabbed twice quickly and feigned an upper cut. I didn't move. My hands stayed at my sides.

He came at me again, this time more aggressive with more intent, nostrils flared. He bobbed his head, an advanced technique. A sheen of sweat was already covering him, like he'd worked himself up to high alert. I stepped forward to meet him. He threw two quick jabs into my face. I pulled my head back for the first. The second jab with his left came in and I ducked right, twisting my feet. He pulled his right shoulder back, signaling a big one. I moved in to shut it down. He changed up and threw the left into my gut, landing it square.

I got a flashing image of him grimacing, white teeth bared as I was projected against the tool station, spitting and choking. He followed up, pouncing on me with a right cross to the jaw. I jerked my head back and braced for impact. The fist narrowly whiffed.

The guy jumped back and smiled, watching me suffer. Luckily I hadn't eaten anything yet. He said, "You done?"

"Not yet." I came back up. The shirt now had a grease stain on it. "Watch the shirt, only just bought it yesterday."

The guy smiled.

I said, "You think that's a joke?"

He came in once more with a flurry of deceptive jabs and tricky footwork. I stepped clear of the jabs and watched for the big one. When it came, I moved inside the heavy punch and knocked it out with my left elbow. I faked a right hook to the temple and came in with a forearm to the throat. The guy bobbed his head back and avoided most of it, but the elbow nicked his windpipe.

He came back hard. A blur of footwork and jabs. The guy switched out of his right-handed stance and came at me southpaw. I could see his eyes darting and focused behind the hands, held high and protective. He bobbed his head deceptively like a turkey. I read a quick set of jabs, but they concealed a big uppercut. The fist came up through my defenses. I watched it coming like it was in slow-motion. Massive fist with scarred knuckles came into perfect focus at a near vertical angle. I knew if that fist landed on my chin it was game over. I'd already committed the hands, extended on my arms to individual tasks, like blocking the jabs that were there, and the one that wasn't. I let my body weight drop to a crouch on soft knees. Got my head quickly out of his target range.

The big fist flew by my face and I was looking straight at his midriff. I sprung off the crouch and launched at him, fully committed. I used my body weight to put a knee into his groin and scored a bull's-eye, big time. The man went down coughing and spitting, full-scale involuntary emergency. He had his head tucked into his chest and was saying something I couldn't understand. I came in closer, wary. He coughed and mumbled. "Got to do more damage, for the cameras."

I tried to be casual and glanced around the room, taking in the two mid-size camera bubbles in opposite corners. I snatched a grease rag from the tool station and wrapped it twice around my hand, gripping the loose cloth in my fist.

I said, "Clench your teeth."

He nodded, eyes squeezed in pain. I stepped in and smashed my fist into the side of his face. Followed that up with a hook to his nose. The guy's head snapped back and blood sprayed out on to the floor. He grunted. I stepped away, unwrapped the rag, threw it on the tool bench, and waited for him to recover. I'd avoided the blood spray, so my shirt was only slightly worse off than it had been.

The man rose to his knees and shook his head a couple of times. He reached up with both hands to his nose and grabbed it firmly. I heard the crack and pop as the cartilage straightened out inside the tightly packed flesh. He lifted his tank top up and over his head and used it as a rag to wipe off the blood and snot. He spit into the rag. "What do you need?"

"I want to know about the keys that get picked up from this place. The house keys. Then I want to know who owns it."

"You said you had one question."

"Now it's two."

The guy nodded and wiped his face. "Yeah ,well, first question is easy. No idea what you are talking about. We've got keys to the vehicles under repair, and to those in the used car lot. Otherwise, I don't know what you're referring to."

I examined him. His face was shiny with sweat and blood. He was mopping it up, but the blood kept coming. I wondered if it was possible that this mechanic hadn't ever gone past the little chain marked *Private*.

"Tilt your head more."

He tilted his head more.

"Tell me about the shop, then."

"Ricardo owns it, technically. But Ricardo owes a dude they call The Bob." His eyes flashed white as he glanced at me. "That's what you're here about, right?"

I tried out the sound. "The Bob. That's, what, a person's name, or an object?"

"It's what they call the big man. You aren't from around here."

It wasn't a question. I said nothing.

He said, "The Bob is the word they use to refer to a person of fearsome reputation and power in this town, and possibly the state. I wouldn't exactly know, as I'm not involved in anything more than getting into the pit and making things work better than they did before they came in."

"That's nice. What is The Bob supposed to be?"

"A loan shark *plus*, is what I'd call him."

"Plus what?"

"Plus the drugs and whatever else they're involved with."

"That it?"

"What I heard. I just work on the cars."

"Who hangs out upstairs?"

The guy blew blood and snot out of his nose into the bunched-up tank top. "Like I said, I just work here. I'm out by six, regular. Sometimes I see them come in and don't see them come out. I never go up there. It's a what-do-you-call-it, a boy's club."

"For The Bob and his friends."

"I suppose, except I've never seen The Bob here, or anywhere for that matter. No idea what The Bob looks like. I just know the name."

"Dumb name."

He glanced up at me then, wary and wise. "Might be, but that doesn't stop people from saying it with a straight face. Always figured there was a good reason behind that."

I looked at the guy, still moving his nose cartilage around like it was going to make a difference. "Thanks for taking the beating. "

He spat into his shirt again. "They should give you a medal or something."

I nodded. "They already gave me a couple."

I picked up the old pistol and shoved it into the waistband behind my back, then pulled my shirt out to cover it. I eased the front door open and walked out, letting it swing closed behind me. My hand ached from hitting the guy, despite the padding I'd wrapped around my fist.

The air was cooler outside, thanks to a nice breeze from the southeast. I looked up at the sound of gravel crunching under tires. The silver van with paneled sides pulled into the parking lot and stopped fifty feet away. The same two Hispanic guys from Linda Cartwright's house were in the cab, looking at me through the windshield.

CHAPTER TWENTY-SIX

I REMEMBERED the two in the silver van. Stocky, tough men who looked like they'd been raised far from Indiana. A world away from regularly spaced suburban houses and freshly watered front lawns. I couldn't see them clearly through the windshield given the glare, so all I got were the silhouettes with some minor detail. Enough to know that the driver was chewing gum. Both men wore aviators, distinct shapes in distinct head formations.

I made a left from the door and walked along the front of the building. I had the tune in my head from the shopping mall, it came easily to my lips as a whistle. I heard the crunch of gravel again as the van crept up on my six. The corner of the building was about ten paces away. I focused on whistling.

Two sets of eyes drilled into my back, like a weight, appraising, calculating. It was no coincidence that they were here. Someone had been alerted by the camera feed coming out of the key cabinet. Maybe some kind of an automated messaging system triggered when I opened the box. I didn't want to turn around, nor did I want to run. That would send out all the wrong signals. The men in the silver van were predators, at least here in Promise, Indiana.

Their problem was they'd confused me for prey.

The two predators were behaving in accordance with what they understood about the habitat. A soft land of suburban families and farmers, with them at the top of the pyramid. I visualized the guy in the passenger seat racking back the slide on a reliable semiautomatic, never taking his eyes off my back. My guess was something practical, like a Glock.

I got to the corner of the building and stepped out of sight around the other side.

I estimated five seconds before the van pulled clear. I was in the narrow alley between building and trees, with the cornfield on the other side. I wanted them to see where I was going, but I needed a head start because I also wanted distance. I sprinted for a four count and stopped abruptly. I glanced back. The van breached the building and the two guys were peering down the side at me. Two pairs of sunglasses turned in my direction. A pause in the gum chewing. Mouth open, the flash of white teeth through the side window.

I took a step across the grass verge and walked into the field.

The corn grew ten feet high, green leaves lush and wide. They'd planted it tight, probably as close together as possible. In an economy of scale, every inch counts. I brushed through the first couple of layers, stopped, and looked back. It was already tough to see beyond even fifteen feet of corn. I got low and put a palm on the soil, grounding myself. I had no real plan, only confidence that I'd figure something out. The dirt was black and rich, peppered with small white stones and detritus from the corn plants. The old pistol rode heavy against the small of my back.

I continued straight through the field for a good minute before stopping again to listen. Nothing was happening, nothing was moving. Only corn growing slow and silent all around me and the blue sky hanging in the heat. It was quiet and the tune I'd been whistling was gone. The only thing in my head was a feeling of calm and the subtle vibration of well-regulated adrenaline and serotonin.

In other words I was in an outstanding mood.

I moved out in a random pattern, making zigzags away from J&S Services. After twenty seconds I stopped once more, crouched and became very still. I got the old pistol out and practiced holding it by the barrel, seeing how I could get the best leverage and grip in relation to the form factor. I'd have to hit hard and move. The last thing I'd want was for the pistol barrel to slip out of my hands. I found a good solution, gripping the middle of the gun and putting my finger backwards through the trigger guard.

Using the pistol as a club struck me as a kind of oxymoron, which made me think about the barrel of a pistol. Which is not something you usually look down, or swing around wildly. Normally you'd only do that after clearing the gun.

I cleared the gun.

It was an old mechanism, from maybe a hundred and fifty years gone by. But it wasn't anything alien. I could figure out how it worked. The breech was operated by a lever that swiveled the chamber up for loading and unloading, down for firing. I pressed the lever to turn the chamber vertical. The mechanism was lubricated and true. The light of day penetrated the scooped out chamber and I saw a little cartridge tucked in there, snug as a bug.

I extracted it with my fingernails and held it up to the light. A dry, well-formed cardboard package. I sniffed it. Gunpowder, probably black powder, and judging by the weight, a cast lead payload. A similar principle to the firearms I was familiar with. The barrel wasn't rifled. I pulled back the spring at the rear, exposing the firing pin, which was more needle than pin. I dropped the little cartridge back into the hole and thumbed the lever, locking the firing mechanism and returning the chamber to an active position. I weighed the gun in my hand, holding it properly by the handle.

Better this way than backwards, that was for damn sure. The pistol felt balanced and true.

Now there was a new plan. Shoot the guy, and if that didn't work, hit him with the angry-faced solid-steel butt. Maybe both if the first and only shot didn't do the job. The wind came through the corn.

Fresh leaves and tassel waved and brushed against other leaves and tassel, making a soft sound.

I took a knee and waited patiently. The two men were in there with me, moving quietly through the corn, looking patiently for an advantage. After a couple of minutes waiting and listening, I moved back toward the place I'd started out. I shuffled in a crab walk, low and quiet, stepping with my heel first, allowing the balls of my feet to roll down. I figured the enemy might have pushed through, looking to circle round and flank me. I assumed they'd split up in the field. I moved, paused and listened, then repeated. Move, pause and listen, move again.

After a couple minutes of that I saw one of them, about fifteen feet away.

It was the movement of the corn that I saw, more than an actual body. A flicker of white and a head of dark hair in the green, passing through at a deliberate pace. I changed direction and came at him, low and slow. The old-time pistol heavy to hand. I had to assume that there would be low accuracy. I'd need to do it point-blank. The smart thing would be to make a semicircle and come up on his six.

I came up on him sooner than I'd anticipated, seeing his back from ten feet away. The corn grew so close that the distances became intimate. I retraced my steps until the visibility dropped off again. It was the man who'd knocked at Cartwright's door. He was talking to his buddy, who I couldn't see very well. Two guys, one potentially unreliable bullet. I figured they'd met up to get their situational awareness aligned and agree on the next step.

I could hear the murmur of a quiet conversation. I could see only the faintest trace of them through the growth. One guy turned and disappeared, the other guy came toward me, angled to pass about six feet in front of my position, moving left to right. He was going slow, crouched and intent on the deep vegetal growth in front of him, like he was trying to suck meaning out of the corn. I backed off even farther, then came around at an angle calculated to flank him.

Two minutes later I was creeping up on his six, slow and quiet, like a cat. I extended the old pistol in front of me. The barrel was around sixteen inches long, like having an extended arm. The spring-loaded needle was pulled back. I was hoping the thing would work. It occurred to me that if it misfired, I'd have to grab a potentially very hot barrel to hit the guy with the angry faced butt.

Too late to withdraw.

I mimicked his footsteps, putting my feet down in time with his. Tracking him perfectly, the alpha predator in a zero-sum game. The muzzle was six inches from the back of his head before the guy sensed it. He froze and flicked his head around in a panicked twitch. I pulled the trigger. The spring released with a click and the old gun made a thick explosion. The round came through the smoothbore barrel exiting at a slight angle and smashed into the left side of his face, tearing through his cheekbone and demolishing a quarter of his head. The shot blew the guy into the corn. A flock of starlings rose fluttering into the blue sky with the faint puff of gun smoke.

My gun arm and the left side of my face had been sprayed with bloody back spatter. I wiped my eye and looked down at the body. The guy had fallen on the missing part of his head, the part facing me was intact. The one remaining eye was open and staring. He had slight beard growth around a mouth that looked unhappy even in death.

A Glock 17 had fallen out of his hand, dull and brutal in the dirt. I bent to take it and heard frantic movement through the corn behind me. There was no time to pause, no time to look. I did a twisting dive across the body and rolled gracelessly. I registered the boom of two heavy rounds fired in quick succession. I sprinted deeper into the corn, disappearing in a zigzag. After a hectic few moments, I stopped and got control of my heart rate. Feeling around carefully, I concluded that I hadn't been wounded.

The shooter must have panicked. It's one thing to go up against civilians who owe money to a loan shark, and another thing entirely to see your partner with half his face shot off and a guy like me leaning over him. I doubled back, slow and calm. A minute later I came across the body. The Glock was gone and the dead man had nothing in his pockets. I was still holding the old pistol by the barrel, which was cooling off in my hand.

The corn was trampled where the second guy had run in. I figured he'd taken his shots and then tended to his dead friend. The starlings were still up in the sky, a murmuration of birds that moved like a morphing infinity symbol. I waited for them to settle down and noticed where they felt comfortable going. Far away from me, and I figured, far away from him.

I triangulated. There was a lot of corn field to cover, but not an infinite amount. Maybe the guy had seen that I was essentially unarmed. Maybe he was professional enough to discern the sound of an antique gun from something more practical. Maybe he'd seen the old pistol and knew. Either way, there wasn't much of a chance that he'd decide to call it a day. Chances were he was trying to figure me out.

I moved away from the starlings, straight for the edge of the cornfield, north of J&S Services. People tend to orient themselves to known locations and objects, like the direction they came come from or the place they parked. The comfort zone can be a deadly drug. I followed the edge west for a while, until I felt myself oriented on a new axis, until I owned the cornfield.

I came back into the battle space with a new point of view. A couple of minutes later I saw him.

The corn on the north side of the field was slightly shorter than over on the south side. The sun must have hit it in a different way. I was holding still with the plant tops at eye level when I saw his head pop up about twenty yards from my position. He scanned in the other direction and then dropped down below the corn.

I came up on him two minutes of slow creeping later. The man was sprawled on the ground in a defensive position. A chrome Desert Eagle was held between his two outstretched hands. The dead guy's Glock was tucked behind him, sticking up out of his waistband. The Desert Eagle looked like too much gun for the little guy, which might have been why he'd missed me. I moved up on him, slow and as quiet as was possible in a densely planted cornfield.

The man must have heard me a little while back. He must have been planning the move, timing it. When I was a couple of strides away he rolled onto his back. The big gun came up at me in front of his concentrated face, muzzle rising fast.

His eyes flashed above the rear sight. I pushed off my right leg and darted to the left. The Desert Eagle boomed once and kicked up in his hand. Big gun, big kick. I needed to close the distance before he could get the gun down again. I pushed off my left leg and dove at him with both hands flailing. The antique pistol went forgotten into the air. The guy managed to pull the trigger but it wasn't pointing in the right direction. The second shot might have scared the birds, but it didn't stop me from landing right on top of him.

We scrambled for a second but I got my body weight up over him. He struggled like he meant it. Eyes bulging and neck thick veined and red. I got into a dominant position and jammed a muscled forearm across his neck. I was holding his arms down with one leg and one free arm. He was wiry and small, but strong. I was starting to choke him out, but the Desert Eagle was still in his hand. The Glock was pinned underneath him.

The man was grunting and breathing heavy. It was an intimate situation, but I was comfortable with that. I relaxed into it. The guy wasn't going to be able to get me off. I took him piece by piece, relaxed and confident. I looked into his face, engaged his eyes. He didn't hold contact. There was a bad bruise on his left temple. The mark of Linda Cartwright's hammer was perfectly formed and plain to see.

Every time he struggled I was able to increase my traction on his body until he was nullified. He knew it; I saw the look in his eyes: bugged out and fearful, desperate in the knowledge that his life was over, yet not capable of giving it up. My face mashed into his armpit and I got a chunk of flesh into my mouth and bit down hard through his shirt. The guy flinched involuntarily. I shifted position and got a knee on his chest, triumphant. The arm that had been across his neck came back and I smashed a fist into his face, striking him between the nose and the upper lip. That was enough to wrench the big pistol out of his hand.

The guy leapt up. Blood flowed freely from where his lip had been split on the sharp edge of a broken tooth. He was holding his hand up to his face, a reflexive action. I saw the Glock on the ground behind him.

I stood up, stepped back, and covered him with the weapon.

I said, "My friend who hit you with the hammer. You know who I'm talking about. Where is she?"

He looked at me like I was speaking a foreign language. It made me think about those Homeland Security agents. Dead now, but definitely interested in some kind of Homeland Security–related issue. I hadn't yet understood why they were involved in all of this. Unless maybe it had to do with some kind of transnational criminal activities. This guy looked like he might be familiar with parts of our two-thousand-mile-long border with Mexico.

I spoke slowly this time. "Easy choices. Either you tell me where you took my friend, or you don't."

A look of pure hatred came over the man's face. The hammer mark had turned red on his flushed face. He screwed his mouth into an ugly twist and tried to spit at me. That was his answer.

I shot him in the chest. Except I didn't. The firing pin clicked uselessly onto the chambered round, which I immediately assumed was either an ammunition issue or a bad primer strike caused by bad maintenance. I pressed forward while ejecting the round and caught a fast flash of the guy's terrified face. He might have gone for the Glock, but that wouldn't have worked. I would have been all over him, with or without a firearm.

By the time I had cleared the gun, and verified that there was no more ammunition in the Desert Eagle, the man was gone through the corn, running for his life. Some kind of a survivor for the time being.

CHAPTER TWENTY-SEVEN

I walked back to J&S Services through the high corn.

The crops didn't look ready for harvest. Tall and healthy, but not yet something you'd want to put on the grill. On the plus side I came out of the field with a different kind of bounty. Cold and angular weapons made from polymer and steel, with modern ballistic projectiles tucked into magazines and chambers, plus the antique pistol.

The Desert Eagle was impressive, which was the attribute its makers had been aiming to convey. The gun weighed around four pounds with an empty magazine. Impressive, but currently as useless as the antique. The Glock 17 was in 9mm parabellum. Seventeen round magazine capacity plus one in the chamber. Practical. Neither of the two men had thought to lock the van.

I opened the driver's side door and vaulted into the seat. Five thousand dollars in hundreds made for a fat wad bunched up in my pocket. I eased it out and laid the cash on the passenger seat. The photograph of William F. Cartwright came with it. I separated the card from the photograph, put the card on the cash and returned Cartwright's photo to my pocket.

The other pocket was stuffed with my wallet and the house keys that I had taken from the upstairs cabinet. I pulled it all out of my pocket and dumped the load onto the passenger seat, right next to the wad of cash.

The cab featured a clean dashboard with a pine tree–shaped air freshener hanging from the rearview mirror. I detected nothing else of note in the cab except the chemical stink of the air freshener. I leaned over and popped open the glove compartment. One burner phone sat there looking at me in silver-colored plastic.

I pulled it out and sat back.

In between the driver and passenger seats was another compartment. I lifted the cover and slid it open. The cavity contained a sunglasses case and a wallet. I flipped open the wallet to find the sullen face of the dead guy who had knocked on Cartwright's door. He peered warily from the top left photo box of an Ohio driver's license made out to Alfredo Celio Remírez. Besides the license, the wallet contained a thin stack of cash.

I thumbed Collins's number into the keypad, watching as the digits appeared on the little screen. She answered with a voice like a finely tuned woodwind instrument.

"This is Tela Collins."

"It's Keeler."

"Oh. One moment." She didn't speak for a couple of seconds, but I heard things moving. A door closed and clothing rustled before her voice came back online. "I had to close the door. Too much noise from the office outside."

"You get home all right?"

"Sure. Took a cab to get my car. I'm at work now."

"How is it?"

"I'm distracted today."

"Unfinished business."

"To put it mildly, yes. You know how it is when stuff gets left undone, like the opposite of a satisfying conclusion."

"I'm tied up at the moment."

"Don't play with me, Keeler." Collins's voice was somewhere between humor and tension. "You want to know what I'm wearing?"

I said nothing.

Her voice was silk. "I want to put a picture into your head, keep you focused.

"Okay."

"First, keep in mind that I've got a private office. There's a door and it's got a lock. And that for work I usually try to dress up."

"Which means what?"

"Which means I'm wearing a business suit, Keeler. Black and formfitting with a sleeveless blouse in white with ruffles. The blouse has pearl buttons, real ones that work both ways, one way to attach, and the other to remove. The blazer's on the other side of the room and my shoes are kicked off on the floor."

I could picture that. I said, "Stockings?"

"Black stockings. I've got my legs up on the desk, leaned back in the office chair. If anyone came in the door now I'd be in a compromised position. You got that image, Keeler?"

"It's vivid in my mind."

"So what do you want me to do now?"

I let that question percolate for a while, drifting in my mind and hers and in between.

Eventually I said, "I want you to meet me at a school and help me figure something out."

"Right now?"

"In about a half hour. Doesn't sound like you're having a very productive day anyway."

She said, "So I might as well just get out of here. Is this related to my wearing a short skirt or to the violent events of last night?"

"Both."

"I see. I can't promise to be well-behaved."

"There has been a new development in the situation."

She let some time pass before speaking. "The situation from last night."

"Correct."

"Okay."

I said, "Your aunt's neighbor Linda Cartwright seems to have been taken, with signs of a struggle."

"Oh."

"I didn't go far last night. Cartwright let me sleep on her sofa. I woke up to her being gone instead of her making coffee."

"That sounds bad."

"School's called Booker T. Washington. I'll be in a vehicle across the street in about twenty minutes."

"Can you be any more specific?"

"About what?"

"The vehicle."

The silver van was facing the wrong direction. I looked into the rearview mirror and saw nothing but a panel wall behind me. I checked the passenger's side mirror. I could see the line of used cars on the other side of the lot, but not in a very detailed way.

I said, "Not at the moment, but you'll find me."

"Booker T. Washington. See you there."

Collins clicked off the line. I looked up at the rearview mirror again. No rear view, only a blank steel wall separating the cabin from the back. Which made me think about the back of the van, and what I might find in there. I leaned to the driver's side mirror and looked at myself. Face flecked with the dead guy's blood and a couple of ancillary wounds from the recent struggles.

I came around to the back of the van. J&S Services was in operation. The garage doors were open, and a car was up on the lift. I couldn't see the guy whose nose I'd broken, but he was probably in there somewhere, no doubt hard at work.

I pulled the latch on the rear door and partially opened the left side. I saw a wire basket just inside containing a pair of work boots, a flashlight, and a thick roll of duct tape. I peeked in farther. No bodies lying in a pool of blood or wrapped in a plastic tarp. I pulled the two doors wide. There was a rolled-up carpet next to two shovels and a pickaxe. I saw a spool of rope and a black backpack shoved to the rear panel wall. Hanging from hooks on the right side was a weed whacker. Closer to the opening were two red plastic jerry cans.

I vaulted into the van and pulled the doors closed a notch for privacy. The carpet was cheap acrylic with a chunky modern design featuring red, black, and white squares. I rolled it open the width of the van. There were no blood stains. I shifted the carpet and unrolled more. Same thing, nothing obvious, which didn't mean there hadn't ever been a body rolled inside, just not a badly bleeding one.

I crab walked to the backpack.

The pack was filled with wood. Specifically, given the color and texture of the wood, I was looking at a bag of broken antique furniture. Given the size of the backpack it would have been either a very small piece of furniture, or a select portion of something.

I thought for a half second and decided there wasn't enough information to draw conclusions. I turned the backpack upside down and emptied out the contents. I crawled back out into the fresh air with the backpack in my hand and closed the van door.

The stuff situation had gone beyond the pocket stage. The backpack was going to be helpful.

Back in the cab, I placed the Glock in the backpack's main compartment. There was a zip pocket in the front. I dropped the phone and the keys into that as well as my wallet and the photograph of William F. Cartwright. The antique gun and the Desert Eagle got wiped and went under the driver's seat.

I had immediate plans for the cash. I shoved the wad into my pocket and closed the van.

There was post-lunch activity around the auto-services bay. A couple of guys moved in and around the raised chassis of a two-door hatchback. The front office door swung open and an older guy egressed. He was absorbed in his phone and didn't notice my coming. The guy laboriously climbed into a civilian vehicle parked out front.

As I peered through the glass front door, I saw a man at the office desk that had previously been vacant. The tough guy I'd taken out had said the place was owned by Ricardo. I figured that was Ricardo, right there, recovering from lunch.

I had a couple of questions.

CHAPTER TWENTY-EIGHT

I CLOSED in on the glass front door and started to get a better look at Ricardo.

He was in his late thirties and was not noticing my approach. The owner remained captivated by whatever it was he had in front of him. As I approached, the object of his attention came into view. He was using a letter opener to slice through the top of an envelope. Ricardo's nose was prominent and wide, maybe the defining feature of his face. He put the opener down and lifted an orange can from the desk. He tilted it up to drink.

That's when he saw me coming.

I was one step away from the door and momentarily refocused on my own reflection. Which was a little surprising in the full light of day, my face was still covered in blood from the back spatter in the cornfield. I'd forgotten about that. I decided to ignore myself and came through the glass door. Ricardo's eyes widened and he spilled foaming orange soda over his shirt.

I said, "Ricardo."

He nodded, distracted by me, and trying to deal with the spilled soda at the same time. I took two strides to the desk, leaned over, and smashed my blood-encrusted fist into Ricardo's face. I got him flush in the nose with a slightly downward angle. His head rocked back on a thick neck. Blood joined the orange soda and dripped all over his shirt and chin.

Time was an issue. I'd told Collins twenty minutes, and I like to be punctual. I needed Ricardo's full attention.

The radio played loudly from the garage to cover the click and whine of a pneumatic air ratchet. Ricardo was trying to get himself together. He was taking too long. I saw the letter opener lying on the desk.

I pinned Ricardo's right hand to the desk, then fetched the letter opener and placed the point in his palm. He struggled weakly for a moment but gave up fast. I got my face a foot away from his and looked into his eyes. "Ricardo."

The guy was all over the place, defocused, disoriented, the whole nine yards. Not exactly condition black, but close to it. He was in some kind of a gray area. Ricardo's eyes finally found mine and settled there, like a shipwreck survivor spotting land.

"Yes."

"You like this hand. You are right-handed. You need this hand."

He looked down at the letter opener. The sharp point was presently making an indentation in the center of his palm. "Yes."

"Good." I applied pressure and allowed a single drop of blood to pool in the callused palm. He struggled to remain calm, snuffling air through crushed nose cartilage. I said, "I have a date to get to, so this needs to be quick, Ricardo." His eyes rolled up at me. "I am interested in the house keys that you give out to people sent by The Bob. Do you understand?"

Ricardo nodded, mute.

I waited. Nothing emerged from Ricardo's mouth. I pushed the letter opener in. More blood came from the pierced skin. He got the message. "I understand."

Ricardo's eyes came off me and went on a little trip around the room. First they aimed at the ceiling corner, then traveled in the direction of the automobile key cabinet on the wall. I followed the direction that his eyes had initially travelled, to the ceiling corner. I hadn't seen it before, but now I did, a little indentation in the wall for the minuscule eye of a camera.

Too late to care about that.

He said, "The house keys. They keep them upstairs. I'm not allowed to go there."

I said, "The Bob records you, in your own place."

He nodded, ashamed.

"What is that, a person who people call The Bob, or some kind of garage band with a dumb name?"

Ricardo licked his lips and bared his teeth in a pained grimace. I don't get concerned with pain; it's not on my list of things to think too much about. Ricardo didn't feel the same way. His eyes rolled up and he glanced at me. "You're coming on a little strong."

"I've got a date to get to. I like her."

He shook his head, like he didn't believe it. "The Bob's got me under his thumb. Yes, it's a person. I think. I've never met The Bob. I don't think he's a musician, at least I have no reason to think that. Most people like music."

"If you don't meet The Bob in person, who do you meet?"

"Various people who I'd prefer not to meet."

"Who brings the keys for the cabinet upstairs."

Ricardo's eyes widened noticeably. "You went upstairs? They aren't going to like that. You better think about leaving town."

"Answer the question."

"I'm not allowed to go up there. Sometimes they leave keys on the desk and I have to give them out. Like, to contractors. I don't know anything else. I get here in the morning and either there are keys on the desk, or there aren't."

I nodded. "What kind of contractors, Ricardo?"

He licked the blood from his lip. "Cleaners, plumbers, electricians, decorators. People who work on buildings. Sometimes it's people who do air conditioners. I only see the trucks when they come for the keys."

"To put it clearly, Ricardo, your shop is being used as a cut out for distributing keys to properties that The Bob acquires through his loan sharking business. I assume that's how he came to have you under his control."

He nodded. "Yes."

"They record sound or just the video on that camera up there?"

"I think just the images. They have cameras all over town. The operation is huge."

"You still owe them?"

He nodded. "Biggest mistake of my life. Look at this shit." He indicated himself, me, the entire situation. "I'll never get out from under it. They keep raising the vig and there's just no way. Once they get their hands on to you they keep squeezing, man."

"What does The Bob do with the residential properties?"

He hung his head and let it droop. "I don't know. You think I'm in a position to go digging into The Bob's business? I'm too busy trying to stay alive."

"You're not looking very good, Ricardo. Your quality of life seems unacceptably diminished. Didn't anyone tell you that offense is the best defense?"

"What do you mean?" Fat tears rolled down Ricardo's face.

I almost felt sorry for him. I released the pressure from the letter opener. "What's your plan, Ricardo?"

"What do you mean, plan?"

"I'm just wondering why you don't terminate The Bob. That could help advance your cause, fix your quality of life issues." He looked at me, uncomprehending. He didn't know how to think outside the box he was in, which was why he was in that position in the first place. "Where does someone go to get close to The Bob?"

A grim smile played upon his lips. "You think this is joke, like you could do better. Nobody finds The Bob. He sends someone to collect; that's it. New kid every other time. I guess it's a job for the new guys.

The Bob's intelligent. Always has a bunch of people between himself and the action, at least as far as I've seen."

"Bullshit. You've had the thoughts. You've gone through the possibilities. You've wondered how you could take that prick out. Early in the game, before you got your tenth beating by The Bob's people. Then you gave it up. But back then you lay awake scheming."

I could see his eyes clouding over, getting the thousand-yard stare. It confirmed what I'd had as a hunch. People aren't all that different from each other. Nobody's that special. Everyone dreams of being a hard ass.

I said, "Where would you go, Ricardo, to have the best chance of getting close to The Bob?"

Ricardo used his free hand to wipe the blood from his upper lip. His face was grim with the memory of failure. "I've thought about it, sure. First, I don't know if he's from Promise. This isn't a city; it's a town. I've heard of people owing The Bob in other towns across the state, but not in the big city."

"He operates in the less-populated areas."

Ricardo nodded. "Exactly. Which means he would be based in the city."

"Indianapolis."

"Right."

"That's all you have, Ricardo?"

He shrugged. "You'd be looking for a place with a lot of camera feeds. The Bob likes cameras."

"That all you've got?"

"Yeah, that's all I've got. I'm not Sun Tzu or something."

Understatement of the month. I released the man and stood back from the desk. "I need a sink. Where do you clean up around here?"

He pointed me to the bathroom.

I splashed water on my face and scrubbed hard with the orange hand cleaner to remove the majority of the dead guy's dried blood. When I came back, Ricardo was using a tissue to clean out the blood from his nostrils.

He looked up at me. "You really needed to break my nose?"

"It was a decision taken at a certain time with the minimal information I possessed. Can you sell me a car within the next three minutes?"

His shoulders slumped. Ricardo delicately pulled the bloody tissue from his nose. "As long as you have identification."

"What do you have that's good?" I saw trepidation on his face. I said, "I'm going to pay you."

"The Crown Vic. If you're taking on The Bob you'll need a decent engine. That thing's souped up with a cold-air intake."

I peeled a thousand dollars in hundreds from the wad, laid them on his desk.

Ricardo looked at the pile for a couple of seconds, like he was considering something. I briefly entertained the idea that he might refuse payment. After all, if I succeeded in taking out the loan shark, Ricardo would get his life back. In any case, he used his wounded right hand to drag the cash toward the edge of the desk and slide it into an open drawer.

Three minutes later I drove away with the title to a brand-new used car in the name of Alfredo Celio Remírez. I bumped off the lot and hit the road back to town. Back to Tela Collins, back to Linda Cartwright and Donna Williams's problems.

Indiana rolled by on both sides, green and pretty flat.

CHAPTER TWENTY-NINE

Booker T. Washington High School was at the crest of a little green hill rolling up from the road. It looked like what it was, a high school. Worse still, it made me remember my own high school. The memories were unclear, like it had all been a dream. I'd gone to a bunch of different schools, one for each place we'd moved when my mother finished one job and got another. She worked in the energy industry, helping her clients guess at what they'd find deep in the ground. She dragged us from one pile of rocks to the next, which meant a new school every year or so.

The bigger schools had featured a hallway with sports trophies in a glass case. No matter what school it was, they'd called that hallway *jock hall*. And the same bullies always hung out near the trophy case, picking on kids as they tried to get through.

I'd learned a lot in jock hall, about cowardice and weakness, but most of all about fighting. The military taught me skills and technique, but for better or worse, the first lessons had been learned in jock hall. Lesson number one: get the first shot in, because it's going to be the last. Which brought up the satisfying memory of my fist connecting with a big blond kid's face and the blond kid's sudden look of shock and fear.

The passenger door opened and Collins was there. The backpack was taking up space. I tossed it into the back. She folded herself into the passenger seat, one leg at a time. She closed the door and looked at me. I looked back at her and felt my brain melt. Business attire with the full monty: stockings, heels, skirt, blouse, and blazer. All put together so you'd never know it had ever been apart.

She raised her eyebrows and glanced around the car. "New wheels, Keeler."

I said, "How do you rate it?"

She ran a hand over the dashboard. "Better than a Kia."

I said, "Crown Victoria."

"Yessir, old police interceptor." Collins slapped the dashboard. "2011 Crown Vic. You've bought into the end of an era."

I said nothing.

She said, "So what's the deal?"

The deal was that she looked damned good in a business suit. I snapped my gaze away from that and indicated the school. "I want to get in there and find a student file. It's got an address on it."

Collins smoothed and straightened her skirt. "Whose address?"

"Donna Williams, the woman who took the shot at your aunt's neighbor Linda Cartwright, then blew her own face out."

"Why is her information at the school?"

"Because Williams has a daughter who attends. Cartwright works as a substitute teacher. She used her contacts to get the file."

"That was a smart place to look."

I nodded. "Cartwright's a competent woman if she's still alive. She had a printout of the school file, but it's not at her house. I think whoever snatched her took that printout as well."

She nodded to herself. "So what you're wondering is how we go in there and get what we need without them getting suspicious."

I liked the way the pronouns had become collective. I said, "That's exactly what I'm wondering."

Collins sank into the seat. "Let's watch for a while, see who comes and goes, see what they do, what they look like, how they interact." She glanced at me. "We need to get a good overall idea of how people are behaving, then we can draw conclusions and make a plan."

We sat in the car looking at the school for ten minutes. Collins didn't break eye contact with the building. People came and people went. Students, staff, and a couple of other individuals who I pegged as outside contractors or maintenance.

Eventually I asked, "You've seen the landscape, you're an expert. What's the verdict?"

She turned and let the green eyes rip into me. "So, I'm wondering what happens when the fire alarm gets pulled. They must have some kind of a protocol, like a fixed way of responding."

I snapped my fingers. "Safety mentality."

I REMOVED the backpack from the rear seat and walked around the car to the back. I popped the trunk and set the bag down. The wad of cash was uncomfortable in my pants pocket, so I slid it into the front compartment of the backpack, where it joined the burner phone and the clutch of house keys. This time, I locked the car.

We walked into the school like we had business. It took us a minute to identify the layout. The school administration offices were past jock hall. The admin section was open plan with wide windows looking in from the hallway. The principal's office was behind the admin desks. Two women and a man were hunched over in office chairs, looking at standard flat screen computer monitors. The man was eating a banana.

Collins pointed to the bathrooms down a short corridor off the main hallway. There were two doors side by side, one for the boys, one for the girls. Straight ahead was a handicapped toilet with the wheelchair sign. On the wall, just in from the water fountain was a red fire alarm pull station. There was a glass bar in front of the trigger, a simple but effective means of deterring false alarms. You didn't pull that thing unless you were ready to break something.

I pulled the switch. The glass fell with a tinkle. The alarm went off immediately, a piercing wail. Collins slipped into the boy's bathroom and I followed. The smell of paper towels hit me like a wall of nostalgia. She opened the door to a toilet stall and motioned me in. Collins sat on the toilet seat and I stood against the partition wall. We waited and listened.

There was the alarm, raising a ruckus, and the reverberated sound of feet pounding polished floors and people talking loudly. Commands were shouted by teachers and staff. There were softer sounds of students not caring one way or another but shuffling into assigned corridors and exit routes.

The positive was that classes were being disrupted. Positive for the students, a pain in the ass for the teachers. I thought of the administrators we had seen. I figured they'd be right up out of their chairs for the fresh air. No problem getting them to take a break.

Collins said, "How long do you think?"

"Five minutes total, two remaining."

She stood up and leaned herself against my chest, hands spread out on either side, cheek touching just below the hollow of my neck. Her touch was like some kind of star dust. I put my hands at her waist, slid one around to the small of her back where it curved in. It felt good there, like a natural place to be. She smelled like lemon-scented soap mixed with some kind of vanilla body lotion. After what seemed like a long time, but was still way too short, she spoke. I could feel her mouth moving through my shirt. "Are you counting?"

"One minute and a half left."

"Okay."

The door to the bathroom banged open. An adult male voice called out. "Anyone in here?"

We didn't answer, we didn't move. She clutched me tighter. The door banged shut.

She said, "You think that's the principal?"

"Or the janitor."

Above the toilet was a small window in textured glass. I disengaged and stepped up on the seat cover. The window opened a crack, allowing me a slim view of the front lawn. Students and staff were milling around. I figured they were following the safety protocol, waiting the prescribed amount of time while the dedicated fire marshal assessed the situation. Maybe that was the guy who had come into the bathroom to check everyone was out. I calculated that we'd have something like five to ten minutes to do a little research in the school administration office.

"Let's go."

CHAPTER THIRTY

The hallway was empty. All the hubbub came from out front, for now. The administrators had picked up and left. I canvassed the computer screens. Two out of three had been switched off, the banana eating guy's screen was active, white and bright, filled with windows and data. I clicked the keyboard to make sure it didn't time out. Collins took a seat at the desk.

I said, "Five minutes and we're out."

"Yes, boss."

Collins dealt with the computer; I took a tour of the principal's office. One side was lined with filing cabinets. I pulled on a drawer but it was locked. I returned to the admin room. Another wall of filing cabinets, also locked.

Collins was focused on the screen in front of her, monitoring my movements at the same time. "I bet the administrators have the cabinet keys attached to their key rings, which are probably in their pockets."

That made a lot of sense. They would be using those cabinets all the time. The way to keep the documents confidential was to keep the cabinets locked. The daily work of an administrator would involve quite a lot of key use.

Collins was clicking the mouse, hunched over and leaning forward in concentration. "Hmmm, but they might have the documents copied digitally as well."

I methodically flipped through the stacks of paper on the administrator's desks. Nothing related to student records. I walked into the principal's office and looked through his correspondence. I found nothing more interesting than the documents piled up on the other desks. I came back out and hovered over Collins.

Four minutes and twenty seconds later we weren't any closer. No Donna Williams, no sign of student records. A lot of administration, like budgets and grade curves and exam board notes. A whole bunch of abstract regulations without the concrete data we required. Collins looked tense. "Maybe it's something they get to through a web browser, Keeler. If that's the case, I won't be able to guess the login or the URL."

Voices came into the admin room from the hallway, bouncing around off the glossy floors and walls. I couldn't understand what was being said. The voices receded when the people speaking turned onto another wing of the building.

Collins said, "You think they can identify which alarm went off?"

"Focus on what you're doing. The alarm triggers a centralized computer, which sends the signal to the fire department. They'll know which one was triggered."

We were running out of time.

I moved back to the principal's office and took a chance. I used a paper clip to pop the lock on his desk drawer. Inside were trays for office hardware, like more paper clips, a stapler with extra staples, and refill cartridges for a fancy pen. Right next to that was a set of two keys on a flimsy ring, backups.

I moved to the filing cabinets right in front of me and tried one of the keys. The first attempt worked. The second key was different. That would be for out front. I pulled off the second key and came through to the open space. I whistled at Collins and tossed her the key.

She caught it left-handed and looked at me.

I said, "Filing cabinets. You're in here, I'm in the principal's office."

The two voices from before were coming back: two colleagues chatting about lunch, going through the fire drill procedure, unworried. Collins got busy with the filing cabinet in the admin office. I went back to the principal's office. Twenty seconds later, I found a whole bunch of historical school records but nothing that told me about the present. Collins's voice called quietly through the door. She was calm now, good under pressure. "Come in here."

I came out to the admin office. Collins was closing the section that she'd been looking into. "This is the A to G section." She pointed to the far right. "That's going to be where we want to look."

Three cabinets, twenty six letters in the alphabet. Which didn't divide easily into three. I stepped aside and Collins put the key into the cabinet on the right and pulled it open. I watched over her shoulder. There were fifteen folders for W, and two were Williams. She pulled both out. The first was a sixteen year old boy named Sasha. The second folder was the one. I saw a photograph of a blond girl and the name Emma Williams. Collins flipped the pages and caught the mother's details, Donna Williams. She flashed a look at me.

I laid the pages on the desk, Collins snapped photos with her phone. Six pages and six photos later she checked the pictures for camera blur. "All good."

I put the folders back in the cabinet and pushed the sliding door in. The latch clicked. The principal's desk drawer was open. I walked back and dropped the keys in. I didn't bother trying to lock the drawer. The paper clip went into a garbage can.

Coming back into the admin area, I had a thought. "Collins, did you see an attendance register?"

Collins was wiping down the keyboard and mouse with an antibacterial wipe from a desk dispenser. She stopped moving and looked at me. "You want to know if the girl's in school." I said nothing. She said, "I didn't see one. Do we have time to keep looking?"

I shook my head. "Negative."

We walked out of the administrator's office. When we were halfway down the hallway, Collins spoke quietly. "We can call the school and I'll pretend to be Donna Williams looking for her daughter. If Emma's not here they'll know."

"Good idea."

We found an exit through the gym and out the back. Behind the school was a baseball diamond. We sat on the bleachers for a minute. The back of the building was all red brick wall. A half-dozen kids were lounging around smoking and posturing.

The air was heavy with humidity. A complete change from the morning.

The sky had been blue and clear when we came in. Now it was covered in swollen clouds, threatening to rain. Collins had her phone in hand, looking at the pictures we'd taken. She read out loud. "Emma Harper Williams, fifteen years of age. Mother is one Donna K. Williams."

Collins looked up at me. I saw the emotion expressed by her eyes, concern, compassion. Something like that.

She said, "What do you think's going on, Keeler?"

I told her about the loan shark they called The Bob and the keys that I had found in the upstairs area of J&S Services. I said, "I don't know what the exact story is, but these people are in trouble."

"The Bob. You think that's a single person or some kind of an organization?"

"I don't know for sure. I'm figuring it's a single person with an organization."

"Right." She was staring into space. She turned to me with a face all screwed into a single good question. "Why do you think those Homeland Security agents were involved with this?"

"You mean, if it's a loan sharking issue."

"Yeah, exactly."

"I don't know. I'm wondering the same thing."

Collins pulled a hair band off and shook out her curls, then tamed the mess of hair in a couple of efficient gestures. She looked at me. "The girl's only fifteen years old. Her mother shot herself in the face? That's a life-changing event for them both. Do you think the girl's gone too?"

I didn't immediately respond. Collins looked back at the sky. It wasn't an answerable question.

"I don't know," I said. "Right now, the operational assumption is that she's missing."

Collins clenched her jaw, shaking her head like there were some things in the world that were simply unacceptable. "We need to find the girl, Keeler." She pulled her phone in front of her face and started flipping and pecking at the screen. Her voice was steady, committed. "Got the address. Berrymore Court. I know where that is." Collins came off the bleachers like we were going to go there together. I stayed, watching her. She turned and looked at me. "What?"

I said, "I appreciate that you're ready to get up and go, that you're in the zone, but this isn't your fight. It's going to get ugly."

Collins's voice was steady, with a steely tone. "It's not your call to make, Keeler. I'm involved now and I'm going to stay involved until it's done. I'm not letting this go any more than you are."

I stared at her for a while, thinking about options. In the end it didn't much matter what I thought; she had already decided. I got up and joined her on the baseball diamond.

"Let's do it."

CHAPTER THIRTY-ONE

Collins led the way in her little red Honda. I followed in the Crown Vic. A single large drop of rain hit the windshield.

Booker T. Washington High School was set on a modest hillside inside a pretty residential neighborhood. That cozy, well-maintained atmosphere fell away once we joined a four-lane artery, split down the middle by a median barrier. I was following the Honda and not thinking too hard about where Collins was leading me. The businesses on either side of the road competed for attention with sign boards in bright colors raised as high as they could get them.

Looking at the eye spam up ahead, I noticed a motel sign in the shape of an eight ball. Round and black with a big number eight in the middle. It dawned on me that this was where the Homeland Security agents had wanted to take us the night before.

The motel was on our left, on the other side of the road. As we came closer to the intersection, I saw a shiny black Chevy Tahoe in the parking lot. I flashed my lights at Collins. She didn't notice, so I came alongside her. I opened the passenger side window and flapped my right hand until I got her attention. Collins lowered her window and looked at me with concern. I pointed to the right side of the road where a low-built strip of stores occupied the center of a crowded parking lot. I shouted to be heard. "Follow me into that lot."

I accelerated ahead of the Honda and jockeyed into the right-turn-only lane.

I parked in front of a Family Eye Care store. Over to the left was a Starbucks. Collins slid her Honda into the space beside me. I got out of the Crown Vic and came over to lean in her window.

I said, "Look across the street."

She twisted around in her seat and examined the other side. "What am I looking at?"

"Eight Ball Motel, where the Homeland Security people wanted to take us last night."

"Okay, I remember. Why did you park on this side?"

"I think there are Homeland Security people over there. Presumably they're unhappy about recent events." I had that Glock 17 in the trunk. A weapon with a potentially dubious history. I might be sympathetic to their loss, but Homeland Security were still law enforcement.

I slapped the roof of Collins's Honda. "I'm going over. You stay here. There's no reason for them to get a look at both of us, if it comes to that."

She didn't look happy. "In that case, why are you going?"

"Because there's a greater than zero chance that I'll learn something."

She scowled. "That's really promising, Keeler."

I gave her a look. "This town is full of promise, Collins."

"Yup, never heard that one before."

I took my chances crossing. The area wasn't designed for pedestrians. Maybe the landscape architect had been into automobiles. Cars and trucks came thick and fast in both directions. I made it over and stepped onto the Eight Ball Motel parking lot.

A guy was loading a box into the Tahoe. I strolled in that direction. The lift gate was up and I could see two brown file boxes in the back. New vehicle. Federal plates. The guy came back again and dropped another box into the back of the Tahoe. He didn't notice me and turned away once the box was in. Young guy in his twenties, probably fresh out of the academy. Pancake holster behind his right hip. I followed him to the motel and watched as he entered one of the rooms at street level. A new four-door Chrysler in white was parked outside the room.

The motel door was open. In addition to the young guy who'd just walked in, at least one other person was occupying space in there. I hung around until the young guy came back out, this time carrying a duffel bag in each hand. Once he was gone, I went to the open doorway. A man was standing, looking pensively in the direction of the wall. He was middle-aged with graying hair and a bald spot above a clean-shaven face and steel-rimmed spectacles resting on the bridge of his nose. A woman sat in a swivel chair with her legs crossed. She was maybe forty and looking serenely at the other wall.

The two wore the same uniform: jeans and a dark polo shirt tucked in at the waist. Like the junior agent, the man in the room wore a pancake holster with the distinctive back end of a Sig Sauer P320 poking out. I assumed these were not the parents of the deceased.

When I came to the door they turned to me as one, as if they'd just been sitting there and waiting for a common object of interest. I got face stabbed by four dead serious eyes. The man dropped his arms defensively and put his right hand on the butt of the Sig Sauer. The woman's body language was a study in contrast since it had not changed one iota. She tilted her head and kicked her toe off the carpet to swivel some more. "Hello there. Can we help you?"

I said, "I'm sorry about what happened to your colleagues."

They stared at me, not in any kindly way. The man strode forward and got close, like he was going to push me out the door. "Who the hell are you?"

I'd been leaning casually against the doorjamb. I straightened up and put my hands up in a gesture of innocence. "I'm just a guy. No need to get in my face."

"Take it easy, Stan," said the woman.

The man stepped back. The woman was looking at me coolly. "Fine, but who are you?"

"Your agents approached me last night. I had some contact with a person of interest in their investigation. They were leading me over here to talk about their case on the record. Maybe in front of you. Instead of doing that, I watched them get killed. Like I said, I'm sorry for your loss."

The man and the woman watched me for a moment without saying anything. The man oriented himself to her, deferring authority. She had a toothpick in her mouth. I watched her chew on it some. She spoke to the guy without taking her eyes from my face. The woman had intense energy. "Special Agent Douglas, how about a couple of sweet teas from that place we went to yesterday. What's it called again?"

"Starbucks."

The woman idly swiveled back and forth. Her toe trailing on the cheap carpet. "That's it. I'll take mine with the peach syrup, no extra bullshit."

I was thinking that the peach syrup was already extra bullshit, but I didn't voice that opinion.

Special Agent Douglas said, "Yeah, okay." He flicked a look at me and lifted his eyebrows.

The woman raised her hand with one finger outstretched, like how you call a waiter for the bill. "Oh, and take the kid with you. He can help carry my tea."

The Special Agent nodded. He glanced up at me. The look wasn't hostile, but it wasn't hospitable either. I stepped out to let him pass. When he had gone I came inside. The woman regarded me calmly. She looked at her watch. "This is going to take less than three minutes, so you can choose to either sit down, or stay on your feet. Personally, I don't give a shit which, but please come a little closer because I don't like to raise my voice."

"Yes, ma'am." I came and perched on the edge of the bed. "So this is the shitty motel in town."

"We specialize in shitty motels."

I said nothing.

She said, "Your name is Tom Keeler, and your curriculum vitae includes neither criminal activity nor corporate dick-sucking jobs. You're a veteran of our military service. From what I was able to gather you have an exotic menu of capabilities. Parts of your service records are classified, but I saw that you're Air Force special tactics." She flicked away the toothpick. "You said you watched them die. What happened after that?"

I yawned and dead-eyed the woman. "Do you have a business card or something?"

She matched my gaze. "Fuck you and answer the damned question. Two and a half minutes left."

I grinned. "Well, ma'am, I pursued the killers but didn't catch up with them."

The woman grimaced. "I think the term *killers* is an overstatement and unjustified by any of the available evidence."

I said nothing.

She continued. "But, it's too bad you didn't catch up with the other party in last night's unfortunate events. With all that training you got from Uncle Sam I was hoping for better results. I am damned disappointed in you."

I didn't respond. If the woman was hoping to surprise me, she was going to be doubly disappointed. Twenty years in special operations had inured me to being surprised by the convoluted ways of desk warriors. When it came to people like her it was always better to avoid any expectations.

She said, "All right, that was my drill sergeant act. So now what?"

"I was hoping you'd tell me that."

"Well, I'll tell you what. This operation is getting shut down as of exactly right now." She indicated the doorway, where Special Agent Douglas had gone. "The morons screwed it up so bad not even I can unscrew it this time. They've got exactly zilch to go on and we're short on man power for other cases where there is shit to work with. What you call a killing is going down as no such thing. It's going down as an automobile accident. You understand."

"No. I don't."

She swung herself back and forth for a second, probably trying to contain her impatience. "Well, then let me explain. If two special agents are killed, what do you suppose happens next?"

"Is this what they call a rhetorical question?"

She half smiled. "What happens is that the killing of two Homeland Security Special Investigators requires an investigation, a deep one, with reports to a whole slew of politicians and administrators and probably press conferences and investigative reporters. Problem with that is *my* morons have already investigated the damned situation with these Cartwright people and found precisely zero. Imagine if you will, launching and completing a failed investigation into the deaths of two Homeland Security Special Investigators. You think that's a solid basis for promotion, Keeler? You think that's a good bet to take?"

"I wouldn't know. Never gave two shits for a promotion, ma'am."

She gave me a disgusted look. "Right. And look at you now."

I looked down at myself. The new shirt wasn't that new anymore, but it was still pretty good by my standards.

I said, "So it's a hit-and-run?"

"Even worse. They got a walk-in at the police station this morning. Town garbage truck driver copped to it. Claims it was an accident. Reason he didn't stop was his traumatic head injury, verified medically by a local doctor. Said injury caused him to momentarily lose his sense of civic duty. Guy wakes up this morning, recalls the events of last night, gets a terrible feeling of guilt, comes in to the station, and turns himself in. Garbage truck driver happens to be three months from retirement with full benefits, but there it is. Case closed as far as the local police are concerned."

I made an ironic expression. "Nice story. That was a hit, one hundred and twenty percent."

She didn't say anything.

I said, "I think the local police helped set it up. I might be tangentially responsible for that. I didn't know your people were law enforcement. I called the locals when I noticed your agents staking out the motel I'm staying at."

She was looking at me, a little bemused smile playing over her face. "Yes. I know all of that and I've made our position clear: it was an accident. None of that is going to change. I'm out of here." She paused a long moment and moved her head in a slow nod until I interrupted.

"But."

" But, you're not the kind of guy who lets a thing like this go, are you?"

"No. I don't suppose that I am."

CHAPTER THIRTY-TWO

THE WOMAN SWIVELED the chair casually back and forth.

"No. I didn't think you were. To tell you the truth, I checked this morning. It costs nearly a quarter of a million bucks to train one of you Air Force special operations people. That's the baseline pararescue pipeline, which even takes into consideration the dweebs who wash out. You know, they count too in terms of the budget. But you aren't a baseline model, Keeler. On top of everything else you got extra training. Like an ice cream sundae with whipped cream, chocolate sauce, cherries, and on top of all that you add sprinkles, crushed peanuts, and maybe fancy shit like macadamia brittle and olive oil. I figured the classified part was everything after the whipped cream. Now I'm thinking an extra two hundred and fifty grand on top of the quarter mil makes it like half a million dollars' worth of muscle standing right here in front of me." She looked at me hard, top to bottom, like a market trader. "And the animal metabolism is still going strong by the looks of it. They chose well."

She was so outrageous that I had to smile. "So you were planning on reaching out, then."

The woman laughed. "Oh, hell no. This is pure coincidence.

There are, like, eight thousand people who up and die every twenty-four hours in this country. Yesterday wasn't any kind of an exception. Today's just another spin of the wheel. Call me a heartless bitch, but shit happens every day."

I agreed. "Shit happens, but here I am."

"So you are." She leaned forward and plucked a thin folder off a short stack in front of her. "Take a gander at this."

I took the folder and opened it to find Linda Cartwright's service records held together by a single paperclip. I leafed through the documents. I didn't see anything more than what I'd already found at her house. I thumbed to a second sheaf of papers.

I was looking at a marriage license from the state of Indiana. Fayaz Nayk Muhammad and Linda Cartwright were married in 2006. Linda Cartwright's place of birth was noted as Hamilton County, Indiana. For Fayaz Nayk Muhammad, the clerk had entered Mazar-i-Sharif, Afghanistan. There were no dependent children.

The woman in front of me was impatiently typing on her phone, as if every second of her life needed to be productive. I decided not to care about her impatience. I thought about the documents in my hands for a moment. At first glance it was confusing. Cartwright marries a guy named Fayaz Nayk Muhammad and then ends up with a guy named William F. Cartwright. Reading the story through her military career brought it into a more comprehensible shape.

Cartwright serves in Afghanistan. Two tours with the 10th, 2001 and 2003. She comes back home and a couple of years later marries an Afghan. Not a common choice, maybe, but not a complete surprise. Overseas deployments are a big deal in a person's life. Cartwright must have been in her early twenties back then. She wouldn't have been the first or the last soldier to have a life-changing experience at war. I figured Fayaz Nayk Muhammad had changed his name to William F. Cartwright. He had taken his wife's last name. The F was for Fayaz, like a reminder of his previous identity.

Big deal. I handed the folder back to the woman. "So what?"

She stopped playing with her phone and took the folder. Laying it delicately on the desk in front of her. She swiveled around to look at me again. "So there's the other thing." She grinned, revealing small white teeth perfectly aligned behind her lips. "The other thing is that our man Fayaz, AKA William F. met Linda Cartwright in Afghanistan when she was on deployment."

Cartwright had been with the 10th mountain division, the first regular United States troops to enter Afghanistan in 2001. As a unit supply specialist, she would have been deployed to headquarters.

"Met as in how?"

"As in Fayaz worked as an interpreter for the US Army. They both worked at army HQ in some shit hole named Karshi-Khanabad. You know it?"

"K2 . I've been there and it's not Afghanistan. They staged the beginning of the war out of an old Soviet airbase across the border in Uzbekistan. Moved everything over to the Ganner later on." I studied the woman in the swivel chair. "So this guy was a terp for the army. All credit to him. He'd have been interfacing with the Northern Alliance people back in 2001." I said his name aloud. "Fayaz Nayk Muhammad." Looked up at the woman and dug my eyes into hers, which were dark brown and did not flinch. "Unsurprising that he'd want to change that name to William F. Cartwright once he gets to Indiana and tries to get a life. Personally, I'm glad he got out in time and I wish him a great life in this country."

She rolled her eyes. "Whatever. Anyway, like I said, two tours and then she's back home. A couple years later he gets a visa by some miracle and they eventually marry in 2006."

I said, "Okay, so what?"

She shrugged. "You see, one of the many issues we face is this Fayaz Nayk Muhammad guy wasn't working directly for Uncle Sam on a military contract. He was employed by a private contractor supplying local services. We reached out but they aren't in business anymore, so there's nothing else to look at regarding Mr. Muhammad slash Cartwright."

"This is what got Homeland Security involved, the Afghan connection."

"Correct. The team was tipped off about a homeland security situation regarding Linda and William F. Cartwright."

"What was the tip-off?"

"Well, now." The woman looked at me carefully. Below the folder that I had handed back was a second folder that she slipped out and held up. "I cannot show you the inside of this folder, Keeler. But it contains the other, other thing."

I said nothing.

"This folder contains documents detailing the marriage histories of nine other male Afghan nationals, or should I say *ex*-Afghan nationals. Ex because each of these men is now a citizen of the United States of America. And like Fayaz Nayk Muhammad, each of them served our military as an interpreter and went on to marry a female veteran of our armed forces."

I said, "I'm assuming there's a connection here."

"Correct. The connection is named Linda Cartwright." The woman switched up her leg-crossing configuration. Right over left became left over right. "Turns out that Linda Cartwright was something of a human rights activist, at least for a time. Not only did she up and marry her own Afghan interpreter, she got busy organizing a kind of marriage circle. Like, a matchmaker, for want of a better term. Cartwright created some kind of an internet group or forum or whatever. She used that to reach out to fellow female veterans and get them interested in the plight of Afghan nationals who had worked with the military. Cartwright claimed that they were in danger over there and made it her mission to get them out."

"That was the tip-off. Cartwright's activities as a matchmaker."

She said nothing, but she tilted her head with an expression that said: not exactly but not so very far either. I thought about it for exactly one second.

Over in Afghanistan, our interpreters had been vital members of the team. Without them we would have been unable to operate. In exchange for facilitating communications, those interpreters received a small sum of money without even a thank-you letter. Once we were out of there, most of them were left high and dry. Many were hunted down by the enemy and killed for collaborating with us. Some escaped, most didn't. Many were still stuck there.

"Cartwright's a hero", I said. "That's a project that I'd get behind in a second. I could convince fifty of my old teammates to do the same. It's just a shame there aren't people like her in the command hierarchy with the guts to put their money where their mouth is."

The woman looked serious for the first time since I'd been there. She stopped twirling and spinning in her seat and faced me properly "That's exactly how I feel. I should say *we*. My people are unanimous about it. This is what we call a complex situation. On the one hand there is the Cartwright project, which we can support as a workaround to the failings of our political masters. Just because my Special Agents are morons doesn't make them completely stupid. They clocked to some kind of a local beef involving William Fayaz Cartwright and maybe his veteran wife Linda. We haven't figured out what the local beef is, or if and how said beef connects to her Afghan adventures. Plus, my special agents found you, who by the way are non-existent in the paperwork. My decision. I control the paperwork. In any case, it's all interesting, isn't it?" The woman slipped the two folders into a leather document sleeve. "But interesting ain't enough for me, Keeler."

The woman stood up. We were face to face, about the same height.

I said, "That's it? You're going to leave Cartwright high and dry."

She shook her head. "You ever have to do triage?"

There had been many occasions in my military career when it had been necessary to let people die in order to save others who had a better chance of living. Triage is when you need to make those kinds of decisions, who lives and who dies. You make the best judgement you can, based upon the information you've got at hand. It doesn't always work out, but you do your best. That's triage. A no-win situation.

I nodded. "That's another rhetorical question."

"Well I'm not any kind of a combat medic, but I'm doing triage all day long, Keeler. Every single day. For every interesting situation that I get my people involved with, there are ten that I don't. Maybe five out of those ten are important. Maybe I make the wrong call and people die, maybe not. That's just the job."

I saw then that she was tired. Tough and experienced, but tired just the same. Fine lines of fatigue ran from her eyes down toward the corners of her mouth. I didn't know how many places she'd had to fly in and out of that week, maybe a whole bunch of them. Each with a terribly important and interesting story that she had to judge against a set of criteria that I couldn't know about.

The woman held out a hand to me and I took it. The hand was warm and dry. Her nails were not ostentatious, but they were long enough to tickle my palm. It was nice to hold her hand and I believe that she felt the same way.

"You do what you think is right, Keeler."

She removed her hand from mine and slid it into her leather document sleeve, extracting a small white card. The card had her name and title. Dr. Amanda Sobell, Director, National Security Investigations, HSI Chicago.

I read her name out loud to hear how it sounded. "Sobell." I looked at her; she looked at me. "I guess you must have had to kill more than a few guys to get into that office."

"More than you can imagine and killing would have been a kindness compared to what I had to do." She held out her hand for the card. "Memorize that and give it back. Call me if it's absolutely necessary."

I took a mental image of the card and handed it back to her.

She said, "If you do survive and make it up to Chiraq sometime, I'll buy you an ice cream sundae. You can have all the bells and whistles too."

CHAPTER THIRTY-THREE

I walked back across the busy road. I could see Collins's red Honda parked out front of the little strip of stores. She wasn't in it, and I didn't see her out of it either. When I came up to the car, she was walking out of the Starbucks balancing two cups of coffee with a brown paper bag.

She held out a cup. "So?"

I kind of raised my eyebrows and wrinkled my forehead in a frown. A way of saying *where do I start?* in body language. She unlocked the car and we got into the seats. The coffee was hot and good. The brown paper bag contained two generous brownies. I sipped at the liquid.

She waited patiently for the debrief.

I told her about Cartwright and the Afghanistan connection. About how William F. Cartwright and Linda had met while she was deployed. The change of name. The Afghan connection explained the Homeland Security interest. I had to do some extra explaining about the interpreter issue. That wasn't common knowledge to civilians.

When I told her that Linda Cartwright had been encouraging

fellow female veterans to help Afghan interpreters get out of the country, I could see that I had Collins's attention. I hadn't processed all of that yet myself and didn't presume to understand the bearing it had on the situation at hand.

Collins was cogitating on the practical ramifications. "Back up one second, Keeler. A lot of people get married for citizenship papers, right?"

I said, "It's a classic."

"Two questions come to mind." She was looking at me intensely, warming to the subject. "First, to what extent are these real marriages? Second, aren't these men already married back in Afghanistan?"

I hadn't thought about that. Domestic practicalities had never been high on my list. It was true that Afghanistan hadn't seemed like any kind of a paradise for bachelors. The terps I had known were from the city, mostly. They weren't villagers from the sticks. But I wasn't any kind of a sociologist either. I hadn't gone over there to study the Afghan society, and most of our business had been up in the mountains taking the fight to the enemy.

"Good questions, Collins. Maybe we'll find answers, maybe not."

"Right."

We were both ruminating, sipping at coffee and nibbling the brownies. I could see that she was disturbed.

"Linda Cartwright's a person with principles," she said. "You don't find those too often, Keeler."

I agreed. "She put her money where her mouth is. A lot of our people over there take exception to being let down by the politicians and upper command chain. Not many of us make that an actionable priority in our lives. Interpreters are just as much team members as anyone else and you don't leave your team members behind, period."

Collins looked at me. "But . . ."

I said, "But what does that have to do with the loan shark?" She looked away. I chewed the last corner of the brownie. "Exactly."

I was looking through the windshield at the Starbucks. Special

Agent Stan Douglas from Homeland Security Investigations stepped out, balancing a little cardboard tray with molded cup holders. Two large ice teas were tucked in there. The young guy came behind holding his own drink, which seemed to be a complicated iced coffee confection with all kinds of whipped stuff on top.

Collins finished her brownie and got the car started.

"Berrymore Court?"

"Let's do it."

Berrymore Court might have been fancy once, but it wasn't fancy any longer.

The place was a faded condominium development of attached two-story buildings with separate apartments on each level. The structure was faced with strips of siding stained the color of dark chocolate. Donna Williams's place was unit 35b, upstairs. I followed Collins and parked the Crown Vic behind her red Honda. I slid the car keys under the seat. We wouldn't be long, but you never know. Maybe Collins would need to drive, maybe someone else.

I could see her through the rear window of her little car, bent over something, which I assumed was her phone. I got out of the vehicle and came around to the trunk. The Glock was in the backpack, dark and mean looking.

I pulled back the action and a round sprung up from the magazine into the chamber. The slide snicked shut. I closed the trunk and pushed the Glock into my waistband, snug at the small of my back. Good to go.

Collins and I walked across the street and climbed a staircase set into the front of the building. The dark wood smelled of recently applied stain.

She said, "Very chalet-inspired over here."

I grunted. "Like climbing to a ski lift."

"You ski, Keeler?"

"No."

We stood looking at the front door of Donna Williams's apartment. A delicate musical mobile hung from the roof awning. Collins pushed it and set off a little jingle. Williams had a green thumb. Her balcony area was lush. Large leafy potted plants were arranged three deep against the walls. Two sturdy macramé holders supported vines that hung in the corners. The sound of the chimes didn't seem to have aroused anybody inside.

Collins thumbed the doorbell, which produced a cacophony of frantic ringing from the interior. Nobody responded to the noise, no panicked footsteps, no flutter of socked feet on polished wood floors. We waited. The wind had picked up and the sky looked threatening.

To the right of the door was a double window. I peered in and saw an orderly kitchen. The opposite wall had an electric stove top and a blond wood kitchen knife block. I examined the window lock mechanism and reckoned that I'd be able to get inside with a screwdriver or a knife. I had neither on me but patted my pockets out of habit.

I got nothing, which reminded me of the keys from J&S Services. I had a bad feeling that one of them was going to fit. I hadn't paid any attention to the addresses on the key tags.

I said, "Hold that thought."

I came down the chalet stairs, two at a time. I unzipped the backpack's front compartment and pulled the seven house keys I'd taken from J&S Services and sorted through them. Each key, or set of keys, had a colored tag holder with an address written in ballpoint pen.

I found 35b Berrymore Court scrawled in blue on the paper strip tucked into a red key tag holder. Collins was watching from the landing. I slammed the trunk closed and came back up. I showed Collins the address on the key tag. Her face darkened. "You think these people have taken Donna Williams's house?"

"Looks like it."

"Seven properties. That's a lot. Keeler. What do they do with all the houses they've taken?"

I didn't know the answer to that question. What I did know was that the cleaners had received the key to the Cartwright house, but not the Williams house. Ricardo at J&S Services had mentioned contractors and remodeling. Maybe there was remodeling planned for the future of Donna Williams's apartment.

I put the key into the door.

Ten seconds later, Collins and I stood in the entrance. I closed the front door behind us.

The apartment wasn't fancy or modest, just a nice-looking comfortable place to live with your daughter. There weren't any big performative nods to the idea of family. No pictures on the wall and no aspirational piano corner. The dining room table was piled with plain cardboard boxes. At first glance I simply assumed that they were normal delivery packages.

Collins didn't even notice the boxes. She said, "What are we looking for?"

"Not sure. Maybe we can find out if there's a father somewhere. Maybe the daughter's staying with him and doesn't know her mom's gone."

"I'll call the school right now. Find out if Emma Williams showed up."

Collins broke off and entered the kitchen. She had her phone out and was looking into it, presumably for the school's contact number. Williams had a landline phone with a cordless handset cradled by a charger next to the microwave oven.

I went to the dining room table and picked up a box. It was small enough that I could get a grip with one hand, and heavy enough to indicate something of substance within. I opened the box and saw plastic wrapping. I pulled the thing out of the cardboard. It was rectangular with rounded edges, made of steel and maybe other stuff. Hard to see in its plastic wrapper. I found the opening and let the object drop into my hand. I was looking at a door-latching mechanism, something that you'd need to fit professionally into a heavy-duty portal. On top of that it had electrical wiring, which made it what they call a "smart" lock.

I opened a few other boxes. One contained a security camera with a powerful lens and a boxy body and bare wires protruding. The other box I opened was smaller and more difficult to explain. It contained six small discs; each had two wires coming out of bare ends.

Collins looked at me from the kitchen. "What's all that?"

"Security upgrades, I guess."

I peeked into another box. More of the same. Security hardware just waiting for installation. Somebody was paranoid.

I left the dining area and walked through the apartment, opening drawers and cabinets at random. Looking to soak up whatever I could gather of Donna Williams's life. The house looked lived in, but anonymous. As if it could have housed anybody, or nobody. The drawers contained the usual objects and items, nothing more and nothing less. What the place lacked was personality.

The kitchen was immediately to the right of the entrance, like a nook or a dead end that went nowhere. The entrance merged with a dining room area, separated from the living room by a shelving unit doing double duty as a space partition. The living room area ended at the wall on the other side of the apartment. Two large windows looked out to the back, which was a section of woods. The back of the building had a skeletal fire escape.

I returned to the living area and followed a hallway that branched into a master bedroom on the right, and a smaller bedroom on the left, presumably for the daughter, Emma.

Emma Williams's room contained a single bed, a desk, and two walls full of neatly arranged teen posters. Another wall was spray painted in multicolored graffiti. The exterior wall featured a window looking out back to a stand of trees. I hunted through the drawers and the closet without finding anything of interest. The priorities seemed to be clothes and cosmetics, including a makeup mirror with lightbulbs framing it. The floor by Emma's bed was littered with phone-charging cables and an electrical multiplug extension for her devices.

Donna Williams's bedroom was immaculately clean. A small desk was tucked underneath the window plants. She had a walk-in closet and her own entrance into the bathroom. Collins came into the room. "School switchboard had me on hold. I'll call again later."

She walked into the closet. I rifled through the papers stacked on the desk. Utility bills in Donna Williams's name. A letter from the school about extracurricular events. A snow globe souvenir from London kept the papers down. Collins's voice came from the walk-in closet. "Keeler." I looked in. Collins was standing in there holding a man's suit, which clung to a hanger. "It's not just Donna Williams here." She pointed to the back of the walk-in space. "Fifty-fifty. The guy's got the back half."

The back of the closet held half a dozen suits on the hanging rail, plus built-in squared-off cubbies for shirts and pants, sweaters, underwear and socks. All of it was organized and folded correctly. I pictured the guy getting down on hands and knees to access his clothes.

I walked out of the closet and out of the bedroom. The hallway ended with another closet door. I turned back out, crossed the living room, and entered the kitchen again. I noticed there were no fridge magnets. Drawers were full of the usual cooking utensils and appliance manuals alongside knickknacks like loose string, batteries, and a pencil stub.

I heard Collins call my name. By the time I returned to the living room, she was sitting on the sofa holding a photo album onto her lap. I sat beside her and watched her open the substantial cover.

CHAPTER THIRTY-FOUR

THE PHOTO ALBUM was a high-quality item with translucent paper and stiff cardstock. It was the kind of thing domestic-minded people acquire at an optimistic milestone in their lives, like birth and marriage.

Collins looked carefully at the photographs. Many of them were of a small baby, and it wasn't easy to tell if it was a boy or a girl. I figured the color of the clothes was a good indication, which were all pink. Donna Williams featured heavily in those first pages, holding the baby in several positions and locations around the house and in parks and playgrounds. The new mother looked happy and tired, either smiling exhausted at the camera, or staring at the baby with a proprietorial eye.

Years passed in only a few turns of the page. Collins stopped at the fifth page. "There's the man with the fancy suits."

I shuffled over next to her and peered down at the pictures. She had a finger next to the photo in question. The picture had been taken right there in the apartment. The scene was a birthday celebration. The baby had become a toddler. But it wasn't her birthday, or her mother's. The cake was frosted white and had *Happy Birthday, Dad* written in blue icing on the top.

Looking at the photograph sent the short hairs on my neck straight up in the air and gave me a nervous tingle. William F. Cartwright, the same handsome man that I'd seen photographed in Linda Cartwright's house, was now squeezed between Donna Williams and little Emma. Both mother and daughter glowed with silly happiness. William F. Cartwright was showing a satisfied white-toothed grin under his mustache. I verified the word *Dad* on the cake again, upside down in the photograph.

I said, "You won't believe this."

Collins turned to me. "What?"

I didn't have the photograph of Cartwright with me. It was in the car.

I pointed my finger. "That's William F. Cartwright, Linda's husband."

Collins looked confused, unbelieving. "You sure?"

"Stay here."

I left the apartment and jogged down the stairs. It was beginning to drizzle out there. I got to the car and retrieved the photograph. When I got back, Collins was still on the couch looking at the photo album. I put the picture of William F. Cartwright in her hand. She flipped to the first picture and we leaned in close to examine the specimens.

"Where did you get that from?"

"Linda Cartwright's house. That's her husband. His name is William, also known as Fayaz. I've seen the marriage certificate."

It was the same guy in the same period of his life.

Collins's eyes had widened as the melodrama sank in. She adjusted her position on the couch and faced me, alert. "No way."

I said nothing.

She looked at me for a long moment. I looked back. Her expression sharpened and she turned once more to the photo album. There were more family pictures featuring William F. Cartwright. Collins paused and examined another one: Cartwright and young Emma locked into rollercoaster seats at an amusement park. The girl had braces but was already pretty.

After a piece I said, "What are you thinking?"

She ignored the question and kept turning pages. She stopped again at a photograph of Emma and the two adults. This time, Cartwright was dressed in a gray suit with a maroon tie and a shiny forehead. Donna Williams wore a white dress and held a bouquet of flowers. The picture was taken against a sky-blue wall. The two adults were beaming with contentment. The girl was maybe eight years old. Emma looked distracted.

Collins didn't respond. She flipped through the remainder of the album and came back to the baby pictures.

"Well it's pretty obvious that the guy had two families. The only question is the extent to which he kept each of them a secret from the other. What did Linda or Donna know about this guy's other domestic situation?"

I leaned back in the sofa and looked over toward the front window. The vines from Donna Williams's little balcony garden were fresh green against the back light. "They live in the same town. Cartwright told me that her husband sold insurance to the hospitality industry. Said it was normal for him to be away for a week or more."

Collins said, "That's the perfect setup for something like this. Maintaining a second family. William F. goes on regular work trips and instead of actually working, he's living the double life."

I said, "Which means the work might be bullshit. Someone who balances two secret families is just as likely to take the risk of borrowing money from loan sharks. He gets in bad with The Bob. Winds up putting two families into jeopardy, not just one. Which would make him asshole of the decade."

"Damn right it does."

My right hand was aching, still feeling the impact of the mechanic's face. I shook it out a couple of times and massaged the knuckles. "It makes sense." I turned to Collins. "That might also account for Donna Williams trying to shoot Linda Cartwright and then trying to take herself out."

Collins blanched. "Because Donna Williams hadn't known about Linda Cartwright!"

"Murphy's law. William F. Cartwright's delicate house of cards comes tumbling down all at the same time. Finally pushed over." I was shaking my head because it wasn't a feel-good story.

Collins was looking at me excitedly. "Donna Williams finds out about Cartwright and then totally loses her shit. By then, the two-timing husband has already gone to ground so she can't shoot him in the head like he deserves."

I was remembering the photograph of Linda Cartwright that Donna Williams was carrying in her purse.

"Cartwright found a photograph of herself in Williams's purse. She said only her husband had that picture, plus the address written on the back wasn't her husband's script."

Collins nodded, "English wasn't his first language."

"Right. It's not out of the realm of possibility that The Bob provoked Williams to go after the other wife. Donna Williams goes over to Linda Cartwright's house with trouble on her mind."

Collins's eyes were wide with fascination and horror. "Yeah, maybe."

I was thinking about Donna Williams's attempted suicide, and the fact of her daughter. "You think she'd kill herself and leave her daughter alone with a guy she just found out was two-timing her?"

Collins was quiet for a ten count. She leaned back on the sofa. Her hair tickled my neck. "Yes, if she was in complete despair, having what they call a psychotic episode."

"Call the school again."

She called the school. This time she made it past the switchboard and was transferred to the receptionist. I only heard one side of the conversation. There was the main question, spoken like a worried mother, "This is Donna Williams, Emma's mom. Can I please speak to my daughter? It's a family emergency."

Followed by a bunch of silent moments, punctuated by "yes," "thank you," and "please," followed by even more nothing. After two minutes her demeanor changed and Collins looked meaningfully at me while nodding vacantly. She said, "Oh not at all, no." Then there was an affirmation, with a nod. "Yes, of course." After that it was all "thank you" and "'goodbye." She hung up the phone. "Emma hasn't been in school for five days."

I said, "That predates her mother's psychotic episode by three days."

"That isn't all, Keeler. They said her dad picked her up from class in the middle of the day. They asked if I didn't know about it. I said I knew." Collins smiled nervously, relieved. "For a minute there the attendance officer got suspicious of me."

I said, "Now we've got even more of a reason for Donna Williams to flip."

"Daughter disappears with dad. Mother gets psychotic."

"Correct."

Collins turned to me. "Maybe The Bob got to Donna Williams first. Told her the daughter was dead. That could kick off the psychotic episode."

"Maybe."

Collins said, "What do you want to do?"

"I see two goals. Find the missing persons, in particular the girl. Then neutralize the threat, The Bob. The order of things isn't important. I'm happy to be opportunistic. The priority would be to save lives and get the missing people safe."

"Which means what exactly, in terms of action?" Collins asked.

"I took a handful of house keys from J&S Services. Each key has an address on it. I'm thinking that those are properties that The Bob has appropriated from people who owe him. Like this place, and the Cartwright house. I'd like to check out the other properties."

Collins was nodding in agreement. She was ready to go. She

folded the photo album and returned it to the glass-topped coffee table. We stood up from the sofa. I could see that Collins's eyes were rimmed with red. She faced me. "I need you to promise me something, Keeler."

I said nothing.

"We go to the wall on this. If that little girl's been let down by the adults in her life, it's got to end with things made right." She used both hands to wipe the tears out of her eyes. "You don't need my entire life story, but I was let down by my parents. It wasn't fair then, and it isn't fair now."

I nodded. "That's what we're going to do, Collins. No doubt."

She punched me hard in the chest. "You're damned right it is."

She was strong. The punch landed very close to a bruised part of me that had already suffered a pummeling earlier in the day. I sucked in the pain.

She stalked off to the door, a committed woman who knew the difference between right and wrong. I watched her open the door and turn back to look at me. She had a strong spirit and intelligence. On top of that she was very good-looking. Outside, the sky glowered behind her with menace. The wind kicked up her curls and brought them to life, like dancing strands of fire.

I followed her out and dug in my pocket for the key. A harsh voice spat out to my immediate right. "Hey, big guy!"

I whipped my head around; nobody there. Collins pointed.

I followed her gaze in through the dense growth over a vine trellis to the wall beside the door. A rectangular plastic object was attached to a trellis crossbeam with a couple of cable ties. It was a doorbell with an integrated camera bubble. Remotely controlled.

A distorted cackle of laughter came out of the fancy doorbell. I realized that someone was speaking through it, and that they were looking at us through the camera bubble. I felt a chill.

The doorbell said, "Well, well, well, if it isn't mister do-good-wants-to-fucking-die." The voice started to cough uncontrollably, which sounded like a malfunctioning machine gun through the tiny speaker. Then the coughing sputtered to a stop and there was a pause.

I looked at Collins. She was staring at the device in rapt silence.

CHAPTER THIRTY-FIVE

The doorbell coughed once more. The voice grated. "Come here and let me tell you something."

Collins stepped forward but I held her back. "Don't go there."

The voice laughed again, an ugly sound turning to static noise. "Don't go there? It's a little too late for that. I'll tell you where you're going. You're going to the farm is where."

I realized what was going on. Whoever it was behind the camera bubble was trying to delay us. They'd clocked us coming into Williams's apartment and had sent a team, but the team wasn't there yet.

I stepped up and grabbed the offending doorbell. The cable ties were tight. I wrenched the device away, and was only half successful. The cover popped off, exposing a small battery and some electronic components. I tilted the battery out with a thumbnail and tossed it off the balcony. The doorbell was now an inert plastic rectangle. The camera was the same as before, dull, indifferent, and ambiguous.

I heard a surprised grunt from Collins just behind my shoulder. I turned around and saw her hands were up in a defensive posture and she was gazing down the passageway. I stepped to my right to see past her. Two men wearing full-face tactical respirator masks with double-inhalation valves were coming up the chalet stairs to the landing. The first guy up had long red hair pulled back in a ponytail. It was the guy from the Silver Inn Motel. The man Cartwright had hammered. He held a large aerosol canister out in front of him. The compressed spray hissed out in a narrow cone. Collins got it point-blank in the face and staggered back.

I got one hand to my waistband for the Glock, and with the other I pulled Collins behind me. I brought the gun up and put two into the redhead's chest at less than two yards. Bang bang. The guy fell back against the railing. I butted Collins through the open front door and kicked it shut behind us. She was staggering, wiping chemicals out of her face. The air was thick with the stench of some kind of medicinal product. I turned the latch to the left and locked the door. Collins was wavering on her feet. I pushed her gently to the back of the apartment. "Fire escape."

She glanced at me wildly, confused and disoriented. Her brain was firing off commands, but her legs weren't listening. She lost her balance and collapsed into the glass coffee table, shattering the top. At the same time the front door shuddered and boomed under someone's boot.

I put three rounds through the door in an upside-down triangular pattern, widely spaced. Nothing came back.

Collins was crumpled on top of the shattered glass amid scattered coffee table items. I moved past the sofa to the window and looked out at the woods. The light rain was showering the inside-out leaves, pale against the dark green canopy.

I put my boot through the glass. It took a couple of kicks to clear the shards enough that I could jump onto the fire escape. I put my head out the window and looked down. The people on the ground floor had miniature cookie-cutter terraces out back, each with a barbecue and a couple of deck chairs around a square of astroturf. Those were fenced off. On the other side of the fence was a flagstone walkway, grass, and then the woods. Nobody was sunning themselves, nobody was barbecuing. All civilians were indoors sheltering from the impending storm.

I came for Collins and pulled her off the broken glass table. She was deeply unconscious. I got her up in a fireman's lift, over my shoulder. There was a sound from the front of the apartment, like the knock of something hard hitting another hard object, two sounds a second apart. Holding Collins like that was not very tactically astute. I laid her carefully on the sofa.

After those sounds there was nothing, only silence, but that knocking sound had tickled my sixth sense. There was a greater than zero chance that I'd shot the guy through the door, but that wasn't anything you could buy lunch with.

I moved to the front of the apartment. Glock up and covering the entry point. Donna Williams had a mirror next to the door, the kind people hang on their wall for a last look before they go out. The mirror was set off to the side. From my approach angle it reflected one corner of the kitchen. A sudden flicker of movement caught my eye. I spun left and got a face full of aerosol discharge, all up in my nose and stinging at my eyes. I had no chance to see the attacker but wasn't in doubt about the situation. One or more of them had come in through the kitchen window. They'd broken in while I had been busy breaking glass out to the fire escape.

I tumbled forward, experiencing the movement like it was happening to someone else. There was a blur of motion in front of me. It felt like a great effort to raise the Glock and squeeze the trigger, but I did it twice, one shot squeezed point-blank at a vague figure.

Whoever I shot made a soft sound like an inflated bag being pierced by a fine needle. The breath released slowly, with an exhausted hiss. I was aware of what was happening. I was being sedated. It made me feel fuzzy and good. I'd done a training course on various incapacitating agents. Some of them had effects close to heroin, I figured this was one of those.

I collapsed forward, with no ability to stop. I managed to turn so that I landed on my back. It was soft and comfortable on the carpet. I felt that I could just relax and stay there forever.

The second guy came into focus, leaning over me, smiling behind the face mask. He was looking at me the way a laboratory scientist looks at a drugged rat, waiting patiently for the effects to kick in, knowing that it was going to happen soon. It was the other guy from the motel, the one Linda Cartwright had hammered in the head.

He came up closer and examined my face. I looked back at him with unfocused eyes. I could hear his voice, muffled by the respirator mask. "Good night." The Glock was too heavy to lift. He examined me even closer, then looked over me at somebody else. "That shit works really good."

The voice came from behind me. "What did I tell you. Never doubt The Bob."

The rain pattered outside, hitting harder on the fire escape. The wind came in, cool over my face. After that the rain came regular and just as hard, like a white noise. Whatever drug they had in that aerosol canister worked. I didn't only hear the rain; I felt it deeply and it felt good.

The guy standing over me chuckled. The tactical respirator made him look like an evil insect. His torso was bulky and I realized that he was wearing body armor under the flannel shirt. I had one last thought before the sucking blackness took me. I'd fired six rounds, which meant twelve left in the magazine. A meaningless number at this point, since the Glock was going to be more than useless. That thought was now nothing but the residue of a strict training regime.

CHAPTER THIRTY-SIX

The first impression of consciousness was my teeth grinding into grit. Hard sand and something that tasted metallic on my tongue. I spit but the taste remained.

Other senses kicked in. I felt an enveloping vibration, like pins being driven into my skin all over the body. That was coupled with the smell of soil and excrement. I opened my eyes. The rain was coming down hard and fast. I was on my knees, sunk in mud. The ground surface quivered and shook from the wretched downpour of heavy drops hitting fast and furious. The air between the drops was hot and humid.

At first I wasn't sure what was what. The ground did not seem solid, a quagmire of dissolved earth furiously shaking. It was only after a couple of seconds that I got my situational awareness.

I was in a large rectangular pen, fenced off with heavy-duty wire. My head was pounding, a dull and frequent thud behind the eyes. The rain obliterated the visibility. What I could see was bleak: rain, mud, fence, and pigs. A whole mess of them, snorting and snuffling and milling around in the mud. They were unconcerned by the inclement weather and my presence.

On the other side of the enclosure was another human figure, maybe twenty feet beyond the animals. She was slumped over and naked, arms and ankles tied back to a sturdy post riding out of the shaking ground. It took me a second to clock that it was Tela Collins, another half second to realize that I was bound the same way, also stripped naked.

My hands and ankles had been pulled back and fixed around a heavy post, slick with wet mud. The binding was tight, and my fingers were numb from the loss of circulation. I pulled upright to take the pressure off my wrists. The pounding rain hammered all around. One of the pigs came closer, ignoring me, completely absorbed in rooting in the mud. The animal's body was pink and gray with brown splotches on taut skin. The splash back from the rain had made the pig filthy. Narrow eyes rolled in sockets and glanced at me. The snout came up and I saw red blood on it and a thin white bone protruding from the pig's mouth.

Which explained why the pigs were concentrating so intensely. They were feeding on remains. The team of hogs separated for an instant. Halfway between Collins and me was a third wooden post, vacated now. I was able to glimpse the base of the post and saw the shredded remains of rope and clothing. The pigs were lapping vigorously at the hellish soup of blood and dirt and gnawing on bones and tough pieces of flesh.

A man walked into the enclosure through a gate.

He wore a hooded olive-green rain slicker and mud boots and carried a long cattle prod. He came directly at me, parting the animals with the prod. The tool crackled and sang with electricity on contact. The pigs scattered noisily. I waited for the prod, but the guy held it in one hand and just stood in front of me, as if something was supposed to happen. The man had a pale face with a couple days' growth of beard. His eyes were set back into hollow depressions. They looked down at me for a while. The man's mouth started working something up and he spat it at me. A glob of spittle landed on my exposed thigh, mixing quickly with the rain.

He shouted to be heard above the cacophonous storm. "Welcome to my farm."

I spat out the dirt and blood from inside my mouth. I said, "So, you're a farmer." I didn't bother to shout, which forced him to lean closer. "You need to pray for a decent death," I said. "You can start by letting my friend go. She's got nothing to do with this."

The man laughed and shook his head. "I'm a simple farmer who does what he's told, pal. I got no beef with you in particular. I've just got a skeptical nature when it comes to the human species. Why does everyone think we're so special? To me you're no different from my pigs, up for slaughter when the time comes." He squatted down so that we were level and looked back at Collins. "And let me tell you something else, *bud*. She's going first and we're going to take our time, just to make an impression on you before you die. That's what the boss says, and whatever the boss says goes."

I nodded and raised my head. Water sluiced over my eyes. "I get it. Still, you heard me. Let her go and you die decently. I'm not planning on saying it again."

The farmer ignored me. "There's the question of the bitch, and where to find her."

"That's not specific enough."

"The bitch married to the guy that owes."

I figured he was talking in a pejorative manner about either Linda Cartwright or Donna Williams. Which meant that the guy who owed was William F. Cartwright, married to both of the women. I couldn't help but laugh. The big farmer looked at me strangely. He reached into his rain slicker and pulled out a toothpick. He stuck it in his mouth and rolled it around a little between his teeth. The pink protrusion of his tongue glistening through the gaps. "Tough guy, huh? We get them once in a while. They go the same way as everyone else, often worse."

I straightened up and looked him in the face. Not a face that I recognized. It was white and fleshy under the stubble, like the fat on a side of beef hanging up in a walk-in refrigerator.

"Who was the last guy you fed to the pigs?"

He snorted and grinned. "I never know who they are, but you shouldn't presume that the people I turn into pig food are all of the masculine gender. We're equal opportunity here at the farm. I just take 'em out to slaughter and let my pigs do the rest." He looked at me like he was observing features on a commodity. "Anyway, you've got some time before that happens." A wide callused hand swept toward the animals. "Pigs are always hungry, they'll wait for you. Those animals are never done eating. They'll eat you and your girlfriend just the same as they ate that one. They'll enjoy every bite. Then I'll sell 'em and they'll end up in someone else's breakfast." He giggled insanely.

Two of the pigs were looking up with small eyes. Their mouths were busy crunching and grinding below the prominent snouts.

The farmer walked out and I watched him disappear behind a dilapidated barn. All around were pasture fields and beyond that trees. The woods were a hazy blur in the rain. The trees in the distance moved with the wind, soft shapes swaying back and forth.

I tugged slowly at my bonds, carefully testing and checking. I let my head loll down onto my chest and shook it around a little. I let my gaze fall on the fence posts and let my eyes roam slowly around the pen. Straight ahead was the barn the guy had gone behind. To the left were fields, then more trees. To my right was a dirt yard bordered by pines.

I began to rock back and forth against the post and then away from it. I wanted to know if the posts in the pigpen had been set in concrete or not. If they hadn't been, there was a greater than zero chance of just ripping the wood out of the ground. It would help if I could dig around it. The post felt solid but you never know.

I turned my attention to the ropes. Like wood, rope is a flexible material that expands and contracts according to its environment. Rope gets slick when wet. The dirt and mud could help with friction. As I rocked back and forth almost imperceptibly, I was expanding and contracting my forearms and leg muscles. The arms were easier to control. I knew that given enough time I'd be able to get those ropes loose a little.

And all I needed was a little, then it was game over in a major way for the people who had brought Collins and me to this place. Neither pity nor remorse could save them then. I got the feeling back in my fingertips and dug them down to the base of the pole. The mud was six inches deep. I felt the hard dirt underneath, and started probing and digging.

CHAPTER THIRTY-SEVEN

A COUPLE of hours later I'd excavated a foot and a half of dirt and mud along the vertical axis of the wood post. I couldn't feel my fingers anymore, only a dull sensation of weight on the parts of my hands that still had blood flow. The effort to continuously move those finger tips was an exercise in body and mind control.

It isn't totally obvious how you're supposed to dig into the ground behind yourself, when you're tied to a post by wrists and ankles in the driving wind and rain. I had to figure it out, like learning a musical instrument or a second language.

What I'd figured out was the importance of controlling the muscles of the entire body, from the legs on up and then out to the arms and wrists, tightening and flexing, relaxing and lengthening. The end result was some kind of a scratching maneuver in the dirt behind me. It probably wasn't pretty, but then again, nobody was watching. I hoped.

Collins was conscious. The rain had slacked off and we'd made eye contact. I'd made a point of not looking at her exposed body. It was out of some kind of respect for whatever remained of her modesty. I had observed her come to and take in the situation. She had reacted as I thought she might. A little surprised, but not shocked. Afraid, but not terrified. Still groggy from the sedation, Collins had seen me and we'd locked eyes for a long time. In that look were a thousand words that didn't need saying, and by the time we broke eye contact she had understood every one of them.

I'd told her I was confident and that she should conserve energy, because she was going to need it. As the situation sunk in, Collins's demeanor had changed. I could see that at twenty feet, in her body language. At first she'd been rigid, trying to get the stress off her ankles and wrists. Then she'd kind of slumped into it. Not slumped like she had no hope. Slumped like she was relaxing and waiting, doing the best she could under the circumstances. She was getting ready for something terrible and off the charts of what normal people think of as being within the realm of possibility.

Which was the opposite of what I was doing. I might have looked slumped to an outside observer, but I was completely activated. Every muscle in my body was dedicated to the task of excavating dirt. It was slow going with the fingernails. The heavy rain and general quagmire situation helped to cover what I'd clawed out.

I felt a different kind of pressure from the digging. I couldn't feel the fingers, but I was sensitive to the pressure moving up the hands, wrists, and into the arms. What I was feeling was something different, more solid. I kept scratching for a couple of minutes longer. It dawned on me that I was scraping my numb and bleeding fingers over concrete.

Which meant the post was solid and there was no way I'd be able to rip it out of the ground.

But defeat wasn't ever going to be an option. I thought it might be a decent idea to try and get some feeling back into my fingers. It wouldn't do to have them fall off, or to rub them numbly until the flesh wore down to bone. I closed my eyes and concentrated on relaxing. I decided five minutes of that would be a good idea.

~

Five minutes probably turned into a whole lot more.

I woke up to the distant sound of dirt bikes tearing through the storm. They started pretty far away, which made me visualize a long driveway. A minute later, the two bikes got to the farm. I had some feeling back in my fingers. The post was definitely embedded into rough concrete. I exercised my fingers by having them push the small stones and dirt back into place, in case somebody came and checked.

The bikes tore past the barn and fishtailed in the mud, carving half circles until they stopped right outside the enclosure. The lead bike was dragging something tied by a rope to the back. When it moved I realized that it was human and alive, wriggling in fits and starts. My first thought was either Linda Cartwright or her husband. I looked over at Collins. She was looking at the dirt bikes, probably wondering the same thing as me: What kind of fresh hell was coming at us?

The rider with cargo had his boots down and revved up the four-stroke engine. I saw that the trailing rope was fixed around a man's neck and the poor guy was still gripping at it with his hands even though it was now slack. I had no way of knowing how long he'd been dragged like that. Those hands were now clenched on like vice grips, the guy's muscles had seized.

The second rider kicked the stand down and got off his bike. He walked to the back of his buddy's ride, thumbed open a clasp knife, and cut the rope. The other rider put his bike on the stand. The two men pulled their captive through the mud, into the enclosure. His body was inert and hard to make out, like a single clot of mud, blood, and bone. The clothing was so shredded that he might as well have been naked. It looked like they'd dragged him for a couple of miles over gravel, at speed.

The helmeted men hitched the victim to the post set between Collins and me, and walked back to their bikes. For a while the man sprawled there, unmoving. There was something odd about his position; I realized it was his legs. Both of them were broken, jutting at wrong angles from his thighs. The two riders revved up and spun out, kicking dirt clods and spraying mud as they carved a semicircle and disappeared behind the barn in a cloud of smoke.

A couple minutes later the rain had washed off the mud from the guy's upturned face. The pigs were gathered around him, curious. He opened his eyes and rolled them around. A tongue came out and tasted the rain. I recognized the face. It was the guy from the corn field. The one who'd gotten away from me when I'd dry shot him with his own Desert Eagle.

Lucky once, not twice. He was one of *them*, which meant that these people were truly without mercy; they'd punish their own for the crime of surviving.

A figure was coming from the barn, walking slowly like he had all the time in the world. It was the farmer again. The man was extra-large. I hadn't noticed before, perhaps on account of the residual sedation. He was almost a giant, with a great pale slab for a face and smaller slabs for hands. He came through the gate to the pen. The farmer was holding a long chrome cylindrical object that shone with a dull light. It was about the size of a short thick baton.

I realized what it was. A captive bolt gun, the old cartridge-firing, penetrating kind they used for animal slaughter. I shouted at Collins across the enclosure. "Don't watch this."

The farmer grinned.

Just as the big farmer looked over at me, I felt something hard and sharp with my left index finger. I probed with my fingers to uncover the object, which wasn't easy since it was buried tight. The farmer looked back to his helpless prey.

The guy hitched to the post was hyperventilating. His eyes were bugged out and fearful, glaring white in a face blackened by blood and grit. Even though he'd suffered terrible abuse, he'd still been hoping for life. He had survived meeting me in the corn field. But now life was moving away from him in a symmetrical relation to the big man's approach. The farmer came up to the guy from the corn field and lifted him by the hair.

My fingers had extracted a section of the sharp thing I'd been uncovering in the dirt. It was a bone fragment, and from the size and shape I figured it might once have been an important part of an unlucky person's leg. Hard to tell by touch, but I was leaning toward a tibia or fibula. Too big for the pigs to eat. I felt triumphant and swiveled to look at Collins.

We locked eyes just as, in my peripheral vision, the farmer brought the captive bolt gun hard against the man's forehead. The impact caused the cartridge to fire with a muted bang. Collins blinked. The guy's head shuddered as the pointed steel bolt penetrated the frontal bone, forcing its way into the brain pan and destroying the first couple of inches of gray matter. The bolt sprung back into the cylindrical barrel with a heavy click. A thick knot of blood and brain leaked out of the hole.

The farmer released his grip on the dead guy's hair and let the corpse flop to the mud.

He looked at me again. "Tough guys go like that, bud. Tonight you'll go the same way."

I said, "Why wait for tonight?"

The farmer stood up, looming over the body at his feet. The pigs were gathered at the other side of the enclosure. They seemed to wither under their master's gaze.

He said, "So you can watch what happens next."

The pigs waited for their master to leave the pen. After that, they didn't waste any time wondering what to do next. Neither did I.

CHAPTER THIRTY-EIGHT

THEY CAME AFTER DARK.

By then I was experiencing issues. More specifically, my body was seriously losing energy. The wind had whipped up and the rain was now horizontal, like a million hot needles in my face, seeking out the eyes. I had the bone shard caught awkwardly between the knuckles of my left hand and was methodically scratching the rope over it as best I could, trying to sever the fibers one at a time. I had no idea how long it had been since the big farmer slaughtered the guy from the cornfield, but it was long enough that whatever there was left of him was no longer in any kind of a human shape.

The pigs were wallowing in the remains, insatiable, cracking bone and ripping flesh and clothing equally.

In the dark storm Collins was a limp shadow. A light had switched on behind her, on the side of the barn. I figured it had a sensor adjusted to flick on after dark. The horizon beyond the barn was a light shade of gray. The silhouettes of five men came around. They staggered to keep upright in the storm.

I was getting somewhere. The rope binding my hands was beginning to fray. That was the good news. The bad news was that I was not even halfway through.

By the time the first man entered the enclosure I realized that the stagger wasn't from the wind alone; they'd been drinking. The first guy to come in hurled his beer bottle at the pigs, who didn't seem to notice. He giggled stupidly. The others filed through the entrance. I kept on poking at the rope with the sharp bone. Three of the men went across to Collins and stood over her. It looked like they were speaking, taunting her, but I couldn't hear anything. Another guy stayed at the door to the enclosure while the fifth came over to me.

He was holding something long and straight. When he got up in my face I saw it was an axe handle. I kept on poking the rope behind my back. The man bent down to look into my face. I guess he thought I was unconscious. I was watching him through lidded eyes. I got another thread cut behind my back. The man rose, stepped away, and whipped the axe shaft in a horizontal blur to thwack me in the ribs.

There was no pain, just a dull numb pressure as the shaft made contact with my left side.

I kept my head down and gave him a theatrical moan. Which caused him to utter a satisfied grunt. He walked back to the entrance, boots sucking in the mud. The men gathered around Collins like a dark knot. I poked another thread loose. I heard the sound of a fist striking flesh and then Collins spit. The men had untied her from the post. I concentrated on the rope behind me, and the bone fragment I was trying to use. It was so slick with the mud and rain that I lost hold of it for a second. I took it up again, carefully, and got another thread cut.

When I looked up, they were leading Collins by her neck. She was hunched over and walking in an uncomfortable position. The man with the axe shaft came back to me. He lit a cigarette in the rain and I saw his face lit up under the brim of a baseball hat. He had a goatee and pockmarked skin. The eyes were pools of black in the gray storm. He shoved the lighter into a pocket and took a hold of his weapon. "We'll take real good care of your girlfriend now. You might even get to see her later on."

I said nothing.

The axe handle blurred. I got it flush in the side of my face and everything went back to black.

When I came to, the rain was even more lively. I lifted my head up from my chest. My face felt a little numb, and my side was bruised. Collins was gone and the pigs were calmer, belly down in the mud. I had no idea how long I'd been out. Too long. I'd lost my grip on the bone fragment and spent a useless minute or two scrambling for it with my fingers. Strong gusts of wind tore through the enclosure and the pigs snorted unhappily. Problem was, the rain had sunk the mud deeper than it had been before. The sharp bone had been helpful, but now it was gone, likely at the bottom of the hole that I'd dug.

I got calm and used my fingers to assess the existing damage to the rope.

There were frayed edges to work on. I started pulling on them, one by one. I got my mind focused on the task at hand and refused to think about what might be happening to Tela Collins. I knew it wasn't my fault that there was evil in the world, but I was okay with shouldering a small part of the responsibility. Whatever was happening up there at the farm was going to end, and there wasn't anything anyone could do to stop me from making sure of that.

In the end I resorted to brute force.

I had been careful, conserving energy for the moment when I could cut loose. Now I needed some of that energy to break the remaining rope threads. There was too much to unpick and nothing left to use as a cutting tool. I surged with energy and howled at the top of my lungs, an inhuman sound. Low and harsh, emptying my entire body of breath. The wind was loud enough that nobody but the pigs could hear me roar. I gave it everything I had. Screamed and roared like a muscle-bound maniac. I was forcing the issue and it was do or die.

At first it wasn't working. I knew that I didn't have an unlimited amount of attempts. I surged again, nothing. And then I felt it give. The rope snapped and the tension pitched me face first into the mud. I lay gasping and spitting for a brief moment, sucking in air. I curled up and worked on the ankle ropes. My fingers were bloodied and it was hard work getting the knots loose.

When I stood up and stretched, my joints crackled like machine-gun fire. I shook myself and howled into the dark sky. Triumphant. Even the pain in my side from that axe handle felt good. Pain can be a good thing, means your body is paying attention. There was nobody around except the pigs, and they didn't care. Then I got my breathing under control. I became calm and felt a smooth alertness flow through me, the way I guess an athlete might feel when they're about to groove.

The barn light shone against the glossy mud. I reached down and grabbed handfuls of the thick stuff. I methodically smeared my naked body with mud until I was covered from head to toe. I imagined how I would appear to the enemy, and that image carried with it a growing surge of well-being and happiness. I was definitely planning on making a strong impression.

CHAPTER THIRTY-NINE

I CAME AT THE BARN, bare feet sticking in the mud, rain sluicing off my chest and shoulders and running in rivulets down my arms and legs. The world was a soaking mire and stank of pigs and blood. Powerful gusts of wind whipped up out of nowhere and sent even more dirt and rain flying from all directions. I moved forward relentlessly.

I considered the enemy. Every one of them I'd seen so far had come around the barn, which meant that there was something the other side of it. Maybe a bunch of people, all in one place. Gathered together like a prize for me to take.

The back of the barn had windows shuttered with roughly nailed-on planks. I gripped a heavy wood piece with my torn fingers and ripped it off the building. The wind hurled part of it across the murk. I held on to whatever remained. It was dark inside the barn. I caved in the window with the broken plank. Nobody was going to hear that in the storm. The glass shattered, and stubborn shards snapped in from the base of the sill as I vaulted over, landing in an empty stall that smelled like hay and manure. Horses fussed farther down.

I kept moving, not too fast, not too slow.

The barn door was ajar at the front, letting in a fat triangle of electric light. Hanging on the wall next to the door was a handheld scythe. The type of thing a farmer would have used to cut the corn, maybe a century ago. I figured you could cut all kinds of things with it, corn being only one of them. The blade was rusty and dull but the point was sharp. Better than the plank of wood I was holding. Maybe I could spear the enemy with the scythe. The old-school oak handle was round and polished with use. If it had been good enough for generations of farmers, it was good enough for me.

I kept to the shadows and gazed through the barn door opening. On the other side of a courtyard was a low set of buildings. Gray geometrical shapes in the wet darkness. Directly across the way was a small stone structure. To the right, a larger building. Maybe a house. The yard in between was on a slight incline, and mud and rainwater were running down the sides from left to right. A single lamp shone from a sconce on the opposite wall. Beside the mud and water, nothing was moving.

I went into the shadows at the left side of the door. Looking to my right I saw three pickup trucks, empty with windows up and nobody in the cab. I looked hard into the night, searching for watchers. Nothing. The two dirt bikes were lined up against a stone wall.

Good.

My eyes had readjusted to the darkness in the barn. Inside the door I made out a series of narrow vertical silhouettes lined up against the whitewashed wall. I got closer and examined them. A shovel, a wicked-looking fork with widely tapered prongs, and a brush. Stable tools. I picked up the fork and held it in my hand. The shaft was aluminum and smooth, light, with fine prongs. It felt dangerous. I figured the stable fork might be better than the scythe. I pictured whipping the fork around, cutting and sticking with the steel points.

Nice.

I stepped back and moved laterally to the right side of the barn door, looking through it to the left. A single building was set apart from the others, its door wide open. The interior was lit up and hazy with cigarette smoke. I could make out figures milling around like rats in a box. The rain was coming hard on the barn roof, so I couldn't hear much. True for me, and equally true for them.

Bingo.

I crossed the yard like a ghost. The light had me for a couple of strides but there wasn't anybody to notice. I settled into the lee of a pickup truck. Felt the hood. Cool. I could hear some chatter from the outbuilding. The thought that they were all in there entertaining themselves with Collins passed through my mind like a malevolent shadow. There was no time to waste. I kept close to the wall and shuffled slowly forward. It was an ugly windowless building, built like a concrete bunker. Light spilled out of the door, making a wedge-shaped pattern on the mud.

Leaning up against the wall outside was a solid-looking axe handle. The shaft was darkly wet from the deluge. Odds were this was the same hard wood haft I'd taken in the ribs and head, which meant it had passed the test of a useful weapon. I leaned the stable fork against the wall and picked up the axe handle. Someone laughed from inside and flicked a cigarette butt out the door, its red glow arcing down into the mud like a rainbow.

The haft was straight-grained wood, hickory or ash. I liked the way it felt. The business end of it was heavy and weighted, while the part on the other side was carved for a good grip. It would work one handed, or with both hands. I gave it a short test swing. Excellent. I could definitely see myself using that, imminently.

I stepped in through the open door, naked, streaked with soaking wet mud and blood.

~

A KNOT of men lined both sides of the narrow entrance, sipping from plastic cups and beer bottles. The walls were bare concrete. The men were big strapping farm types, red faced and young, jolly with alcohol. I counted seven of them. The two dirt bike riders and the five men who had come for Collins. They were big boys, well-fed and muscled. Eyes flicked up at me when I entered, and then pupils dilated in panic.

I head-butted the first guy in the nose. The bony part of my forehead went right through his flesh and cartilage. I felt the bounce and didn't pay any attention to what happened to him next. Another man's panicked face appeared in front of me and I slammed the axe handle directly into it with a satisfying impact. Hard enough to know that I'd done serious damage. I changed grips and swung smoothly into the head of a third guy. He was turning away from me when I struck and got it behind the ear. The impact made a solid smacking sound. I followed up with another rapid blow, harder even. I got splatter in my left eye from whatever the hard wood had knocked loose in his skull.

Another guy was turned away, trying to get past his buddies. I grabbed him by the collar and pulled him back. I caught the white of one eye flash at me in terror. The guy was definitely condition black, full-on horror show. He lost his footing and wobbled. I swung down on him, hard and brutal. The axe handle caught him on the neck. The glint of steel appeared in my peripheral vision. I whipped the haft across onto the knife holder's wrist, nailing it perfectly. Bone snapped and the blade clattered to the floor. The thin end of the axe handle landed neat into the knife holder's horrified face, shattering teeth and splitting his mouth in a bloody gash.

I was in the flow, feeling like DJ LeMahieu on a good day with the Yankees.

Another man was trying to get away. I got low and swung across the back of his knees. He stumbled and I swung at his head, but the blow glanced off awkwardly. The second swing landed hard and I could feel the skull crush in. Home run.

Six down, one to go.

I looked back and saw movement from the first guy, whom I'd

head-butted. I adjusted my stance and came down on his head three times in quick succession until there was no more head left to speak of. I still had one man to account for, plus the big farmer somewhere. There was motion in my peripheral vision and I twisted around to see another guy I'd hit. He was struggling to pull a firearm out of his jeans.

The man's face was already a mass of bloody pulp, but he still managed to get a handgun up. I took one stride between the bodies writhing on the killing floor and nailed him in the side of the head with the axe handle. The guy tottered over, looking at me with the one good eye bulging strangely. I stomped him down and got my bloody hands on the weapon.

The gun was the Remington version of a 1911. A solid firearm in .45 caliber. The body was in blued steel with walnut-checkered grips. I appreciated the heft. Holding it felt like coming home after a long time away. I made sure there was one in the chamber and clicked the regular safety down. The hammer thumbed back and I was good to go. One of the men on the floor made the mistake of moaning and shifting. I put a round into the back of his head.

Now the place smelled correct. Blood, fear, and burnt sugar.

The room ended in a hallway. I put my head around and looked left. The figure of a man was rapidly moving away. I squeezed a round and his plaid shirt tore up and darkened between the shoulder blades. He fell over like he'd been hit in the back by a train. Seven men accounted for.

I looked to the right. Nothing but an open door, through which I could see a toilet bowl. It went dark in the hallway; someone had hit the lights. There was movement from down the hall where the guy in the plaid shirt had fallen on his face. I ducked back into the killing room and narrowly avoided being hit by a shotgun blast.

One extra guy, or the big farmer.

I waited a breath and then popped out from cover again, crouched real low. I put two rounds down the corridor and sprinted after them, hugging the wall on the right side.

The shooter had ducked into cover, but he hadn't expected me to come up on him so fast. I swung around the corner and pushed the Remington's muzzle into his chest, squeezing off a round point-blank. The man fell back looking surprised. The shotgun released from his hands. I fired a second round into his forehead and he was done.

Not the farmer, someone else. The fresh dead guy was older than the other boys and plump.

Six rounds gone. There aren't more than eight rounds in a regular 1911 magazine.

I felt a presence before I saw or heard anything. I twisted around with the weapon up. My eyes came around first and a shadow loomed in front of me. My gun arm came around. The big figure in front of me hammered a fist onto my arm. The Remington clattered to the floor. I surged into the attacker, knocking him over. I felt the contours of a face and attempted to get a thumb into his eye socket. The face was sweaty and my thumb slipped off to the side.

The guy was good enough to use that small slice of momentum and twist. His thick arm slipped around my neck and then tightened, firm and strong like a steel bar. It happened fast. Before I knew it, the other forearm was pressing into the back of my neck. I was being put into a sleeper hold.

The man was grunting in my ear, taking hard breaths that smelled like tobacco. I didn't fight the arm, I knew there was no time to waste. The only advantage I had was the fact that I was wet and slippery with blood, mud, and rainwater. So I wriggled and shook like a maniac until I was able to get up into a crouch and use my legs to slam him back into a wall.

The hold loosened a millimeter.

I looked down at his shoes. Mud boots. I hooked my hand behind the guy's knee, fighting for a good grip, one finger at a time. He tried to step back to keep the hold tight. I pushed against him and kept the contact. When I got a good hold I hauled him up. The man was heavy and big and struggled not to allow me the leverage. But the bigger they are, the harder they fall. I got a tenuous finger grip and hauled him up and raised him as high as I could. The attacker was wriggling hard. I dropped harder, using everything I had to come down. We hit the ground and I dug an elbow into his gut.

The wind came out of him, which was enough to get loose.

I twisted fast and slipped out of the hold so that I was over him and dominating. It was the murderous farmer with the slab for a face. He was staring at me, surprised that the tables had turned. I put a thumb directly into his eye and pushed in, gouging deep into the socket and hooking my thumb around the eyeball. The man didn't make a sound, which made him a veritable tough guy. I hit him hard in the throat with the edge of my hand and he coughed and choked. I looked up past him. There was a door to another space. A light was on in there. Through the narrow opening I could make out a naked leg with a foot, female. Collins. She was on the floor and immobile.

CHAPTER FORTY

I GOT off the farmer and got my hands on the shotgun. It was a Weatherby semi-auto tactical model, 12 gauge in matte black with a pistol grip. The farmer stayed down, working hard to get air back into his pipes. His wounded eye was red and closed, puffing up. The left side of his face had four fresh cuts on it, like he'd been hit with a rake. I opened the action and looked into the breech with the light from the other room. Good to go. I stepped over to the big man and put the barrel in his direction. He was eyeballing me and trying to say something.

"We didn't touch her."

I assumed he meant that he and his men had not been inappropriate with Collins. I wasn't impressed with that statement. Nobody ever got a medal for not violating another person. I slid the Remington handgun behind me with a bare foot and kept it there while I looked into the room.

It was some kind of a farm product processing room, lit by overhead fluorescents. Steel-topped work tables and containers were squared away at right angles. I figured it had something to do with milk.

My eye was drawn to the captive bolt gun up on one of the shelves. It looked clean. I pictured the farmer washing it after use. Collins was lying unmoving on the floor, her face turned away from the door, hair splayed out, naked as a newborn. She appeared cold and exposed under the fluorescents. I didn't like how vulnerable she looked in there. Angry and pissed off didn't begin to describe how I was feeling. *Murderous* was a word that came closer.

The Weatherby stayed on the man, like an unblinking and pitiless eye. He was tracking the muzzle and keeping quiet. I didn't like the way he looked, the man was dangerous and scoping for a way out of his predicament. I pulled out of the room and stood over the farmer. "Take your clothes off."

The guy hesitated, maybe running down options, maybe testing me. Whatever, even a quarter second hesitation was too long for me. I drove the steel capped stock into his face. The big man's cheekbone cracked in. The stock glanced off and crushed nose cartilage. Blood cut loose, painting the wall in a crimson arc. I pressed the muzzle hard under his chin.

"You carrying?"

He blew blood out of his nose and shook his head. I patted him down with my free hand. When I stepped back it only took him a half second to start unbuttoning his shirt. I noticed that his finger and good eye were steady.

At least his motivation had improved.

He said, "Underwear too?"

"No."

I picked up the Remington pistol and placed it on a surface just inside the door.

While the farmer worked on his shirt and pants and socks and boots, I started on the plump guy across the hall. I laid the shotgun on the ground and dragged the corpse by the feet. A part of me was hoping that the farmer would go for it. I had big doubts about allowing his continued survival under the circumstances, in light of what I had seen him do. I was struggling to resist imagining the things that I hadn't seen.

But I had questions.

I said, "What is this place?"

The big farmer was methodically removing his boots like a fussy child. His face was busted up, but he ignored that. The guy was mumbling something to himself. When he got the second boot off he removed and folded his socks.

He said, "What're you gonna do with me?"

"I don't know. Answer the question."

He looked up. "This is the farm. We take care of what needs taking care of. I don't know how else you want me to explain it, *bud*."

I said nothing.

He got his clothing off, slid the pile at me and sat back against the wall in a pair of clean white boxer shorts. He was a big guy, but there wasn't any kind of baby fat on his body. It was all hard bone and muscle, sinewy like something that even the homicidal pigs wouldn't want to get involved with.

By the time he was out of his clothes I had stripped the other body. I put the Weatherby's muzzle up, angled so that I'd blow the farmer's head down the corridor if he twitched the wrong way.

He said, "You want to know anything, I'll tell you. I don't give a shit."

"What is it you want to tell me?"

He looked at me coolly, the good eye a slit in the big slab of a face. The bad eye had turned into a reddened bulge. He blew his nose hard into the wall. "Whatever. You ask, I'll answer. No problem."

"I want to know about Bob."

"*The* Bob. Boss man out of Indianapolis. Runs the action around here. I don't work exclusive for him, but he's the man."

"He got a second name?"

The farmer shook his head. "Not that I know of."

"Where do I find The Bob?"

"He's up in the city. Meridian Hills, living like a rich guy. Got a big house up there I've never been to and wouldn't recognize if you showed it to me. Never been invited."

I said, "Run it down for me, how this all works. The Bob gets in touch with you, gives you a name, you go out and grab them?"

"Negative, partner. I don't do delivery or retrieval, just processing."

"The redhead and the other guy who brought us here. Who are they?"

"The Bob's people, not mine."

"But you know them."

"I've dealt with them before. More than once. Doesn't mean I know them. Doesn't mean I like them."

"So what, they just show up? Who's the point of contact?"

The farmer looked at me casual. Like it was easy to talk with a broken face. He said, "They don't just show up. They need to be booked in advance." A little curve formed on his thin and busted line of a mouth. "You really want to know the point of contact?"

I said nothing.

He nodded. "Local police come over when The Bob wants to make a reservation at the farm." The farmer had a triumphant glow in his eye, like he'd just made some kind of an interesting point. "New cop every time. Take that one and chew on it slow. Even if you kill me now you won't make it out of town alive."

"We'll see about that. Who scratched your face?"

He said, "Your girlfriend's a hoot, bud."

I indicated the direction of the farmer's pigpen. "Tell me about the last person you killed in there, before the guy just now." He said nothing, just looked at me. I moved the Weatherby's muzzle from his head to his knee. I said, "You know how this could go, don't you? One knee at a time, then the arms, one by one. After that I'll make sure you're alert and conscious and put a round into your guts with the pistol. That's one way it could go and I don't know how long you'd last. Could be a while. The other way you just tell it straight and I blow your head off down the hall here and we're all done."

The farmer laughed and started coughing. The line in his face curved slightly. "Goddammit you're some kind of real life superhero. The way you came through the boys all naked like that. Bet those boys shit their pants before you sent them to hell." He shook his head, coughing more. "They should put up warnings when special ops veterans of the GWOT come through town." He liked that idea and went off into another round of laughing and coughing, a true maniac. "Maybe they could make it like a legal compulsion of some kind, like a mandatory vaccination against psycho superheroes."

I said nothing.

He said nothing. Any humor that the farmer might have retained in the situation was bluff. His grim expression returned. I knew then that there was something more to find, something he didn't want me to see.

I got the Weatherby up at his head. "Close your eyes if you don't want to see it coming."

The farmer looked at me for a piece and then turned away so that I had a good shot of the side of his large head. The scratch marks on his face came into relief again. I didn't want to kill him just yet. I wanted to go scout the farm for a bit and come back if I had more questions.

I flipped the Weatherby and hammered the stock into his temple. He flopped loose and crumpled.

I pulled on the big man's clothes. They fit baggy, but I could work with that. He had a belt, which was helpful. There was a noise from inside the milk room. I looked in on Collins. She was pushing herself up off the floor. Her face had bruising on one side and her eyes lost focus when she looked at me. I brought in the pile of clothing I'd stripped from the corpse in the corridor and set it in front of her. "Put those on."

I lifted the Remington .45 from inside the milk room and checked it. There was one in the chamber and an empty magazine. I came back out to the hallway while Collins got dressed. The farmer was still unconscious.

Collins egressed from the room.

I said, "What did you have on you?"

"What do you mean?"

"When they took us. What were you carrying, besides the clothes?"

"Just the car keys. I locked my purse in the car."

"Nothing else you need to get back?"

Collins shook her head. Then she realized. Her face crumpled. "The bracelet. My niece's bracelet."

I handed her the Weatherby. "Someone comes beside me, you pull this hard into your shoulder and pull the trigger. Do the same if this guy tries to get up. And keep your distance from him."

"Where are you going?"

"Give me a minute. I'll get that bracelet back for you."

Collins was shocked. "It's not important, Keeler."

Which was true. But I wanted to look around. I had half an idea that Cartwright might be somewhere in the compound, or Donna Williams. But the bracelet was a good enough excuse. Little things matter.

I said, "If that's not important, nothing's important. What're you going to say on Thanksgiving, when she asks you where it went?"

Collins stared at me, astonished, but not confused. She nodded, unsmiling and grim. Same way that I was feeling. She squatted along the wall across from the unconscious farmer.

I said, "You okay?"

"I don't know if *okay* would be the word I'd choose, Keeler."

I got situated. Milk room was behind me. To the right and down the hall was the entrance, what I'd turned into a killing room. Straight across was darkness. I took the right and tracked back to the entrance room, where I'd done the most damage. The place was a mess of blood and bodies. I stepped over the corpses.

The farmer's boots were big on me, slipping in the gore.

CHAPTER FORTY-ONE

OUTSIDE IT WAS A MISERABLE DRIZZLE, quieter now that the hard rain had stopped. A horse whinnied in the barn, spooked. I moved left along the wall. Nobody was out there as far as I could see. I stopped and took a knee.

I mapped out the situation. Barn across the yard. To my left was the small stone building, then the house. There could be interesting things to find in each of those buildings. I'd already seen the barn. I moved to the small stone structure. The door opened easily. I flicked the light switch right inside and the place lit up with naked fluorescents. I was in a storage room. Shelves of boxed product were stacked in obsessively ordered columns. There were containers and vats and implements that I assumed to be farm related.

One side of the room was taken by a chipped white laminate worktable. I recognized the objects there. Two respirator masks and an aerosol canister were parked, fat and guilty on the white top. A couple of large cardboard boxes were pushed against the wall. They featured logos and company names that I didn't recognize. I came in closer for a look at the fine print. Some kind of a bovine sedative.

They'd managed to get that into aerosol form and had used it on us. Collins and I were lucky to be alive.

Which I took to mean that the redhead and his buddy were still around and the farmer had lied. He wasn't just running a slaughterhouse for The Bob. The farmer was involved in the procurement as well. The redhead and friend had been messing with Linda Cartwright from the very beginning.

There was nothing else of interest in the room. No wallet, no clothes. Only the rows of industrial shelving. I turned off the lights and put my hand on the door handle. I was just about to open the door, but the back of my mind was telling me that something wasn't right.

It wasn't anything I could hear, or not hear. It was something about the space in which I was standing. I turned the light back on and saw it immediately. The room was a confined space, but it didn't match up to what I'd seen from the outside. The shelving units were too close to the door. I went up to the shelf and looked through it to the wall behind.

There was no wall. Behind the shelving unit was some kind of heavy-duty PVC sheeting. I began to methodically inspect the shelves. These were strong steel units, bolted together. If there was something important on the other side of them, they would have made it accessible. I found the way through at the right side of the shelf. The center plank held dummy cardboard boxes and had a catch at the hinge. The steel shelves dropped down and I passed through a slit in the black PVC sheet. Behind the curtain, a single fluorescent light bar illuminated a machine taking up the central area.

The object was some kind of an industrial processing unit. There was a big steel chamber with a fat pipe going up into the ceiling. Thick wires connected the machine to the wall. I figured that was a power supply. There was a round door right in the front of it secured by a set of heavy-duty latches. The kind of thing you need to really think about before opening, like the hatch on a submarine.

There were two buttons next to the hatch, big and round in red and black. Next to the red button was a single word: *Incinerate*.

I touched the outside of the steel chamber. Cold steel and smooth. I pulled open the latches and saw darkness inside the chamber. I put a hand in and ran it through cool ash. I pushed through to the bottom of the chamber. A heavy steel plate that retained a modicum of residual heat from the last time it had been lit up.

My fingertip pushed a tiny object. I managed to get it between thumb and forefinger. Some kind of hard pebble. I pulled it out. A small ceramic cube with the corners rounded off lay in the center of my palm. I pushed the cube over with my thumb and blew the ash away. The letter L was sculpted into one side of the cube, the glaze had burned off. I knew immediately what it was: the bracelet that Collins had been wearing. They'd burned our clothing and belongings.

It took me a minute to collect the remaining three bracelet cubes. I let them tumble into the front pocket of the farmer's jeans. Collins would make it to the next family Thanksgiving celebration. I'd make damned sure of that. I flicked off the light and moved into the front room. The door was ajar. I looked out into the night. The yard was still empty and silent in the drizzle. Nothing moved, nothing spoke, except the horse snorting in the barn.

I took a step back inside. There was something else that bothered me.

I went back through to the incinerator room. At the left side of the room, butted against the steel shelving unit with the heavy PVC sheet in between, was another industrial shelving unit. I walked over. The shelves were mostly empty. A handheld vacuum cleaner and its charging unit took up one of them. The shelf at chest height had a shoebox. I opened the lid and looked down on three piles. On the left, a pile of cash neatly banded together. Next to that was a pile of gold and silver jewelry. Necklaces and bracelets and other miscellaneous items. On the far right side was a pile of fancy watches. I figured, jewelry for the ladies, watches for the men.

My eye picked out a familiar shape from the pile of jewelry. Even before I had it in hand, I knew what it was. A gold pendulum earring. I bent and took it between my thumb and forefinger. The earring was in the shape of a tear drop. The same earring I had seen hanging from Donna Williams's ear just a couple of days ago.

They had executed her. The thought made me angry in a resolute way. I pocketed the earrings and left everything else where it was.

When I came out of the building, I got low against the stone wall and observed. The drizzle was still coming down. I crouched with my back against the hard cold stone for two minutes, listening. I rose slowly and heard the squeak of a large chassis on an old suspension. That was followed by the sound of tires running slow in the mud.

I slipped behind the door and into the storage building again. The vehicle was some kind of a truck or a four-wheel drive. A car door snicked open quietly. I had one round in the Remington's chamber and that was it. I braced myself to come out hard and fast. The vehicle had entered the compound from the left, which meant the passenger side was facing me. I figured I'd go for a shot at the driver first and take out the passenger manually since he'd be closer. I waited silently for the sound of the second door opening.

The motor cut out and the driver's door clicked open. I put an eye to the crack in the door and saw the vehicle just in front of me. It was the red Pontiac GTO, which meant the redhead and his friend. I felt a swelling of adrenaline. I had been looking forward to my next encounter with those two. The area was flooded with light from a second vehicle maneuvering into the yard. The headlights flicked off and it cut the engine and coasted to a stop, tires rolling over the mud, brakes squeaking a touch.

Two vehicles, minimum three combatants, maybe more if the second vehicle had passengers in the back seat. I didn't have a good view of the new arrival. The situation was getting complicated. There was no other way out of the storage shed. That door was all I had.

Everything changed when a shotgun blast came from the outhouse. The boom from the Weatherby was loud, even though it was muffled by distance and walls. The shotgun was fired a second time. Collins was in trouble.

CHAPTER FORTY-TWO

The doors of the second vehicle opened and closed in short order. Two doors. Booted feet splashed mud past the shed door. I figured they were responding to the shotgun blast with some kind of urgency.

I waited for a five count and pulled the door open wide enough for me to slip out. The second parked vehicle was a Promise, Indiana, police cruiser. The interior was dark. The light drizzle hung in the air, pushed around by a wild wind. I figured the police hadn't come up to the farm to help us out, that was for damned sure.

Four armed reinforcements headed into battle. One round left in the Remington. It was like a puzzle. Things were definitely getting interesting.

Another Weatherby twelve gauge blast came from the outhouse, this time less muffled than before. Which meant that Collins had come closer to the entrance. She was under pressure but moving forward. All good signs. The problem was that I'd counted three shells out of the Weatherby. Maximum capacity was going to be five plus one in the breech. Collins had no more than three bites of the apple left.

I shouldn't have left her alone with that big farmer. I took a risk.

You always need to take risks, sometimes they work out, sometimes they don't.

I kept close to the wall and snuck up on the outhouse. The stable fork was leaning against the wall where I'd left it. The prongs were just as tapered and thin and wicked looking as they'd been before. I got the fork in my right hand and held the Remington in my left. I balanced the two weapons; they felt good. I put my back to the wall just outside the door and listened. The men were arguing in whispers.

I peered around the doorway.

Three men standing, huddled near the corridor entrance. Two of them in police uniforms, one of them with red hair in a ponytail. Bodies littered the floor, now thick with congealed blood and muddy boot tracks. I assessed the situation. They'd come in like gangbusters and Collins had blown away the first unlucky man who'd entered the hallway. Good for her. She'd be hunkered down waiting for the next guy. Maybe waiting on me to come help out.

Whether or not she'd taken out the big farmer was an open question.

I came around the corner and into the outhouse, stepping carefully. The men had their backs to me, oriented to the hallway and their friend.

He was floundering on the floor like a landed fish, not quite dead yet.

The two cops were closer to me than the redhead, who was squatting. Looked like he was going to try dragging his friend out of the hallway. I shot the first cop in the back of his head. The impact blew a hole out of his face onto the back of the second cop's head. The second cop turned, like an instinctive and involuntary reaction. I saw the look of shock and horror on his face and stabbed the fork one-handed into his neck. Two prongs went in at the level of his windpipe, like fine needles penetrating a soft cushion. He had been holding a weapon, which dropped. I held him up with the fork and kicked him hard. My boot unthreaded his neck from the impaling pitchfork and slammed him into the redhead behind him.

The cop's weight unbalanced the redhead. He staggered out of cover and right into Collins's line of fire in the hallway. The redhead managed one terrified look at me, his eyes rolling back in their sockets. The Weatherby kicked loose. The spread was tight and on target. The redhead's chest exploded and he was thrown a yard back.

I waited a second and spoke in a measured tone. "Collins, it's clear. Come through."

Her voice came from the dark. "Keeler?"

"Roger that. Move."

Collins came fast. Hustling around the corner. The clothes hung loose off her and she looked like a warrior. She carried the Weatherby up and ready. Her eyes went wide when she saw the room. It was like an abattoir at that point. Piles of corpses and blood, all beginning to smell bad. Her shoulders were up high just below the ears, tense and alert.

I put a hand on her shoulder and looked her in the eyes. She breathed out deeply. Her shoulders sunk back into place. I couldn't help reflecting that Collins would have passed the drown-proofing test as a combat diver. Everybody freaks out. Not everyone recovers in time. It's an experience.

The second policeman was alive. The fork had left red dots on his bare neck. He had dropped his weapon and looked bad, like he'd be having a real hard time speaking. Collins looked down at him, writhing on the floor. Both cops had been carrying Glock 17s. I stepped to the wounded man and picked up his weapon. I turned to face Collins. "You know that this guy cannot be a survivor. He can't be allowed to recognize you."

She nodded. "He wasn't here to help." I shook my head. Collins said, "If he came here to harm us, then he's a traitor to the law and the oath he swore to. Without the law there's nothing left, Keeler." She didn't avert her eyes. "Do it."

I put a round into his face from a yard away with his own weapon. The policeman's ethical problems were over.

I said, "Something is definitely not copacetic in the town of Promise, Indiana."

"Not after this, that's for sure."

"Not before either. Remember that: we didn't start anything."

She was looking at me, a strange glint in her eyes. "So, what if we hadn't stumbled into it?"

"Simple, it'd be over and these people would have won."

"Right, and now?"

I dropped the Remington on the floor next to the dead policeman. I examined the two Glocks. Both of the police-issue service weapons had full loads, minus the round I'd just fired.

I looked up at her. "What about now? Isn't it obvious? Now they're going to lose." I took the Weatherby from her hands and gave her one of the Glocks. "You just pull the trigger on that thing."

"I know."

She was looking at me strangely, like she'd discovered a new aspect to something.

"Good."

I placed the shotgun on the ground and squatted by the redhead's corpse. I went hunting through his pockets. No car keys. Maybe he'd left them inside the GTO. It was time to get the hell out of there. I looked up at Collins, who was looking back at me. Her face was pale and bruised, her eyes wounded.

"From now on we move together," I said. "You stay right behind me. Keep touch, so I know where you are if the shit hits the fan. I'm not leaving you alone again."

She nodded. "Okay."

"I need to know what happened back there with the big guy." I jerked my thumb toward the back, where the farmer had been under Collins's guard.

She inhaled deeply, then expelled the breath and told me.

Collins had kept the gun on the big man, guarding her distance.

What she hadn't considered was the guy's speed. The big farmer had waited for her concentration to drop off and then he'd made his move. Collins hadn't dropped her guard much, just enough for the guy to leap up and punch away the Weatherby. She'd fumbled and gotten the gun up again. By then, he was gone. Listening to her speak, I was just happy he hadn't taken the shotgun out of her hands.

I said, "Gone where?"

"He went straight up into the dark. I didn't see."

I flipped the light switch. The hallway fluorescents blinked on, exposing the rampage in bright and gory detail. I didn't stick around to examine the carnage. Collins and I moved as a unit. At the end of the hallway there was nothing but bodies and blood. To the left was the milk room. The farmer was gone. To the right was a short section of corridor that led to another room. That was the direction through which the big farmer had disappeared. I didn't figure he'd still be in there.

The room was large and well lit. It contained a cluster of connected steel vats and pumps and pipes set on sturdy legs. Like a machine for processing something. A central work table was stacked with blue milk crates and empty round plastic containers.

Collins said, "They make yogurt here."

"Isn't that cute."

None of which resolved the mystery of where the farmer had gone; there were no windows to escape through.

I said, "You sure he came this way?"

"I think so."

I shrugged. We weren't going to spend a whole lot of time looking for him. It was time to get out.

Out in the yard it was still dark, but dawn was coming. There were no residual stars to see, no moon either, only a brooding low cloud cover with dense dark patches, all moving fast and transforming. The horizon was strangely blue and the wind was whipping up hard. The air was humid and hot.

The red Pontiac GTO was open. The keys were pinned behind the sun visor on the driver's side. Collins got in on the passenger side. The interior smelled like pine.

"You recognize that smell, Keeler?"

"No."

"I think they brought us here in this car. I remember the stink."

She pulled at the air freshener hanging from the rearview mirror. It was shaped like a Christmas tree and gave off a chemical stench that approximated the scent of pine needles. The logo of a carwash establishment adorned both sides of the cardboard tree. Collins read it under her breath. "Gresham's Drive-Through Hand Wash." She flicked the tree so it spun. "I hate that fake pine smell."

I said nothing, but I was thinking that fake pine was better than cherry or bubble gum—or whatever we smelled like. My thoughts turned to the silver van back at J&S Services. There had been a pine tree air freshener hanging from its useless rearview mirror as well. I hadn't bothered to look at it with any care.

I had my hand around the ignition key and had just started to exert pressure when I saw a movement in the side mirror. The silhouette of a black SUV was approaching. Lights off, running dark. It was maybe fifty yards away and moving in slow and steady. I eased up on the ignition and found the interior light switch between the sun visors. I thumbed the switch so that the light would not be triggered by opening a door. The passenger side was closest to the buildings. I leaned across Collins and popped the door latch.

She had already understood the situation so I didn't need to waste any energy or time making the obvious stale.

She slipped out and I followed. We got very low and moved with speed, purpose, and stealth. Behind us came the soft creep and crunch of more vehicles, all running dark. We slipped through the gap between stone buildings, screened by parked pickup trucks. A couple seconds later we had our backs to the building, listening. Car doors opened and closed discreetly.

I was thinking about the big farmer. Looked like he'd found a phone and had called for reinforcements. The big man was at the top of my list. He needed to be sent to hell.

CHAPTER FORTY-THREE

THE FARM BUILDINGS were on a gentle rise overlooking a line of trees. Beyond that, it was all fields. We tracked close to the buildings along the rise, arriving at a space between the last structure and the dairy production facility. I stopped at the corner. Collins's hand was a light touch at my belt, keeping the contact.

I looked to my left, down the gap separating the outhouse from the last farm building. A man was silhouetted at the corner. He was armed with an AR-15-style assault rifle and had a squared off beard jutting from a chin that moved slowly up and down, chewing and then squirting a thin stream of tobacco juice into the mud. I recognized his shape as the same guy I'd seen when the garbage truck had mowed down the Homeland Security agents.

On the other side of the yard, another sentry stood in the shadow of a big tree. He was sectioning off the area with his eyes, head moving slowly, left and then right and then swinging back again. This was the other guy I had seen that night. Beyond him were fields.

There were more guys like that egressing from the vehicles, spreading out and taking positions.

I considered the situation.

These were no longer rank amateurs bumbling into action and getting picked off from the front and from the rear. By considering those two silhouettes and the new atmosphere of competence, I could discern a disciplined force moving together, in harmony. The remaining men were carefully positioning themselves, getting the battle space organized before considering offensive action.

The SUV had looked familiar, the shape of the grill was identical to the vehicle that had come up on Collins and me after the two Homeland Security agents had been crushed to death. Which reminded me of the Lincoln, and the pile of shredded metal that it had become.

Collins was gazing intently at something past me. I raised my eyebrows. She jutted a chin at the other side of the dairy building, leaned in, and whispered, "Vents from a storm shelter. Maybe where that big guy went."

I saw what she was referring to. Behind the dairy facility were two ventilation pipes sticking up out of the ground. Tufts of long grass clustered around them, neglected by the weed whacker. I had seen those as well but hadn't clocked them as being anything remarkable. I figured she looked at things differently than your average person, being a professional landscape architect.

I wasn't too familiar with storm shelters. They didn't seem like a very good place to hide. More like a great place to be caught and trapped, with no way out. I looked at the landscape on that side of the farm. There were routes the big guy might have used to egress. He would have known the terrain.

I touched Collins's wrist and signaled to the trees below. We moved down the rise and to the other side of the tree line. The field was edged with an irrigation ditch, thick with mud and rain water. I got in first; Collins followed.

We slithered on elbows and knees, keeping our heads low. I did the army crawl, Collins did whatever she could. Moving silently was slow going and very hard work. By the time we got to the other side of the field, she was exhausted. I let her catch her breath for five minutes. Nobody was coming after us. I figured it was morning, but you wouldn't know it to look at it. The rain was coming down again and the clouds were moving fast and furious. Dark shadows swirled and unfurled within lighter shades of gray. It was a hellish landscape and both Collins and I looked the part.

She kicked back against the ditch and gulped air slowly. I could sense her deep fatigue. Collins was running out of physical resources and it was time to get her safe.

We worked our way around the field and into a section of deep woods behind it. Carrying the Glock was a hindrance. I took the gun from Collins. I made both of the Glocks safe and put one in each of the farmer's pants pockets. After that we hiked wordlessly through the forest. The pistols slapping against my thighs through heavy and wet textile. The wind was kicking up, ripping the leaves off the trees and sending them flying around. Eventually we came to a highway and found an access road with a sidewalk.

I kept us back in the woods for a while, observing the road.

"Let's just get out of here," Collins said.

I said nothing and kept my eyes rotating between left and right. She settled down. Five minutes later a big Chevy SUV rolled past on the access road. The Chevy was white with Promise Police Department logos. We were in cover, but I could see the cops up front. Wrap around black shades in the storm, scanning both sides of the road. The female police officer drove and chewed gum rhythmically.

Once they'd passed I waited a ten count and stood up. Collins followed and we resumed the march. Ten minutes later we came to a big Exxon sign between the access road and the highway. I asked Collins if she knew where we were.

"Out on route I-70, Pretty far east, I'd guess"

"Out of Promise's jurisdiction."

"Far out."

We looked like hell, but Collins managed to get us a ride with a friendly truck driver. The driver didn't mind us being wet and dirty; she just put a couple of pieces of cardboard down on the big seat and didn't stop talking until we got back to town. Collins fell asleep five minutes into the ride. I just sat there staring into space and listening to the driver babble, until I clocked that she was babbling about the storm that was coming.

I looked at her, a large woman with short hair wearing feather earrings. "Storm coming, you mean it's not here yet?"

"Oh, hell no, this isn't the storm, man. This is the little shit before the storm. You are in Tornado Alley, mister, and we're smack in the middle of tornado season. I were you, I'd get somewhere with easy access to an underground shelter, and I'd choose one with a decent refrigerator and air-con unit. That, or keep riding with me. I'm headed northwest out of here."

I said, "How long until the tornado hits?"

She glanced at me across Collins's sleeping form. "Nobody can say with any exactitude where or when a tornado is going to land, though they try to make predictions about it."

"And they're predicting it will land here soon."

"You betcha. The conditions get a certain way, the tornado forms." She looked at me and grinned. "Boom-chaka!"

The truck driver dropped us off at the closest exit ramp to Collins's place. Collins threaded her arm through mine and we trudged another twenty minutes through the driving rain. Her house was a small two-bedroom on a quiet street. The wind was blowing so hard that she had a tough time pulling the door open.

Once we got inside it wasn't hard to figure out what to do next.

I said, "Shower."

Collins said, "Later."

She pushed into me and buried her head in my chest. Her hands pulled at my clothes and then I got into the game. We didn't bother with buttons and proper undressing. She tore the shirt right off my back and then I did the same to hers. She giggled insanely and kissed me hard. Her body was muscled and soft, all at the same time. Warm and smooth and perfect, locked together with mine. I clutched her long curly hair in my fingers, while she raked nails across my back.

Collins led the choreography. We ended up entangled for a while on a deep pile rug in some part of her house. Things got complicated and wonderful. Deep, mellow, and hair-raising, if that's all possible to have together. At some point after that we were in the shower, where everything was at least as good, if not better. Hot and soapy and filled with steam. Later we lay on her bed. The sheets were dry and clean and smelled like lavender. I had my eyes closed and felt her fingers idly caressing me. She lingered on the scars and kissed my chest. I turned lazily and got behind her. I felt her settle into a spoon formation, but not exactly passively. She began to idly push back at me, which made me do other things, just as a matter of instinct. From there things got even more interesting.

At some point there wasn't anything more we could do. We were truly spent. Just before we fell into a deep slumber, she was spooned in my arms. She said, "That was insane."

I wasn't sure if she was talking about what we'd done just then, or what had happened at the farm. I figured the farm. I moved closer to her. Her body was warm and silky smooth. I pushed my face into her hair, right by her ear and whispered softly. "You've pulled back my curtain. It's dark in there."

She stirred and turned her head so that my nose touched the warm soft skin behind her ear. "You pull that curtain back a lot, Keeler?"

"It happens."

There wasn't anything more to say, or any energy remaining to say it.

CHAPTER FORTY-FOUR

SOMETIME LATER I WOKE, clearheaded and feeling good.

A single image was held front and center in my mind. A cluster of keys, lying in the palm of a hand. Piled up and clumped together in disorder. It wasn't a dream exactly, more like some kind of half-awake fantasy. I sorted through the keys. Six sets, each with a tag attached and an address noted in ballpoint ink.

Each address was a story. Probably not an uplifting story. Maybe a tragic story.

I wondered why there had been six sets in the dream, not seven. I realized that the seventh had been Donna Williams's apartment, and now she was definitively out of the game. Worse than dead. Killed and fed to the pigs.

I opened my eyes.

Collins was right in front of me. We were face to face, covered with a single sheet. She was asleep, her lips perfectly pursed. I could feel her breath on my face, sweet and cool and fresh. Her lids flipped up and her eyes looked into mine. I felt an electric charge pass through me, from the eyes to the brain and then out through the limbs, making them feel even better than they had before, if that was at all possible. Her irises were green, the color of glacial lakes I'd seen up in the Canadian Rockies. She shifted closer to me and closed her eyes. She pushed her nose into my neck, at first warm and then warmer. She began doing things with her hands and her body, slowly.

Which took my mind off the keys.

I must have gone back to sleep after that. The next time I woke I was alone. The smell of bacon and coffee was thick in the air. And like an obedient animal, I wanted to make my way to it.

First, I stretched out my limbs like a cat. All limbs working and feeling good, muscles loose and tendons relaxed, ready to coil and spring or just wait for the occasion.

I had no clothes, so I wrapped the blanket around myself.

Collins was wearing gym shorts and a tank top. Her hair was piled on her head and she looked about as good as it was possible to imagine. A small kitchen radio was playing old country music. She was multitasking breakfast at the stove top. She registered my awakened condition. "This will be ready in a minute, but you might want to go look out the living room window first."

I walked out of the kitchen to the living room and looked out the window.

The sky was clear, with white clouds spotting the blue. The street was a scene of destruction. Large pieces of aluminum siding and a car bumper were strewn in the front yard, alongside assorted junk like torn home insulation material and a plastic lawn gnome. The mailbox was a splintered stump, the box part of it gone. On the road were the remains of a bicycle and the scattered pieces of somebody's shed. Farther along I saw a sofa settled on the curb, foam stuffing poking out of large tears in the fabric.

The pants I'd taken from the big farmer were in a tangle under the coffee table. I crouched down and removed Donna Williams's earrings from the front pocket. The remnants of Collins's bracelet joined them in my palm.

When I came back into the kitchen there was food on the table, a lot of it. I spilled the contents of my hand onto free space. Collins came over and looked down at the two sets of objects. She recognized the bracelet cubes.

"You found them?"

"Found that."

Collins picked up one of the earrings. "What's this?"

"Those were Donna Williams's earrings. Found them in the same place I found the leftovers of your bracelet. They used an incinerator for non-valuables." I nudged one of the ceramic cubes. "Those don't burn." I didn't mention the other things that I had found, the jewelry and cash that those murderers had looted from their victims.

Collins fingered the teardrop shape of the earring. She spoke very quietly in a small voice. "So that woman was killed." She looked up at me, her eyes brimming with tears. "She was killed before we got there, in that same place."

I nodded. For a while we didn't say anything. But hunger is a place, and I was definitely there. I waited a decent amount of time before speaking, like eleven seconds.

"I guess the tornado hit." I pointed vaguely in the direction of the living room window.

Collins grunted. "Not exactly." She pointed at the radio. "They just said the storm's coming back and a tornado watch is still on." She glanced at me. "Apparently that wasn't the tornado. The storm is building up again. It just drifted out of town for a while. See the blue sky?"

Out the window there was a backyard and then the backyards of other neighbors. The sky was clear and the air felt less humid than before.

I said, "Looks nice out."

"Looks can be deceiving. The radio said it isn't nice out, just temporarily calm, right here and right now. The storm front is out there sucking in moisture and building up power." She perched against the counter facing me and illustrated with her hands. "You know the funnel thing on a tornado." I nodded. "It's filled with moisture, condensation. Everyone thinks that's what a tornado is, but it isn't. That thing's not the tornado, it's what you see *before* the tornado hits."

Which was some kind of a meteorological concept that went over my head. I nodded along.

She continued, gesturing at the sky. "Right here we've got the dry and cool air, because the storm's sucking in the mean stuff. They just talked about it on the radio."

Collins poured coffee into two cups. We got busy. We were done talking and got involved in breakfast, with zero hesitation or formality. Delicious things were consumed and more of them appeared, then were consumed. When we had slowed down sufficiently, I stood up and cleared some of the empty dishes off the table and took them to the sink. I hunted around in her cabinets. She had fancy taste, which I'd been counting on. Olive oil can be a good household product for gun cleaning. Collins watched me making myself at home. She even gave me a couple of spare cleaning rags.

I brought the two Glocks into the kitchen and got busy taking them apart and cleaning off the mud and junk with small pieces of clean cloth dipped in olive oil. While I did that, she made more coffee.

She said, "So?"

I used a bent fork tine to get the rag into a difficult crevice. "So we're going to visit some properties in the area. Keys are in my car, if it's still where we left it." She was nodding absently, accepting the program. "Maybe we'll learn something."

"Okay."

The big farmer had said something about The Bob being from Indianapolis. I kept that in the back of my head, but not as anything to actually believe, more of an example of what not to believe. I snapped one of Glocks back together again and set it aside. Collins was following my movements with curiosity. "You've definitely done that before." I grunted in the affirmative, picked up a triangle of toast and spread butter on it. I bit off the end. "That big farmer guy asked me about Cartwright. He called her *the bitch married to the guy that owes*."

Collins shifted position, a tell which meant that she had a contrary argument. "Well, how do you know he wasn't referring to the other one, Donna Williams?"

"Because Williams was already dead. Cartwright is missing, I had presumed that she was in deep shit, which she probably still is. But I'm now thinking that she's undead."

Collins choked on her coffee. "You mean alive."

"I mean undead." Collins was looking at me, argumentation on her lips, all ready to go. "The military isn't any kind of a sentimental place. We have an expression. If you're fucked, you need to get unfucked. It's like your responsibility to unfuck yourself. Nobody's going to do it for you."

"All right, I get it. Cartwright is undead. But not yet unfucked."

"Correct. I see Cartwright as the survivor type. She could have been dead, like Donna Williams, but she made herself undead."

Collins buttered a remaining piece of toast and spread grape jelly on it. She held it delicately and pointed the end at me. "Donna Williams ate her gun. You're saying that Cartwright wouldn't do that, in your estimation. Only the truly fucked would eat their own gun. Cartwright would have the wherewithal to unfuck herself before it got to that." Collins leaned back and looked proud of herself.

I chewed the remainder of my toast and followed it down with the black coffee. "Right. I was surprised that the guy asked me about Linda Cartwright, because I assumed that they had taken her. But maybe they didn't. It's possible that what I saw in her house was a struggle that she escaped from."

Collins lifted a coffee cup. "Here's to Linda Cartwright. More power to her." We clinked.

The guns were clean and buffed. The polymer frames matte and angular. They looked pretty good in the middle of the kitchen table. Like a still life. Breakfast with guns. The blue sky was beginning to draw in puffs of thin white cloud. Collins was staring out the window. She shook her head.

"What is it?" I asked.

"I'm thinking about the daughter. Emma Williams, fifteen years old." She looked at me, and I saw her eyes had reddened again.

I drummed fingers onto the table. "Mother out of the game, father gone to ground. Emma's got to be somewhere, which means we'll find her."

"You promise we'll find her, Keeler?"

I locked eyes with her. "Not the slightest doubt. No let up until we get her safe."

Collins's eyes were shining now. "Let's do it."

There was green flame in her eyes as they bore into me, the burning core of righteous anger that we shared. I would have kissed her right there and then, but there was a cup of coffee to finish first.

CHAPTER FORTY-FIVE

The initial problem was trivial: I had no clothes.

I could walk around in what I'd stripped from the farmer, minus the shirt Collins had torn off with her fingernails. The farmer's textiles had been saturated in mud, which had dried while we slept. That wasn't an issue, as long as I could break them in a little. Good thing about dried mud is that it crumbles off easily. That could work for me, but Collins wasn't on board. For one thing, she knew the bus driver.

When we boarded the bus, I was wearing an oversize Cardinals t-shirt and a pair of sweatpants over the farmer's mud boots. Collins and the driver weren't on speaking terms, more like nodding terms. She climbed the steps before me. I watched the driver deliver a deep affirmative nod to her that did nothing to unsettle the opaque aviator shades clamped firmly to the bridge of his nose. She delivered a strong nod in return and emptied a handful of loose change into the tray. The driver let the change sort itself out with a made for purpose gizmo. I came behind, a Glock in each pocket and the bulges covered by the oversize t-shirt.

I made eye contact but didn't nod. The driver looked away.

The bus dropped us off at the corner of the main road and the entrance to Berrymore Court. We trudged up the slight incline to Donna Williams's address. When we crested the rise, the red Honda and Crown Victoria came into view. Both vehicles were intact and accounted for.

Like choreographed swimmers, we directed our gaze across the street to Donna Williams's apartment. The door was shut and it almost looked normal. Collins spoke softly. "They covered the kitchen window."

A plywood sheet had been nailed over the opening. It did not look out of place in a town getting ready to receive a tornado. Many street-front businesses and domestic go-getters had nailed up plywood protection. The plants on Williams's chalet landing had taken a beating in the storm. I guess Donna Williams would have taken them inside, if she'd been alive.

The Crown Vic was unlocked, the keys under the seat where I'd left them. Collins had a spare set for the Honda. She opened the passenger side, retrieved her purse, then locked the small red car and came back to the join me. I had the backpack open in the trunk. Six sets of keys were cradled in my hand.

We started going through addresses on the key tags.

Collins dug out the phone from her purse. She knew some of the addresses; others she had to look up. The locations were spread out in and around the town of Promise and the county more generally. "That one's close to my aunt's house." Collins tapped a finger on a set of keys with a blue tag. "You can follow me and I'll park in her driveway."

"To your aunt's house?"

She nodded. "Yes. I'll drop off the Honda and we'll travel in yours."

We made a small convoy over to Springhurst. Collins driving her little red Honda in front, me following in the Crown Victoria. I twisted the knob on the radio. Jazz guitar music came through a surprisingly decent set of speakers.

I was reminded of the unfinished business with the guitar case. Gus Simmons and his fancy house. The thought brought an internal chuckle up from some place where I had a funny bone. I was looking forward to seeing Simmons's expression when I turned the screws on him. I figured everything had its time and its place. I certainly wasn't going to be deterred by his maid and the best security system money could buy.

Collins parked in the driveway of her aunt Ginny's. She shot me a look and then went into the house. I let the Crown Vic idle, listening to the music with the window open. Hot air from the storm front blew in a chaotic pattern, left to right and up and down, in all kinds of combinations. With the storm winds came the smell of humid soil and fresh corn.

Across the street, the laundry hanging in Linda Cartwright's yard hadn't faired too well. She'd used clothes pegs, but I guess they hadn't been designed to withstand a big storm. Pillow cases and sheets were strewn about, caught up and tangled around immovable objects like fence posts, tree branches, and subterranean ventilation units.

Which made me pause and reflect. There were two kinds of steel ventilation units. One with a rotating turbine, another that was straight. I'd seen those vents before but had assumed they were part of the basement. Now, I realized that the Cartwrights had a storm shelter. The rectangle of cement was the size of a modest room.

Collins came to the driver's side. "Slide over, I'm driving."

I slid into the passenger seat and She got in. I figured I was better suited to be a double-fisted gunman, while she'd already proved herself at the wheel. I looked at her adjusting the steering wheel and the rearview mirror. Love and combat, two of my favorite things, combined neatly into a package named Tela Collins.

I pointed across the street at the Cartwright house. "They have a storm shelter."

She looked at the yard, examined the ground level protrusions.

"Yup, looks like they do." She chuckled softly. "Unsurprising when there are tornados almost every other year."

Collins moved the shifter into drive. I put my hand over hers. "Wait."

She shifted back into park and looked at me. We had been thinking the same thing. "The storm shelter?"

I didn't need to say anything, Collins killed the engine.

I USED the key under the flowerpot. The house was empty, nothing happening. It didn't smell of freshly brewed coffee, or homemade lasagna, or anything besides cleaning product. The women of Lopez Cleaning Service had done an outstanding job. Every surface gleamed and the plant had been repotted. Cartwright's hammer was drying in the dish rack perfectly clean, the steel business end gleaming.

I came down the basement stairs as quiet as possible. Collins was right behind me. I had the Glock in my right hand and did not put on the lights. I remembered my first trip down to the basement. There hadn't been any door leading to a storm shelter, not that I recalled. I checked again. No door visible, no obvious place for a hidden door. But there was a door leading to the garage, the only place in the house that I hadn't thoroughly searched.

I stood in the basement doorway. The automatic folding garage door was on my left, closed with light streaming in through four square windows. The garage contained no vehicles, but it did smell like motor oil and cardboard. The cement floor was stained. A storage shelving unit was straight ahead of me. I stepped in and sideways. The shelves contained automobile products. A lawn mower was fitted into the bottom shelf along with a gas can and a pile of rags.

On the other side of the shelving unit was a narrow door.

I looked back at Collins and nodded. She raised her eyebrows. I stepped up and twisted the door knob. It wasn't locked. The door came open and I was looking into a narrow corridor with a low ceiling, almost like a tunnel. Light from the garage door windows came through and I saw yet another door about fifteen feet in and made of steel.

The door handle had a lock set in it. It looked like a tough door to break down swiftly, without the help of an explosive device, or the mother of all battering rams. Which meant that surprise wasn't going to be readily achieved. Usually I'd make a little calculation in my head before going through a door. I'd consider the probabilities of getting shot in the head by an amateur on the other side. Those were usually low probabilities. Coming in hot and heavy on a bunch of poorly trained and undisciplined Taliban was always going to give you a decent chance.

But if you take out the surprise factor, you give a lot of opportunity to the other side.

I knocked three times and waited. Nothing moved, no sounds came from the other side of the door. I looked back at Collins. She was wedged in there with me. I shook my head, as in no way it's empty. She gave me a confirmatory nod, as in you're right, no way. I knocked again and called out speculatively. "I'm here to help. Open the door."

No response. I called again, trying to be very precise and clear in my language. "I'm a friend of Linda Cartwright's. I am here to help. Open the door."

Collins said, "Kick it down."

I counted down from ten. I wasn't going to kick it down. I was planning a little raid on the toolbox back in the basement. When I got to four I heard movement on the other side. A shuffling sound that turned into someone doing something with the other side of the door. Latches popped and a jangle of keys twisted in locks. I watched as the bronze knob turned. The latch popped from the doorjamb and the door finally opened.

Young Emma Williams stood in front of me. She was holding an old Colt Python in .357 that was larger than her two hands put together, and she looked pretty much like her photograph. One problem was that her large revolver was aimed at my chest. The other problem was that the girl was shaking like a leaf, which made me somewhat concerned that she'd shoot me, despite the eight pound trigger pull.

CHAPTER FORTY-SIX

I SLID the Glock into the waistband behind my back and held up my hands.

"I'm not a threat; I'm a friend." I was about one and a half seconds away from disarming her.

Collins brushed past my shoulder, her hands were up and reaching. "Put the gun down, honey. We're just worried about you."

She didn't wait for the girl's reaction. She just folded her fingers over the Colt and brought it down. Emma Williams didn't fight; she was terrified. I was already looking behind the fifteen-year-old and examining the storm shelter. What I saw was a tight living space with a sofa, coffee table, and several chairs. Behind that was a door. A man was propped on the sofa pillows. He was staring at us through a big blue ice pack held on his face.

A tear rolled down Emma Williams's cheek and she stepped back to make room. I went past her and looked at the guy on the sofa.

Both of the man's eyes were inflated to the point that his face was insectile. His inflamed skin was smooth and purple. I understood why he had the ice pack going. He was trying to keep the inflammation down. It wasn't only the eyes; there was also something wrong with the lower part of his face. I came closer. The one recognizable feature was the thin mustache that, in the photographs, had made Fayaz look like a fun and dashing guy. At the moment he looked like a guy who had received a significant beating at the hands of an experienced torturer. He turned his head a little to face me, which meant that he was capable of seeing. But it didn't look like he was capable of speaking.

I stepped in and took a seat on the oak coffee table. The guy looked frightened. "Hold still, I'm going to examine you." I took his face in my hands and probed with my fingers. He grunted and groaned when I touched sensitive spots, which were all over him and in particular around the jawline. I hardly used any pressure with my fingers, but it wasn't too hard to understand what had happened. Collins and Emma were looking on, Fayaz was avoiding eye contact and allowing the examination to happen.

I sat back. "You've got a broken jaw. Otherwise you'll live. You need to go to a hospital eventually and get your mouth wired shut." Williams nodded and looked like he was about to speak. I held up my hand. "Don't speak. Just keep everything as still as you can and hope for the best until you can get treatment."

I turned to Emma. "Who did this to him?"

Emma backed off a little, smiling nervously. "Who are you guys?"

I said, "We're here to help. Take it from the top, Emma, and tell us what's happened."

"How do you know my name?"

I rolled my eyes. "It's a long story, and I don't have the time to tell it. Did the lady who lives here do this to your dad, or was it the other people?"

Emma Williams was looking from me to Collins and back. She had suspicions, mixed with hope. She said, "That lady who lives here, Linda. She went apeshit on Dad."

Emma looked at her father, who had been following with his eyes, careful not to move his head unnecessarily. There was a notepad and pencil on the coffee table. He reached for it and began to scribble. After a minute he tore off the page and held it up. The note read, *Why should I trust you?*

Collins shook her head and laughed.

I said, "I couldn't give a shit if you trust me." I indicated Emma. "I don't know what you've told your daughter, but the issue of trust between you and your close relations needs to be examined. That is once you're done trying to stay alive."

Collins was pissed off, shaking her head. She was looking at Emma. The girl had her head hung down.

"Did you see my mom?" she blubbered, then hid her face. "Is she still okay?"

Emma Williams turned away. Her body was wracked with grief. I remembered her bedroom. The floor and a tangle of phone-charging cables near her bed. Some sign of a normal adolescent life. It seemed far away from the storm shelter where she now hid with her father.

Collins looked at me; I looked back at her. Her face was alarmed and anxious and unable to respond. I made the call intuitively. Emma knew her mom was gone. I could see that knowledge in the grief already on display. What she required was confirmation, then there was the hope she'd get past it in her life.

I said, "She's dead. We're pretty sure." Emma choked and turned, her eyes bloated and wide and shocked. She staggered back. Tears ran freely down her cheeks, flushed and red. Collins was stabbing me to death with her eyes. I ignored her. The girl needed the truth, not bullshit. "There isn't going to be some kind of a better way of finding out, Emma. Right now there's serious ongoing danger from the people that killed your mother. Nobody's safe until we put those people down."

Emma sputtered. "What does *pretty sure* mean?"

"Means what you think. I didn't verify her body, if that's what you want to know. Best position for you to take would be that your mom's dead. If she turns out to be undead, you'll deal with that when it comes."

Collins folded an arm around Emma's shoulders. The young girl shrugged it off and gave her a bitter glance. "I'm not a baby. I can handle it."

I stepped forward so that she had no option but to pay attention. "Good. Now tell me everything from the beginning."

Emma Williams sobbed into her sleeve. She howled for a whole minute, her face bright red and eyes streaming tears. After that she got ahold of herself and blew her nose directly into her shirt sleeve. She shook her head and cursed violently at her father, who put the ice pack back over his face, itself a mess of tears and shame. Emma took a seat next to her father, composed herself and between the two of them we got the story.

Fayaz had picked up Emma from school and taken her into hiding on a friend's farm out of town. At that point he divulged most of the truth. First up was the fact that he was married, and not to Emma's mother. Emma had not been surprised, being fifteen years old and intelligent. She'd already known that her father was not a reliable person.

The next revelation had to do with her dad's debts.

At that point in her life, debt was tough to get a grip on mentally. Her dad owed money, and the people he owed it to were coming to get them and maybe do very bad things to them. At that point I intervened in the storytelling. After what I'd seen in Donna Williams's apartment, I already had a theory.

I spoke to the idiot on the couch. "You gave up Emma's mom's apartment as collateral on your debt?"

He couldn't speak, of course. Emma was looking at him with an expression that was tough to judge. Collins wasn't even trying to suppress her disgust. Fayaz looked away and nodded affirmative. He scrawled a long note on his notepad. In short, saving Donna Williams hadn't been an option. He'd needed to decide at that point, save the kid or her mother. He'd made his choice.

Collins was appalled anyway. "Scumbag."

The worst thing about it was that Donna Williams had discovered the truth through an interaction with the loan sharks. That and the disappearance of her daughter had been enough to set off the psychotic episode.

Emma didn't even try to defend her father. She continued the story. Hiding out at the friend's house worked for a couple of days, but the friend wasn't *that* much of a friend. With the storm coming, Fayaz got the bright idea of using the shelter back at Springhurst Road. That was a couple of days ago. The shit hit the fan when Linda Cartwright came down to escape from the two men in the silver paneled van.

I said, "Linda came down here, same way as us?"

Emma hadn't thought about it or hadn't paid attention. Fayaz raised his hand. I waited patiently while he wrote down a note. He showed us the notepad and pointed to the back. The note read: *She came through the back. Two ways out of here, or into here.*

I went back through a door into a small kitchen. Shelves contained canned goods. I figured Fayaz was going to run through the soup section pretty quick, since he wasn't able to chew. A ladder was fixed to the far wall, going up to a hatch. The storm shelter had a garden entrance. Linda Cartwright had been tactically astute. She'd managed to escape from the two guys who had invaded her house to snatch her. Then, instead of just running away out the front door, she doubled back through the yard and got into the shelter. The hanging sheets would have helped obscure her entry. The two men must have just assumed that she'd run off.

I came back to the living area. Collins was looking at me, demanding information.

I said, "Cartwright came down here from the yard."

Collins looked at Emma. She said, "Linda Cartwright didn't know about you when she came down here. You'd heard about her, but she had no idea about you. That right?"

Emma's eyes were on her father. Fayaz nodded affirmative. His daughter looked at the floor. "She must hate me and my mom."

Collins couldn't help herself. She spoke to the man on the couch.

"You don't deserve to live, let alone enjoy the love of this beautiful girl."

Emma gave a little snort of a laugh to herself. She shook her head and her eyes blazed at Collins. "What's your point? If you're trying to accuse my dad of being irresponsible, an idiot, and a menace to himself, you can save your breath. We all know that already. What you don't know is that he's a good dad in other ways. Even Linda admitted that he was a good man, after she broke his face."

Collins became equally defiant. "Good how and in what universe?"

I stepped in.

"Save it for later. I personally don't care how good of a dad anyone is. I had a dad, he was all right. Maybe he's still alive. Point is, I got over it and you will too, Emma. People get over their parents." I pointed at Fayaz on the sofa. "The issue isn't you anymore. It's everyone else who's getting blowback from your actions. You got in trouble with the wrong people and now your daughter's mother is dead as a consequence." I looked directly at Emma. "That's going to be up to you to deal with." Collins had backed away and was staring at me. I said, "The task at hand now is to eliminate the danger, take that variable out of the equation." I looked back at Emma and then her father. "Afterwards, you two can be alive to enjoy therapy for the rest of your lives." I looked at Fayaz. Do you know where Linda went?"

He shook his head.

Emma said, "She stormed out of here and we haven't seen her since."

"When was that?"

"Yesterday. During the storm."

Collins said, "She left the storm shelter, during the storm."

Emma nodded. "Yeah. She's completely insane."

None of which surprised me in the least. I spoke again to the guy on the couch. "You have any idea where we can find The Bob?"

Again, he shook his head. Useless, and once again, I was not surprised. None of these people were capable of standing up to The Bob. Except for Linda Cartwright. She was the only one willing to go out on a limb for herself and her people. Guys like Ricardo and Fayaz would get in trouble with the loan shark and then just roll over and hope for the best. They lived in a fantasy world of denial.

There was another dimension to Fayaz, however. He was a useless and dangerously irresponsible individual but also one who attracted love and affection from those who surrounded him. A complicated man with a complicated life.

Collins spoke to me. "This all leaves us where, exactly?"

"We're working off the basics, Collins. Remember the mission." I indicated Emma. "This girl's alive, which is a good thing. That's one less thing we need to think about." I pointed at Fayaz "That guy's hanging in there somehow. Now it's about Linda Cartwright. She's out there somewhere, probably engaged in some kind of rash and courageous activity. I imagine she's on the warpath. I don't think she can go up against these people alone."

"So, back to the other thing?"

"Correct."

CHAPTER FORTY-SEVEN

On the way back to the Crown Victoria, Collins wanted to talk over the sequence of events.

I said, "Cartwright went down there the afternoon or evening before last. She was just trying to get away from the two guys who'd come to attack her." Another thought entered my mind. "Could be that she intended to come back up the basement way and get them from behind."

"She does sound very aggressive."

I agreed. "I imagine that she's taking the fight to the enemy. Maybe she knows where to find him, maybe not. If we go looking for The Bob we might end up finding Linda Cartwright."

"Before she gets herself killed, you mean."

"Correct."

We crossed the street and got in the Crown Vic. I looked back at Cartwright's yard. I didn't know exactly how to think about it. The only word that came to mind was *complicated.* Collins got the Crown Vic running. She looked at what I was looking at, the Cartwright yard. She had a thought. "You know the beginning, Keeler? When Donna Williams tried to kill Cartwright, and then shot herself?" I grunted affirmative. "They don't know about that, do they, Fayaz and Emma?"

We looked at each other. She was right.

Collins got the vehicle moving and my attention shifted to the current task. The first address we'd chosen was only three miles away. While Collins drove, I examined the horizon. The sky was sectioned off. The side of it closest to town was clear but getting hazier. Over on the other side, out of town a piece, was a boiling cloud system crackling with lightning. It was dark and brooding in there, a rolling swirl of black and gray. Collins caught me looking at it. "You ever see a tornado?"

"No."

She said, "Impressive weather coming."

"You've seen one before?"

Collins nodded. "Couple of years ago, out east of town. They had a couple out there."

I had the feeling that a lot more than just the weather was coming our way. We drove without speaking for several minutes. The streets and front yards were littered with detritus from the storm. Town employees had been deployed in pickup trucks to clean it up. We saw a couple of groups picking up the larger items and hauling them into truck beds. The music on the radio was pretty good. Collins nodded to the beat, contented, mission focused.

Her phone was propped up behind the steering wheel and she multitasked, shifting attention between the map on her small rectangular screen and the real world outside. We came around a turn. She glanced at the map, looked up through the windshield at a street sign. "We're coming up on it now. Next block I think."

I started to pay attention.

The neighborhood was solid middle class. Flat ranch houses on widely spaced lawns. Like Springhurst but with more yard space. The density thinned out as we moved away from the town center.

Collins guided the car across another intersection and the road curved gently to the right. She was driving slowly. When we got halfway around the bend she slowed the Crown Vic down to a crawl. A town police interceptor was parked up ahead. Police tape marked off a big yard at the corner.

The smell hit first, like burned candy.

At first I didn't notice the house. I was busy noticing the fire hydrant. The sidewalk around it was still wet with pools of water forming in the grass and at a dip in the pavement. The hydrant had been painted in red, white and blue, like the figure of Uncle Sam. Collins muttered under her breath. "Holy shit."

By then the stink was pervasive. Burnt candy, mixed with chemical flame retardant. The yard that was taped off had the remnants of a house in the middle of it. Most of it was gone and what remained was a smoking black ruin. The ground was a slurry of soggy charred wood and ashes. Collins looked at the burned house, then down at the map. The house must have burned during the night. It would have happened after the storm.

"I think that's the address we're looking for, Keeler."

I could see two cops in the prowler.

"Don't stop. Drive past the police car."

She was about to say something. She closed her mouth and put the accelerator down nice and easy. The Crown Vic purred. We swept past the police car at an even keel. I looked into the prowler until we were parallel. Then I turned away. The two inside were drinking from paper coffee cups, exchanging some kind of banter.

When we were two blocks away from the site, Collins pulled over.

She slid the shifter into park. "That was weird."

"Maybe. Aren't there always fires after a storm? Electricity lines knocked over, stuff like that."

Collins shrugged. "Sure."

I said, "The rule of threes. First one's an accident. What's the next address?"

She had it noted in her phone, like an itinerary. She looked into the device. "Five miles away."

"Let's go."

She slid her finger across the phone's screen. Jabbed at it twice. A new icon appeared in the reduced rectangular vision of the world. Like a red teardrop. She poked the teardrop and the phone started speaking to her. Her foot went down on the gas and the Crown Victoria moved away from the curb and back into circulation.

CHAPTER FORTY-EIGHT

THE COLUMN of smoke streaming skyward was visible from a mile out.

As we approached, the thin dark plume continued like a beacon, front and center of the windshield.

We let the scenery go by without comment and sat tight in the moving car, thinking and looking and listening. The road rose slightly. On either side, mailboxes and driveways and low-slung ranch houses cruised by. Some of the driveways featured basketball hoops, but no basketball players appeared. The homeowners had varying degrees of ambition when it came to landscape architecture.

When we arrived at the summit of the rise, another scene of destruction lay before us.

This fire had taken out the garage entirely. The skeletal remains of a four-door SUV were framed inside a crumpled square of burnt timber and blackened aluminum siding. Behind the destroyed garage were the ruins of a home: charred and black remnants, piled in uneven mounds. A brick chimney remained, blackened but standing strong. The domestic disaster had been squared off by police tape, as if it required a formal outline to be made comprehensible. Firemen were still present, hosing off smoldering remains. The police had moved bystanders across the street.

Collins guided the Crown Vic down the rise and pulled over a block away from the zone. We got out of the vehicle and took a walk.

I said, "Look for a homeowner. We need to speak to somebody."

Collins said, "Where does this sit in your rule of threes?"

"The first one's an accident, second one's a coincidence."

She waited a beat, expecting something else. "And the third?"

"There's no such thing as a coincidence, so I never bother with the third."

No homeowners were visible. We had come late to the game. Survivors would have been already removed by ambulance. The burn zone was being tamed. Pretty soon it would be only ruins and a bad smell. After a while it would turn into a construction site. That would require paperwork and legal action. One day, another house would stand there and memory of the old one would be reduced to old photographs in someone's picture album.

I guess The Bob planned on being far away by then. Maybe on a luxury yacht, sipping cocktails and watching hard bodied twenty-year-olds forming tan lines underneath barely existent bikinis. That was an outcome that I planned on frustrating. Polar opposite visions of an outcome made The Bob and I bad enemies.

We came back to the car. Collins started the engine and executed a K-turn out of there. Two minutes later we hit a major artery with traffic lights and a gas station on the corner.

I said, "Pull into the gas station."

She glanced at the fuel gauge. The needle was up near the top, maybe ten percent off from being full. She made no comment, simply pulled in and stopped the car in a parking spot. I got out and walked across the stained asphalt surface. The farmer's mud boots squelched rhythmically.

The store was air-conditioned enough to freeze a sweaty elephant. Luckily the map rack was right there in front of the cash register. I paid for a red Sharpie and an old-fashioned folded map of the county. I felt lucky to get out of there without catching pneumonia. Back at the car, I spread the map on the warm hood. Collins egressed from the vehicle.

I anticipated the questions. "Better to see the situation from up on high, like a bird's eye view. That way we can look for patterns."

The county was shaped like a vertical rectangle with a squared off nub at the top right and a squiggled extrusion following a river line at the bottom left. The town of Promise maintained prime position in the top middle of the county. Collins brought out her phone and reeled off the addresses. We included Donna Williams's house and the Cartwright's in the list. Once we found one of them on the map, I made a circle with the red pen. The two burned houses we'd already seen got marked with a large X. Once we had all eight locations mapped out, I stood back and looked at it.

The eight properties were roughly spread around the county, with the epicenter being the Promise municipality. The two houses that we had already visited were the closest to the town center.

I heard Collins grunt, like she'd understood something. I looked at her.

She said, "They burned the closest ones first. Maybe they're moving out from the middle." She looked at me for my view.

"That's possible, depending."

"Depending on what?"

"On what they're doing with the houses in the first place."

Collins was shaking her head. "Why burn them?"

"Only reason to burn them is to destroy evidence."

I was calm, reflecting upon the events. I recalled the boxed items on Donna Williams's table. Security hardware. The Bob was using his loan sharking business to gain control of properties, then he was doing something with them. There were the contractors that Ricardo had noticed. Whatever The Bob was doing with the houses, he felt it required additional security measures. Looking at the map was a good exercise. The bird's eye view made me feel removed from the situation, like it wasn't me down there doing the do-or-die. Collins's eyes were intense, demanding answers that were unanswerable at that point.

Collins said, "Burn evidence of what?"

"We're going to find out. The important thing to note is that The Bob has reacted to what happened at the farm."

She was thoughtful. "You think so?"

I looked at her. "Why else would he start burning his own assets? Think about the business of a loan shark. He makes money off other people's assets once he's got them locked up in debt. I'm assuming he only loans to people with collateral. Guys take out a loan from him as a last resort. In the end he makes money from their assets. Now he's like a farmer burning his own field."

Collins laughed. "You make it sound like we're winning."

My eyes burned confidence. "Hell yes, we are. The guy's locking down. His plan is to wait us out. That won't work."

Collins stared at me for a long moment. She looked back at the map and fingered one of the locations farthest from the Promise town center, in the southern part of the county. "Maybe we should check this one?"

I examined what she was pointing at. Out there the land was sectioned into rural parcels, divided into increasingly large grids by increasingly narrow farm roads. Maybe it would take longer for The Bob's people to get out there and commit arson. If they had begun the operation after the rain, how many houses could they have done before daylight?

The property in question was around forty miles from our location. Small roads and then dirt roads were involved. An hour and change.

By the time we were halfway there the topography had transformed. Flat had turned to undulating, farmland had ended and woodland begun. Collins's phone had been speaking to her in an Australian accent. A male voice, giving directions. Left, right, but mostly straight ahead. At the point where the undulations eased into the tree line, the voice just stopped altogether.

Collins pressed the screen with agile fingers. "Don't need it anyway."

I had the map up on the dashboard. The place we were looking for wasn't far away. Straight for five more miles, then we'd turn left and see it a mile and a half up the road. I watched the odometer. Five miles later there was a road on the left, no stop sign. No traffic either. Collins made the turn. We hadn't seen another vehicle for twenty minutes. The last house had been ten miles back. The tires hummed over fine gravel and splashed through the occasional puddle left from the rain. She took it slow.

A mile and a half later a driveway appeared on the right.

Tall grass and two ruts for tires. It didn't look like any kind of sedan had been coming up this driveway. It was a rough track and the grass brushed against the Crown Vic's underside, making a constant whooshing sound. The occasional rock scraped and bumped. We slowly followed a series of lazy curves and undulations. I was examining the map. The property was large, but not endless. Looking at the topography I guessed we'd be coming up on the house pretty soon.

I pointed to a grassy area off to the side of the driveway. "Pull into that. We'll go on foot from here."

She didn't comment. She pulled the Crown Vic over to the side and got it into the weeds on solid ground. She cut the engine and handed me the keys. The vehicle was nosed into tall grass. On the other side of it were old-growth white oaks mixed with scrub pine. I prepared the weapons. Two Glock 17s, clean and good to go. I handed one to Collins and kept the other.

I said, "Let's approach through the woods, maybe circle around to observe the place."

A few minutes later we came over a rise and I saw the house up ahead. Collins was right behind me walking carefully through the old forest. It was beautiful out there after the storm. Fresh and green and vital. I eased down into a prone position and indicated for her to do the same. We crawled up behind a fallen tree, a position with an excellent view.

Below and straight ahead of us was a solidly built two-story ranch house constructed from hardwood timber and stone. It wasn't an old house. The people who had built it had done so with pride and with an eye toward durability for the future. They weren't going to flip that place for profit; they were there to stay.

The driveway opened up to a gravel area out front. A carport off to our right protected two vehicles. One large silver SUV and another sportier car. We were far enough away that I couldn't make out the brands or models. The front door was shut and there was nothing to see in the windows. The driveway was separated from the grassy yard beyond by white stone curbing.

The carport side of the house hosted a rectangular central air unit. The cream colored steel box was sunk into an area covered with small white pebbles and curbed with the same stone used for the driveway. Good modern ventilation. Another vehicle was parked on the gravel driveway, unprotected by the carport. It was a brown truck that looked old.

Collins said, "Ford Bronco, 1992."

I said, "Visitor or intruder?"

She said, "Could just as easily be a son or a daughter. Carport fits mom and dad's cars. Kids have to park in the driveway."

"Right. They'd all need a vehicle out here. How else would they get anywhere?"

"Exactly."

I was noticing something. I said, "Look at the front door. Is it closed?"

Collins looked, thought about it. Looked harder. "I can't tell. You're thinking about the angle of the paneling."

"Yes." The door was white with squared-off ornamental paneling. "The perspective doesn't match the frame. The door is slightly open."

I glanced at Collins. She held my gaze. I nodded, she reciprocated.

We came off the rise and approached the house. A minute later we arrived at the brown truck. Nobody was inside the Bronco. The hood wasn't warm. Collins pointed into the cab. I followed with my eyes and saw nothing. My eyes asked the question.

Collins said, "Air freshener."

A Christmas tree air freshener hung from the rearview. We got close and examined it. From an angle near the mirror on the passenger side it was possible to see a logo printed on the tree-shaped cardboard wedge. *Gresham's Drive-Through Hand Wash.*

Collins glanced at me and I raised my eyebrows.

I approached with the Glock held behind my leg. Not exactly subtle, but not full Rambo either. Collins was right behind me, checking our six and the peripheral while I scanned the windows, but they were sealed off by wooden plantation shutters. I came up the front steps.

The door was slightly ajar. A red oriental rug with tasseled edges covered the entrance area. A wedge of daylight spilled in and illuminated the detailed design. A rotund object took up space on the carpet. I came closer to examine it. A decapitated human head lay on its side. The eyes were open and looking out past me.

CHAPTER FORTY-NINE

WHEN COLLINS SAW the head she sucked in her breath and froze up.

I pushed the door open with a boot toe. It was dark inside and the blinds were all closed. I looked around for a body that might once have hosted the head. To the left was a carpeted staircase. To the right, a wall. Straight ahead was another wall with a security door that had a camera mounted over it. The camera would have been pointing right down at me, but it had been destroyed and now consisted of a collection of shattered plastic, wires, and the destroyed drywall behind it. The security door was made of brushed steel with a biometric sensor off to the side.

The door was half open, with a corpse wedged between it and the doorjamb. The corpse had no head, or neck, or chest.

What was clear to me was that the head hadn't been decapitated in any kind of a clean way. It wasn't like the headless person had been sent to the guillotine, more like the headless person had run into a tight hail of buckshot fired at close range. It did not smell pleasant.

Weirder yet was the interior design. We weren't standing in the entrance to anything that resembled a domestic abode. I'd come in the door expecting an airy entrance leading out to the living room, or a big farm-style kitchen. What I got was a tight, claustrophobic space between the external skin of the ranch house, and an internal chamber that had been shoved inside it.

The plantation shutters were closed over windows that nobody would be looking out of since they were almost flush against another wall. A box within a box.

The house creaked. I got very still and quiet and listened. Collins stood paralyzed, eyes wide open staring at the unattached head on the carpet. Nothing happened.

I peered in through the half-open security door. The decapitated person had fallen with feet facing into the darkened interior carpet. It was a male head, as far as I could make out. The dead man's hands were encased in high-quality black silicone gloves. I came through quietly, stepping over the corpse and entering the inner room. I noticed something gleaming at the dead man's front jeans pocket. It was a clip from a folding knife.

I slipped it out. A Gerber clasp knife. I slid it into my pocket. The darkness in there was almost complete. My left hand located a fancy light switch exactly where you'd expect to find it. The switch had a round shape that clicked in to activate.

The lights faded up theatrically. No bare bulbs or lamps in sight. Light sources were hidden in recessed nooks and crannies built into the interior structure. I was standing inside a generous vestibule. To my right was a wall with two doors evenly spaced along it. To my left was a horseshoe-shaped sofa with two velvet ottomans. It was like being in someone's idea of heaven, or a music video, or a fancy massage parlor. I couldn't decide which.

I was leaning toward the music video idea. One of the ottomans hosted a hiking backpack. The second had a heavy-duty sledgehammer, leaned neatly against it. At the far end was a closed door. The dry wall on either side had been violently perforated. That had been the role played by the sledge hammer. Large gaping holes had been punched in at regularly spaced intervals.

I unsnapped the top of the backpack and flipped it open. Peering inside I was looking at a neatly packed collection of around a dozen injection tubes. Half the tubes were upside down, the other half had the long nozzle facing up. Each plastic nozzle had been snipped and capped with a twist of plastic wrap. All ready to go with no fussing around on site. I pulled out an upside-down tube. It was empty. The bottom of the backpack was protected by a layer of folded newspaper. I examined the tube's label. This wasn't silicone sealer for a bathtub, it was liquid superglue. I showed the label to Collins. She mouthed the question without actually saying it. "Flammable materials?"

I shrugged in the affirmative. Must be an arsonist's toolkit. I could smell the stench of burnt chemicals coming from somewhere. I figured the layer of newspaper served to protect the backpack against the spilling of superglue from a used tube. The headless guy had been a professional arsonist.

Collins was crawling on the plush carpet examining the base of the wall. She reached under the sofa and pulled out an injection tool. The kind of thing you fit a tube into and then pull the trigger to get the stuff out of the plastic nozzle. She came to me and whispered. "Guy was applying this to the base of the walls." She pointed at the punctured drywall. "Maybe that also helps the burn."

I said nothing. She was right.

The house creaked again, in a different way than before. I stopped moving again. Collins gripped my sleeve. Nothing happened, nothing else creaked. I figured it might just be the regular noise that a house made. Perhaps the storm had knocked something loose.

I opened the first door to the right. As was the case with the entrance, there were no windows and it was dark. I found the lights and punched the switch. This time the recessed luminance faded onto something that more closely approximated a domestic scene. It was a bedroom, and at first glance that was it. However the bed was an oval and of a size that could fit half a football team. Aside from the bed, the room had a small bar and a leather recliner. There was a plush-looking square bench between the bed and the recliner.

Collins toured the perimeter. She opened a bedside drawer and fished out a handful of packaged condoms. She raised her eyebrows at me and let them rain back into the drawer. I backed out to the entrance area once more. Collins followed me into the next room. I flicked the switch and a new kind of experience was illuminated.

The second room was much larger. It contained four identical felt-covered symmetrically arranged card tables. Not the kind guys use for Saturday night poker. These were professional level croupier tables with all the accoutrements. The seating was leather and mahogany. Along the walls were armchairs, side tables, and good-looking lamps. A bar occupied one of the short sides of the rectangle. There was no bartender, and no croupiers. But there was space allocated and designed for maybe five or six employees. Collins looked in and the frown on her face got deeper.

I backed out to the entrance area again. There remained one more door to check out, directly across from the security entrance where the acephalous body had wedged itself.

This door was not actually closed. An inch wide gap let air flow between the door and the framing. Closer to the door the smell of burnt chemicals became more pronounced. I pushed the door open and stepped through. Collins clicked on the light switch behind me. Recessed lighting swelled up from the hidden crevices built into ceiling molding. But this room wasn't the same.

For one thing, there was another dead guy. This one was sprawled back against the far wall. I approached with the Glock up, fixing him in the sights. He had a head, but the buckshot had perforated a portion of his groin and abdomen. Blood had leaked onto the espresso-brown carpeting. The dead guy's eyes were closed and his face was drawn and white from the loss of blood.

Collins said, "Oh wow."

Which made me look away from the dead man.

The walls were wood paneled. It looked as if the design intention had been to lend the space a private VIP backroom vibe, except this room had been torched at multiple points. The scorched and blackened walls indicated a fire that had burned hot for some non-negligible period of time. At that point someone had decided they didn't want the place burned down. They'd come in like gangbusters with some kind of a shotgun, first taking out the guy at the entrance, then this guy.

Otherwise, it looked like a great place to hang out.

The furniture was all velvet sofas and recliners and fancy leather-backed antique loungers. There were two low tables and a couple of floor cushions. A couple of solid marble planters were placed against the wood-paneled walls. An exotic wood shelving unit hosted a fancy hi-fi system. Not that I know anything about hi-fi systems, but this one looked both vintage and modern, an indication that it would have been an expensive purchase made by a knowledgeable connoisseur.

Collins moved to one of the low tables and studied the items arranged on the glossy surface. An ornate brass tray held an odd assortment of antique objects. They looked expensive and rare, like they belonged in a museum. The tray held a compact ornate brass oil lamp with a wick and glass bulb cover, brass bowls and a variety of small utensils including a pair of scissors, a couple of solid metal picks, a brush, tweezers, and other implements. At first I had no idea what I was looking at, then it dawned on me. I'd spent a lot of time in Afghanistan.

Collins plucked a two-foot long cylindrical tube and held it up for examination. It was engraved ivory with inlaid filigree patterns and a telltale small bowl popping out of one end. She looked at me with raised eyebrows. "This is an opium den, Keeler."

I said nothing. The dead guy over by the wall wasn't speaking either. But I had heard a pounding sound, soft, like a heartbeat. I looked at Collins. "You hear that?"

She had moved to a side table near the door, also an impressive piece of furniture in dark mahogany. "Hear what?" I came up as Collins pulled open the top drawer. Sealed hypodermic needles were lined up and ready to go. Collins picked up one of the packaged needles and held it between thumb and forefinger. "Not just opium in this opium den."

I said, "Let's clear the house. Then we can discuss the war on drugs."

She said nothing. She was listening. The soft pounding was there again, as if the house had a heartbeat. It was getting faster and louder. I moved laterally and backwards, seeking a good view out into the entrance area with the velvet ottomans and the horseshoe shaped sofa.

I saw immediately what was making the soft pounding sounds.

A woman was sprinting hard, coming right at me. She looked like a fierce soccer mom. Eyes wide open and teeth clenched in a grimace. Her blond hair bob bounced with each heavy step as her pink bare feet pounded the plush carpeting.

It was happening in a matter of seconds. The woman was getting closer and I saw that she carried something in both hands. I hadn't thought of her as an immediate threat, but I was wrong. When she was two steps from the door I realized the object raised in her hands was a shotgun. I was working under the assumption that it had been used before, at least twice.

The woman's mouth opened in preparation for a scream that hadn't yet exited her throat. The twin side by side muzzles of the long gun were black orbs rising up to greet me.

CHAPTER FIFTY

I DID my best to preempt the woman's scream. I raised my hands in a gesture of compliance. I got a sound out of my mouth, something incomprehensible and animalistic and related in tone to the concept of *no*. The woman wasn't listening, maybe couldn't even hear me. A couple of things happened, more or less simultaneously, but in the heat of the moment it might as well have been a slow-motion movie.

The woman's scream succeeded in exiting her mouth as she spilled into the room at full speed. Like my verbalization, there were no consonants or vowels. But the woman's scream was a clear primal warning to get out of her house and leave her alone.

I glanced at Collins.

She looked horrified, which was understandable. But she hadn't yet seen the approaching woman, couldn't have known what was coming down the line. She had seen me pointing and gesturing and screaming. She'd heard the woman's cries. But her horrified expression was focused right behind me. She pointed and spoke calmly. "Undead."

I twisted and turned. The dead guy who had been crumpled against the wall in the back was now moving, he was undead. His eyes were open and he was raising a large chrome pistol. The woman came through the door. Collins had been anticipating those softly padded and urgent steps. She intercepted the woman as she came in, shouldered her to the side. The woman lost balance. The momentum of her run, combined with Collins's tackle, launched her into the side of a leather sofa. The shotgun boomed as the two barrels went off at more or less the same time, sending buckshot into the wood paneling.

The undead guy fired. Another booming shot. I got the Glock up and squeezed two quieter rounds into his face. The guy barely budged. There was only a subtle double quiver as the metal slapped through flesh. The twin holes freshly drilled into his cheek and forehead were pretty good indicators of his status as a truly dead person. I moved to the woman, sprawled on the ground. She was regaining her balance and fumbling for a reload.

I locked her arms to her sides and got eye contact. "Not an enemy. Put it down."

She stared at me, uncomprehending. The woman had watery blue eyes and wore gold stud earrings.

I said it again. "I'm here to help. Put the weapon down."

She took a sobbing breath. "I thought you were with them."

"I know you did."

Her grip on the shotgun relaxed. I pulled it away and took a deep breath of my own. The woman fell back on the carpet and sobbed mightily. The watery blue eyes moved to me again, confused and defeated. I saw her focus drift from my face, beyond my shoulder.

The woman said, "Oh."

Collins was sprawled awkwardly, face down in the carpet. She was trying to regain her composure, like something had happened to surprise and embarrass her. I was there in two strides. She twisted onto her back and looked up at me. "Dammit I think I'm shot."

I looked down. An oval of blood was growing on Collins's denim-clad lower left leg.

She said, "I don't feel any pain. Is that a bad sign?"

I ran my hands over her, head to toe. Checked her in the back, everywhere. No damage besides the lower leg, which was damage enough. Collins had no obvious arterial bleeding, and I didn't find an exit wound.

I tried to look composed and reassuring. "Don't worry. You'll get the pain eventually."

I took her under the arms and hauled her into a seated position with her back against the wall. I pulled the legs straight out. The wound wasn't bleeding terribly, but you never know. I pulled the Cardinals t-shirt over my head and ripped a long piece out of it. I fashioned that into a tourniquet above the entry wound.

I went back to the homeowner. She was weeping silently.

"I'm Tom Keeler. What's your name?"

"Jane Starmer." She looked me in the eyes, serious and sad. "Larry's gone."

"Your husband?"

She nodded. "Upstairs."

"It's over now. Your husband's gone, but you're alive and you defended yourself. We need to take care of my friend, then I'm going to need to talk to you."

Starmer sniffed and nodded. "What do you need?"

"Do you have any first aid supplies?"

The Starmers had a kit. The husband was upstairs. I found him crumpled and dead with his back against the wall. Blood had pooled below the body. Blood-soaked bandages lay on the floor around him, along with discarded first aid packaging. The man had been gut shot by a large caliber round. The abdomen was all gore and the imploded remains of a prodigious beer belly. His head slumped off to the side, like a ragdoll. The eyes were rolled up, staring lifelessly in the direction of the ceiling.

A first aid kit was scattered around him, like a still-life expression of panic. There was a red plastic box. The Starmers had dumped the contents onto the floor and wasted about half of it. I collected everything useful that remained and brought the box downstairs. Collins was looking alert and not yet in pain. Jane Starmer was weeping softly to herself.

I put the first aid kit down next to Collins. I went to Starmer and guided her over. "I'm going to ask you for items from your first aid kit here; you're either going to give them to me, or we'll find the next best thing."

She nodded again. "Okay."

"Start with the scissors."

Two seconds later, a pair landed into my outstretched hand. I cut away the denim on Collins's leg, exposing the wound.

"Get me water. A bottle of it, or whatever's closest."

Jane ran out, padding away over the soft carpet.

Collins had a case of dry mouth. "Thirsty."

"It's coming. You're going to be okay."

Jane came back with a bottle of water and put it in my hand. I washed the blood away from the wound with the torn leftovers of the Cardinals t-shirt. When I was done cleaning the blood away, I handed the water bottle to Collins to drink from.

The wound wasn't deep enough to have been a direct hit. I looked around and my eyes fell on one of the marble planters. The corner had been smashed and fragments of stone lay scattered across the carpet. The planter had absorbed much of the bullet's force and momentum. The squashed slug from the dead man's big chrome pistol had spun off into Collins's shin. The tibia was broken and the round was lodged in there somewhere. Collins was still in the adrenaline phase, but she was going to feel the pain soon. I didn't want to mess around trying to extract the metal object from her leg.

I looked at Starmer, kneeling beside me. "We need gauze from a sealed pack and a set of tweezers. Either medical from the kit, or whatever you use to take care of those perfect eyebrows."

"Is that it?"

"Some kind of disinfectant like alcohol or a gel and a bandage, if you can find it all easily."

Starmer scuttled over and hunted through the box. She came

back quickly with everything I needed. I needed to disinfect the area and pack the bullet hole with gauze.

"While I work on this, run me through what happened here."

Starmer stared at me. "What?"

I began to take up the gauze with the pair of tweezers. "Obviously Starmer, your house is a little unusual, but we can speak about that later. Tell me what happened last night."

"Oh." Her mouth stayed in a circle until it broke down into quivering and finally settled. "Larry got out of bed and went downstairs. I was half awake. I don't know what got him up exactly. I heard the banging from the gunfire. I didn't know what to do, but I got up and was going to go downstairs." She broke down into more sobbing. "Larry came up the stairs. He gave me the gun and said, 'I got 'em, Janey.' Then he sat down on the carpet. I asked him what I was supposed to do with the gun. He said he was real tired and wanted to take a nap."

I glanced at Starmer. Her eyes were wide. She'd been through one hell of an experience.

I said, "What did you do then?"

She was pleading. "I'm not trained in first aid."

"I know you aren't. You aren't supposed to need to be, ma'am."

She nodded. "Okay." After a while she said, "Well, he slipped away I guess. And I stayed next to him and just couldn't do anything at all except sleep and not think. And then you came and I wanted to kill you." She sobbed quietly.

I had a lot of that gauze stuffed into the hole. "Hold her leg up."

Starmer lifted Collins's leg, so I could wrap it tight with a clean bandage. I taped the bandage and we put her leg down. Collins's face was getting pale and I could see that she didn't have a lot of time remaining as a pain-free patient. I briefly considered the concept of opium, and if I'd be able to source it quickly. I discarded the idea. If this was a well-organized operation; they wouldn't keep the product on site. They would maintain a fluid supply chain and keep the main stash away from the users.

I turned again to Starmer. "Were there only the two men?"

She looked at me, uncomprehending. "What?"

"The men who attacked your house. Two of them?"

"I think so."

"That's good. We're going to talk while we drive. My friend needs to go to the hospital."

She said, "What about Larry?"

"Larry's dead. I guess there's a reason you didn't call the police?"

Starmer was looking in my direction, but her thousand-yard stare saw something else. Her lips pursed and she whispered her response. "Yes. There is a reason."

CHAPTER FIFTY-ONE

I CARRIED COLLINS PIGGYBACK. She held on tight with her arms and the one good leg.

Starmer came after us, scrambling barefoot out the door. "I'll get the car."

I laid Collins down. Her hair splayed out on the pale gravel, framing her face. Her expression was strained but smiling when we made eye contact. I lifted her leg and positioned it so that the wounded leg was laid over my thigh, elevating the injury. Collins grunted when the leg was touched. The pain was kicking in.

Over at the carport, the silver SUV's engine turned over. The taillights came on and the vehicle backed out toward us. The carport was set on a solid concrete foundation. The wheels sounded wrong from the get-go. I saw immediately that the vehicle was running on rims, the tires had been slashed. I looked at the other vehicle in the carport, which was likewise disabled. The first dead guy must have used his Gerber knife to slice open the only possible escape vector that Jane and Larry Starmer had left to them.

I let down Collins's leg. Starmer was flustered, knowing something was wrong but not realizing exactly what it was. I came to the

SUV and rapped on the window. She glanced at me, panicked. She couldn't figure out what to do. I opened the door.

"Turn the car off and come down. They slashed your tires. We aren't going anywhere in that."

Starmer looked bewildered. I left her to figure it out and set off jogging down the drive. A couple of minutes later I was at the Crown Victoria. I backed out of the grass and drove up to the house. By then Starmer had gotten with the program. We lifted Collins into the back and got rolling.

THE CLOSEST HOSPITAL was a place called County General.

Starmer gave me directions. We stayed silent and concentrated while the car was rolling and bumping over the driveway and the gravel road. I adjusted the rearview mirror to keep an eye on Collins in the back. She was biting her lip and grimacing. The bumping and pitching wasn't helping much with the pain now shooting out from her wounded leg. Once we were cruising on smooth blacktop, I looked at Starmer. "Now you tell me everything, from the beginning."

Once Starmer got to talking, it was like a faucet had been turned on that couldn't be turned back off again. Behind it was an ocean of regret and bitterness, backed up and collecting for years with nowhere to go. Her red mouth moved rapidly, the eyes glassy, staring sightlessly at the horizon.

The reason they hadn't called the police was that Starmer's deceased husband, Larry, was up to his eyes in debt to The Bob. He was also now an accomplice in the drug and sex business. At least that's how it would look to an inquisitive prosecutor.

When Larry had been alive, he'd worked in IT sales. By middle age he had acquired the veneer of a successful man. He was also an ex-felon who'd gone down for dealing pot with extenuating circumstances, ten days after his eighteenth birthday. Starmer made a tutting sound and shook her head. Dumb kid, but still, prison time and a felony rap for *that*? After the six-month stint in Wabash Valley Correctional, he'd come out reformed and educated, with a GED and everything. Right after prison Larry had gone on to the community college and gotten his associate's degree in Business Operations, Management and Technology. He'd managed to find an initial job and then he and Jane had married. After the marriage and the kids came, Larry had gotten serious. Over time he'd worked his way up the ladder of his profession.

By the time the kids were both in college, Larry was an account executive with a local company helping farmers take advantage of the supposedly revolutionary advances that fancy internet technologies now promised. Then, he'd seen an opening in the market that nobody had spotted. He figured he could strike out on his own and get a piece of the dream for himself and his family. The kids were already halfway out of the house and he could take the risk.

But none of that had helped when it came time to get a loan from the bank. A felon is a felon for life, and felons don't get bank loans.

I was watching Starmer talk. She was angry. Not only at her husband and The Bob, but at the world for being unfair. She shook her head in a fierce internal dialogue. I made eye contact with Collins. She was listening. Starmer started up again, this time with even more venom in her voice. What Larry should have done, was confide in his wife. She could have secured the loan in her own name. But damn it if Larry wasn't a proud man. That was when and why he'd started down the road where dreams and folly meet tragedy.

Starmer looked at me. I nodded at her. "Go on."

It had started off as a small loan of ten grand, which had been manageable on his salary. Larry had figured the ten k would be enough to buy time and figure out the business plan with some help from a consultant he knew. Then, he could get other investors on board. But it hadn't worked out that way. The Bob had the noose set, and the rope had slowly tightened around Larry's unsuspecting neck. Next thing he knew the ten had turned into a hundred, which was less manageable. A year later it was another multiple of ten.

Starmer paused to blow her nose on the hem of her shirt.

I said, "What happened then, the contractors showed up or did they threaten you first?"

She looked at me with pure burning anger and held up her right hand. The middle finger had been chopped off at the knuckle joint. "They got me first. Larry kept his problems from me for as long as he could, the dumb shit. But the problems came for me in the end."

By the time the contractors had shown up to the house there wasn't anything left to discuss. They were both in deep. They bowed to the superior power of criminal violence. A few months later they were hosting a franchise of The Bob's entertainment business in the shell of their own house. Not only were they prisoners in their own home, but active participants in a criminal enterprise.

I said, "Hosting, as in you were involved in the operation?"

"No. They didn't trust us. We weren't allowed to be downstairs at all. You didn't see it, but the kids' bedroom is set up with a hot plate and fridge. We've been living like tenants in our own house."

"I see. How did it work, then?"

"Members club, like a pyramid scheme. They get like a dozen men involved. They tell their wives they're going over to Larry's for a poker game. In fact they're going gambling and smoking and worse. They always had a girl working nights, three nights a week. Thursday through Saturday."

Now Larry was dead and Jane Starmer was left clutching the hem of her shirt, weeping copiously in the passenger seat.

I glanced at her. "You know they've got more of them around the county. Maybe around the state."

Starmer cleaned up her eyes with her shirt sleeve. Blew her nose again on the hem. "I'm not surprised, but I don't know anything about that. I was living my own personal nightmare, you know? It was like being in a locked room."

"Yeah."

I looked back at Collins, who was stretched out on the backseat and staring up at the passing sky. By now the clouds were all rolling thunder and darkness. The big one was on its way, that was for damned sure. I pulled the Crown Victoria up to the County General emergency entrance.

I turned to Starmer. "Take her in and make sure everything goes all right. I'm counting on you, Starmer. This is your mission."

She said, "What are you going to do?"

"Bad things to bad people."

Starmer looked at me for a moment, pupils dilated, gazing into the wrong side of that curtain. She disengaged and unlocked her seat belt. I came around and helped Collins out of the car. She was doing okay, considering the bandage was soaked through with blood and she was looking weak. Starmer took over and supported her.

Collins gazed at me for one long moment and then they were walking to the hospital entrance. Starmer supporting, Collins limping on her good leg. I got back into the Crown Victoria and moved it out of the hospital driveway and into traffic. I was angry and tired. More angry than tired, and I knew that the tired part could wait. I could stay awake for weeks hunting these people down. I was feeling it, a remorseless calm right before the shit kicked off in a big way.

CHAPTER FIFTY-TWO

I NAVIGATED BACK TO TOWN. Two hands placed on the wheel at ten and two. I was running down the variables in my mind, barely paying attention to where I was going. I was almost surprised when I felt compelled to look more carefully in the rearview mirror. Something had shifted from the back to the front of my mind. An object of animal perception passed like a football from quarterback to running back. My focus narrowed to a pickup truck a couple of vehicles back.

I soaked up the details. Ford F-150 in some kind of a metallic blue color. Not the latest model, but not a relic either.

I took the next exit off the highway. The off-ramp resolved in a traffic light. Two vehicles stacked up behind me before the light changed. The Ford truck wasn't one of them. Which didn't mean anything. I respected my animal instincts. Nothing surprised me about being followed. I figured they'd picked me up coming back into town. The Bob had people and eyes, that was for damned sure.

I passed a home-improvement store with a parking lot the size of a football field. Serious-minded men and women were strapping plywood boards and other supplies onto all kinds of vehicles. Looked like a good time to be in the home-improvement business. Since everyone else was getting prepared for the storm, I figured that was the smart thing to do.

The security guard wasn't happy about my lack of a shirt, but it wasn't a deal breaker. I went in with a mental list and an open mind.

The first item on the list was a good pair of safety goggles. From what I'd seen so far, a tornado means things flying through the air at high speeds. Big things weren't going to be an issue for the eye, little things could get tricky. Eye protection was therefore prudent. I went with a model that had an elasticated band and a single fully enclosed scratch resistant visor with ventilation to avoid fogging. Next up was the heavy tool section.

I knew what I wanted. I had been inspired by the sledgehammer back at the Starmer property. For my purposes I wanted heavy, but not burdensome. The store had a wide variety of sledgehammers. From three pounds all the way to twenty. I chose one in between, ten pounds of high strength steel with the promise of an unbreakable handle. I had tactical thoughts, and this item fit right into them.

A woman in a store uniform was stocking a shelf from a heavy cardboard box. She was removing steel objects—shaped like wedges, lining them up, and sticking price tags on them. I bent down to where she was kneeling. "Excuse me, ma'am. What are those?"

She looked up at me through a pair of thick-framed glasses. The woman stood up and her knees cracked loudly. "Well, now." She held up one of the objects. "I'm no expert, but I just got these in yesterday. They're called splitting wedges." She smiled, and twirled it around between her fingers. "Quite the specialty item, but I know my customers. I'm also the owner, so I need to vet all the stuff the distributor wants me to sell. Last night, I watched a video on the internet. A guy was splitting stone with one of these at a quarry." She pointed to the thin shaft at one end of the wedge. "That's called the feather. You hammer that end into the stone or the concrete or whatever. You get it in there good." She pointed to the sledgehammer in my hand. "Then you get busy with something like that. Nothing to it."

I said, "It's called a splitting wedge."

She smiled. "That's right. If you need to split something, this is going to make life easier."

The wedge was the width of my hand and twice as long. I took the one she was offering. "Thank you, ma'am. That looks just about perfect."

She said, "My pleasure." I watched a dreamy film come over her eyes. She was philosophizing. "People rarely know exactly what they really need. One day you don't know that you need it, then you can't do without it. You have a great day, sir."

Right next to the heavy tool section was a shelf of work boots. Definitely on the list. I settled on a steel-toed boot built from leather and mesh with a good-looking sole. Right next to that was a rack of work gloves. Not on the list, but interesting. I chose black canvas with rubberized finger grips. Opposite the work glove shelf hung a rack of one-piece coveralls in black canvas. Not on the list, but definitely a desirable product. I chose extra-large. The coveralls were heavy duty, with special pockets in all kinds of useful places. Collins's sweatpants could do the job, but these looked like they'd go that extra mile.

I got side-tracked by the hunting section. What I noticed first was a fancy spotting scope sitting up on a high shelf, a nice-looking object in dark green with a white duck logo on the front. It was a monocular scope with a wide body for the grip, plus it came with a strap for hanging around your neck. The price tag was steep, but I was flush with cash.

I threw a roll of duct tape and a good-quality duffle bag into the basket.

All of that cost me close to two thousand of The Bob's dollars.

On my way out I stopped by the bathroom and changed into the coveralls. I ripped the tags off and tore the packaging up and stuffed it all into a garbage can. The sledgehammer fit nicely into the duffle bag. The other items got piled in there as well. I left the mud boots neatly lined up under the sink. Maybe someone would be in need of foot protection.

The coveralls were stiff and new and felt solid and resistant to weather and minor scratches. This choice was more than vindicated the moment I stepped out of the store. The rain had started again. Thin and meager but strengthened by the wind and needling exposed skin. I zipped up the front and admired the selection of pockets.

Twenty minutes later, I pulled into the Silver Inn parking lot.

I sat for a while in the Crown Victoria feeling the engine's vibrations. Smooth and slow and perfectly tuned. I was thinking about what needed to be done and how I was going to do it. I was mission minded and target driven. The enemy knew I was in town.

But it was tough to deny the environmental situation in relation to weather. It wasn't very late, certainly not yet night, but the sky was charcoal gray. Headlights were on and the general mood was cautious and pragmatic. Stray objects were already getting kicked up off the streets by strong winds. Plastic bags and fragments of paper spiraled high over the buildings and got caught in trees. It was hard to believe that the night before had only been a dress rehearsal for the main event. But that's what it looked like. People caught on foot were walking fast. Vehicles seemed to be navigating with even less patience than before.

Through the open car window I could smell the greasy smoke coming out of the ventilator around the back of the Grill and Banquet. I was hungry. I killed the engine and fisted the key. I retrieved the backpack from the trunk and locked up the car. Up on the balcony I fit the key into room number ten. I turned and looked across the street to scan the line of cars where the silver sports car had been. Nobody there watching the motel. Nobody at all walking on the street. Only speedy vehicles getting the hell out of there, thinking about deep cover and supplies.

I opened the door and set the duffle bag down.

I spread out my belongings on the bed. Someone had been in there to clean things up and straighten sheets. I had the duffle bag with sledgehammer, splitting wedge, goggles, gloves, and the duct tape. Two Glock 17 pistols with a decent amount of ammunition remaining. Approximately two thousand dollars in cash. One Gerber clasp knife, sharp enough to cut through good quality tires.

I was feeling pretty good about all of that.

My mood moved up a notch higher when I started putting gear into pockets. The Gerber knife clipped into a side pocket on my right thigh. The two Glocks fit perfectly into symmetrically arranged diagonal zip pockets across the chest. They showed as bumps, but you'd need a wicked imagination to know what the bumps were.

I figured that was enough for dinner. The bad feeling faded and hunger took its place.

CHAPTER FIFTY-THREE

A COUPLE of minutes later I was on a stool, elbows resting on the chipped Formica countertop at the Grill and Banquet. I was feeling well-dressed. The grill guy slapped the meat on the fire and the fat sizzled perfectly. I'd given Nancy the order, same as before with bacon and cheese, hold the onions and double down on the pickles.

The coffee mug slid in front of me and I looked up to see Nancy. I said, "Do you own a phone?"

She was a little surprised by the question but recovered quickly. "Sure." Her right hand moved to her apron, tracing the form of the rectangular device. Nancy's eyes darted to the right. I figured another customer was trying to get her attention. I sipped from the mug. Good, strong, hot and black, nice. Nancy was watching and waiting, looking a little nervous.

I figured she wanted to know what I thought about the coffee. I tilted my head to the side while nodding in approval. The gesture indicated very good and even a little bit extra good. But my approval did not make Nancy happy. Her eyes moved again to the right, then straight ahead, meeting my own, and shifting right again.

I said, "Smile, Nancy, and tell me where."

Nancy paused for a breath. She forced a smile. Her voice quivered. "Back of the restaurant, same booth that Linda was in the other day."

I smiled broadly and nodded. "Outstanding."

I could see the booth. The partition was high enough to conceal whoever was in there. I glanced to my right. Behind the counter was a steel mirror, ancient and dented. It was clear enough that my gaze fell directly into the stare of a bearded man. He was sitting at the far bench of the booth, back to the wall, observing the place through the old mirror. I held his stare, neither of us dropped. I couldn't tell if he was alone or with a partner.

I was not surprised that they knew where I was staying. After what I'd done at the farm it was logical that The Bob would have major concerns. Equally logical that his people would find me here, and that a welcome party would be arranged. There were two in here, which meant someone with half a brain had anticipated that I'd come down to eat. There was also the possibility that the two here were decoys. Could be more out there, getting ready to act on their bad intentions.

I said, "Just the one guy?"

"No. Two of them." Nancy said, "I've got a kid."

"Nothing's going to happen here."

"Why did you ask about the phone?"

I dropped the staring contest with the bearded guy and looked at Nancy. "I'm interested in a specific car wash in town. It's supposed to be excellent. Gresham's Drive-Through Hand Wash. Do you think you could help me out with directions?"

Nancy bit her lip. She was anxious. I tried to convey relaxation and tranquility. She shook her head quickly, as if shaking out the dust, and removed the slim rectangle from her apron. She put the phone into her left palm and began to nudge and sweep the fingers on her right hand over its surface. She was good, employing a few gestures from the left thumb. Soon she had it all figured out and showed me the rectangle vertically. I looked into a map, which even showed our position, and the direction in which the phone was facing.

I pointed into the screen. "South side of town, right?"

Nancy screwed up her face. "Not exactly. It's kind of in between. We call it Little Ohio."

I examined the positions, each point relative to the other. The destination, The Grill and Banquet, the municipal building. I swiped my fingers across Nancy's screen, pinched in and pinched out. I got located, pinned the mega-church and the shopping center in my mental map. Gresham's Drive-Through was definitely somewhere between the south and the southwest. Like a Venn diagram where two circles overlap. I shrugged and repeated the neighborhood's nickname. "Little Ohio. Is that a nice neighborhood?"

"No, I wouldn't say so. But then again, you're just looking for a car wash."

"Why Little Ohio?"

"I guess a bunch of people moved there from Ohio and their friends and family came out to join them. Before you knew it they had their own restaurants and stores and ways of talking and doing things." She shrugged. "It's smaller than the real Ohio. So, Little Ohio."

"Because people from Ohio are so different from Indianans."

"Hoosiers, and yes, we are very different."

I looked into the dented mirror again. The bearded guy was still there, still staring right at me. I tried to discern some kind of a pattern in the few features I could see that would indicate if he or his ancestors had originally derived from Ohio. It was tough, bordering on impossible to form an opinion.

Behind Nancy, the grill guy was putting the finishing touches on my burger. He made none of the common errors, like sliced tomatoes, which could make the burger hard to handle, or lettuce leaves, which would wilt with the heat. Just the extra pickles, American cheese, bacon. A sprinkle each of salt and pepper. He turned to look at me watching him. "You want I put marinated hot peppers on it? Got them right here." He pointed the tongs at a deep steel tray with a pile of slippery looking peppers.

Unorthodox but not uninteresting.

"Sure, why not?"

The burger came. My attention shifted. Nancy's attention drifted to customers in more urgent need of her assistance. I chewed. I thought about things, like places to go and people to do things to. A world of things out there. When I finished the burger, Nancy brought the carafe over and refilled the coffee. Like an automatic gesture that nobody would ever dispute.

The guy in the mirror was still staring, still bearded, and still sipping slowly from a mug of coffee. I wondered if it was cold or still retained residual heat. I felt lucky knowing that my own beverage was fresh and hot. I got up from the counter and walked my coffee cup over to the booth in the back. As I approached, the guy started shifting. By the time I stood over him, he was sitting in the booth like a normal person: upright against the seat back, looking across at his buddy, who also had a beard and a cup of cold coffee.

I recognized them by their profiles. These were the two guys I'd planned on killing with my first pitchfork the night the Homeland Security agents had been murdered. Probably the same guys I'd seen at the farm, who'd come to save the big farmer's hide. Both men turned their heads simultaneously. One to the left, the other to the right. Two sets of eyes landed on me.

I grinned. Neither of my interlocutors found any reason to smile in return.

The beards were healthy and full, dark and trimmed in severe geometrical angles. Aggressive beards grown over tough faces. Both men were in their midthirties, like me. Each of them looked like they could bench-press two-fifty to three hundred, but not more, which meant they'd be agile and limber opponents in any kind of a wrestling match.

I said, "You guys from Ohio?"

They looked at me with blank, stony faces. The guy on my left said, "Why do you ask?"

I took a sip from my mug. Hot and good and necessary. "Was just wondering which team you two were on."

The guy on the right said, "You think this is a game?"

I shrugged. "Isn't it?"

"No. We're not playing."

I said, "That's not very sporting of you."

The guy on the left said, "Whatever, it's game over for you anyway. Who cares which team we're on?"

I sat down on the bench to my right and bumped the bearded man over. "Scoot over, Ed."

Both men involuntarily flinched, but hands did not fly for objects secreted in waistbands or accessible pockets. All four of their hands stayed up on the table. I put both of mine where they could be seen, along with the mug.

The guy across from me said, "Ed?"

"Ed from Ohio. Has a ring to it."

He shook his head. "Boss said you were original."

The guy next to me said, "You've got some balls coming over here like this, give you that."

I said, "Rules of the game. We'll do the tussling somewhere else. I don't want these people getting in trouble after I kill you both. It's a good restaurant and a couple of murders could change its reputation."

The guy across from me laughed and shook his head. "Man, you're something else."

I nodded at him smiling. I picked up my mug of coffee and sipped from it, grinning along to the good humor. I'd confirmed my suspicion. These two weren't there to do the deed. They were more like middle management, there to check up on the product and verify my identity. While we were sitting there chatting, the team was setting up on me elsewhere.

I stood up. "If you need any help writing your last will and testament, I suggest you ask the internet. These days they've got all kinds of templates for free. That's what I've heard. Wouldn't waste time on a lawyer, unless you've got a complicated situation with intellectual property or something of that nature."

The two beards looked at me like strange fish. I returned the mug to the counter, empty now. I paid the bill and left the restaurant.

CHAPTER FIFTY-FOUR

THE SILVER INN was a left turn out the door, then another left diagonal across a stretch of grass between the two parking lots. The wind was so strong and unpredictable that I wasn't concerned about anyone aiming a long gun through a scope. I leaned my head into the tempest and moved forward.

They'd need to come in for me and get up close and personal.

I was looking forward to that.

I stood on the balcony in front of room number ten, looking over the parking lot, the street with the line of parked cars, then left to the main road. Not exactly buzzing with traffic, but active. On the far side of the lot was a paneled van that I hadn't seen before. There were no metallic blue Ford F-150 pickup trucks in sight. Aside from my Crown Victoria there were just three other vehicles parked close to the building. Maybe customers at the restaurant, maybe new guests at the motel. I catalogued the parked cars and shifted them to the back of my mind.

The van was farther away, outside the lot. I couldn't tell if it was occupied. The suspension wasn't sagging, and there was only darkness and the reflected exterior visible in the windshield. I wondered if anyone was waiting for me in the room. I stood for a moment, weighing the pluses and minuses of the situation. It was noisy out. The usual, plus the storm.

I had a plan; it involved architecture and perception, thinking outside of the box.

I put the key in and opened the door. Nobody in there. I removed my sledgehammer from the duffel bag. Ten pounds of steel at the end of an unbreakable shaft. All of that for fifty three bucks and change. The gloves fit nicely. The goggles were high-quality, clear and well ventilated.

The wall itself presented no obstacle. The Silver Inn's owners had not gone for the expensive option, with soundproofing and high-quality materials. They'd gone for the baseline. I rapped my knuckles on a section near the dresser. The studs were twenty-four inches apart. I measured approximately twelve inches in from the stud, nudged gently with the heavy steel and dented a little target in the drywall.

I got in position, legs widely spaced for stability. Everything felt just about right. When I let it rip, ten pounds of steel, multiplied and leveraged by the long handle and my muscular energy, punched through the wall and out the other side. It took five hard blows to outline a good hole. I finished it by kicking in the residual drywall with my new boots. It wasn't a doorway, exactly, but enough of a hole to get through.

I tossed the sledge hammer onto the bed and ducked through into room eleven.

I emerged hunched over in a low crouch. A man was standing over by the bathroom wearing a white terrycloth robe. He looked very frightened. Holding out a fistful of cash, he said, "This is all I've got. Just take it." I almost laughed. The man must have taken the time to hide his wallet while I was breaking through the wall.

I stood up. "When did you check in?" The question obviously confused him. I said, "Not a trick question."

He said, "Maybe two hours ago."

"One second."

I ducked back through the hole and got a grip on the dresser. I was able to drag it toward me and cover the hole, at least from a casual inspection. I stepped back into room eleven. The man was where he'd been before, hands at his sides this time and quivering. I saw a large rectangular phone on the dresser near the bed. I slipped it into my hip pocket.

I brushed drywall dust off my new coveralls. "You'll get the phone back. This is a temporary confiscation." I moved to the window. The man's suitcase was on the floor between the bed and the window. It presented an obstacle. I grunted and pointed to the luggage rack just behind him. "You know they put the luggage rack there on purpose, for your suitcase. Why don't you use it?"

It took him a moment to understand. "You want me to move my suitcase?"

"If you don't mind." I removed one of the Glock 17s from my excellent pair of coveralls. Worked the slide back and let it snick shut all by itself, a round slipped up from the magazine into the chamber.

The man coughed and I looked at his face. The expression projected anxiety and fear. I gestured for him to pass, that the pistol was not his concern. The communication worked, he looked relieved. He may not have had a clue as to what was going on, but he was rolling with it admirably. I moved away to allow access to his suitcase. The television was on, the sound muted. The slim flat screen was showing images of natural devastation. I realized that he'd been watching the news.

Once he'd removed the suitcase, I used my forefinger to shift the curtain just a tad. I was able to see out across the parking lot. The paneled van had not moved. The rear doors were open and I could see two men gathered back there, busy in some way. I couldn't see what they were doing, but I could use my imagination. In it, I saw duffle bags with weapons and ammunition. Maybe gun-cleaning kits and suppressors. I was probably overestimating their ambition, but it's better to plan for the worst and hope for the best. These people were not very subtle.

"What's on the news?" I looked at the man.

"Just the storm." He was looking me up and down, considering what kind of mortal threat I posed. He said, "You aren't here to rob me?"

"For once it's not about you." I examined his face. I couldn't figure out if I'd hit a mark; I'm no psychotherapist. I said, "There's going to be some imminent rumble. There won't be any survivors, except for me and maybe you, provided you do what I say when I say it. Doable?"

He nodded. "I was just about to order Chinese food."

"This won't take long. If you can still eat after it goes down, I recommend The Grill and Banquet, just down and around the corner. Chinese is disappointing nine out of ten times. The idea of it is better than the actual experience."

He sat on the bed. "I didn't know they had a restaurant here. What's the longest you've gone without eating?"

Out the window, three men were walking toward the motel. They looked confident and wore long raincoats. I assumed the coats were intended to hide long-barreled firearms. Good thing I was in that room, where a long gun would be less useful than out in an open-air environment like a parking lot. Unless they'd planned for the close quarters context, in which case shotguns would make more sense.

Shotguns would be messier. There would be more chance of collateral damage. I glanced at the guy, now watching the big flat-screen television. He'd asked me a question about eating. I said, "A couple of weeks I guess, without eating. We had water."

The television was showing a tornado chewing through a neighborhood. A caption insisted that the footage was "illustrative." The man looked up from the news. "That's a long time." His eyes examined me.

I said, "What are you doing here in town?"

He shrugged. "I just got divorced. My wife had a midlife crisis. I decided to take a road trip across the country. West to east. After that, I'll see. Thinking of maybe buying an organic farm in New Hampshire. Figured I'd wait out the storm. Someone said they have good coffee here. I'm from the West Coast; coffee's important to me."

I ignored the suggestion that West Coast people had a monopoly on the appreciation of good things. "Coffee's good here, so's everything else. You're in safe hands, as long as you survive the next couple of minutes."

His face froze for a second and then he laughed loudly. I grinned, liking him. We were getting along just fine. I couldn't see the three men in the parking lot anymore, which meant that they were getting close. I ran it through my head like a real-time movie. They'd be coming up the stairs now. I looked at the guy sitting on the edge of his bed watching TV. He didn't look like any kind of a farmer. I said, "Go lie in the bathtub and meditate or something."

The guy looked alarmed. "Right now? I'm not sure they have a bathtub."

"Whatever they've got, it's going to be better than where you are right now. Shower will do. Get in there and curl into a ball. I'll come and get you when it's done."

The man rose and disappeared into the bathroom. Everything got quiet. I stepped over and stood behind the door. I couldn't see through the curtains, but shadows moved and something paused in front of the window for a moment. I figured it was one of the men trying to see in. They'd be bracing the door to room number ten and getting ready to make an entry. I started up the real-time movie again. Two men, one on either side of the door. One guy bent over picking the lock.

I considered letting them enter room ten and then shooting them through the wall. The construction materials posed no problem. The bullets would move through the drywall as if it was paper. The issue was location and visibility. I wouldn't be able to see them and would have to rely on estimated targets. Definitely a greater than zero chance of missing. I discounted that option.

The building made a very small but perceptible shudder as the entrance to room number ten was breached.

I had another idea.

I crept back to the bathroom. The guy was in the shower stall doing just as I'd asked. He'd hung the bathrobe on the door. Without it, he had what teenagers call a dad bod: Slim shoulders and a rounded waist, like a pale pear. He was dressed in boxers and a tank top. He was looking at me with questions. I just nodded and removed the bathrobe from the hook.

I put the robe on over my coveralls. It might give me a couple of seconds extra. I waited a ten count and opened the door. I stepped out of room eleven. A man I had never seen before stood outside of room ten. He wore a baseball hat and had a beard. I walked toward him, steadily, not too fast, not too slow.

Like magic. Guy walks into one room, comes out of another. Simple, but effective.

It took the man exactly three and a half of my steps to understand that key elements of the situation had changed. The bathrobe got me an important second and a half. By then, I was there and the ugly end of the Glock was pushing into his chest. He wore body armor and a sour expression. It looked as though his day was turning out worse than expected. A short-barreled assault rifle was inside his coat. I shook my head, the rifle was a terrible idea for a confined space. I raised the Glock above the body armor, squeezed the trigger and a single round punched into his jugular notch.

The man fell and began to shudder and shake, making a rattling sound. He wasn't looking capable of a coherent response, so I sidestepped his twitching body to look through the doorway to number ten. Two more men with baseball hats and beards stood in the room, looking angry and disappointed. Whatever it was they'd been hoping for hadn't materialized as they'd planned.

The men in my room had just heard the bell toll for their friend standing guard outside. They had turned to face the danger and were in an advanced state of getting short-barrel assault rifles up and ready. The problem was physical as much as mental. Even a short-barreled assault rifle takes longer to get up and ready than a pistol.

I already had the Glock up. My eye was already aligned with where it was pointing. I wasn't worried about acquiring a target through the sights, I'm an instinctive point shooter. I moved into the room, relentlessly changing the angles on the two men.

I put one round into the guy closer to me. The bullet formed a red flower in his forehead and his eyes rolled up as hot metal rattled around his brain pan like a loose food processor blade. The man collapsed to the bed, bounced off and ended his travels in an ungainly position on the floor. By then I had turned to the next guy. He had his gun up and ready.

I dropped against the bed to my left. The guy's gun was an AR-15 platform with the shortened-barrel options and some extra gear on the top rail. The muzzle flared and a triple burst sang over my head and thwacked into the wall like three hammers hitting in very quick succession. I allowed myself to bounce off the mattress and, at the top of the gravitational arc, shot him once through his right thigh.

The impact tossed him back against the dresser. A moment later I was pushing his gun to the side. The wicked cyclops eye of my Glock nailed him in place.

I said, "Take me to The Bob. I guarantee your life."

The man gulped and I knew what was happening in his mind. A second later the guy had run through the options. He was in a cold sweat but the conclusion was unavoidable. "Can't do that."

"The Bob's that bad?"

He nodded. The guy had pissed himself. I'd seen the farm, which had been bad. Maybe The Bob was even worse than that. None of which made the guy into a victim. He was old enough to know the consequences of his actions and associations.

I said, "Sure about that?"

He shook his head and glanced at me bravely. "I've got family here. Can't take the risk. I don't want to die, but I'm not going to put all my chips on you surviving. The Bob's been around for a long time."

"This isn't your first miscalculation, but it's your last."

I squeezed the trigger. Hot metal spat out of a rifled barrel, along with powder and various other chemicals and gases. A small hole opened in the man's forehead. The round was lead with a copper jacket. It was hard and fast as hell. The exit wound sucked blood, bone, brain, and the remains of the bullet out into the drywall behind him. The result was him gone limp to the floor, and the drywall even more damaged than it had been.

They'd definitely be needing a redecoration crew.

I walked back to the door. The guy who had been outside was no longer in the land of the living. He still looked surprised and shocked at his fate, which was pretty stupid given what he'd set out to do in the first place. I looked out from the balcony. Cars were moving around with headlights on. The wind was even worse than before and the rain came diagonally from several directions at once. It was a mess out there. Nobody walking, nobody looking, nobody paying any attention to happenings other than their own retreat from the storm.

More importantly, there was no sign of the two middle managers I'd seen at the Grill and Banquet.

I grabbed the top of the first dead guy's armored vest and dragged the corpse into the room. I closed the door to room ten. Everything was quieter now. I pushed aside the dresser and entered room eleven. The guy was in the shower stall, still curled up like a large baby. I removed his bathrobe and returned it to the door hook.

He said, "Is it over?"

"Almost. Hold tight. I need the password to your phone."

"Why?"

"To make a call."

"Five zero two three two six."

I went into the bedroom and sat down. The television was cycling through the same scenes of destruction from before. I dialed. The Director, National Security Investigations, HSI Chicago answered after a single ring. "Sobell."

I said, "There's a motel in town called The Silver Inn."

"And?"

"Room ten has issues."

"Issues how?"

"Issues that require a cleaning service. I'm worried that the motel will charge me extra for the damage."

"Room ten."

"Correct."

"So this is how it's going to be, you call me when you need customer service."

I said, "Nobody answers phones these days; it's all about robots and apps. I like the human touch."

She paused, maybe considering the implications. "I take it you don't yet deserve the ice cream sundae."

"No, not yet."

Sobell ended the call.

The guy was in the bathroom, wrapped up in a large white towel, sitting on the toilet. He looked up expectantly. I handed him his phone. He reached for it. I withheld.

"What are we not going to do?"

He said, "I'm not going to call the police."

"Why not?"

He wasn't sure. His voice had questions. "Because you don't want me to?"

I shook my head. "No, because there's an outside chance that the police will kill you."

The man just stared at me.

I said, "And the other thing is the motel. This one's not a good option anymore. People will be coming. You don't want to get on a list. I suggest you move to the Eight Ball. Coffee isn't as good, but sometimes you need to compromise."

"But I already paid for the room here."

I shrugged and handed him back the phone. "Good luck becoming a farmer."

CHAPTER FIFTY-FIVE

I LIBERATED the dead of their burdens.

Specifically, their weapons and ammunition. I only took one of the rifles, but I threw all of the magazines I could find into the duffle bag with the sledgehammer and my other accessories. The loads were sixty grain V-max in .223 with the polymer tip. Good and responsible choices for urban warfare, since the rounds would frag against walls. Each of the dead men had carried their weapon and the loaded standard magazine plus an extra. All in, I was a well-armed predator with one hundred and eighty rounds, give or take the shots already fired and those already chambered.

By the time I had everything packed into the Crown Victoria, the roads were less populated and the storm was closer. The stuff being picked up and flung around by the wind was heavier and larger. Driving south, I noticed a red trench coat maintaining a holding pattern fifty feet above a franchise restaurant sign.

I've been to the state of Ohio a number of times. It's a diverse and varied place, and not one that you could fit into an area thirty-six blocks square. There was a sign indicating the neighborhood, Little Ohio. Six blocks later another sign, *Thank You For Visiting Little*

Ohio. I took a left and then another left, doubling back and driving through the neighborhood one more time. Little Ohio was a light industrial zone of low-slung single-story warehouses, old multistory brick buildings and newer concrete structures that were more stained and weather damaged than the century-old brick.

I crossed a main road, took a left and another left onto First Avenue, a main drag I imagined was normally bristling with commerce. Now it was subdued and darkened. A minute later I saw the car wash. The sign didn't say Gresham's Drive-Through Hand Wash, it just read *Hand Wash.* The intersection was First Avenue and Gresham Street. I put it together and figured this was it, the place I'd come to see. The facility was closed, windows boarded up with plywood. Looked like the proprietors of Gresham's Drive-Through Hand Wash were pragmatic types who acted quickly on an approaching threat horizon.

Not that the absence of car washing activity presented a problem. My assumption was that Gresham's Drive-Through Hand Wash would be the central point of an axis, around which The Bob's people frequently orbited. My theory was that I'd find The Bob's local headquarters near there. The car wash building was two stories tall and had a flat roof. That would make a decent observation post for an initial reconnaissance.

I bumped the Crown Vic into the parking lot. The driver's side window wiper needed a new blade, the current one left a blurry streak. I nudged the gas and nosed the vehicle into a good spot between a dumpster and the whitewashed side wall. The fire escape on the back side looked underused and rusted. I made it up to the second story without incident but had to take my chances getting any higher. I ended up scaling a wet and slippery vertical pipe. The gloves and boots gripped nicely.

Up on the roof I had an excellent view of the area, including the storm front. It had looked distant previously. Now, it was a black and boiling wall of weather, maybe a half mile away. The wind was moving in all kinds of directions so it was tough to anticipate where that storm was headed.

I conducted a cursory examination of the surrounding buildings and routes in and out. The car wash was smack dab in the middle of Little Ohio. Looking out over the rooftops, I had three blocks to worry about in each direction. I spent some time turning clockwise in a slow three sixty, looking over the rooftops and wondering what it was I needed to be paying attention to. Little Ohio was a scruffy neighborhood pretty much shut down by the impending storm. The rain remained light, swirling in and around on gusting winds.

I was thinking of coming down and doing a slow cruise through the zone, when I remembered the cameras.

The Bob was a heavy user of security cameras and remote imaging technologies. Like Ricardo at J&S had said, The Bob would need some kind of place where all of those cameras could feed into. I did another slow spin counterclockwise, vaguely remembering something that the back of my mind had noticed. As soon as I hit the eleven o'clock mark, that something slotted right into the front of my mind.

It was a building two blocks to the north, a two-story concrete building with a roof full of cell phone equipment, something of an unremarkable sight these days.

The roof surface was crowded with gear. Vertical rectangular masts formed the perimeter. Deeper in was a welter of support structures with white discs and even more vertical rectangles clamped onto the scaffolding. I got out the spotting scope and looked closer. Thick cables in white housing coiled out in multiples from weatherproof junction boxes, snaking into weather-sealed perforations in the roof structure. There would be an attic below housing even more gear.

I wasn't able to see much more than the roof and the top of a line of windows. The building deserved a closer look. I came down from my observation post on Gresham's Drive-Through Hand Wash and returned to the Crown Victoria.

The streets were now almost deserted and darkness was descending. I kept the lights off and cruised slow. I got two blocks over and found a dead end between two low warehouse buildings. It was a decently concealed location to use as base. I opened my trunk and got to work duct taping magazines into pairs. I had no idea what I'd be facing, so it was better to be over prepared.

Each pair of magazines was ready for quick reload. I had three pairs. One set went into the rifle, the other two got left in the trunk.

I climbed an access ladder to the roof of the warehouse closest to my target. Up there I found a flat asphalt landscape split up by boxy air-conditioning installations and two stairwell access points. The roof edging was around three feet high with widely distributed runoff ducts that dipped below the edging. I set up next to one of the ducts and was able to get a very good view of the building across the street.

I assumed a prone position. The rifle was positioned next to me, the spotting scope strap looped around my neck. The building wasn't huge. There were six windows on each floor. The front was a blank, with the entrance taking up one of the corners. It was a stepped entrance with pillars on either side, all of it stone and designed to impress. The entrance side of the building was separated from its neighbor by a narrow alley. The other side was connected to a larger two-story building in brick.

I put up the spotting scope.

The roof was a complicated situation that I had few qualifications to decipher. As far as I could tell there were at least five different telecommunications standards going on, with maybe ten different companies renting space up there. I was willing to assume that a building like that wasn't going to be residential. That was mostly because I assumed that people wouldn't want to live with all of that electromagnetic activity buzzing around over their heads.

I scanned the windows. Nothing going on there because each window was covered by an institutional gray roller blind. The corners were interesting. Solid-looking security cameras mounted in groups of two. Each one facing a different way. The cameras were gray, blending in with the concrete structure. Cables looped from the back of each device into the concrete facing. The entrance had an additional situation. From my angle, I could see into the other side of the recessed stone vestibule. A round black camera was installed in position to observe those entering. The lens was larger and the circular exterior pulsed with a subdued red glow.

My peripheral vision registered movement. I took the scope away from my eye. A vehicle was coming down from the northeast. It was an older Volvo model, in some kind of pale color. I'd seen the car before of course, on Sherisse's junkyard lot: Gus Simmons's old car, which he'd given up for the champagne-colored Audi I'd seen him driving.

The Volvo crept slowly, no headlights. I watched the car get closer and come to a halt a block away. I put the scope up and found the range. The driver was sitting motionless. It was all shadow in there and I could see only indentations of two eyes in a dark oval. A car came the other way, headlights on.

The light slashed across for half a second, enough time for me to recognize Linda Cartwright's expressionless face.

CHAPTER FIFTY-SIX

I WATCHED Cartwright through the scope.

The headlights passed and it was dark again. I didn't know what her plan was, or if she had one. I knew that a standard assault on The Bob's place was a suicide mission. He had too much security invested into the doorways and passages. She'd be killed fast.

I could either sit around waiting for her to reveal a plan, or I could preempt it and start up a useful collaboration.

I picked up the rifle and put one in the chamber. I sighted on the side view mirror, passenger side. I pulled and the rifle popped. The round pinged into the appendage, shattering the plastic and fragging off into the street. Nothing happened, Cartwright hadn't even noticed. The howling wind was too loud, or else she was listening to music in the car, or the radio.

Whatever.

The next round went into the windshield, snapping through the shatterproof glass and puffing into the passenger seat behind. That seemed to get her attention.

The effect was near instantaneous. Cartwright jammed the vehicle into reverse and backed it fifty yards up the road in a manic swerving line. She made a hard turn into the cover of an alley. I came down off the roof and got the Crown Victoria in gear. This time I let the headlights do their work and cruised at a normal speed, like a normal person.

When I had arrived at the alley I slowed. The passage was narrow with just enough space for parked vehicles on one side. Cartwright's sedan was stopped in front of a closed rollup garage door. I nosed in and flashed her once with my high beams. I cut the engine.

We looked at each other through the glass. Mine clear except for that windshield wiper smear, hers damaged. I opened the door and kept my hands where she could see them. I walked over and looked in through the driver's side window. Cartwright wasn't happy, far from it. She looked to be in a state of glowering anger and betrayal. I noticed that she hadn't shot at me yet, so I figured I was safe from her homicidal rage.

I came around to the passenger side and got in. The seat was too far forward. I racked it back and looked at her. Cartwright was dressed in tactical black, like a ninja soldier. Her short cropped hair was speckled with gray. In her lap was a sandwich wrapped in foil. I stared at her, she stared back.

I said, "What are you doing, Cartwright?"

"I was fixing to eat dinner before you so rudely interrupted me."

I pointed through the window at what I was pretty sure was The Bob's building. "Nothing to do with that building over there?"

She shook her head. "No. What's there?"

I laughed. Cartwright picked up her sandwich and took a bite. I examined the contents. Looked like a meatball wedge. I said, "How'd you figure that for the enemy's location?"

She chewed quietly and swallowed. "I nosed around a little. Figured it out eventually. That asshole isn't subtle. And there are many people who'd be happy to see him in the ground."

"Not many brave enough to help put him there."

"No."

I said, "I recognize the car. Far as I know it's got a bad oil leak. What happened, you went over the tracks to Sherisse's junkyard after they tried to grab you?"

Cartwright looked at me, tore off a bite of her sandwich and spoke through it. "Car isn't registered anymore. Can just ditch it no questions asked. I already knew Sherisse; we're neighbors. Better to get to know the local thieves." She finished the bite and spoke more clearly. "How did you know I was going to be here, Keeler?"

I shrugged. "Short answer is, I didn't." Cartwright looked at me uncomprehending. I said, "You invited me to stay at your place, remember? Key's under the flowerpot."

She looked at me a moment in the same way, but the light came to her face eventually. "Oh."

I nodded. "I woke up on your sofa and you weren't there. I saw the hammer and blood. I got worried about you. So I started looking. Short version is that I ended up right back at your place. Figured out there was a storm shelter, found your husband, Fayaz, in there with his daughter, Emma. Looked like you had a one-sided marital dispute."

Cartwright said nothing.

I said, "Is your husband into The Bob for just the loan sharking or is there something else going on?"

"Something else like what?"

"Like sourcing heroin for him from back home in Afghanistan."

Cartwright looked away, through the windshield into the stormy dark. "No, luckily not." She glanced at me. "So you found out about him. Afghanistan and all that."

"The Homeland Security people told me."

Cartwright looked at me sharply. "Oh, they came?"

She seemed suspiciously unsurprised that I'd mentioned Homeland Security, but somewhat surprised that they'd actually made an appearance.

I said, "You're the one who got them involved? Good move. I like your game. It didn't work out so well, but the idea was smart and you managed to get attention."

Cartwright glared at me and looked away again. "Weak sisters. What happened with them?"

I said, "My guess is that you sent some kind of tip-off about Afghan nationals because you figured that'd be enough to get their panties in a twist. At least that worked out."

Cartwright grunted. "But."

"But a couple of things. You should know that they approved of your project, getting interpreters out by way of naturalization. You put yourself on the line doing the right thing where the political people and the command failed."

"Spineless assholes. Tell me something I don't know."

"What you don't know is that two Homeland Security agents got killed trying to figure out the issue with The Bob, you, and your husband. Maybe you didn't give them enough clues."

Cartwright withdrew into herself. "I'm sorry to hear that. I was hoping they'd come heavy. I guess that was a wish too far." She looked at me. "You served over there?"

I nodded. "Air Force Pararescue. Embedded with a bunch of teams out of KAF. A little after your time."

She finished the last of her sandwich. "Figured something like that, given how you . . ." she found the words. "How you carry yourself." Cartwright was staring off into the night. "Given the Afghan thing, I thought there was a chance Homeland Security would come figure out what was going on with The Bob and put him down. That evil man is out of control."

"I think the local police caused problems with your plan. The Homeland Security team was small. They didn't come heavy and couldn't hack it. Their command didn't have patience or belief, so once the first team was taken out, HSI command moved on."

Cartwright shook her head. "Wishful thinking." She looked at me. "Should have known better after all those years of service right?"

"Don't blame yourself. Those guys died in the line of duty. Now we're following up. We're here to make sure they didn't die for nothing, Cartwright. The cause is righteous, but I need to know the full deal with your husband, Fayaz."

"Deal is that I never met someone like that before. Fayaz blew me away, Keeler. He wasn't helping us out for the money. The man was a true believer. He was educated. He bought into freedom, liberty, and equality before the law." Cartwright shifted her body language, turning to me, engaging me. "Deal is that we just left them there. We betrayed people who thought they'd been on the same team as us. Fayaz was married when I got with him over there. We were in love, but he still loved his family. Him and his wife were together because their families matched them up. It isn't like over here, where you meet at a party or a bar. Doesn't mean they don't love their own like we love ours. He loved them exactly the same. His entire family was murdered because of what he did helping us out. Wife and four kids, parents, grandparents, and any other relatives those scumbags could find."

"Where did that happen?"

"Fayaz's family was from Kabul, hers from up north in Mazar-i-Sharif. The Taliban tried to do it all in one night, a coordinated strike on the families of interpreters and other allies. Fayaz was up in K2 at the time, Uzbekistan. I wasn't around anymore. Not that I could have helped out. The state department didn't give a shit, wouldn't expedite anything, or help in any way. Fayaz and a couple of other guys who'd worked with us had to go into hiding for like, *two years.*" Cartwright glared at me, still angry about it. "He was in touch with me over the internet. I got him out eventually. I guess you know that we got married and Fayaz became William."

"Yeah."

"You know how it is for a lot of our people who come back. Guys who've been in combat or whatever."

"We all have issues, some get it bad, some get it worse."

"I call him Bill now, not Fayaz. His choice. *Issues* doesn't begin to describe it. Bill grew up over there, in Kabul. Lived his life, you know? But losing the family changed him. He wasn't the same once he got stateside. Shows up in suburban Indiana after everything that happened to him. It's no exaggeration to say that he completely lost his mind."

"Specifically?"

"Specifically, Bill wasn't a good husband. He was damaged goods. Over here he became a loser, a liar, a philanderer, a gambler, and maybe even a thief. That woman who tried to take me out wasn't the first one he got with."

"Donna Williams. You knew about her before it all went down?"

Cartwright shook her head, grim. "I knew she existed. Didn't know her name." She engaged me with her eyes. "You were over there, you know. What would you do, Keeler? A man does things in the prime of his life. Actions that are brave and exceptional. Risks his life on multiple occasions. He's a hero for a time. But then he loses himself and he isn't a hero anymore. He doesn't act like a hero, he acts like an idiot. What do we do, toss him away?"

"No. He gets to always be that hero. No matter what."

"Right. We tolerate him and we do damage control. He's one of ours."

"Correct. He's one of ours."

She said nothing. I knew that she was split. The topic was confusing. How do you reconcile two facets of the same person?

I said, "I don't see any moral confusion on the issue. People aren't one thing or the other, they're complicated and multiple. Your husband may be an idiot now, and all of the other things you said. But he's a hero at the same time. He didn't stop being a hero just because he lost his way."

For once, Cartwright had nothing to say in return.

I said, "Donna Williams is dead. The Bob had her killed. He would have done the same to you if you hadn't escaped."

Cartwright looked away and cursed. "You know what Bill did?" She didn't wait for a response. "He put up my house as collateral with The Bob." She shook her head slowly. "Like that was ever going to be okay with me. Like I was going to allow it."

I said, "They underestimated you."

"Damned right they did."

I gestured to the car we were sitting inside. "What's the deal with this? I recognize the car."

Cartwright scowled. "When I came out of the shelter I went back the same way you did, across the tracks. Sherisse let me stay there, gave me the car."

"So what's next?"

Cartwright looked at me, a wary and shrewd but committed look. "Next is do or die, buddy."

I deadpanned. "Yeah, I mean after that. What's the end game with your husband and the girl?"

"Oh." Cartwright looked surprised. "You mean, now that Donna Williams is dead. Girl's got no mother."

I said nothing.

"Hadn't thought about that." Cartwright's head tilted back and forth, as if she was weighing competing ideas against each other, then checking the winning idea against another standard. Finally she looked at me with clarity in her eyes. "I guess I'll take the girl and we'll live like that. Give her a life like she deserves. That kid didn't do anything wrong; she's an innocent." She considered something else again. "Not sure she should stay at Booker T. Washington though, I know some people there. Not the best school." She gazed at me. "We'll see after this. But there's one thing I do know for sure."

"What's that?"

"Her dad can't do it alone."

"Good. Now that the family planning is out of the way, let's talk about this. You're fixing on going straight through, I guess. Linda Cartwright's way of the hammer."

"Correct."

"Wrong."

Cartwright shook her head and rolled her eyes, like the entire world was filled with incompetent morons. "Okay, mister special soldier. What's your idea?"

I pointed out the windshield, past my car, to the two-story brick building that adjoined the target. The words *National Building* were engraved above an ornate double doorway. To the right of that was a neon pink sign that read *Mind and Body Meditation.*

I said, "We go in there like normal people, like we're going to meditate." I waved my hand to the right. "Once we're at the far side of it, at the wall meeting the target, we start thinking differently."

"How so?"

"Consider the enemy. The Bob is hunkered down in there somewhere. He's thinking of his own safety and security. He sees doors and windows and alleys that need securing."

"I'm not following you, Keeler. You're making no sense."

"He's thinking like an architect. Doorways, windows, alleys, streets, those are all passages and entry points." I shook my head. "Not for us, they aren't. We're going to think differently. The last thing we're going to do is walk through a doorway, down an alley, or climb through a window."

Cartwright snorted in derision. "So what do we do?"

"We walk through walls."

CHAPTER FIFTY-SEVEN

I OPENED the trunk of the Crown Victoria. The duffle bag unzipped, revealing its bounty. The two extra duct-taped magazine bundles slotted into back pockets. The knife clipped into place in a slim thigh pocket of my coveralls. The splitting wedge fit into another neat pocket slit at the other side. I was good to go. The last element was the roll of duct tape itself. I cut off a length and twisted it so that it became a rope. I threaded that through a belt loop and tied the roll of duct tape to the coveralls.

Cartwright had a standard Mossberg 500 that she carried with two hands. A pistol was out front in a chest holster. I stepped back to examine her. She was ready to rock in tactical black with all the trimmings.

I said, "Where'd you get the outfit?"

Cartwright was tightening the rip-stop webbing. "Found a tactical gear store on East Eighty-Sixth up in the city."

We stood at the corner of the alley and the street, looking at the building in question. By now there was nothing moving except the wind howling in the urban canyon. All manner of debris was coming down and over. I put the goggles on. Cartwright squinted.

Cartwright had to yell to be heard above the wind. "So?"

I was looking at the big picture window. It was dark in there now, and nobody had thought to cover it with plywood. Maybe a case of an absentee landlord, or one with a good insurance policy.

I crossed the alley and pushed the sledgehammer into the window. The plate glass tinkled, almost silent in the overwhelming cacophony of the storm. A couple more gentle taps cleared any hanging pieces of glass and we were in.

~

NOBODY WAS MEDITATING. There was no yoga going on and the Pilates machines were silent as skeletons before a dance. I had a hard time imagining what the National Building had been before the meditators moved in. Half of the space was a large exercise studio with glossy wood floors. A wall of wire rack shelving hosted long pillows and yoga mats stacked by the dozen.

I was interested in the far wall. The sledgehammer in my hand was heavy and hungry and needed to be fed.

Cartwright was waiting for me to explain my plan. Truth was, it was more of a tactical feeling than a full on plan. I was thinking about breaking through the wall. Once I got to the other side, I'd see. Over in northern Syria the urban conflict had been intense. Any kind of movement was the equivalent of suicide. Every door was booby-trapped, every window had a sniper buried a couple of rooms back. The alleys and streets were under observation from feral children put up on the rooftops by rough men.

It was the stage in a war where anyone still alive and operational was a seriously dangerous person, man, woman, and child. But there were rules and we weren't allowed to shoot the kids. Which meant that we couldn't walk through the streets or the alleys, or enter doorways, and going through a window was an invitation to get dead.

We'd had an Israeli guy with us for the ride. He'd been sent up from Tel-Aviv to get some schooling in American special tactics.

We'd had plenty to teach him and he'd been a good student. But up there one day in Idlib he'd been the man with the plan. The team was in a situation. We were tactically stuck. We needed to get into a specific apartment in a specific building but there was no non-suicidal way of getting there.

The Israeli guy had a little coffee kit with him. We were gathered around it, drinking coffee from small cups. I was in command and I hadn't asked his opinion, so he hadn't offered it. He was a visitor, not exactly a team member. I noticed him dragging on his cigarette with a weird look on his face.

I'd said, "What?"

He said, "What, what?"

I said, "What're you thinking?"

He shrugged and stubbed out the cigarette. "I'm thinking that you're thinking like they want you to think. Maybe you should consider thinking differently."

He looked up at me with big and round blue eyes. That day, I learned the way of the sledgehammer.

Now, I was looking at the wall and thinking about materials and tensile strength, and all kinds of things that I was unqualified to evaluate. The wall looked like it was regular drywall. Which meant cardboard and chalk and maybe some other stuff. Inside would be insulation and wiring and pipes and more stuff. I expected to find something on the other side, like brick, or cement.

I selected a spot, waist high on the wall to the left of a motivational poster of a young and limber athlete next to the words *Just Do It*.

I set down the AR-15 and got busy busting a large hole in the drywall. In a couple of minutes I'd ripped through it and made an opening roughly the size of a door. There was insulation material. I ripped that out. There were no pipes and I soon arrived at a flat gray concrete slab. I figured, poured concrete wall.

I said, "You have your hammer?"

Cartwright said, "Never go anywhere without it."

She produced a hammer with a rubberized grip from a Velcro pocket at the small of her back. I removed the steel splitting wedge. Cartwright stepped back and I put the goggles on. I positioned the thin end of the wedge, what the lady at the store had called a feather. It took three good thwacks to get it stuck into the concrete. I returned Cartwright's hammer and took up the sledgehammer. I needed to hit it straight on or else the wedge would just come out.

I assumed the position.

Cartwright got into a stance and aimed her shotgun at the spot.

I said, "Do or die."

She said, "No doubt."

"This thing's supposed to have an unbreakable handle. What are the odds?"

"I don't care. Just do it."

I laughed. My first hit drove the wedge in an extra inch. Now, it was firmly engaged. The third hit cracked the concrete wall right down the middle. The steel wedge pushed into it about five inches, the damage was done. The next hit propelled the wedge all the way through. I swung three more times in quick succession, using the best sledgehammer technique I could get under the circumstances. A couple of minutes into the operation we had a good hole into a dark cavity on the other side. It wasn't exactly a doorway, but it was big enough to climb through one at a time.

Cartwright's phone doubled as a flashlight. We were inside of a narrow cavity. I retrieved the wedge. The wall in front of us was concrete, but it wasn't the same as what I'd just come through. The color was darker and the texture smoother. It looked a hell of a lot more solid. Cartwright swung her light up and over.

There was nothing above, and nothing to the left or the right.

We were in an empty space, like some kind of a clean zone. I realized that's exactly what this was, a box within a box. The Bob's architectural style. I was listening, but there was nothing to hear. I estimated that we were far from the external walls. I moved right.

Cartwright followed with her light. She spoke quietly to my back. "Where are you going?"

I whispered. "Somewhere noisier."

A minute later we got to a part of the building that was closer to the outdoors. I put my ear to the wall. I looked at Cartwright. "Hear that?"

She listened. "Storm is going wild out there."

I listened for half a minute. There was a banging sound, monotonous and regular. A cable had come loose from the outside of the building. I figured that was suitable cover. I got on my belly and put an ear to the floor. I motioned to Cartwright. "Hammer."

The hammer came into my hand and I knocked carefully on the concrete floor. There was nothing back but the dull sound of steel on an absolutely solid foundation. I stood up and put my ear to the wall facing us. I tapped with the hammer. It was a solid sound, but this time there was reverberation from some kind of cavity on the other side.

I positioned the wedge against the wall. Hammered it lightly until it was well fixed. I handed the hammer back to Cartwright and assumed the stance once more. She gave me space and kept the light on the wedge. The sledgehammer whipped through the air on its unbreakable handle. The extra flexibility of that shaft added a multiplied force which equaled extra power. The first strike buried the wedge almost totally. The second hit made a hole. Two more hits and we were through.

I put Cartwright's light into the hole. Another cavity. We came through and looked around. There was a tubular shaft, the width of a very big person, running horizontally along the wall above head height. The space rose about fifteen feet up. I pointed at the thick tube and spoke quietly. "Maybe network cables?"

Cartwright shook her head. "Utility shaft."

I said nothing.

She said, "Cables plus ventilation and maybe other stuff, would be my guess, anyway." Cartwright pointed at the large shaft. "Too big to be only network cables. They put whatever they needed inside a single conduit for everything, instead of multiple units."

I moved to the left. We came to a steel railing twenty feet in. Half of the cable ducts elbowed vertically into a hole cut in the floor. A skeletal ladder was fixed into the curved concrete edge. I went down first and Cartwright shone the light for me. The ladder ended in a narrow vestibule with a door. The fat shaft fed into the floor.

There wasn't enough room for both of us down there. The duct took up most of the access. Cartwright had to wait a couple of rungs up the ladder, holding the light. The door was locked from the other side. I used the Gerber knife to jimmy the latch. I gestured for her to switch off the light. There were no sounds coming from the other side of the door. I pushed until I saw a half-inch crack open.

I put my eye to the crack in the door. A light breeze came through. I was looking at a white painted concrete wall with a horizontal red line. I positioned myself so that I could see to the right. The wall ended and beyond it was an underground parking bay. The floor was polished concrete painted in sky blue. Light came from overhead fluorescents. I moved again to see left. The only thing visible was more wall. There were no human beings that I could see, hear, or smell.

I moved through the access door fast, gun up and ready for a living and breathing enemy. Cartwright followed. To my left was a long corridor with that white wall and the red line going off to the far end where I could make out a stairwell on one side and a door on the other. The stairwell went both up and down. The door was painted red.

The garage had three vehicles. One Ford F-150 in metallic blue and two identical black SUVs in matte black. On the other side of the cars was a ramp. I was suspecting that the inner core of The Bob's little army had come together here to wait out the storm.

I was also thinking about the box within the box. A parking garage and ramp implied an exit of some kind. How would they get their vehicles down there without compromising security? Some kind of secure access, like an elevator or multiple chambers with separate key codes.

I'd be finding out, one way or another. Murmurs and soft laughter came from the direction of the stairwell.

It wasn't possible to know if the human sounds were coming from above, or from below. Cartwright and I were stock still, listening hard. The distant sounds came reverberating along the hard corridor walls, floor, and ceiling. A man thought something was funny. A second man said something that I didn't hear well enough to understand.

I made sure the rifle was ready to go.

Cartwright's eyes were almost popping out of her head and she was sweating. Slick face, large dark circles around her eyes. I chin pointed at the Mossberg. She had no idea what I was trying to say. I considered the situation. Cartwright had been a unit supply specialist with the 10th, which meant a lot of things that were good and respectable. But, none of it meant that she could perform adequately in a high-intensity combat situation.

I pushed her out into the parking garage and gently backed her against the wall with a palm on the shoulder. She closed her eyes and breathed in and out for around a minute. She opened her eyes again and looked at me with a gaze that said she was done freaking out. I touched the Mossberg and gave her a questioning look. Cartwright checked the breech and gave me an affirmative nod.

She was good to go.

CHAPTER FIFTY-EIGHT

We moved out. I took the lead, creeping along the wall toward the stairwell and the sound of voices. I had the AR-15 assault rifle up and ready. Cartwright held the shotgun at port arms, something she'd learned in basic training. Good enough for rock and roll. We moved slow. Each step had to be very carefully placed because the concrete floor, ceiling, and walls reverberated and amplified the slightest sound.

We might have been only one floor under the ground but it was silent in there. I could hear the radiator ticking from one of the vehicles in the garage. I heard a faint scraping sound and stopped. We were halfway down the corridor toward the stairs. The sound was faint but regular and getting closer. Cartwright was concentrated and alert. No more sweat, no more dark circles. She was looking positive.

The sound again. Not a scrape, something else.

I identified the shuffling of feet. Somebody was coming up the stairs, sliding one foot into each step, slowly, one after the other. I relaxed and got into a more comfortable position. About a half minute later a man emerged onto the landing and stopped still. He was looking at a phone in his hand. I figured that's why he'd come up so slow. It was one of the guys from the Grill and Banquet. The one I'd called Ed from Ohio. In profile, his beard jutted out at an even sharper geometrical angle than before. He was laughing quietly to himself, reading something on the screen. His plaid shirt was untucked and the free hand idly scratched.

My selector switch was set to single. I had a bead on him, ready for the head shot. The guy thumbed something into his phone, stepped off and shouldered through the red door. He disappeared and the door swung closed on its spring. I looked back at Cartwright. She'd started sweating again.

I moved forward toward the stairwell. There was no telling how many of them were down there. The red door across the way had no sign on it. I wasn't sure what I was going to find in there. But this was an opportunity to take an enemy out while he was separated from the others. Ed from Ohio wasn't going to be permitted back down the stairs.

I glanced at Cartwright and held up a finger, as if to say, just a minute. I couldn't hear anything through the door. A slight wind blew through the corridors, maybe from the parking garage. It was like listening to the inside of a sea shell. There was no indication that outside, a bad storm was tearing the town apart.

I toed the red door open an inch and looked in. A white painted room starkly lit by overhead fluorescents. I slipped inside. The wall to my left was a makeshift kitchen. Folding tables with items for the preparation of food. A camping stove with a couple of unused pans. There was an open bag of sliced white bread and a cutting board with the remains of a sliced tomato and a knife. Tucked below the table was a small refrigerator. On the far side of the room was a white painted door, slightly ajar. Since the bearded man wasn't in the same room as me, I figured he'd passed into the next one.

I set down the assault rifle against the wall. My right hand slipped the knife from the painter's pocket on my leg. I thumbed the blade open and passed it to the left hand. I drew the Glock with the right. Knife in the left, Glock in the right. Like plan A and plan B.

The white door was cracked, showing three inches of nothing. I crept forward. Halfway across the room, I registered movement through the three-inch crack. The door kicked open with a thwap and the guy was standing there staring at me. He was surprised and vulnerable. It looked as if his good mood was draining out of him fast. He had his hands busy buckling a belt, which is why he'd opened the door with his boot. Behind him was a white ceramic toilet that he hadn't flushed.

The tightly trimmed beard began a quarter inch above his Adam's apple. Below that I could see the pale flesh of his throat coloring, like a blush. The man's options were slim. Go for his weapon and call out to his buddies or do something related to asking for mercy. He wasn't dumb enough to think he'd get mercy.

I pointed the Glock down and put my finger to my lips. I didn't plan on allowing him to survive, but I did want him to avoid making a ruckus. I thought I could gain a second or two.

His right hand left the buckle and slipped behind his waist. It was a move that said he'd be going for a gun tucked behind him. I went on instinct and leapt forward. I wanted to use the knife because any kind of pistol shot was going to be way too loud. I'd hoped to preempt his pistol hand being drawn. But I hadn't figured on him having a tricky belt buckle. The move behind his back had been a ruse. There was no handgun. The guy's left hand drew a blade out of the belt sheath. It was a short and mean stabbing knife in matte black. The belt buckle served as a grip, blade protruding between big knuckles.

The guy stepped into my path. I was over committed in my movement. I saw his face light up with excitement, he was counting on winning the engagement. The knife hand punched in at me and the blade tore into my chest on the left side. It was aimed correctly, a strike that intended to push the knife between my upper left ribs and directly penetrate the heart.

The contact came and I had to be a useless observer while the knife cut into my new outfit. There, the point was blunted on the steel barrel of that second Glock 17 I'd slipped into the diagonal zip pocket at my chest.

The man grunted in disappointment. The little grin on his face turned south. Once lucky, I wasn't going to waste the opportunity. I sank the Gerber's blade into his Adam's apple, pushing deep until my fist around the handle was pressing into hot blood. The bearded man reeled back. He kept his footing for a couple of staggered steps but couldn't maintain. When he fell, the back of his head hit the toilet's rectangular cistern. There was a loud crack as the ceramic lid broke in half. The whole upper section crashed to the concrete floor around the man's thrashing body.

Messy and about ten times noisier than a 9mm pistol shot. Definitely not what I had wanted.

I cut the man's neck bleeder to make sure that he wasn't going to get undead. I put my knee on his chest until the thrashing had gone out of him. The man's eyes were open and brown, staring into the wall behind the broken toilet. Ed from Ohio was dead.

I hoped that his friends wouldn't react to the sound of a broken ceramic toilet cistern lid. Maybe they'd think Ed had just been careless.

CHAPTER FIFTY-NINE

I CAME BACK to the red door, walking on eggshells. The sound of the bearded man's head crashing through the ceramic toilet cistern had been enormous. But had it been contained?

I picked up my rifle and pulled the red door open. On the other side of the corridor, Cartwright was backed against the wall, looking tense. The Mossberg was gripped tight in both hands. Sweat gleamed in a film over her face. She saw me coming, and darted her eyes to her left, my right, and the direction of the stairs.

I stopped and listened to what she was already hearing. There was a guy down there. I could hear breathing and the shifting movement of indecision. Then he voiced his concern. "Tommy."

Ed from Ohio's name was Tommy.

I took a single step across the corridor to get alongside Cartwright. In case the concerned man came up the stairs looking for his friend. Another man's voice came from a little farther behind the first. "Leave him alone. He's making a sandwich."

The concerned man didn't move. I could feel and hear him down there. He was suspicious, thinking, worried, debating with himself.

He spoke quietly, probably to the second man and himself. "I'm closing the door anyway. Tommy can use the code."

There were three tentative and defensive footsteps, like someone retreating backward. Then we heard the sound of a soft object against something hard, like felt against concrete, followed by the heavy snick and thud of a large door closing with a high-end security mechanism locking into place.

How long would they wait for Tommy to make himself a sandwich, three minutes? I spun out and looked over the banister. Nothing down there but a landing and floor space. I whispered to Cartwright. "Wait."

She didn't respond. I moved like a cat. AR-15 up and traveling along with my sight lines. I came down the stairs and verified. The landing was a mezzanine with a chrome banister. The stairs resolved to the left, but straight ahead was a double-wide steel door, presently closed. Above the door was a camera aimed in a diagonal to capture the image of any person that might come through it. I was high enough not to be in the frame.

I backed off and returned. There wasn't going to be a way of breaking through that steel door.

What I did remember was the initial penetration of The Bob's lair. We'd come in through the external skin of it, like a virus worming itself through the epidermis. I remembered what Cartwright had said, the large tube wasn't a network cable conduit; it was a utility shaft. Which must mean a multipurpose way of getting stuff from out in the world into the secure zone. There is no such thing as a hermetic seal.

I pulled Cartwright along the corridor with me.

We got back behind the first door, with the utility shaft running into the floor.

I pointed Cartwright up on to the ladder again. Whispered, "Hammer."

The hammer entered my hand. I snicked open the Gerber knife. The blade was bloody, so I wiped it on my thigh without thinking.

The shaft was made of some kind of heavy duty, but flexible plastic. I positioned the knife point and pushed it in. A couple of taps from the hammer and the blade was through. It wasn't exactly easy to cut my way into the shaft, but it wasn't impossible either. A minute later I had cut a rough hole. Small and tight, but big enough to squeeze into.

Cartwright looked at me as if I was insane. I wondered if she was claustrophobic, but I wasn't going to wait to find out. She was breathing heavily and sweating even more. I leveled a look at her and spoke softly. "I'm not going to reassure you. This might end badly for both of us, or just one of us. But this is the best option for ending it for them too."

Do or die.

The hammer fit into a cargo pocket on my left leg, secured with a Velcro flap. The coveralls had been an excellent purchase. The rifle wasn't going to make it in that confined area. I tucked it against the wall behind the shaft. Cartwright did the same with her Mossberg. She shook her head, as if this kind of collective suicide wasn't really to her taste. I grinned at her. She suppressed a smile. We weren't that different, when you got down to the heart of it.

I squeezed in through the rough hole. The shaft was vertical at that point, so the only way to do it was to push in opposite directions with my back and my legs, squeezing myself in there. I descended, releasing pressure from my feet and back, applying pressure again. I guess if I hadn't been inside of that tube, the move might have looked like modern dance.

Cartwright was examining the technique. I gave her a thumbs up. She was slim and wiry and came through faster than I had. The 9mm Smith & Wesson was holstered in front of her chest, a great place to carry in this kind of an acrobatic situation. The two Glocks were zipped into the diagonal pockets of my coveralls. The knife back in its little leg sheath, probably designed for a detailing brush.

We moved down. It was completely dark in there. The imperative was speed and stealth, which was going to be hard. We had one thing going for us, air flow. Cartwright had been correct when she'd estimated that this multipurpose utility shaft would be used for both cable and air flow. One side of the tube was thick with cable conduit, fixed together like a coiled snake. The rest of it was empty.

About ten feet down I came to an elbow joint. Vertical transitioned to horizontal. I had been moving feet first, now I needed to get into a plank position head first. The only way to do that was to spin around inside the vertical tube, maintaining pressure and tension on each side until I was able to lower myself to rest on the bottom.

It wasn't easy, or comfortable, and the air in there wasn't enough to stop me from breaking into a sweat.

The weird back and leg pushing resolved into a crawl. The cable snaked above and scuttled out of Cartwright's way. Once she was behind me, I resumed the movement. I figured the shaft was running along the underside of a ceiling, traveling back to some utility area. It would make sense that from there, the cables and the air would be distributed.

It was hard to be quiet in there. Everything sounded loud. The shuffling sounds of crawling, the increasingly heavy breathing coming from both Cartwright and me. After crawling slowly for maybe twenty feet, I stopped to listen. Because I thought I'd heard something from below, through the shaft.

I settled my breathing. Cartwright did the same behind me. Half a minute later I heard the voice. It was conversational and calm. "Wish you'd let us bring the girls down here."

Another guy made a sound like kissing teeth. "The Bob wouldn't be The Bob, if he wasn't The Bob."

A third person cut in, his voice, gravelly and authoritarian. A voice that I found familiar. "You boys need to think about this like a warrior ceremony. Like an initiation."

"We're not boys anymore," the first guy said.

The third man said, "Just be glad I'm not making you do that Indian Fire-Ant ceremony, because I will, if you don't shut the fuck up."

Nobody spoke after that. But someone did put on music, which came in muffled through the plastic tubing. It was a cowboy ballad which I would normally not have a chance in hell of recognizing, but this one was famous. A tune called "El Paso." I liked that song, had a buddy in the military who played and sang it real good on the banjo.

I anticipated the lyrics.

Out in the West Texas town of El Paso

I fell in love with a Mexican girl.

The third guy's rough and familiar voice murmured along with the recording. The low bass quality of his gravelly voice carried through into the utility shaft, amplifying the low end.

Nighttime would find me in Rosa's Cantina

Music would play and Faleena would whirl

More importantly, the tune gave me the chance to keep going. My hope was that we'd reach a utility closet. I was hoping to open a hole in the utility shaft and get this over with.

But hope is a four letter word.

The utility shaft we were crawling through ended ten feet deeper. A strong-looking steel grill blocked further access. The cables snaked through without any issues, but after the grill there was no more crawl space. This was the end of the road. Linda Cartwright and I were stuck in the utility shaft, while the enemy below was relaxing to a cowboy ballad.

CHAPTER SIXTY

I REMAINED calm and considered the options, which wasn't hard because we didn't have any.

Going backward was impossible, would never happen. The only way was straight ahead, and that was blocked by the steel grill and the narrowing of the shaft beyond it. There weren't two ways out of there. I carefully removed the Glock from my chest pocket on the right side. Cartwright was behind me, but I was unable to turn to look at her or speak or make good hand signals.

I raised the Glock and waved it twice, like a flag. I figured she'd get the idea.

I set the gun in front of me. My right hand slid the Gerber knife out of the painter's pocket. I flicked it open. I'm tall for a man, and my reach is well north of three feet. I stretched my arms out in front of me horizontally and positioned the point of the knife against the plastic shaft floor. I dug it in and let the Gerber stand on its own while my right hand fit the Glock between my teeth.

I had a plan, but it was going to be risky. I felt like an athlete who's about to go for a low-percentage shot. If it comes off it's going to be memorable, but the chances are slim. Death or glory. The important thing was that it was a positive move. You can't stay on the defensive and hope to win.

Glock firmly between the teeth, both hands gripped the Gerber handle. Below, the song played on. I heard the pop fizz of a can being opened. The familiar gravelly voice was still murmuring the lyrics to "El Paso." We were at the second chorus.

Out through the back door of Rosa's, I ran

Out where the horses were tied

I caught a good one, it looked like it could run

Up on its back and away, I did ride

I pushed the knife as hard as I could into the shaft floor and achieved penetration with effort. The tune below had gone into a banjo solo, slightly noisier than the voice. I drew the embedded blade toward me, slicing the thick semirigid plastic along its length until I couldn't pull any more. I shuffled forward, breathing through my nose and trying my best to do so quietly with the gun clenched in my mouth. I experimented with pushing in through the slit pipe. Very tight. It was going to be possible to get through there, but I didn't know if I'd be able to come out the other side clean.

Time to find out.

The guy down there was mumbling lyrics again, so I figured he hadn't seen my blade emerging from the utility shaft above his head. The only way to get through the sliced pipe was to get on top of the cut and push off hard against the roof of the shaft with my feet. Kind of like giving birth to yourself. I didn't know what Cartwright was thinking, but I had faith in her ability to figure it out and get with the program. I pocketed the knife and got the Glock in hand.

I made sure everything was correct with the weapon. I gripped the gun in both hands. My boots found the top of the shaft. Now or never.

I launched through the cut pipe. The strong kick off the ceiling put my shoulders through, free for a moment until my waist got stuck. I ended hanging upside down from the slit pipe, feet trying to find purchase, but not finding any. I was stuck up there. Not that I was worrying too much about my feet. I was concerned with the enemy down below.

The older guy was the first one to notice me. He was ensconced in an arm chair, head oriented in a diagonal to where the ceiling met the wall. I knew immediately why his voice had been familiar, it was the big farmer. The cruel killer who had gotten away from Tela Collins and disappeared. I should have known that someone that evil couldn't be a simple killer.

They called him The Bob.

The only reason The Bob hadn't clocked onto me earlier was because his eyes were closed. He had been relaxing, holding a can of Bud. Now he was staring at me, the beer can held against the arm rest. The Bob wasn't an immediate threat. There were two other men in the room, not encumbered with beer cans or positions of relaxation.

Both men had geometrically severe beards. One of them was the other guy from the Grill and Banquet. He was twenty degrees to my left, drawing from a holster at his waist. I had to twist, and ended up looking at him upside down, but that made no difference to my target acquisition. I drilled two rounds into his chest, squeezing off quickly.

Meanwhile, I could feel Cartwright up there in the utility shaft, busy messing with my legs in an attempt to get me through. I hadn't spoken to Cartwright, but I assumed that she was concerned with me being stuck. Which, while inconvenient in one regard, did give me a stable platform from which to shoot. I had the Glock homing in on the second bearded guy. I was trying to aim true while Cartwright twisted and pushed at my legs. I squeezed one shot off at his chest. The round missed widely, because the firing pin impact coincided with Cartwright's success in releasing me from the plastic shaft's grip.

The projectile entered the bearded man's muscular thigh.

His lower body was punched back, throwing the leg out and bringing him down on the other knee. The guy was brave and solid. He managed to compensate for all of that adverse force and brought his weapon to bear. I saw the muzzle coming my way while I tumbled gracelessly from the ceiling to the floor. The dark hole at the end of the pistol barrel flickered and I felt the hot zip of a round passing an eighth of an inch from my nose.

It all happened within two seconds.

I hit the ground, flailing and adjusting my center of gravity like a house cat and had the sense to roll away. Another round punched into the floor where I'd been half a second before. A third round slammed into the floor near my head. I lost my grip on the Glock and caught peripheral movement from where The Bob had been. The bearded guy was still the main concern.

My gun hand went for the second Glock, tucked awkwardly into the zipped pocket where it had earlier saved my life. I wasn't going to make it. The bearded man stared, like he was enjoying having the drop on me. I was watching his trigger finger beginning to squeeze when his eyes widened. The man's neck opened up in an explosion of red, as if a fish knife had flickered in there for an invisible filleting job. For an instant, it was like some kind of a late spring flower had come up. But spring was short. An instant later the red flower was just blood splatter on the wall behind him.

I heard the sound of Cartwright's Smith & Wesson after she'd shot the guy in the neck. I glanced up to see her hanging out of the shaft.

The bearded man who had come close to ending my game collapsed onto an armchair. The shock of being hit, combined with near instantaneous blood loss, meant that he wasn't in control of his muscular operations anymore. He couldn't maintain his position over the chair and his body slid down until he was prone on the carpet, head settled under the chair.

Cartwright had come through the pipe's epidermis and was just as stuck as I'd been.

I guess The Bob had taken the temperature and found it a little cold in there. He was making haste for the door, in the manner of a big man. I tugged at the Glock and got it out and pointed in his direction. Cartwright was turned the wrong way to get him in her sights. Before he passed through the doorway, The Bob put up a large chrome handgun and let a round loose, casually, without properly aiming. I saw the casing fly into the steel doorjamb, hit it, then tumble over catching the light as it flew off into the next room.

I leapt up and followed. When I reached the door The Bob was gone. Before me was the large double-wide steel door. To the right was a smaller door, still swinging open. I looked back. Cartwright was still hanging upside down from the utility shaft. She'd been shot in the abdomen and her expression was even more grim than usual.

I went to each of the bearded men and put a single round through their brain pans. They couldn't be allowed to get undead. I pulled Cartwright down from the shaft above and laid her on the carpet. She was looking up at me with clear eyes, screwing up her endless courage. She said something, but I wasn't paying any attention to her words. I had moved into another level of consciousness, saving her life.

I tore away her clothing. The entry and exit wounds were clean. The Bob had loaded his weapon with non-expanding full metal jacket rounds. Maybe he preferred keeping his victims alive to bring the pain at a future date. I scanned the room, eyes taking in the potential materials I had available for immediate first aid.

I mapped the situation. Secure quarters with the steel door out front. This room was a lounge area. To the left was a room filled with computers. I ignored that and found a zone with sleeping cots and wire shelving. I went in there and saw a stack of t-shirt triple packs, still in their packaging. I grabbed one, tore open the plastic, and removed the shirts.

I worked as my feet moved me back to Cartwright. The t-shirts got sliced into thin strips. I used one of the shirts to wipe off the blood. The torn strips packed her wounds on both sides. The plastic packaging got split in two and each side duct taped over one of her wounds. I tried not to tape it too tight, but it needed to be tight enough for traveling.

When I was done and ready, I made eye contact with Cartwright. She was looking strangely peaceful, like she was out of the game now and finally able to relax.

Cartwright said, "Don't let him get away."

"I won't."

"You can leave me here."

"No, I can't."

CHAPTER SIXTY-ONE

There wasn't any perfect way of carrying Cartwright. I slung her over my shoulder and moved out. She was light and easy to maneuver. The heavy steel door sucked open at the push of a button, changing the air pressure. I came through and heard the sound of an engine starting up. The Bob had made use of some kind of an emergency exit.

I came up the stairs fast, Cartwright uncomplaining. By the time I was at the garage there was one black SUV gone, replaced by the strong odor of auto fumes. The Bob's main issue was going to be getting his SUV out of there quickly. You don't build a box within a box without making it at least some kind of a chore to get out again. I figured he'd have to stop the car, maybe punch in a couple of codes, or do some kind of manual latch release, and then reseal it behind him.

All of that hassle might be enough to win me a minute or two.

I opened the red door and started to retrace our path. I got Cartwright through the initial hole in the wall between the Mind and Body Meditation Center and The Bob's hideout. I had taken out the front window with the sledgehammer. Now the space was open to the elements, and the full impact of the weather became apparent.

The current weather situation was extreme.

I staggered across the road with Cartwright's thin frame draped over my shoulder. It wasn't tough because she was heavy, but because the wind was so strong that it was difficult just staying upright. I didn't know if I was on the inside of a tornado, but I was definitely inside of some serious weather. Debris was flying through the air randomly. I had the goggles on, so I wasn't worried about my eyes. Most of it ranged from small things like dirt and leaves and rain, to bigger things like cans and bottles and torn-off aluminum siding.

There wasn't any sign of human life. No lights in windows, no vehicles, and certainly no pedestrians or cyclists. I got across the street and into the alley, finally feeling protected on both sides by brick walls. Something thunked into the top of my goggles. I felt up there with a gloved hand and pulled out an embedded shard of broken glass. The environment was hostile.

We made it to the Crown Victoria and I got Cartwright across the back seat. I had a decision to make. Go for The Bob, or get her to a hospital. I thought about it for half a second and decided to split the difference. I would circle the block once, in case I could find The Bob's exit hole. If I didn't find it fast, or see a sign of him, I'd get Cartwright to safety.

I negotiated a couple of large branches, torn off from trees and strewn around. Lines had been ripped out of buildings. No longer stable or fixed to the structures, they whipped around in the wind like angry tentacles. I circled the block, momentarily mounting the sidewalk to get around a fallen utility pole. I figured if I saw taillights it'd be The Bob. Any sane person was huddling underground.

I knew that even if I discovered where he'd come out, estimating where The Bob had gone was going to be tough, bordering on impossible. That was all true, and hope isn't any kind of a plan, but the weather proved to be an unexpected ally. I made it to the other side of the building and saw the red glow of taillights in the blackness up ahead. They disappeared quickly, but I knew which direction he'd gone. I also saw what had delayed The Bob.

A thick fallen tree lay across the road, perfectly blocking my way.

The Bob's exit had been a conventional ramp, sealed by a regular garage door. He'd come out of that and anticipated being followed. The Bob had taken the time to block my path, probably with a hook and winch on that black SUV. I wasn't getting the Crown Vic over that tree. There was no obvious way of going around it either. On the left side was a wall, I wasn't going through that again in a hurry. The right side of the street was a business that had been boarded up. The leafy part of the tree crushed up against the plywood.

I didn't know yet what that business was, but the plywood went all the way to the ground. I called to Cartwright. "Hold on."

She didn't respond. I glanced back there to see her grimly securing the seat belt. I gunned the engine and launched the Crown Vic into the plywood sheets. We bumped in over the short skirting, through the plywood and plate glass sandwich. On the other side of that was the interior of a coffee shop. The car scattered and crushed a few retro chairs. I wrenched the wheel left and the Crown Vic demolished the corner of an espresso bar. I got her oriented to the covered window again and launched the car out the other side.

Insurance claims on acts of god were going to be popular in the town of Promise, Indiana.

I cut back and forth, weaving a path out of Little Ohio, and trying to formulate an estimation of The Bob's probable escape route. I was thinking that he'd go for open spaces. Maybe a farmhouse. So I made my way south, scouting the edges of darkness as I went.

I threaded my way back and forth, crisscrossing the gridded streets until the more densely built part of Promise approached the farmland beyond the town line. I came out from under an overpass and spotted red taillights disappearing up a clover leaf on-ramp, heading hot out to the highway.

Instinctively, I cut the headlights and ran dark.

I maneuvered to the on-ramp and hit the gas. Tela Collins had said the Crown Vic was an old police interceptor. The engine responded well to encouragement. It felt good in there, driving south to some kind of a confrontation. Now that I had The Bob on the run and in my sights, there wasn't any question of his getting away. The Bob had abused the luck of his birth. I hadn't been there for that event, but I'd be there for the final act.

A minute later I was gunning it on the highway. No traffic, no rules, no speed limit, only airborne hazards and debris littered across the asphalt. A pale and rectangular shape came spinning out of the black. I saw it in my peripheral vision from the left and had to suppress the urge to abuse the steering wheel. The object hit the Crown Vic's front left fender and careened into the darkness, carried by strong winds.

A quarter second after it was gone, I realized the object had been a refrigerator door.

I stayed focused on those small red lights in the distance. The Bob wasn't going to be seeing me running dark in his rearview. There was too much visual interference from the slanting rain and airborne debris. For a while it was all straight lines and the intense concentration of driving at high speed with no headlights on. For five miles I pushed the Crown Victoria to its limits. The Bob's SUV remained out of reach; maybe we had equally powerful motors.

It took me a while to realize that the distance was closing. Those red taillights weren't moving as fast as before. In fact, after a piece I recognized that they weren't moving at all. The Bob had stopped driving completely. From a quarter mile back I could see the black SUV stopped diagonal across an empty highway. When I got closer I saw why he'd stopped.

Twenty yards past The Bob was a massive, angry-looking wall of weather. I hadn't ever seen a live tornado before. Not up close and personal. It was a dark night, but the tornado was a lighter shade, I guess because of all the stuff raised up and spun into its centrifugal forces. The base of the tornado was chewing up a ground area the size of a neighborhood. Dirt and objects were being captured and raised, adding to the spinning mass of debris and humidity and loose soil and all manner of other objects. The tornado whirled from the ground all the way up to a low dark cloud formation.

lightning flickered within.

Through the SUV's windows I could see The Bob, silhouette against the spinning column of weather behind him. Maybe he was deciding what to do, or just staring mutely at the sublime wonders of nature. Either way he was my target. I aimed the car directly at the SUV and hit the gas. The speedometer needle climbed. Cartwright coughed in the back seat. "I'm not feeling especially suicidal tonight, Keeler."

The needle was approaching one hundred and twenty miles per hour.

I said, "This person needs to die."

Cartwright's voice was casual. "You'll just have to do it the hard way. Think about the girl, Emma."

CHAPTER SIXTY-TWO

The hard way.

I let up on the gas. The Bob's silhouette shifted and I knew that we'd been spotted. I flicked on the headlights to kill his night vision. I was focused on the enemy, but the tornado behind him was difficult to ignore. The highway was completely blocked by its spinning mass. Off to the left side was a vast corn field. The column of rotating weather chewed into a barn, which came apart as if it were being plucked by the fingers of an invisible giant, plank by plank. Each piece got sucked into the centrifuge.

The highway was bordered by deep ditches, which weren't going to be traversed by either of our vehicles. The Bob was stuck between the weather and me. I closed in on him, fifty yards away. He moved fast for a big man. He egressed from the vehicle and took up a firing position over the hood, protected by the engine block. I didn't try and swerve, or divert my course in any way. I went straight at him.

The muzzle flashed and rounds were incoming. Two missed completely, one came through the windshield and out the back, making starred holes. I thought, full metal jacket. Shrugged internally. I'll bet The Bob was wishing he'd packed a messier kind of ammunition. I could see the man's flat pale face behind the gun. He was concentrated, calm, focused, and unfortunately firing into heavy wind gusting in unpredictable ways. The chances of one of his rounds hitting me was slim but getting better the closer I got.

At the same time, the closer I got, the harder it would be for him to hold his nerve. I noticed myself grinning widely.

I pushed the pedal to the metal and closed the last twenty yards. The Bob squeezed off one more round before calling it quits. The muzzle flashed. The windshield starred in front of my face and my left earlobe stung as if from an angry wasp. The big man spun away from the vehicle. He'd left it a little too late and staggered back in a hurry. The Crown Victoria hit the black SUV. The crash bars crunched in, the powerful force shoved the larger vehicle a couple of yards.

The airbag hit me full in the face and I felt my nose fracture. I snatched the Gerber and flicked it open. The blade sliced the airbag away and I got out of the car. I blew blood out of my crushed nasal passages. The Bob was halfway between his damaged SUV and the rotating tornado. He was concentrating on the big gun in his hand. The Glock was zipped into my coveralls and I instinctively ignored it. No time to waste pulling that thing out.

Cartwright had wanted it the hard way.

The slide had gotten stuck on The Bob's weapon. By the time I noticed that I was already there with the knife. He dropped the handgun and shifted his feet to face me in a good fighting stance. He was a big guy, a credible menace. The storm behind him was noisy, I'd never heard or seen anything like it before. Something very different from the artificial madness of mechanized warfare. I was enjoying the ambience. The Bob must have seen me smile, because a look of uncertainty passed over his face.

I went in for a quick kill. Knife slash at his neck, going for the artery. He stepped inside and punched my arm out. Not exactly what I was expecting. Most people move away from a knife blade. I caught a fast movement in the darkness and The Bob's elbow dug into my gut. I sucked in the pain and kicked him in the knee. He stepped back.

A flash of something pale came out of the dark to my left and I was hit in the face by a wet piece of fabric, maybe someone's laundry that had been ripped apart by the twister. I flicked it away, but The Bob had taken his chance and come at me, quick as the lightning shivering through the storm. He clamped an enormous hand around my wrist. The guy's fingers were like steel bolts. It was like being held and squeezed by a man-size crab.

Sometimes it's better to go with the flow.

I let my knife hand go soft, allowing him to rip the weapon away. His hand unclamped from my wrist. Behind The Bob, the wall of weather spun. A nightmare vision, insane and sublime. Either we were getting closer to it, or it was getting closer to us, maybe both. The Gerber went skittering over the asphalt, drawn into the spinning tornado and disappeared among the whirling debris. The Bob looked happy about getting the blade away. It was a small victory for him, and an important one for me.

My left hand unstuck the Velcro flap and I pulled out Cartwright's hammer by the steel head. The Bob's face was lit up in a grin. I tossed the hammer from my left hand to my right. Fingers securely latched on to the rubberized grip. I stepped in and swung. The hammer nailed The Bob hard in the center of his pale forehead. The grin stayed stapled on his slab of a face until I hit him again and wiped it off. Another shot, perfectly timed and aimed exactly in the center of his forehead. The Bob staggered back, stunned like a condemned farm animal.

That close to the spinning tornado, I could see the things that were caught up in it and rendered airborne: planks of wood and construction material, torn cloth and plastic sheeting. I noticed a giant green snake, about three or four feet off the ground, dipping and floating and approaching across the vast spinning storm. Literally on the edge of being sucked into the tornado, The Bob was trying to stay on his feet. The green snake came from the left. I only recognized what it was at the last instant, a twenty-five-foot-long garden hose spinning through the air, like a weird flying serpent. It was an old-school hose, with a heavy bronze spigot at the end of it.

I guess the heavy bronze plug had flattened out the shape of it, like a kind of flexible arrow.

The leading metal spigot impacted The Bob like a large caliber bullet. It punched right through his chest and out the other side, impaling him and threading his body on the long green hose. I watched, horrified and fascinated in equal measure. The big man tottered on his heavy legs and remained in place, like a puppet. I realized that there was some kind of equilibrium at play. His weight, the force of the tornado's centrifuge, the balancing contribution of the rubber hose and the heavy spigot behind, tugging at him.

That perfect moment didn't last. The Bob fell back and was captured into the storm. As The Bob drifted a foot off the ground, his head lolled onto his chest. His arms were out on either side of him, raised by the storm. The figure was sucked deeper into the gray whirl, and a few seconds later he was gone.

CHAPTER SIXTY-THREE

I MADE it back to the Crown Victoria against the sucking wind. The tornado was moving away, drifting southwest over farmland and ripping up the corn as it went. Cartwright was in the backseat, strapped in and unconscious. I took her pulse: strong and regular. The duct taped wound dressing was clean and hadn't bled through. Cartwright's eyes flicked open and locked into mine. She said something but I couldn't hear it. I put my ear close.

She said, "You look surprised."

"I'm wondering why you're not dead is all."

"I'm resting, taking it easy." She hovered a palm over her wounded abdomen. "If you're worried about that, don't be. There's nothing in there. All I have is pain, and I can do pain, Keeler."

"What do you mean?"

"Nothing inside. I had a colectomy a couple of years ago. They removed the colon." She laughed softly. "The bullet probably went in the same place as the scalpel."

Which meant The Bob's full metal jacket round had gone in and out through skin and muscle and that was it. No danger of organ failure or a leaking colon, because she didn't have one. She closed her eyes again. Cartwright was weak but hanging in there, a true survivor whom you could put your bets on.

I got into the driver's seat and backed the Crown Vic away from the black SUV. The front end was damaged but the engine buzzed nicely. I turned the car around and headed back to the town of Promise, Indiana. Cartwright was conscious. "We're south; get me to County General, if it's still there. Maybe I'll get the same doctor as before." She laughed quietly, a rasping sound, like sandpaper on wood.

County General, where I'd dropped off Collins not long ago. As we came back on the highway, I saw it was possible to trace the direction the tornado had taken. On one side of the road, there were destroyed buildings and shredded corn fields, while the other side had sustained no damage at all. The hospital was southeast, and the tornado had skirted the edges of town, churning north to south along the west side.

I carried Cartwright into the emergency entrance and deposited her on a stretcher wheeled by a concerned orderly in a mint-green uniform. A half-dozen people sat in chairs, waiting for someone to come and fetch them. A kid was crying, sucking at a wounded thumb. There was a guy sitting in an odd position, like he'd swallowed something the wrong way and didn't want it dislodged the wrong way. Most of them were gazing at a television that was tuned to the weather channel. It was showing the heavy weather, but everything at the hospital was operating normally, like nothing special was going on.

Cartwright let her head relax when she got horizontal on the stretcher. She turned her head and glanced at me, the whites of her eyes flashed briefly. I could feel some kind of an acknowledgement from her, like we were at least on the same team. A nurse stepped over and administered an oxygen mask. Cartwright settled, relaxing her body onto the stretcher and she disengaged from me. The orderly spun the stretcher trolley around and sped his patient through the double doors into the hospital complex.

That was the last I saw of Linda Cartwright.

Once I'd seen her into safe hands, I asked at reception for Tela Collins, figured now might be a good time for a visit. The young guy there looked fresh and alert, primed for information retrieval. He reached into his computer and dug out the conclusion that Collins had checked herself out, all set to recuperate at home. The address she'd given was 1250 North Springhurst, her aunt's house.

Out in the parking lot, the Crown Vic was waiting and eager to eat up gas and prowl the open road. I cruised back into town the way I remembered. The road from County General passed through the southwest. The whole area had been well chewed and spat out by the twister.

By then the storm had moved on and the moon was out and shining bright. The damaged areas of town had a blue glow around the edges, like a scene from a disaster movie with an unlimited budget. I passed an intersection that looked familiar. Not because of the houses, which were not in good order, but because of the familiar lay of the land. I made a U-turn and came back through, slower this time. I had an intuition.

I stopped the Crown Vic next to a street sign pole, bent over backwards, and twisted in three places. I read the sign upside down, Church Street.

I'd been there before, specifically on my way out to the neighboring development up on Sycamore Circle. More specifically still, number seven Sycamore Circle, the home of Gus Simmons. I recalled my important business with Mr. Simmons. I figured that had priority over sleep and food and even Collins. I drove up the circle and past the first six gates. The woods were pretty torn up, but the walls around the expensive south side properties were solid and unchanged. I couldn't see past the stonework; maybe the houses had withstood the carnage, maybe not.

I'd left my patience back on the road, somewhere that only a hell of a lot of sleep and a good breakfast could hope to penetrate. So I wasn't in any mood for security cameras, intercoms, house maids, or any obstacles at all. I drove past number seven and pulled the car to a stop. I killed the engine and sat there for a moment, thinking things through.

A moment later I had a plan. Not a complicated plan but a very simple one involving brute force and direct confrontation. I egressed from the car, mounted the hood, and stepped up on to the roof. I got hold of the top of the wall with a good solid leap and hauled myself over, all in one smooth move. I landed on the other side in a stable crouch, boots dug into dirt. All the important muscles and related appendages were working well.

I stood on a wooded rise that looked down at Gus Simmons's property below. The forest glade where the house stood was now perfectly lit by the full moon. The tornado had come through Sycamore Circle like a gigantic lawn mower. The house wasn't really a house anymore, it was a spectacular-looking and untidy pile of expensive sticks and shattered glass. It was remarkable that even in ruins one could tell that the house had been pretty and photogenic and probably designed by a renowned architect. No doubt that house had featured in glossy magazine spreads.

On the other side of the glade, the kidney-shaped swimming pool was littered with the detritus of Gus Simmons's living room.

When I got closer still, I could see that most of what floated there were the shattered remains of his significant collection of stringed instruments. There was a ton of floating wood shards in all different sizes. Broken strings had remained attached to shattered headstocks, their pearl inlaid logos gleaming in the moonlight.

I assumed Simmons was underground somewhere, maybe sleeping comfortably in a well-built storm shelter. Alone, or with the woman who'd come out to confront me before. He could be right there on the property for all I knew, even under the pool. I had no idea and didn't plan to stick around to find out. There was an equal probability that he'd been helicoptered out to a stronger redoubt, maybe over in the Rockies. Something impossible to penetrate, like a Mormon genetic data center.

The important thing was that there was no sign of either Simmons or his maid. Whatever security system he'd put in place hadn't been enough to protect his special house from a tornado. No doubt he was fully insured. I found what I was looking for, not in the pool, but farther out in Simmons's garden, stuck into a compost heap.

The guitar case was unscathed and in the same condition it had been after its first tornado. The lock was still secured and I didn't have the key. But maybe Collins's aunt Ginny did. It was time to complete the mission.

CHAPTER SIXTY-FOUR

I LOOPED UP through town and slingshot around the municipal building.

The houses on Springhurst were still standing, unscathed as if nothing had happened farther south. Collins's red Honda was squared away up the driveway of number 1250. I pulled the Crown Vic over to the curb and killed the engine. The issue was the time; it was the middle of the night, and it would be considered rude to go banging on Aunt Ginny's door just then.

I'd spent twenty years in the United States Air Force, so I didn't have much appreciation for sleep as a sacred institution. But I'm aware that normal people can get upset if their sleep is disturbed. The last thing I wanted was to disturb or upset Collins's aunt. On the contrary, I wanted Aunt Ginny pleased and happy and feeling as good as possible. I pushed back the driver's seat and closed my eyes. Sleep came sixty seconds later.

I woke to a sharp knock on the passenger side window. A small and wizened old face was looking at me through coke-bottle glasses. I looked back at her. The old lady's eyes were huge behind the lenses. She looked worried. I leaned over and opened the window.

She said, "You can't just sleep in your car around here. There's a storm going on."

The woman was in her nineties. She wore a pink robe and had just a few remaining bleached hairs feathering up off her cranium. Behind her was the driveway to 1250 Springhurst and Tela Collins's red Honda. It was daylight. The sun was out, the sky was blue, and everything was brightly lit. The green grass glistened brilliantly in the morning dew.

I said, "I think the storm's passed, ma'am."

She looked up at the sky. "Maybe, but that doesn't mean it's gone for good."

I yawned and stretched but it was confined in there and I felt an urgent need to stretch. I didn't want to scare aunt Ginny, so I asked permission. "Do you mind if I get out of the car?"

Ginny stood back from the window and waited on the grassy verge. I stepped out and yawned and stretched and shook out my legs and arms and rolled my shoulders and neck and head until I was good and loose.

She said, "It's bad for the circulation, sleeping in your car. Don't you have a place to live?"

Aunt Ginny was examining the damaged Crown Vic, and she wasn't seeing anything that she liked.

I reached in back and pulled out the guitar case. "I'm here to make a delivery. This is for you." I held up the object so that she could see it. Pointed to the tag. "1250 Springhurst."

Aunt Ginny tilted her head and checked me out, like she was seeing me in a new light. "You're the man Tela told me about. It's your fault she almost died." She pointed at the house. "Tela's inside if you're here to see her." Ginny looked again at the guitar case in my hand. She shook her head. "That's ridiculous. I've never heard anything so absurd in my entire life. I don't play guitar, never played guitar, and never even liked the guitar."

I came around the car. "I'll bring this inside for you. Then you can decide what you want to do with it. Is Tela awake?"

Ginny took my arm. "You're a big fellow, that's for sure."

Her two hands gripped my forearm tight until we crossed the threshold to her house. The entrance gave on to a linoleum-floored kitchen on the left and a living room straight ahead with olive shag carpeting and gold motifs adorning the wallpaper. The television was on, showing violent imagery from last night's storm. I figured that's why Aunt Ginny had assumed it was still happening.

Ginny leaned on the kitchen counter and got her breath back. "Go on inside and make your first left. Down the hallway second door on the right. Tela's awake all right. I just brought her breakfast. She needs to recuperate, so don't go bothering her for too long." She fetched a ceramic mug from a cabinet and handed it to me. "Coffee. It's good for the heart. Don't let anyone tell you otherwise."

I held out the mug while Aunt Ginny filled it with hot black liquid from a Pyrex carafe. I watched the bean juice flow and began to feel better just looking at it. "Thank you. I won't."

Aunt Ginny waved me away. I saw her eyes flicker to the guitar case and I figured she needed some time alone with it, to let the past and the present wander together again. I was hoping the old memories would catch up with her. As it stood, Ginny didn't look either happy or grateful that I'd lugged that thing all the way up from Alabama. Of course, she was unaware of the complications the journey had involved.

But sometimes complications have their compensations. Collins was in bed. The room was small and cozy. A window on the other side of the bed gave out to the backyard. She'd been gazing dreamily out there when I came in the room. Now she was gazing dreamily at me.

"You made it, so it's finished."

"Done."

Collins nodded. "Good." I tilted my head, as in a question. She said, "What?"

I said, "Not only good, excellent."

Collins blushed. She looked about as good as it's possible to look.

Better than any super model I ever saw, and she'd only just gotten started for the day. She was still wearing her mint-green hospital gown under the covers. She caught me looking at her outfit. "I wanted to make it out of the hospital before the storm. You never know. I got them to release me and called a cab. Got in the car and got here. Now here you are." Her eyes locked on mine, direct. "We're good right Keeler?"

I nodded. "Everything a positive, zero regrets. I'm feeling unbelievably good."

Collins smiled. "I like that. Perfection is only ever a temporary condition, i'm happy to leave it at perfect."

I said nothing. There was a very comfortable pause, us looking at each other patiently, taking in and absorbing the sensory data. I could feel the information populating my body with urgent instructions, sending blood out to all of the important places. I could see that the same thing was happening to Collins. Her eyes had become defocused, pupils dilated, skin flushed.

She broke the silence with a practical instruction. "Go close that door."

I glanced back. The door to the hallway was wide open. I closed it.

"Let me show you something for you to remember me by."

I said nothing.

Collins pulled back the covers. Her left leg was encased in a fiberglass cast. I was going to ask her what the final diagnosis had been, but she preempted the question by pulling the gown a little higher up her leg. "You see what I'm trying to show you, Keeler?"

I wasn't completely sure, although I had an inkling. The cast ended below her knee. The gown kept on traveling, sliding smoothly north. Collins said, "You know what you wear under these hospital gowns?"

I didn't, and I said so.

Collins was staring at me, but I was looking at what she was demonstrating. She said, "Nothing. It's all about facility of access."

~

Aunt Ginny was sitting in her chair watching the television. Nothing had changed, and the storm was still happening on screen. Close up and violent and loud and threatening. Ginny was captivated, but she muted the thing out of politeness when I came in the room. I placed the coffee mug on her kitchen counter. "Thanks for the coffee, and great to meet you."

Ginny stood up and tottered toward the guitar case, which had its own chair now. She patted the old leather. "Take this with you. You got it wrong; it isn't for me."

"Well, it's yours now, ma'am. It's got your address on it. If you don't want it you could sell it."

She was still shaking her head, like there was something I didn't understand. Ginny pointed to the tag. "No. I'm not making it up. You got it wrong. This doesn't say 1250 Springhurst. It says 1250 *South* Springhurst." She was fingering the label. "Look. You must be blind."

I bent down to look. It was suddenly all clear. The label was smudged, I'd gotten that part right. There was a capital S and then Springhurst, the ink blurred together. I had assumed the doubled letter was a result of water leaking in there, but now I was seeing it clearly for what it was.

"There are two Springhursts?"

"Of course there are. There's two of everything, didn't you ever read about Noah's ark? I live on North Springhurst. You need to bring this to *South* Springhurst. Capiche? You need me to find you a compass, son?"

I nodded to her. "Mind if I use your phone, ma'am?"

Aunt Ginny didn't mind. She returned to the television. I dialed the old kitchen phone she had. Sobell answered after the first ring. "Sobell."

I said, "There isn't any HSI angle here."

There was a slight pause. "So what, then?"

"Local trouble."

She said, "What about the local law enforcement."

"A drone strike would be appropriate."

"All of them?"

"Far as I can make out. If they didn't know then they weren't paying attention, which is arguably worse."

"Yeah." Sobell sipped something. "Thanks for letting me know."

A minute later I was shoving the guitar into the back seat of the Crown Victoria. I stood up and looked over the roof of the car to Linda Cartwright's house. The laundry had been taken in. Maybe William F. Cartwright was doing the chores now. I came around to the driver's side door and looked back at 1250 *North* Springhurst. Aunt Ginny was closing the front door. I folded myself into the car.

The county map that I'd bought with Collins was in the glove compartment. I unfolded it and spread it out in front of me against the steering wheel. I found the north part of Springhurst, designated with a capital N and a period. I ran my finger down. South Springhurst wasn't exactly a continuation, it was on the other side of town, but more west. I figured the distance from the municipal building to number 1250 on the south side would be similar to the same number on the north side.

I was wrong.

CHAPTER SIXTY-FIVE

South Springhurst was closer to the municipal building. The properties directly south of the center were more densely packed together. The property in question was a few miles west of where Gus Simmons lived. A few miles made a big difference, in terms of property value and population density. I came up on number 1250 with a little trepidation. The street had been badly hit by the storm, with a couple of houses straight-up flattened, while others were just damaged with maybe a porch shredded, or half a roof torn off.

I didn't have a hard time finding the address because the sign announcing number 1250 was still standing. A proud and solid plank of wood was bolted to sturdy posts and sunk deep into the front yard, clearly set with concrete. The number was at the top of the sign, four digits on a path that traced the concave line of the wood. Below the number, the words Montgomery Baptist Church were painted in thick brown letters against the cream background.

I pulled the Crown Vic to the curb and observed the proceedings.

The church was a converted house, undamaged by the storm. A small crowd had gathered in the front yard. I wasn't able to immediately recognize the purpose of the congregation. I didn't think it was Sunday, but I wasn't completely sure about that. I stepped from the vehicle and pulled the guitar case out. The mission needed to be completed. I was ready to do whatever it took. I was done with Promise, Indiana. Nice place, but not nearly as nice as the beach.

On the approach, I quickly realized that breakfast was being served. Folks of all ages were in a line leading to a set of folding tables. I could already smell it. The tables were laden with heavy machinery of the culinary practice. A serious-looking set of waffle irons took up the real estate on one side. On the other half were two gas burners hosting one iron skillet for the bacon and a secondary skillet for the eggs. Secondary but no less important.

The equipment was being operated by individuals in deep concentration who definitely looked as if they took their responsibilities seriously. I was happy for them, and hungry. But I didn't presume that I'd be welcome to partake of this communal breakfast. I stood just outside of the small crowd and scanned for an authority figure who could take the guitar case off my hands.

There were over two dozen people present of all ages, shapes, and sizes. Many of them were eating at a row of picnic benches set up beneath the front windows of the church. Others were on line for breakfast, making it, or clustered in small conversational groups. One person looked more authoritative than the others. She was tall and striking, with complicated braided hair that involved colored beads. Definitely not a person that it was possible to ignore. The kind of person who enters the room and ends conversations. She wasn't restless, but active, moving from cluster to cluster, like she was verifying and taking notes all at the same time.

I saw her give an instruction to a rotund man. He nodded and scuttled to the front door. I figured that was it, she was in charge. I made my approach. The woman was alert, highly tuned to movement in that space. I made eye contact with her. We were the same height, the same approximate age, and neither one of us needed to look up or down at the other. Her glance was straightforward, but indifferent. It didn't linger, and I realized that my look hadn't been questioning enough.

She was looking for problems, not people.

The woman was already talking to someone else, so I came at her from another angle. She sensed me and turned.

I said, "Excuse me."

"Sorry for ignoring you just then. I didn't think you had any issues. I'm a little busy, performing triage over here." Even busy, the woman was giving me her full attention. Her attention made me feel blessed, which is of course the definition of charisma.

I knocked myself out of the spell. "Just one thing." I showed her the guitar case. "I'm delivering to this address."

She glanced at the guitar case and then back at me, curious and a little surprised. "Okay. I thought you were here to help with, you know." She smiled showing healthy white teeth and cast a strong hand over the proceedings. "This."

"What's going on?"

"Neighborhood cleanup. From the storm last night." Her large eyes sought mine. "People need help, so we're going to help them. Got a lot of folks out here to handle that. Going to turn a bad situation into a good one." She touched the guitar case and flipped the tag so that she could read it.

I said, "1250 South Springhurst."

"Yes. That's correct." She agreed but looked confused.

I said, "What's the issue?"

The woman chose her words carefully. "The issue is, I need to find my grandmother, and there's no reason that you should wait for me, standing like that." She examined me from the feet up. "You look hungry, permanently." She was right. I said nothing. My silence was more than enough confirmation for her. She laughed then. Pointed a finger at me, like I was guilty. "Right. You *are* hungry."

The woman took my arm and led me to a bench at the picnic table. "You sit right there. I'm going to totally hook you up."

A minute and a half later I was sitting in front of a plate double stacked with waffles, a triple portion of bacon, and three fried eggs. There was a small coffee cup filled with syrup, a container of ketchup, hot sauce, and another coffee cup filled with small paper packets of salt and pepper. A half minute after that I was presented with an extra-large cardboard cup of black coffee. The tall woman touched me on the shoulder with her long fancy nails.

Blessed.

I began to get involved with breakfast, watching her walk over to a group of elders ensconced on deck chairs over by the side of the church. She knelt by a wizened old prune and began to speak. I couldn't hear the words, but I could understand the gestures and the looks. Many of them were toward me, and the guitar. I nodded and smiled each time they looked over at me.

The older lady gestured into the house. The younger woman nodded and disappeared around the back. My benefactor came back around the time I'd finished up the first waffle. I was pouring syrup on number two, when she sat across from me. She looked happy. I was happy too.

She said, "Can I see it?"

I passed the guitar case across the table to her. She set it down in front of her. She reached into a pocket of her dress and produced a small key on a twist of hemp rope. A look of concentration came over her face as she focused on the business at hand. I took a big bite of the second waffle, even better than the first. Perfectly crunchy on the outside, fluffy and soft inside. Hot and good. The coffee worked together with the waffle, like a pitcher and the batter. Can't have one without the other. What would be the point?

The woman got the old lock open and lifted the lid. I couldn't see inside, but I could see her expression. She was gazing in wonder at the contents. A small crowd began to gather behind her. Whatever was inside the case was making a good impression. I saw grins and smiles and looks of appreciation. Not for me, for the instrument. The woman looked at me radiantly. "You know who this guitar belonged to right?"

I shook my head. "No, I don't."

She grinned. "A great musician." The woman pointed her well-formed finger at the sign out front. "The church is named for him."

I read it again. Montgomery Baptist Church. The name rang a bell somewhere in the back of my mind. Mostly, I was aware of a budding desire to be of assistance. The breakfast was beginning to do its work, feeding minerals and vitamins and fats and proteins and carbs into the necessary corners of my body. The woman in front of me was helping out, just by existing. I had the right outfit for the job, and Florida was still going to be there when the work was done.

GET A FREE NOVELLA

Building a relationship with my readers is the best thing about writing. I send the occasional newsletter with details on writing, new releases, and other news related to the adventures of Tom Keeler.

And if you register for my Reader Group I'll send you a copy of Switch Back, a Tom Keeler Novella.

Get your free copy of Switch Back by signing up at my website.

jacklively.com

See you there.

JL

ENJOY THIS BOOK?

You can make a big difference.

Reviews are the most powerful tools in my arsenal when it comes getting attention for my books. Much as I'd like to, I don't have the financial muscle of a New York publisher. I can't take out full page ads in the newspaper or put posters on the subway.

(Not yet, anyway).

But I hope to have something much more powerful and effective than that, and it's something that those publishers would kill to get their hands on.

A committed and loyal bunch of readers.

Honest reviews of my books help bring them to the attention of other readers.

If you've enjoyed this book I would be very grateful if you could spend just five minutes leaving a review (it can be as short as you like).

Thank you very much.

JL

ALSO BY JACK LIVELY

The Tom Keeler Novels

Straight Shot

Breacher

The Tom Keeler novels can be read in any order.

ABOUT THE AUTHOR

Jack Lively was born in Sheffield, in the UK. He grew up in the United States of America. He has worked as a fisherman, an ice cream truck driver, underwater cinematographer, gas station attendant, and outboard engine repairman. The other thing about Jack is that since he grew up without a TV, before the internet, he was always reading. And later on, Jack started writing. All through those long years working odd jobs and traveling around, Jack wrote. He'd write in bars and cafes, on boats and trains and even on long haul bus trips.

Eventually Jack finished a book and figured he might as well see if anyone wanted to read it.

Tom Keeler is a veteran combat medic who served in a special tactics unit of United States Air Force. The series begins when Keeler receives his discharge from the military. Keeler just wants to roam free. But stuff happens, and Keeler's not the kind of guy who just walks away.

Jack Lively lives in London with his family.

Impact

First Print Edition

ISBN 978-1-7397891-0-7

General Projects Ltd.

London, UK.

jacklively.com